PRAISE FOR *NEW YORK TIMES* BESTSELLING AUTHOR BETH KERY

Recipient of the *All About Romance* Reader Poll for Best Erotica

"Wicked good storytelling."
—Jaci Burton, *New York Times* bestselling author of
Hope Flames

"One of the sexiest, most erotic love stories that I have read in a long time."
—*Affair de Coeur*

"A sleek, sexy thrill ride."
—Jo Davis, author of *Sworn to Protect*

"One of the best erotic romances I've ever read."
—*All About Romance*

"Nearly singed my eyebrows."
—*Dear Author*

"Fabulous, sizzling hot . . . You'll be addicted."
—Julie James, *New York Times* bestselling author of
Love Irresistibly

"Action and sex and plenty of spins and twists."
—*Genre Go Round Reviews*

"Intoxicating and exhilarating."
—*Fresh Fiction*

"The heat between Kery's main characters is molten."
—*RT Book Reviews*

"Some of the sexiest love scenes I have read this year."
—*Romance Junkies*

"Scorching hot! I was held spellbound."
—*Wild on Books*

"Nuclear-grade hot."
—*USA Today*

SWEET
RESTRAINT

BETH KERY

BERKLEY SENSATION, NEW YORK

THE BERKLEY PUBLISHING GROUP
Published by the Penguin Group
Penguin Group (USA) LLC
375 Hudson Street, New York, New York 10014

USA • Canada • UK • Ireland • Australia • New Zealand • India • South Africa • China

penguin.com

A Penguin Random House Company

SWEET RESTRAINT

A Berkley Sensation Book / published by arrangement with the author

Berkley Sensation Books are published by The Berkley Publishing Group.
BERKLEY SENSATION® is a registered trademark of Penguin Group (USA) LLC.
The "B" design is a trademark of Penguin Group (USA) LLC.

For information, address: The Berkley Publishing Group,
a division of Penguin Group (USA) LLC,
375 Hudson Street, New York, New York 10014.

ISBN: 978-0-425-26652-6

PUBLISHING HISTORY
Heat trade paperback edition / July 2009
Berkley Sensation mass-market edition / December 2013

PRINTED IN THE UNITED STATES OF AMERICA

10 9 8 7 6 5 4 3 2 1

Cover photograph © ImageBrief Alex.
Cover design by Jason Gill.
Interior text design by Tiffany Estreicher

PROLOGUE

His mouth flattened in contempt when he picked the second lock on the backdoor basement entrance with ease. He'd seen it dozens of times before so he didn't know why the evidence of Huey Mays's cockiness should surprise him. How someone could live by a code of intimidation, corruption, and violence and yet never imagine that crime might waltz through his own back door remained an enigma to him.

Maybe it was just as simple as the fact that there was no need to imagine evil "out there" when it resided right here in your cozy little home.

He went utterly still when he heard the sound of footsteps above him. Light, quick . . . undoubtedly the tread of a woman. His nostrils flared as he stared up, an image of her flashing into his mind as clear and vivid as if he possessed X-ray vision and could see straight through the ceiling.

He'd planned his mission carefully, but he hadn't expected her to still be awake. He'd have to occupy himself down here until she slept.

He surveyed the room in which he found himself. Mays had decorated his basement lair to resemble one of the many Chicago sports bars that he and his flock of followers patronized.

Three large flat-screen televisions were arranged at varying angles. He could see the room fairly easily with the help of three glowing beer signs that hung over the back of the bar. The red and blue neon cast lurid light on two pinups of nude platinum blondes, one of whom was bending over, her oiled, glistening bare ass beckoning an invitation to one and all.

He walked silently past the mahogany pool table. A quick glance behind the bar told him that it was fully stocked with premium liquor. He had no doubt that if he opened the humidor on the lower shelf it would contain the finest Cubans.

For a moment he stood behind the bar and looked out over the tacky playground. He slid a finger through a residue of white dust along the mahogany ledge and placed it to his tongue.

Nothing but the best for Huey Mays—the most expensive cocaine, booze, cars, tickets to high-profile sporting events . . .

Women.

His gaze flickered toward the ceiling again before he continued his inspection. He examined several photos of coaches and players for the Chicago Bears, Bulls, Black-hawks, Cubs, and White Sox, most of them signed with personal messages to Mays.

He tried to open the wooden cabinet beneath the shrine of sports photos but the doors were locked. It took him three times as long to pick the lock on the cabinet as it had the back door. He got a clear glimpse into Huey Mays's priorities when the lock finally gave.

His eyes fell first on a large dildo, then several sets of handcuffs, a flogger, two paddles, and several ball gags. Some of the large assortment of sex toys had been un-wrapped and previously used while other items were still in their original packaging.

He started to reach for a sleek mini-camcorder sitting next to several video cassettes but picked up a stack of photos instead. His hand remained steady as he shuffled through the photos portraying two blondes with large breasts being flogged and then sodomized by Huey and a brown-haired, wiry man he immediately recognized.

He paused at one photo and examined Huey's face. It was twisted and red with a mixture of lust and what appeared to be undisguised fury. He gripped the woman's long hair in one hand, his body poised to plunge forward in what promised to be a harsh jolt of flesh against flesh.

He wasn't wearing a condom.

From the two women's overly dramatic expressions of red-lipsticked, wide-mouthed ecstasy directed toward the camera while they both took it in the ass at once, they'd been agreeable to the sport.

And more than likely paid well for it.

He put the photos back where he'd found them and refastened the lock.

The lurid images flashed across his brain as he stood. Just because she hadn't been in the photos didn't mean she hadn't been there. Who'd been taking the photos, for instance? The incendiary thought caused a wave of nausea to sweep through his gut.

His gaze flickered upward. As if she'd grown restless due to his thoughts of her, she moved again upstairs.

She wouldn't be entangled in Huey's sleazy web.

Chances are that she was, though. He had enough experience at this point in his life to know anything was possible. The woman upstairs had slammed that lesson home to him hardest of all.

But she *couldn't* be.

Fuck. How could she *not* be?

The sound of a shower being turned on penetrated his bitter ambivalence. His hand pressed to the package inside the breast pocket of his jacket. His chest seemed to burn beneath it.

A litany of curses and insults paraded across his consciousness, every one of them aimed at himself . . . at his immense stupidity. Despite his mental self-flogging, he didn't head for the back door like he should have if he'd possessed even a single working neural pathway in his brain. Instead he waited for the sound of the shower door closing and ascended the stairs silently.

He'd come here with a mission and he'd complete it. Maybe it'd give him some peace of mind.

Maybe.

But he doubted it.

The upstairs of the prairie-style home was in direct opposition to the tacky basement. It would have been convenient to say that her character reigned upstairs while her husband's ruled below, but the only trace he caught of her was the elegance and simplicity of the décor. Otherwise he might have been in any handsome, historical Hyde Park home.

The original maple floors had been lovingly restored. They gleamed in the dim light from the living room and a room down the hallway to the right. High ceilings, original crown molding, and graceful archways bespoke an era of elegance and attention to the smallest architectural detail. The furnishings were eclectic, but tastefully chosen—a mixture of antiques and modern furniture with clean, sophisticated lines.

He frowned in puzzlement. The walls were bare . . . the credenza, mantel, and tables free of sculpture. No art.

Once he entered the hallway his nose caught the odor of damp clay. He paused, his gaze cast hungrily toward the partially opened bathroom door eight feet in front of him on the right.

Nevertheless, he stepped into the room on the left, his stance wary. He knew for a fact that Huey Mays was out of town, but Mays was a dangerous man. He wouldn't put anything past him.

Sure enough the room was her studio. The small twelve-by-twelve-foot room had no windows. It looked as if it were originally meant to serve as some sort of large closet or utility room. She must use the bathroom across the hall where she showered presently for the water she required for her sculpture.

The sculpture that she'd been working on stood on a table, wetted down and covered in plastic. He stared at an array of maquettes set out on the floor and on a bench—her working models for larger pieces. His forehead crinkled in bemusement when his gaze landed on one portraying a young man sitting on a bench, his longish hair covering one eye as he leaned over and read a book with almost tangible intensity.

He started toward her work in progress when he heard the sound of water splashing against the tub extra hard, like she'd just squeezed the moisture out of her hair.

His outstretched hand jerked back.

He silently stalked farther down the hallway to the entrance of the bathroom. She hadn't closed the door all the way. He might have denied himself the opportunity to look at her art but he wouldn't deny himself a glimpse of her body.

Why should he, goddamn it? She owed him that . . . and a hell of a lot more.

He placed his fingertips on the door. It silently opened a few more inches. The shower was situated on the opposite wall from the door. Steam clung to the glass but he saw her nonetheless. She was turned in profile, her head back, eyes closed as water streamed down her face, neck, breasts, and belly.

His body went rigid—a fixed flame.

A minute later he located the hidden jewelry box in her underwear drawer. The leather box hadn't been stashed amid her fine silk and satin lingerie. No, instead she'd hidden her jewelry among her everyday underwear—worn cotton briefs and exercise bras.

He smiled coldly at that fact. Perhaps she had some inkling about the true nature of the glittering pieces of paste Huey gave her as gifts.

The large emerald sparkled and winked at him as he held it up in the stream of his flashlight. He held up the facsimile next to it.

"Pretty little fake," he whispered into the darkness.

He pocketed the glittering lump of paste and placed the exquisite gem with the trapped fires into her jewelry box.

Then he exited Laura's life just as silently as he'd entered.

CHAPTER **ONE**

TWELVE YEARS LATER

The man sitting in the driver's seat of the car parked in an abandoned parking lot near the Cal-Sag Channel was a keg of dynamite about to blow. In fact Randall Moody had come here on this cold January Chicago night to ensure that he did. He wanted to be the one to toss the igniting match in his own good time, however, and he didn't want to be anywhere near the explosion when it occurred.

He cautiously tapped twice on the car window.

"What the hell? How'd you find me?" Huey Mays asked after he'd peered through the window and unlocked the car door. Moody got into the passenger seat. His nose wrinkled in distaste.

"Smells like a distillery in here." He glared repressively at Mays when he saw the other man had drawn his gun when he heard the knocking on the window, but didn't tell him to put it away. He planned on Huey using that gun sometime soon, after all. Huey'd need it handy.

Moody shivered uncontrollably for a moment, cursing his aching joints and aging body. Dammit, Huey Mays's life was about to come to an end. What he wouldn't give to have his younger, more virile body, even though Mays had wasted much of his health on alcohol, drugs, and multiple daily doses of rich, fatty foods. Moody was pushing sixty but he worked out at his health club vigilantly and was fastidious about what he drank and ate. He considered aging a weakness, but what he despised even more was Huey's lack of discipline and tendency to wallow in his carnal nature.

"One of the patrolmen saw your car out here," Moody replied, his tone smooth and warm, carrying no hint of the bitter resentment he felt. There was no reason to elaborate further. Mays knew as well as anyone Moody had one of the best information networks in the city. If something significant was going down in Chicago, chances are Randall Moody knew about it. Thirty-five years in the Chicago Police Department and carefully established contacts in both government and the underworld had seen to that.

"I'm glad you're here," Huey muttered. His hands moved nervously along his thighs as he wiped the sweat off his palms, but Moody was glad to see he merely placed his gun in his lap instead of putting it away. "You've gotta help me get out of this mess. The feds are breathing down my back to name names, you know."

"I told you they would. I also told you why it wouldn't be in your best interest to do so," Moody said calmly.

"They say it'll reduce my sentence to almost nothing."

"Almost nothing? Your best scenario—*best*, mind you—would be five years in federal lockup. Might as well say an eternity when it comes to you, Huey. Have you thought about what that'd be like? No cocktail available every time you get nervous. No cocaine to give you a nice jolt." Moody slowly removed his leather gloves and stacked them neatly on his black cashmere overcoat. He inspected his well-manicured nails. "And, of course . . . you'll be on the receiving end instead of the instigator in the type of sex you prefer—"

"There's not a chance in hell!" Huey shouted. His eyes looked bloodshot and wild. Moody was pleased to see he looked like a man who stood right on the edge.

"And the fact of the matter remains, Huey. Any benefit you receive from pointing fingers will be very short-lived. It's time you took responsibility for your own actions."

"Nothing?" Huey entreated gruffly. "There's nothing you can do for me?"

"Your fate is in your own hands, I'm afraid," Moody said, his gaze flickering down to the gun in Huey's lap.

"I should have gotten rid of Shane Dominic years ago."

"When the time is right, Dominic will be taken care of, I assure you of that."

"Or better yet, we should have just whacked her back then."

"Your wife is a lovely woman. We aren't such monsters that we kill something so delicate and rare," Moody remonstrated.

"Better you would have married the bitch, then." Huey's smile resembled a snarl as he stared blankly out the front window, obviously picturing something much more pleasant in his mind than the black winter's night. "I got her good, though. Both her and that asshole Dominic."

Moody shook his head sadly and reached for the handle on the passenger door. "This is your chance, Huey, to show your wife she married a strong man, a disciplined man. Do yourself a favor and take advantage of the opportunity while you still possess not only your freedom and your honor, but your manhood. Don't let Shane Dominic take *that* away from you as well."

Moody patted Huey's knee in a gesture of paternal encouragement before he exited the car.

Shane Dominic noticed Clarissa's sharp brown eyes on him in the reflection of the mirror on the antique armoire and coat tree. He dropped his hand from where he'd been pressing his fingertips to his scalding eyelids and caught her in his arms as she spun around.

"You know how horny this dress makes me," he murmured next to her neck. "You wore it to the City Club dinner last fall. I could barely string two words together during my speech because I kept thinking about getting you into bed and stripping you out of it."

Clarissa's laughter vibrated into his lips as he pressed them to her throat.

"That was last fall, Dom. What about tonight?"

His fingers found the zipper on the sexy burgundy cocktail dress and lowered it. "Tonight I can't wait for bed. I'm going to have to take you right here in the hallway, I think."

He smiled when he felt her shiver beneath his marauding mouth. Her fingers delved into his hair, urging him down to the breast that he'd just revealed by sweeping aside the clinging fabric of her bra. He paused, however, and grabbed her wrist. When he pushed it behind her it forced her back into an arch. She moaned as he inspected her small, pink-tipped breast. He blew on it softly.

"You're such a tease, Dom," she mumbled. But she arched higher for him, pushing her nipple closer to his mouth.

He chuckled before he licked her nipple lightly. "You're the one who teased me all night by wearing this dress. Now you're going to have to pay for it."

"I can't wait," she whispered.

He glanced up at her. His eyes chose that unfortunate moment to burn and water. He clenched his eyelids shut for a brief second to get relief.

"Do you want to know what I think?" Clarissa asked.

"What?" he mumbled, not really paying attention. He lowered his head to Clarissa's beading nipple, his entire attention focused on the sensation of every tiny bump rolling across his tongue. Single-minded, that's how Clarissa always described him.

She moaned in pleasure, so it surprised him when she jerked at his hair with the hand he wasn't restraining behind her back. He glanced up at her.

"I think you're trying to change the subject. I think you're exhausted, that's what I think. You've worked nonstop this week on that corrupt cop investigation only to have another speaking engagement tonight at the Magellan Club. You're burning the wick at both ends, Dom. Why do you feel you have to hide your fatigue from me?"

"I don't feel the need to hide anything from you, Clarissa," he assured her before he bent his head again to attend to a tight nipple.

She snorted.

Shane regretfully straightened to his full height. He didn't need to be an expert on human behavior to know that she wasn't going to allow him to make love to her until she said whatever was on her mind.

"If you refer to my work, you know I can't tell you much beyond what the press releases about any Bureau investigations," he said as he removed his overcoat and hung it on the entryway armoire. The jacket to his tuxedo followed.

"Give me a break, Dom. You know that's not what I'm talking about."

He hid a grimace when he saw the expression of stark annoyance on her face. He'd let the familiar phrase out of his mouth before he'd had time to censor himself. But worse, he'd apparently delivered the line in that brusque manner that never failed to push his fiancée's red button of irritation.

Don't you dare use that Special-Agent-in-Charge tone with me. Christ, no wonder they say you've got a heart of stone, Dom.

Clarissa's past accusation echoed in his head as he gently pulled the fabric of her dress back into place on her shoulder.

She had a right to be pissed at him. He'd barely spoken with her in a week and a half, he realized guiltily. Robert Elliot, the United States Attorney for the northern district of Illinois, had just handed him those much-sought-after arrest warrants four nights ago designated for several cops in the Chicago Police Department.

But no matter how good his reasons for doing so, Clarissa wasn't likely to appreciate him ignoring her for the past ten days only to have him maul her the second he had her to himself.

He led her into his book-lined study and sat her down on the leather couch.

"I know I haven't been able to see you much this week. Tell you what," he said softly. "Let me go and get out of this monkey suit. I'll make us a drink and we'll talk."

Her dark eyes swam with tears as she looked up at him. Clarissa was one of the smartest and most successful financial analysts on LaSalle Street. She didn't cry easily.

"We're going to be married in two months, Dom. Why can't you even admit to me that you're exhausted? Can't you show even a shred of vulnerability in front of your future wife?"

He smiled. "You want me to tell you that I'm exhausted? Okay. I'm about ready to fall flat on my face. I've probably slept a total of eight hours in the past week and my eyeballs feel like they're going to burn through my eyelids. My vision is so blurry that I told the president of the Magellan Club that he needn't bother with getting me a drink from the bar because another gentleman was already getting me one."

"What's so terrible about that?"

"That other *gentleman* was his wife."

Clarissa's lips twitched with humor. "You didn't."

Shane shrugged sheepishly.

"You also told the superintendent of police that you were going to give a nice Liverpool kiss to the next man who ribbed you about being named the 'Sexiest Man in Chicago' by *Chicago* magazine. I didn't understand that you were threatening him until John McNamara explained to me that a Liverpool kiss was a street-fighting technique—a brutal head-to-head blow."

"That threat counts for women, too," Shane said with a mock somber expression. Clarissa grinned.

"Maybe you should have threatened someone besides the superintendent of police, considering the fact that more than half the city sees you as being responsible for taking away their trust in the Chicago Police Department."

Shane's eyebrows went up at that. "Operation Serve and Protect exists for the sole purpose of returning the public's trust in the CPD. Jake Moriarity knows that. That's why he's backed the FBI's investigations of CPD corruption one hundred percent."

"Are you sure that's the only motivation behind your mania for this investigation?"

Shane paused in the process of untying his bow tie. "*Mania?* That's a bit harsh."

Clarissa didn't break their stare.

"This case falls directly under several FBI directives for investigation. Christ, we've uncovered the largest organized theft ring in known history, one that crosses multiple state lines and is run by public officials. What other motivation do we need?"

Clarissa looked vaguely uncomfortable at the question but she didn't look away, nonetheless. "Well . . . there are those insinuations that Channel Six News made about your connections to the Vasquez family."

Shane rolled his eyes. "I know a quarter of the cops and most of the detectives on the CPD. I not only have worked with dozens of Chicago cops, I call many of them friends . . . including Joey Vasquez."

"But how many of those cops did you attend elementary school with like you did Joey Vasquez?" Clarissa persisted. "And . . . and that news report said Huey Mays's wife is Joey Vasquez's sister and that you've known her for ages . . ."

She trailed off but continued to study his face hungrily.

Shane froze before he jerked the bow tie off his neck, the sliding silk making a hissing sound. "I *knew* Laura Vasquez, Clarissa. I haven't spoken to her in over a dozen years. What's your point?"

Clarissa exhaled slowly. "I don't know what my point is. You've just seemed so obsessed with this case."

"You tell me I'm always single-minded about whatever's on my plate."

"You are. You have a one-track mind, Dom." She shook her head and laughed softly when he lifted an eyebrow and lowered his gaze to her still erect nipple pressing against thin fabric.

"They showed a picture of her, you know," Clarissa said, laughter still clinging to her lips. "On the news. Laura Mays, I mean. She's extremely beautiful."

"Is *that* what this is about?"

"Maybe. I don't know." Her expression turned a little sheepish. "Of *course* you have good reason to be obsessed with this case. Some of the things those cops were doing . . ." She shook her head in mixed disbelief and disgust as she removed a clip at the back of her head. Her dark blonde hair fell around her shoulders. "I mean, using the police department resources to steal from innocent people, severely beating some of those innocent people, three of them nearly to death in the process, extorting untold amounts of cash from drug dealers and other criminals . . . it boggles the mind, to be honest. They were nothing more than a vicious organized gang operating out of the offices of the CPD.

"*Hello?* Dom? Where'd you go?" Clarissa asked a few seconds later.

Shane blinked, realizing that once again he'd been lost in his thoughts.

Lost in this case.

Why Clarissa put up with his late hours and divided attention was beyond him. She even was good enough not to hold over his head the fact that he'd postponed their wedding—not once now, but twice—every time they got in a spat. He'd been starting to experience those old, familiar doubts about marrying her yet again, and he knew as well as anyone what a jerk that made him.

"I don't deserve you, Clarissa," Shane muttered, wishing for the thousandth time that he could rid himself of these uncertainties. Surely it was just the longtime bachelor in him getting the jitters?

But at the same time he couldn't help but think that if Clarissa was truly the woman for him, there wasn't a chance in hell thoughts of her would so rarely cross his mind for ten days in a row, no matter *how* compelling his work was.

The sultry expression she wore as she looked up at him went a long way toward erasing his doubts for the time being. His eyelids narrowed as he watched her lean forward and plant a kiss on the root of his cock. Despite his fatigue he felt himself stir with arousal.

"You're right. You don't deserve me. I have to admit one thing though. *Chicago* magazine was dead-on. You're downright edible in this tux, Dom."

"Is that a promise?"

She arched her golden eyebrows. "Why don't you go and get comfortable and pour us a drink. Then we'll decide if you're in the mood to sleep or fuck."

"I know what I'm in the mood for and it's not sleeping. I owe you after this week, Clarissa," he murmured as he pressed his thumb to her lower lip.

"We'll see if you're up for it."

"Oh, I'm *up* for it all right," he assured her.

The sound of Clarissa's appreciative laughter followed him out of the den. He grinned. She really was an amazing woman. She'd just thrown down the gauntlet, knowing full well that he never walked away from a challenge. He may be tired as hell but it was the exhaustion that came after a bloody battle. Some lusty sex would be the perfect way to celebrate his triumph.

Not to mention make him forget his doubts in regard to marriage.

He wasn't a young man anymore. He needed to settle down. So what if he wasn't necessarily eager to rush home to see Clarissa at the end of a workday? He'd just have to try harder to be considerate, that's all. She was a fine woman. He enjoyed her company. There weren't a lot of smart, independent women out there who could meet his needs sexually, but once they were behind bedroom doors, Clarissa submitted very sweetly to him.

Still . . . those doubts lingered.

Thirteen and a half years, for Christ's sake. How lame could he be to carry a torch for a woman for so long? Not just any woman, either. A woman who clearly didn't want him.

A woman he obviously shouldn't want.

Clarissa was standing directly in front of the television set when he returned a few minutes later wearing pajama bottoms and carrying two brandy snifters. He was used to her occasionally switching on CNN business news for any recent headlines, but he was a little surprised that her attention remained fixed on the screen when he came up beside her.

"Oh no, Dom," she whispered.

"What?" he asked.

"Look . . ."

His gaze shot to the television screen. It showed a handsome man with dark hair graying at the temples dressed in an expensive, immaculately tailored gray suit exiting the doors of the Dirksen Federal Building. Shane knew the footage had been taken two days ago, just after Huey Mays had been released after posting bail.

A feeling of profound hatred swelled in Shane's chest, the magnitude of it shocking him a little. It must have been the unexpectedness of the image that had taken him off guard.

"Yeah, that's Huey Mays. They'll be running the story about the arrest of a captain of the Organized Crime Division running the most extensive jewel, fur, and rare coin theft ring in history from the offices of the Chicago Police Department for quite a while," he muttered with grim satisfaction.

"That's not the story they're running," Clarissa said as she looked up at him anxiously. She took the drink that he offered her without seeming to be aware of what she was doing. "Or at least that's only part of it. The story is that Huey Mays shot himself earlier this evening. He was just pronounced dead at Northwestern Memorial a half hour ago, Dom."

Shane slowed his car on Erie Street next to the entrance of Northwestern Memorial Hospital. He spotted one of his nemeses, Blaine Howard, a reporter for Channel Eight News, dashing toward the doors leading to the east side of the massive building, his cameraman huffing and puffing to keep up with his long-legged sprint.

In Shane's experience the only characteristic that exceeded Howard's ignorance was his arrogance. It wasn't a pretty combination. But if there was one thing Blaine could do it was smell blood.

Shane recognized her immediately when she exited the

glass doors and jogged down the sidewalk. A bevy of reporters and cameramen followed several feet behind her, shouting questions and clicking off photo after photo. Shane saw the trace of panic in her rigid features as they closed in on her.

He knew how much she hated crowds. When they were teenagers her brother Joey had slacked off on studying for his entrance exams to Whitney Young Magnet High School and had had to attend St. Ignatius instead. So when Laura had started at Whitney as a freshman and Shane had been a senior, he'd taken Joey's kid sister under his wing. He'd coached her in order to get her through a required public-speaking class. She was a bright student and a brilliant artist, but she was reserved. Not shy necessarily.

The public arena just wasn't Laura's domain.

Or at least it hadn't been when he'd known her, when innocence still clung to her like morning dew to an exquisite, unopened rose. Things were different now, of course. Huey Mays had seen to that. Huey and whoever else he'd granted rights to the use of his stunning wife's body.

To his stunning slave's body.

There were a lot of things an officer of the law learned from electronic surveillance that he'd rather not hear. In Laura's case they'd been things Shane would have paid any price to permanently erase from his memory banks.

She abruptly broke free and sprinted ahead of the pursuing reporters and photographers. He pulled up a few feet in front of her as she ran down Erie Street and slammed on the brakes.

"Get in," he barked through the lowered window.

She pulled up short, her eyes widening when she saw him. She hesitated.

"Get in the damn car, Laura. They'll be all over you in a second."

Once she'd made her decision she moved fleetly. He stomped on the accelerator the second she'd slammed the door. One of the members of the rushing media slapped the back of his car in frustration as it took off down the street.

For almost a minute neither of them spoke as he merged onto Lake Shore Drive south. It struck him as surreal to be driving a car with Laura Vasquez in the passenger seat. This morning he'd never have guessed in a million years that this was how his day would end.

"You shouldn't have done that, Shane. One of them might have seen your license plate and figured out that I was just picked up by the Special Agent in Charge of the FBI's Chicago offices—the same man who was responsible for Huey's arrest."

"*Huey* was responsible for his arrest, Laura."

His stern tone might have been an attempt to neutralize the effect her low, husky voice had on his body. She was one of three people on the face of the earth who actually called him by his given name—his mother and father being the other two. He hadn't heard it coming off her tongue for more than a dozen years now.

He glanced over at her, taking in the clean, harmonious curves and angles of her profile against the lights of the city, a flawless diamond set among glittering rhinestones. She appeared calm and untouched by his provocative statement.

How did she really feel about her husband's death? He forced his stare back to the road.

As usual it was impossible to plumb her depths. She was the one person he'd ever encountered who represented incontrovertible truth that his ability to judge another human being's character was grievously flawed. His peers would say that was Shane's expertise—the ability to comprehend people's motivations, to predict how they'd act given a certain set of circumstances.

The fact that his feelings toward Laura were such a stark discrepancy of what they *should* be given reality bugged the shit out of him. It'd been like a burr under his skin for thirteen and a half years, a wound that just wouldn't heal no matter how he tried to forget her and move on with his life.

"So what if they do realize it was me?" he muttered. "I'll say that I picked you up for questioning."

"Is that really what you're doing?"

For a brief second their eyes met in the shadows. "Questioning you has never gotten me anywhere in the past, has it, Laura?"

She looked like she was about to say something but then she stopped herself. Her face looked set and pale—the most beautiful mask he'd ever seen in his life. He resisted an urge to pull the car over and shake her until she showed him something. Her rage. Her sadness. Her passion.

Anything but this cold indifference.

"Where are you taking me?"

He blinked at the mundane question in the midst of such a charged moment. Charged for *him*, anyway.

"I don't know. Where do you want to go?"

"So you're really not taking me in for questioning?"

He cast a hard look in her direction. "Didn't the police question you?"

"Yes. At the hospital. They said they'd be contacting me in the morning to clarify a few other things. I received the news that Huey had passed away as they were questioning me . . ."

He didn't say anything for a few seconds when she trailed off. Huey Mays's unexpected death by suicide pissed him off so much that he'd practically been blind with rage for a few seconds as he stood there in front of his television set forty-five minutes ago.

Oily little weasel to the finish, wriggling free of the snare he'd caught himself in like the coward that he was. Shane seethed.

Mays had been the linchpin to the FBI's continued investigations into corruption at the CPD. The man was slimier than the stuff that got stuck to the bottom of your shoe in a sleazy dive's john. Except Mays was worse because he was handsome enough to appear on the front of a men's magazine and just as slick as the glossy cover.

Shane suspected that Mays would have spilled names to save his own neck, and his instinct was rarely wrong in such matters. He had hoped that he'd sing one name loud and clear—that of the current chief of the Organized Crime Division of the CPD, Randall Moody.

"Did they tell you that Huey left a note?" he asked Laura. He'd spoken to the commander in charge of the precinct where Huey's body had been found and knew the basic details of the case.

"Yes," she replied.

He took in her unruffled composure. Shane sighed, ineffectively venting an almost fourteen-year-long frustration at the sight.

"His body will still be examined by one of the Bureau's agents at the crime lab, but as long as everything checks out with their report and the note is genuine, there won't be a formal investigation. It'll be ruled a clear-cut case of suicide. Picking you up on the street just now wasn't official business. It was a spur of the moment thing," he mumbled after a few seconds when he saw her smooth brow wrinkle in puzzlement. "I saw the media charging you. I spend half my life escaping from those jackals."

A small smile tilted her full lips. "Still saving me from the bad guys, Shane?"

"That would require you *allowing* me to save you, wouldn't it? You've swum way too deep now, sweetheart," he snarled.

He paused when he noticed the glaze of shock in her wide eyes. He inhaled slowly and fixed his stare on the road. Jesus, what the hell was wrong with him?

"I'm sorry. You didn't deserve that. Not tonight." He felt her gaze on him, making his skin prickle, but she didn't speak for several moments. Finally she cleared her throat.

"I suppose they would have told you that he . . . he did it in his car?" she asked. "Another police officer found him. Huey had parked in a deserted area near the Cal-Sag Channel. The police officer thought the car had been abandoned and went to investigate. Huey was still alive but unconscious. He never woke up."

"Who was the officer?"

"Josh Hannigan, from the Sixth Precinct."

"Do you know him?"

Laura shook her head.

He peered at her suspiciously through the darkness. Laura came from a family of cops. Her uncle Derrick—her guardian—had been a twice-decorated sergeant. Her older brother, Joey, was a vice detective.

And, of course, her husband had been a cop—though Huey'd made a mockery of the title. Now it looked as if Joey might be entangled in the whole affair as well.

And Laura sat in the midst of it all, silent and inexplicable. Who was she protecting with her aloofness? Her husband? Joey?

Herself?

He blinked to clear the blurriness from his sleep-deprived eyes and took stock of his surroundings. He realized he'd been driving south on Lake Shore Drive without a clue as to where he was going. He got over into the right lane and narrowly made the closest exit.

Joey Vasquez might be a person of interest in the CPD theft ring case, but he also was an important part of Shane's history and Laura's only living immediate family. Joey and he hadn't seen much of each other since Shane had returned to his hometown, this time to head up the Chicago offices of the FBI. Still, he knew that Joey lived in Hyde Park. He ducked his head and tried to make out the street sign as he passed to get his bearings.

"You shouldn't be alone right now. I'll take you over to Joey's," he muttered.

"No, not to Joey's. Take me to my house, please."

"*Laura*, you just—"

"Joey is out of town," she interrupted calmly. She noticed his skeptical glance. "I'm telling the truth, Shane. He and Shelly took a van-load of kids to Springfield for the high school girls state volleyball championship. Carlotta is playing in the finals."

"Carlotta can*not* be in high school," Shane proclaimed flatly, referring to Joey's daughter.

His gaze caught and stuck on the tantalizing image of Laura's small, wistful smile. "She's a junior at Marie Curie High School."

Shane shook his head. You could ignore your advancing age as much as you wanted, but the next generation refused to allow you to remain secure in your denial.

"You're thirty-four years old," he said as he drove down the silent, dimly lit city street.

"Since November," Laura replied in a hushed voice.

It took him a half a minute to realize that she was crying. She never made a sound as she stared straight ahead, the tears clinging like ice crystals against her smooth cheek.

CHAPTER **TWO**

Of course it was natural that she should cry under these circumstances, Shane reminded himself. Huey Mays may have been a scumbag, but he was her husband. And he'd just chosen to kill himself instead of confronting the circumstances of his crimes—circumstances that Shane had forced him to face. He didn't know how to soothe Laura without sounding like a hypocrite, so he drove in silence for the next five minutes.

"You shouldn't come in," she said when he pulled into the long driveway of the prairie-style home and unbuckled his seat belt. He noticed that her cheeks were dry now, as though the tears had never existed. "It's only a matter of time before those reporters converge on the house."

"Which is all the more reason for you not to stay here," he said loudly.

She smiled at him. Not the wan, half smile that occasionally had tilted her lips during the car ride, but a full grin. He inhaled slowly to stave off the blow that smile imparted. She'd once gifted him with them regularly, lighting up his world.

"You haven't changed, Shane."

He rubbed his eyes with his fingertips and tried to ignore the burn. God, he needed to sleep. He felt raw—volatile. Christ, what luck to be so exhausted and vulnerable for his first meeting with Laura in more than a dozen years.

"If you won't let me take you to a friend's house, then what about a hotel?"

"No. I told the police I'd be here in the morning."

He sensed her once-familiar steely determination but opened his car door anyway. He gave her a quelling look, cutting off her inevitable protest.

"I'm just going to check out your house—make sure everything is okay. It's the least Joey would expect of me in these circumstances."

He didn't like the quick, almost furtive manner in which she glanced out the window. Was she expecting someone? On the night that her husband had committed suicide? Don't even tell him she expected one of his crime buddies—or worse, one of Huey's sleazy sex pals.

His well-honed sense for potential threat ratcheted up several degrees as they walked up the dim driveway and mounted the steps to the front porch, Laura several steps in front of him. Nothing unusual happened, however. Not while Laura unlocked the front door and not while Shane did a thorough search of the premises.

When he returned downstairs he found her in the kitchen leaning against the counter, the steam beginning to rise off a teapot on the stove behind her. She studied him with those exotic, slightly slanted green eyes that still occasionally haunted his dreams . . . although with less and less frequency, thank God.

She'd removed her long wool coat and wore an ivory-colored, soft-looking sweater and jeans beneath it. Her dark brown hair hung loose around her shoulders. He could just make out a chain on the side of her neck, but the pendant hung beneath her loose sweater. Other than that glimpse of gold she wore no jewelry. She didn't wear a trace of makeup.

Not that she required either.

He set the manila folder he'd found upstairs on the counter. The small bedroom where he'd found it appeared to be occupied solely by Laura. A surprisingly sparse amount of Huey's clothing and personal items were in the master bedroom suite. The majority of his personal items were in the basement. Shane tried to ignore his satisfaction at the evidence of their separate existences within the house. Lots of married couples slept apart after thirteen years, after all.

He flipped open the manila folder, revealing dozens of travel brochures to exotic locations.

"Planning on going somewhere sometime soon?"

Irritation and something else—was it embarrassment?—flashed across her impassive face. She shut the folder quickly.

"Not that it's any of your business, but the answer is 'no.' I just like to . . . think about getting away." Her gaze flicked up to meet his. "You know how Chicago is in the wintertime."

"Yeah, the snow in Banff looks like it'd be much more relaxing than Chicago snow," Shane deadpanned, referring to one of the brochures he'd seen. She merely turned away without responding in typical, infuriating Laura fashion. "Were you in bed? When they called earlier about Huey?" he asked, thinking of the unmade bed he'd seen in her room.

"Yes. I hadn't fallen asleep yet, though. I had a show at my gallery this evening. It went well, but I was exhausted from all the preparation. I was in bed by ten."

"What time did you leave your gallery?"

"I had a wine-and-cheese party for the showing. It started at six-thirty. I locked up at around nine-thirty."

He nodded his head slowly. She straightened from her leaning position, obviously sensing the tension that suddenly seemed to thicken the air between them.

"I thought you said you weren't here to interrogate me."

"I asked. You answered. Some people call that conversation. Don't you think you could use something stronger than tea?" he asked, glancing pointedly at the teapot when it started to whistle.

"Huey has a bar downstairs if you'd care for something stronger."

He frowned as he watched her pour the hot water into two mugs. He'd rather drink the probably foul-tasting herbal tea she prepared than take a sip of Huey Mays's premium party-time liquor.

She hesitated when she turned around to hand him the tea. "Would you . . . would you like to sit down in the living room?"

He nodded once and followed her into the subtly lit living room. She sat in an upholstered chair and he took a seat on the couch. When he glanced up after sipping his tea, trying to hide his grimace at the bitter taste, he noticed the queer expression on her face as she studied him.

"What's wrong?" he asked, the cup still an inch from his lips.

"I just recalled that Joey told me you were going to be married earlier this year. I suppose by now congratulations are long overdue."

He set down the tea on the coffee table in front of him. "Joey and you talk about me?"

She started in surprise at the question. "Not much. Occasionally. Why?"

He shrugged. "He and I never discuss you. Ever. He seems to think you're a taboo topic where I'm concerned."

"I see," she said after a pause. He watched as she took a sip of the tea, momentarily mesmerized by the sensual movement of her throat as she swallowed. "Just like family, isn't it? Never to talk out loud about their ugly secrets?"

He leaned forward, his elbows on his knees. "Joey was never ashamed of you. *You're* the one who kept the secrets, Laura. And not the Vasquez family's—Huey Mays's secrets."

She just stared at him, as calm and enigmatic as the Sphinx. Years of frustration, fury, and thwarted desire bubbled up to the surface. He found himself engaging in a full-fledged offensive when he'd never even planned for battle.

"You realize, don't you, that your husband and his little gang represented everything that your father hated? All the government corruption, the selfish grappling for power and money at the expense of the people—all of those things he wrote about in his books . . . what he lived to defeat?" Shane prodded, referring to Laura's father, who had been a Cuban political dissident. Shane had liked and respected Richard Vasquez enormously, and he'd always sensed the regard had been mutual.

When Laura's father was finally released from a Cuban prison he'd fled to the United States where he'd eventually become a respected professor at the University of Chicago. He'd published extensively on the topic of the crushing effect of corrupt government and dictatorships on the human psyche and spirit.

"And how could his daughter have turned around and married the devil? Is that what you're thinking, Shane?"

Her quiet voice infuriated him even further.

"How his daughter could have bedded down with him, sold her soul to him, bent over for him or any one of his greasy pals whenever he demanded it. *Yeah*, I'll bet your father'd love to know the answer to that if he were still alive. I know I'd give my left nut to hear that explanation myself—not that I'm holding out for any substantial answers. The only thing I ever got from you was that crap you fed me thirteen years ago after you married Huey about your undying love for your saintly husband."

She set down her mug stiffly. "What are you talking about?"

"Electronic surveillance, Laura."

"You had this house bugged?"

He shook his head in mixed frustration and disgust when he saw the last vestiges of color drain out of her face.

"That's right. We were lawfully intercepting Huey's phone and Internet conversations for almost a year, but he was careful about what he revealed. He was a suspicious guy, your husband. I finally convinced a federal judge that wiretaps weren't enough. We got a court order to listen in on his little playpen downstairs. It never paid off in regard to the case in the way that I'd hoped. It took a jewel and fur thief who also just happened to be a Chicago cop for a period of time—a little weasel who's in the witness protection program—in order to get the names, written documents, and details that we needed to pin Huey. *Everything* about how they would use police computers to track jewelry, fur, and rare coin salesmen's car rental and hotel information, all the dirt on their little extortion ring . . . how they took regular payments from known criminals in return for keeping silent about their rackets.

"So the bugs down in your basement didn't pay off in the way I'd hoped," Shane continued, "but the agents who got assigned the monitoring detail weren't complaining much even though it's usually a *shit* job that nobody wants." He leaned forward intently. Despite his intense anger, he kept his voice low, although he couldn't dull the bitter edge of his sarcasm. "Especially when Huey threw one of his little sex parties for his friends. You know about those parties. Don't you, Laura?"

She just stared at him, her silence and coldness sending his fury near the boiling point.

He stood up abruptly and grabbed her shoulders. She didn't resist him when he pulled her up. He pressed her to him, crushing her full breasts into his lower chest, the sensation of her distended nipples making his cock harden with amazing alacrity. Her scent—soap mixing with the once-familiar underlying odor of sweet, succulent woman—entered his nostrils, sending him further into a spinning chaos of desire and rage.

He leaned down and spoke in a soft, vibrating voice just inches away from her parted lips.

"Nothing to say, Laura? Always so controlled. But you weren't so silent down in the basement entertaining Huey and his friends, were you? You screamed and moaned and begged like a good little whore while they took their turns with you, double-teamed you—whatever Huey demanded of you, you *did*. Yeah, your father would have been so proud to know about his daughter's generous hospitality to her husband's friends."

Her green eyes flashed. "How do you know it was me?"

He gave a harsh bark of laughter. "Let's see—what was my first clue? Oh yeah—*'That's right, Laura, suck him nice and deep like a good little wife. Show him how nice we treat our guests.'*"

He blinked in shock when she slapped his cheek, the evidence of her crumbling façade shattering his own brittle control once and for all. He grabbed the wrist of the offending hand and twisted it behind her back, pressing her tighter against him in the process. She cried out in surprise and discomfort.

"Is this how you like it, Laura?" he growled. Their eyes met briefly, her startled stare searing right through his shattered defenses. "*How* could you do it? How could you let those assholes touch you? You're *mine*."

He saw her eyes go wide but he didn't give her a chance to respond to his totally irrational proclamation before he covered her mouth with his own.

He drank from her furiously. Pain vibrated through his flesh. Not the discomfort of a wound or an injury, but the raw, searing pain that came from exposing a desire that had long been denied.

At that moment he *needed* Laura Vasquez just like he *needed* to breathe.

Later he wouldn't be able to say at what point she stopped struggling, precisely when her tongue began to tangle with his, or when her hands rose to caress his neck and her fingers delved through his hair. She pressed against him almost frantically, the abrupt appearance of her need shocking him . . . and nearly blinding him with lust.

The sensation of the hard centers of her breasts pressing against his chest, the feminine softness between her thighs rubbing subtly against his hard cock, the incredible silkiness of her skin, all combined to form a powerful ward against logic.

Desire, distilled and potent, overcame Shane's anger. His tongue was just as demanding in its actions, but as he plunged into her exquisite taste he also paused to linger on her full lips, using his teeth and tongue to mold and nip at them, before he plunged into her once again, drowning in her sweetness.

When he felt her hands cup his ass and pull him even tighter against her body, he groaned and maneuvered her over to the couch, pushing her down. He tore roughly at the button fly of her jeans. She lifted her hips compliantly, all the while watching him with huge, desire-glazed eyes.

He pulled off her socks, palming one of her heels in the process and stroking her. She moaned softly. He glanced up at the sound. Her white underwear created an erotic contrast to her smooth, honey-colored flesh.

He slid his hands along her skin beneath the elastic band of her panties and lowered the tiny garment slowly, caressing the silky skin of her thighs as he did so.

"I've never touched anyone with skin like yours. It's like warm satin," he muttered. His nostrils flared in feral lust at the sight of her long, shapely legs, naked hips, and the delicate pink folds of her labia peeking out through neatly trimmed dark brown pubic hair.

He placed his hands between her thighs, spreading her farther, looking his fill at a sight that had been cruelly stolen from him. It was pitiful to think it, but Shane was still shell-shocked by that theft.

Still stunned by Laura's treachery.

An ache of anticipation stabbed through his cock, the strength of his reaction like nothing he'd ever known. He yanked his gaze from her pussy and looked into her eyes. She stared up at him with an expression of wide-eyed, stunned arousal. He couldn't resist the invitation of her parted lips. He leaned down and dipped his tongue into her mouth again and again.

He saw nothing but a red haze of pure lust. A primitive mandate to mate hard, fast, and well overcame him. If he didn't bury himself deep inside her within seconds he would lose it. Explode . . . implode, he couldn't tell which. He no longer knew up from down, right from wrong. An unstoppable tsunami of desire rolled him along helplessly in its wake.

"I'm sorry for rushing but I can't wait . . ." he muttered apologetically as he raised himself off her and reached for the button on his jeans.

"I don't want to wait, either."

Her husky whisper made him even more frantic. He hastily extracted a condom from his wallet before he ripped at the fastenings of his own jeans, his breath sounding harsh and ragged in the otherwise still room. Within seconds he lay between her parted thighs, positioning himself.

Mindlessly he nuzzled at her breasts through the soft sweater, inserting one thrusting, stiffened tip between his front teeth and biting lightly. She cried out in surprised pleasure, the sound deepening his already intense excitement. Her fingertips pressed to his scalp, urging him on.

He shifted his hips, pressing the head of his cock against her pussy. He grimaced in frustration when he thrust and went nowhere. She was warm and deliciously slick but he wasn't a small man and the couch was narrow . . .

And so was she.

"Put your leg on the back of the couch," he said. He waited, a bead of sweat rolling down his abdomen as she complied. He sensed the slight give in her flesh. He flexed his hips and drove into her.

She screamed. His own shout sounded guttural . . . triumphant.

She moaned shakily as he began to fuck her. He watched her through narrowed eyelids as she stretched back her neck and raised her hips to meet his demanding thrusts. Her back arched off the couch. Her full breasts pressed tightly against the sweater, the promise of their softness taunting him.

He growled and braced himself on one hand. With the other he shoved up her sweater to reveal the elegant lines of her stretched torso. His fingertips slid beneath the clinging satin of her bra, plumping the pale, firm flesh over the restraining fabric.

It felt like more sharp, agonizing pleasure than he could bear to lean down and suckle the large pink nipple that he'd exposed while he plunged his cock into Laura again and again. Her nipple distended against his thrashing tongue. She whimpered in pleasure.

Their mating became maddened, his thrusts hard and forceful, the tempo of their briskly slapping flesh increasing with each passing second. She met him stroke for stroke, her hips pistoning his cock into the wet, sleek tunnel of her pussy in a perfect, driving rhythm.

Her catchy, anguished cries drove him wild. He hooked the leg that wasn't on the back of the couch into the crook of his elbow and took her even deeper, as though he were desperate to find some answer at Laura's farthest reaches. She grew taut beneath him. She clenched her eyes shut and ground her pelvis against him, trying to get friction on her clit.

He reached between their bodies and separated the swollen folds of her labia. When she pressed back against him her exposed, erect clit rubbed directly against his skin. Her warm juices anointed him. She gyrated her hips, grinding against him in small circles. Her pussy squeezed tightly around him.

His eyes crossed at the sensation.

When he felt her break and shudder around him he gave up trying for even an ounce of restraint. He fucked her fast and furious while she shuddered beneath him and uneven cries erupted from her throat, her pussy pulling and convulsing around his stabbing cock.

He slammed into her one last time and roared as he leapt into the inferno with her.

A moment later he fell heavily on her, his breath falling in jagged pants along her neck.

He didn't want to move, wanted to stay in that mindless state of bliss with his sated cock buried inside Laura for an eternity. Her pussy tightened around him and he quickly changed his opinion.

He'd be more than happy to hop straight from satiation to another bout of brain-frying lust. Just as long as he didn't have to think . . .

He nuzzled her neck languidly, pressing his lips to her leaping pulse. His eyes clenched tight when he felt her blood running wildly in her veins.

No one tasted like Laura. No one smelled like her.

The first time he'd kissed her she'd been twenty years old. Earlier that day she'd been suntanning out on the roof of Sunny Days, the West Side diner and cop bar that her uncle bought after he'd retired from the CPD. She'd worn a white sundress. Her sun-drenched, dark honey-colored skin had set off her exotically tilted green eyes to stunning effect.

It had been the first time that he'd realized Laura Vasquez wasn't just an extremely pretty girl, but a singularly beautiful woman. And when he'd tasted her lips and dipped his tongue into the sweetness that lay behind them, Shane'd been a goner.

He leaned up and brushed kisses on her nose and cheek, eventually settling on her parted lips, all too eager to relive the sins and follies of the past. After a few moments of rubbing and nipping at the plump flesh of her lips he sank his tongue between them. He groaned and flexed his hips, stroking her warm, snug channel.

Being surrounded in her taste made him burn all over again. Yes . . . if there was one thing that could make him forget, surely it was this.

As their kiss grew wilder Laura made a sound in her throat of mixed desire and anguish, making him pause. He leaned up and studied her in the dim light. His cock lurched inside her clasping pussy at the vision before him. Her full lips looked red and swollen from his kisses, her eyes limpid.

She looked anything but aloof at that moment. The realization struck like a hammer to a gong, vibrating deep inside of him. She wasn't as impervious to him as she pretended to be. Logic, threats, and fury bounced off Laura, but sexual desire pierced straight through her thick defensive armor.

Was she like this with any man who dominated her and bent her to his will?

Certainly that's what Huey must have done to her years ago. Shane had been her lover . . . a besotted, devoted one. Huey had been ten years older than her when Laura married him, seemingly out of nowhere. She must have been fascinated by the handsome older man.

Shane had only been twenty-four at the time of their all-too-brief love affair. In his opinion, Laura's and his sex life had been phenomenal . . . electrifying, even. But it obviously had been lacking for Laura. He hadn't tied her down, after all, or used sex toys on her.

He'd already guessed Laura was a natural submissive,

but they hadn't gotten around to exploring those avenues when their relationship abruptly ended. She'd been so young, after all, and Shane himself hadn't been much older. He would have loved to be the one to introduce her to the BDSM lifestyle, but it'd been Huey who had done it instead. Not that Shane's domination of Laura would have been anything like Huey's. The mere thought of sharing her with other men made Shane nauseous with rage.

He'd suspected the nature of Huey and Laura's relationship. Feared it even. And after hearing those tapes several weeks ago all of his suspicions had been confirmed. Even though he'd begun to think of Laura less and less frequently over the years, after hearing those tapes it'd all started again.

The worrying. The needing. The anger at her treachery.

"I'm not married yet," he said, realizing that he had never corrected her earlier.

"Yet?"

"In two months."

She gave a tremulous smile and leaned up slightly from the couch, averting her gaze from him.

"*Please*, Shane."

He cursed under his breath and moved. It just about killed him to withdraw from the one place where he knew for a fact that Laura wasn't indifferent . . . from the place where she burned hot.

As soon as he'd removed his weight she sat up and grabbed the afghan off the back of the couch, covering herself.

He ground his back teeth together in frustration as he walked to the bathroom down the hall, disposing of the condom. "You're *not* going to pretend that just didn't happen," he warned when he reentered the living room, buttoning his jeans.

She looked up at him slowly, her lustrous dark hair falling away from her exquisitely chiseled jawbone. The evidence of her weariness made his follow-up comment freeze on his tongue. Her eyes were like mirrors reflecting the harsh reality of what he'd just done.

She'd just discovered that the man she'd been married to

for thirteen years, and who she apparently worshipped in some warped manner like a slave did its master, had shot himself in the head. And Shane's reaction had been to shove her down on a couch and fuck her like there was no tomorrow.

Regret lanced through him, sharp and burning.

She glanced down, avoiding his gaze. "You need to go, Shane."

For a full ten seconds he stood paralyzed.

Of *course* he should go. He not only had risked all the hard work that his agents on the Organized Crime Squad at the FBI had put into the CPD theft ring case by having sex with Laura, he'd just sounded the death knell on his relationship with Clarissa.

But still he remained unmoving.

"Joey?" he asked harshly.

She jerked her head up.

"Is that why you did it, Laura? Why you *do* it?"

Her expression settled into a mask, but he didn't miss the flash of panic in her green eyes.

"Why don't you trust me to help you? Goddamn it, *tell* me." His whisper cut like a serrated knife through the weighty, poisonous silence.

"Tell you what? That I regret it? That it was a mistake?" She drew the afghan tighter around her torso. "Do you expect me to reveal some detail to help your investigation just because of *this*?" She glanced down pointedly at the couch. Despite her disdainful expression he saw how she trembled.

"You know damn well that's not what I wanted you to tell me, Laura."

He felt her eyes on him as he walked out. But as usual, Laura remained mute.

CHAPTER **THREE**

Laura waited, her posture rigid, until she heard the sound of Shane shutting the front door behind him with an angry click of finality. Her body sagged. An almost debilitating fatigue suffused her, weighting her limbs so greatly that for a moment she wondered if she would move again . . . ever.

The explosive encounter with Shane had made her feel the heaviness of her choices a hundredfold.

Her head fell back onto the couch. *That's right, Laura, suck him nice and deep like a good little wife. Show him how nice we treat our guests.*

It felt like pouring acid on a raw wound every time she replayed it in her mind.

She clenched her eyelids shut, trying to rid herself of the image of Shane's furious, disdainful expression as he'd looked down at her and said those ugly words. There'd been something else there on his face—something that cut even deeper than his contempt.

Hurt. What he'd said pained him deeply.

How could you do it? How could you let those assholes touch you? You're mine.

He still loved her. Shane—the object of her single-minded, worshipful devotion since she was a small girl of six—still cared for her. Despite everything.

Her face collapsed. It was the sweetest knowledge. The bitterest.

A sob tore at her throat. Her anguish was so great that her body must have instinctively tried to protect her from the unbearable weight of it combined with everything else the fateful night had brought her.

The sound of her cell phone ringing insistently pierced her consciousness. She sat up wearily, confused. Her eyes widened in shock when they fell on the antique grandfather clock. She'd been sleeping for more than two hours.

She paused when she saw that the number had been blocked on her caller ID. Her heartbeat quickened. It might be the anonymous caller—the one who had hinted he possessed some evidence that could help her. She pressed the receive button and put the phone to her ear without speaking.

"My condolences, Laura," Randall Moody said. She shut her eyes in disappointment. Not the anonymous caller who hinted at a means for freedom from the devil's snare, then.

It was the devil himself calling.

"What do you want?"

"Is it a crime to check in on the grieving widow?"

That comment warranted icy silence, which is precisely what it received.

"I know who was there earlier this evening."

"Does it surprise you? Huey was his trump card. He's furious about Huey's death," she hissed, injecting as much cold disdain into her tone as she could muster. Of course Moody was having her watched. The devil didn't miss much that went on in his domain.

"Does he suspect anything?" he asked.

Laura felt like all the blood in her head surged down to her feet in a dizzying rush. She reached out blindly, her hand finding the back of the couch, steadying her vertigo.

"Are you asking if Shane Dominic suspects that Huey was murdered?"

"That's right."

"No. He believes it was a suicide."

"Are you sure he wasn't after anything else, Laura? Not interested in rekindling the old flame?"

"I could care less if he were. You know as well as I do the only thing Dominic wants is to find a way to nail Huey along with any other neck he can wrap his hands around. He was just here to badger me for details about the case."

Moody made a sound of disgust. "He must be pretty desperate, roughing up a woman who just discovered her husband killed himself."

"Did he kill himself?" Laura asked, hoping Moody didn't hear the tremor in her voice. There was no love lost on her part when it came to Huey. He'd lived by a code of violence. It didn't surprise her that he'd died by one. But the thought of yet another murder to cover the tracks of these men's crimes made her physically ill.

A gravid pause ensued. When Moody resumed speaking, however, he sounded entirely calm.

"That's what it looks like. You and I both know Huey didn't have what it takes to weather the difficult times. Weak. Huey couldn't face the day unless he thought riches were going to fall into his lap simply because he blessed the rest of the world with his presence. And I'd be careful about voicing any doubts about Huey's suicide, Laura. It just struck me that if an investigation were to be launched and certain unsavory details were revealed, you could be a prime suspect."

Laura glanced around her living room warily while he spoke. Shane had said that the basement had been bugged. Surely he wouldn't have had sex with her on that couch if they were being listened to by members of his own staff. He might have been half-crazed with fury and lust, but Shane was also a vastly intelligent, methodical man—the consummate professional. He didn't make stupid mistakes like that.

But what if *other* ears were listening . . .

"Huey's death doesn't change a thing in regard to you, Laura. I just wanted you to know that."

Laura found herself staring fixedly at the antique grandfather clock. It had been one of several pieces that she'd inherited from her uncle Derrick when he'd died in a car wreck thirteen years ago. Derrick hadn't been the only tragedy of that accident. Laura's younger brother, Peter, had died later in the hospital from injuries sustained during the crash.

"I'm aware that nothing has changed," she replied coldly.

"Good, I'm glad to hear it. You know how fond I am of you, Laura. Huey was a top-notch soldier and you've always been a *good* wife to him . . . but there are others who could take his place."

"Not a chance," Laura hissed before she could stop herself.

"Your loyalty to Huey is touching, of course. I've got my eye on you, though, Laura. You won't appreciate my methods if you should do anything rash," he warned, all the while using that warm, grandfatherly tone that made her skin crawl. "These are difficult times for you—for all of us. Joey and his family will be there for you, of course. He's always been a good brother to you, hasn't he? Invaluable. That's what family is at times like these. Wouldn't you agree?"

Laura hit the disconnect button. Her hands shook uncontrollably as she placed the phone back in her purse and wrapped the afghan tightly around her. She started to curl up in the corner of the couch once again but veered off in the opposite direction.

The last thing she needed at a time like this was a reminder of how completely she had melted beneath Shane's touch.

Still. After all these years.

A cold sweat broke out on her forehead and upper lip when she recalled how Shane had asked about Joey there at the end. Remorse flooded through her, bringing another wave of dizziness with it.

She paused on the stairwell, her hand going out to the banister to brace her suddenly limp, ineffective muscles. It terrified her to think of how easily she'd succumbed to him . . . how much control he had over her.

She needed to avoid Shane Dominic at all costs.

He thought since she'd surrendered her body to him he had a right to her mind . . . her spirit. But Shane Dominic had another thing coming. She hadn't done what she'd done for the past thirteen and a half years only to have him spit in the face of her efforts now.

John McNamara cast a doubtful look out the windows of the headquarters of the Federal Bureau of Investigation's Chicago field office. A lethal-looking lake wind whipped up the recently fallen snow on Roosevelt Road and rattled the panes of glass.

"Why do we let him talk us into this?" John mumbled under his breath to the woman standing beside him, who was in the process of pulling a ski mask down over her smooth, brown face.

"Because he's not only our boss, he's our boss's boss. And what he says is true—"

"I do think better when I'm running outside. Treadmill just doesn't do it for me," Shane finished for Mavis Bertram, the supervising agent on the FBI's Organized Crime Squad. He grinned when he saw McNamara's sheepish expression at being overheard.

"Come on, Mac, it'll put hair on your chest," Shane said as he unceremoniously shoved a Georgetown Hoyas knit hat onto his head. The temperature was a bitter sixteen degrees this morning, and that didn't include the chilling effect of the brutal wind.

"If I'm lucky it'll freeze the hair off my legs permanently and I won't have to shave anymore," Mavis said wryly as she did some quick stretches. "How far are we going this morning, Dom?" she asked when she stood again and the three of them headed for the revolving doors.

Shane shrugged. "Just around the block."

He caught Mavis giving Mac a long-suffering glance and laughed. Mavis shivered noticeably once they stepped outside.

"Why couldn't we have gotten ourselves a normal, paper-pushing SAC, the administrative kind who does his best work in an office?" Mavis joked as they started jogging.

"You guys are in charge of Operation Serve and Protect. But a case like this requires just as much administration and diplomacy as it does investigation," Shane muttered wryly. "Makes the people of Chicago uneasy . . . and angry to consider so much corruption in their police department."

"Yeah, and not just at the CPD, either. At us for exposing them," Mavis muttered under her breath.

Neither he nor the other two special agents spoke for the first ten minutes as they jogged, allowing their bodies to become accustomed to the paradoxical stresses of heat-producing exercise and bitter cold exterior temperatures. Which was fine with Shane, because he wasn't in the mood for jocular camaraderie.

What he was in the mood for was regaining some footing on the CPD theft ring case. For regaining some much-needed perspective after what had happened with Laura three nights ago.

He'd found it increasingly difficult to separate that charged episode from any aspect of his life over the weekend—whether it was personal or professional. Clarissa was currently refusing to talk to him because of his aloofness since returning home on Friday night.

Her fury at him served his purpose. He needed time to think, to clear his head. Because he knew he was going to have to talk to Clarissa about their future.

Or their lack of a future, to be more precise.

He wasn't just going to postpone their wedding this time, but call if off for good.

Best to admit the truth. What he'd done thirteen years ago said it all. There was never any real doubt where his heart lay. Cold, hard logic suggested that he was behaving irrationally; but something else—Shane suspected it was pure stubbornness on his part—argued loudly that he should resist the smug security of cold, hard logic at all costs when it came to Laura.

Clarissa deserved better than to be married to a man who couldn't forget another woman, even if that other woman didn't want anything to do with him.

Something else had been preoccupying him all weekend long. In the shadowy background of his methodical brain, he'd been planning something. Something outlandish.

A desperate plan for a desperate man.

"Aren't you going to ask us if we have any good news for you, like you usually do?" Mavis asked eventually.

"Not if you're going to tell me 'no' like you usually do."

"We're gonna break the precedent on all sides on this lovely Chicago Monday morning," Mavis assured him. "Go on, Mac."

"Okay, get this, Dom—you're never gonna guess who Vince Lazar's first cousin is," Mac said, referring to one of the four cops that had been arrested along with Huey Mays last week.

"The mayor?"

Mavis snorted, sending a jet of white vapor through her ski mask. "Even better. Vince Lazar's cousin is Eddie Mercado."

Shane broke stride slightly at that, one shoe nearly losing its grip on the pavement. Eddie Mercado used to be Alvie Castaneda's first lieutenant before he was found shot in the alley of a high-class strip joint on the North Side several years ago.

Alvie Castaneda was the head of the Chicago mob.

Mac smiled, clearly pleased by Shane's surprise. He nodded. "We need to firm it up some, but we have reason to believe that Lazar was involved in extorting money from bookies and small-time thieves for Mercado and Castaneda back in the early nineties."

"That wasn't in our file," Shane said. "How'd something like that get by Lazar's pre-employment screening at the CPD?"

Mac shrugged. "Huey Mays was a sergeant in the Organized Crime Division when Lazar came on board. He could have easily covered up that little detail."

"He could have," Shane said as he stared down the

plowed, quiet urban street, his mind churning. "So could have Randall Moody. Moody would have been a captain of the division at that time."

When neither agent said anything, he glanced over at them in time to see Mac meeting Mavis's gaze.

"What?" Shane asked. "You think I'm just saying that because I'm gunning for Moody now that Mays has gone and ruined our case by taking the low road?"

"Dom, we've got nothing on Moody but Deangelo Stout's confession that he believed there was someone in the CPD above Huey Mays who masterminded all the plans—which jewelry exhibition to target next, which fur shows, which salesman they'd hit, what supplies they'd steal from the stores of the CPD. Stout said he *suspected* it was Randall Moody. What makes you so positive we can nail a respected, thirty-five-year veteran of the CPD? Stout's a worm—you know that. Shit, for all we know, he's got a grudge because Moody disciplined him at some point while Stout was under his command."

Shane didn't respond for a moment as he jogged, letting Mavis's words filter through the rest of the morass of thoughts in his brain. Yeah, Deangelo Stout—the ex-cop turned jewel and fur thief who had given evidence on Huey Mays and several other cops from the safety of a witness protection program—was no choirboy. Mavis was right. It wasn't uncommon for those who finally decided to roll on past crime buddies to throw in one or two personal vendettas to sweeten the sour taste left over from squealing.

Still, Shane was convinced Randall Moody was their man. And when he became this sure about something, he was usually right.

His mind whirred as they jogged along at a brisk pace and sleet stung his face. It felt great. Shane felt better than he had in days. Warm, sharp, and hyperalert.

Nothing like a good run in a Chicago sleet storm to rid oneself of the mental fog.

"Mays had a charisma that mixed with his ruthlessness. It made the guys beneath him look up to him like a hero.

And he may have had the brains to carry out something as vast as this operation," Shane mused. "But he didn't have the patience.

"Mays was an addict—booze, drugs, money, gambling, women—and he had the personality of an addict," Shane continued. "He needed his fix and he got nervous and irritable when he couldn't get it. He would have cut corners if he had the chance, been sloppy in order to get the high an addict lives for, pulled jobs in too quick of a succession or in locations that were convenient versus wise."

"But they didn't," Mac agreed as they turned east, their pounding feet making a hollow thumping sound on the frozen pavement. "Those thefts were spread out over eighteen states and fifteen years. We didn't start to connect the dots until eighteen months ago."

Shane grunted.

"What?" Mavis asked, her brown eyes sharp and curious behind the ski mask.

"Fifteen years?" Shane muttered. "That's one of the reasons I think Moody's involved in this. There's good reason to believe that he's been pulling off these jobs for nearly twice that time."

There was another reason he suspected Moody and it was too vague, unformed, and illogical for Shane to speak out loud to Mavis and Mac.

Shane recalled all too clearly seeing a younger, leaner Moody sitting in a booth at Derrick Vasquez's restaurant Sunny Days, shooting the shit with Derrick and two other uniformed cops. Shane had come to meet Laura after her shift waitressing during the all-too-brief six-month period when they'd been involved.

They'd kept the fact that they were dating a secret, which Shane had reason to be thankful about presently with news reporters nosing around and talking about his past connections and friendship to Laura's brother Joey. Laura's uncle was very protective of her, and even though Laura had been twenty years old and a college student at the Art Institute at the time, she still lived in Derrick's house.

At the time, Laura and he had been crazed, couldn't-keep-their-hands-off-each-other, barking mad in love.

Or at least that's what Shane had thought. He had second-guessed that assumption when she'd eloped with Huey Mays while Laura and he were supposedly in the ecstatic midst of that love affair.

But Shane hadn't had a hint of future calamity almost fourteen years ago on that brilliant fall afternoon as he'd walked into the crowded restaurant. Laura was an angel, as far as he was concerned, and he'd only wanted to glory in her existence like a man who'd come upon a treasure and reveled in unexpected riches.

As Shane had searched the crowded restaurant for a glimpse of Laura, Derrick had called out a greeting to him from a booth. Randall Moody had turned to look at Shane. Their eyes had met for all of two seconds, but a singular sensation had gone through Shane at that moment . . . something he'd never forgotten in almost fourteen years.

Moody had still worn the shadow of his winning smile around his lips, but it was his pale blue eyes that told the true story. Shane had seen something primitive and feral in that gaze . . . something that called to mind a calculating, deadly viper.

Maybe it had just been his imagination. But the thought had struck Shane more than once over the intervening years that it was precisely in that moment, when he'd unintentionally caught Moody with his mask down, that everything had started to go wrong with Laura and him.

He yanked his thoughts away from the past.

"Maybe you're right about me being off base about Randall Moody," Shane told Mavis and McNamara several minutes later. "But I don't think so. We may have lost Mays, but we have solid cases against the four cops working for him. And now we find out that Vince Lazar had connections to Eddie Mercado . . . and possibly to Alvie Castaneda, the biggest crime boss in the city."

"You really think it's possible that Moody could be working with the mob?" McNamara asked doubtfully.

Shane shrugged. "We're talking about the largest organized theft ring in known history, Mac. A hundred and three million dollars. That's the amount of money we think this operation has amassed in the past fifteen years—and that's just from the theft ring. These cops were a law unto themselves. Stout has testified that they regularly shook down drug dealers and other hoods. They'd had plenty of time to expand and perfect a racketeering operation that's gone unchecked now for at *least* fifteen years. How many operations of that caliber do you know of that the mob hasn't been involved with?"

Shane didn't wait for Mac to answer before he plunged ahead. "Personally I don't give a rat's ass about whether or not we ever pin mob connections on Moody. I want to nail him any way I can, and maybe this'll help us. I want you two to dig into this mob angle further. We've got an airtight case against Lazar. If he does have ties to Castaneda, he'll do whatever he can to protect them. He knows damn well Castaneda can reach him behind bars. He'll be more willing to sing about a higher-up in the Chicago Police Department than he would about any connections to the mob."

"You think he wouldn't be worried in the lockup if he gave evidence against Moody?"

"He's not in the county jail, Mac. He's in federal. Besides, I see Dom's point. If I were Lazar, I'd risk Moody's wrath before I would Castaneda's."

Mac raised frost-coated eyebrows. "Too true."

"Problem is, Lazar couldn't make bail like Mays did. He must be on both Castaneda's and Moody's shit list for some reason if they're letting him rot. Or worse, he doesn't know anything. If the higher-ups aren't concerned, there's a good chance they think Lazar's got nothing of consequence to spill," Shane muttered grimly.

Several hours later Shane looked up from a paper-strewn desk when his administrative assistant buzzed him.

"Mavis Bertram to see you, Dom."

"Send her in."

Mavis poked her head in the door a second later. "You feel like taking a ride?"

"It depends on where we're going. I'm up to my ass in paperwork," he said distractedly.

"How about to Laura Mays's house?"

He glanced up sharply.

"She placed a nine-one-one call to the police not fifteen minutes ago from her home phone. She said there was an intruder in her house. There was a click on the line and Laura Mays told the operator that whoever was in the house was on the line with them. Then the phone went dead."

Shane stood and grabbed his jacket off the back of the chair. "Let's go."

CHAPTER **FOUR**

Laura parked on the street near Joey's house. She turned off the car, her eyes trained on the rearview mirror.

The driver of the silver Camry turned right down a side street. It'd been five days now since her house had been broken into, but she was still nervous and jumpy. Nothing had been taken from the house. The police had assumed that Laura had interrupted a burglary by unexpectedly being home from work that day.

Shane Dominic had suspected otherwise. She'd been shocked to see him pull up to her house next to the cop car. He'd listened while the police questioned her about the break-in, then pulled her aside and questioned her privately.

"Your car is parked out front, Laura. Unless the burglar was brain-dead, he would have assumed you were here, not at work."

"So?" she'd asked.

"Whoever broke into this house *knew* you were here, dammit. They only ran because they heard you on the phone with the police. They weren't on a burglary mission. It was *you* they were after. Now . . . are you going to tell me what's going on, or are you going to wait until some asshole hurts you?" he'd asked her, his blue eyes blazing fiercely.

Of course Laura had denied his allegations. She'd also refused to talk to him the three other times Shane had called her during the week. She couldn't afford to have Shane interfering now. The anonymous caller who'd promised evidence against Moody had never called back, but Laura somehow equated the elusive caller with the break-in.

In other words, she suspected Shane had been right in his allegations. But surely if the anonymous caller and the intruder were one and the same man, he didn't want to hurt her, only talk to her.

So why was she so jumpy and nervous?

She glanced outside warily but nothing looked unusual on the dark, cold January night except the large number of cars lining the street—guests for the party Joey and Shelly were throwing for Carlotta and her volleyball teammates.

The heels of her boots hitting the frozen pavement echoed around the still neighborhood, the hollow sound making her feel prickly and vulnerable—like a deer in a clearing with a bull's-eye trained on it.

She grinned hugely several moments later as she hugged her niece, all anxieties momentarily forgotten.

"Thank you so much for coming, Aunt Laura. I told Dad that maybe we shouldn't have a party, with everything you're going through and all."

"Don't be ridiculous. You win the state volleyball finals once in a lifetime," Laura reassured her.

"There's always next year, you know," Joey Vasquez said as he approached. He kissed his sister's cheek. Despite his friendly, cheerful façade, Laura sensed the tension in her older brother's rigid posture.

"Dad's a little overconfident," Carlotta commented ruefully.

"It's a father's prerogative," Laura said before she handed Carlotta a small wrapped gift. "Congratulations. I wish my showing at the gallery hadn't fallen on the same date and that I could have seen the championship game."

"Oh, you shouldn't have!" Carlotta exclaimed as she accepted the box. She grinned excitedly at one of her teammates standing nearby. "Aunt Laura gives awesome gifts," Laura heard her tell the teenage girl before they walked away.

Joey chuckled. "High praise."

Laura fondly watched Carlotta unwrap her gift surrounded by eight or nine other volleyball players. Joey's energetic wife, Shelly, had decorated the large family room and adjoining dining room with an assortment of congratulatory signs and streamers in the girls' school colors.

A crowd of more than fifty people glanced over when Carlotta withdrew the silver volleyball charm and squealed in delight.

"To be sixteen again," Joey muttered with undisguised envy.

Laura studied him as he watched his daughter. With every passing day he seemed to resemble their father more and more: the same thin, angular face, the aquiline nose, the warm brown eyes.

Even as she watched, however, those expressive eyes flickered across the room furtively. She opened her mouth to ask him why he seemed so anxious when her gaze followed Joey's. Her expression stiffened.

She faced her brother. "What's he doing here?" she hissed under her breath.

Joey looked down at her, his expression stricken. "I'm sorry, Laura. I meant to warn you before you saw him. I was as surprised as you are when he showed up. I saw him down at Headquarters today and invited him to the party. I never guessed Dom would actually come."

"Shane?" Laura asked incredulously. That hadn't been the person to whom she'd referred.

Her head swung around.

Their eyes met immediately. Laura had no idea how she could have missed him. His presence commanded the entire room. He sat in a lounge chair close to the fireplace, long legs bent, his knees slightly spread. She was relieved to see that he wore jeans and not his work attire, hoping that meant he hadn't come to Joey's house in any official capacity. He pinned her steadily with his stare, his blue eyes seeming all the more brilliant set off as they were by his dark complexion and a black knit shirt.

Despite his impassivity, Laura knew with some second sense she possessed when it came to Shane that he directed a powerful beam of concentrated anger at her. Shane had always possessed a singular brand of intensity. He was furious, yes, but there was something else in his gaze.

Frustration.

She forced her expression into a neutrality that matched his, her eyes skimming past the white-haired, distinguished-looking man who stood on the other side of the fireplace. Randall Moody's pale blue eyes watched her with a predator's focus, his gaze eerily at odds with his benevolent countenance.

It had been Moody's presence that had caught her attention when she'd glanced into the crowded room. That's why she hadn't immediately noticed Shane.

Laura swallowed thickly, trying to ignore the prickly sensation on the back of her neck undoubtedly caused by Shane's continued stare.

"I meant Moody," she whispered to her brother. "Since when do you socialize with the likes of him?"

Joey looked uncomfortable. "Moody's not so bad."

"Not so bad?" Laura muttered, stunned. It suddenly struck her that Joey had assumed she was anxious because of Shane's presence because *he* was more nervous about Shane being there than Randall Moody. The realization created a sensation like a lead ball settling in her stomach.

"Is Shane here because of the CPD investigation?" she asked. She stepped closer, forcing her brother to look at her when he'd just glanced away uneasily. "Has he been asking you questions?"

"A few," Joey said evasively.

"Why are you acting so nervous, Joey?"

Joey gave her an insulted look. "There isn't a cop in the department that wouldn't be shitting bricks if Dom came within a hundred feet of him at this point."

She opened her mouth to ask Joey whether Shane was asking questions as a friend or in an official capacity, but Carlotta touched her arm.

"Thank you so much, Aunt Laura," the vibrant girl said excitedly. She held up her hand. The silver charm bracelet that Laura had given her when she turned eight years old glittered on her wrist, the tiny inscribed volleyball having been added to the other charms Laura had given her over the years.

"It looks great," Laura complimented.

"We're going to cut the cake," Shelly called out from the dining room.

Laura had difficulty concentrating for the next ten minutes. On the surface she appeared to be chatting amiably with Carlotta and her teammates as they ate blue-and-gold-frosted cake and the girls related all the details of their championship game to Laura. In reality she was hyperaware of the small group that stood several feet away from her that consisted of Joey, Shane, Shelly, and Randall Moody. The cake she tried to eat felt like dry dust when she saw the way Shane pinned Moody with his steady stare.

Laura could tell by Shelly's broad smile and frequent laughter as they ate the cake that their conversation had nothing to do with the FBI investigation of the CPD. Still, icy fingers of panic uncurled inside of her when Moody glanced over and gave her a friendly nod. For a few tense seconds she thought he was about to come over to talk to her.

"How about if we help your mom out and clear up some of these dishes?" Laura asked Carlotta briskly.

"Sure," Carlotta agreed.

Carlotta and her friends retrieved glasses and plates from the kitchen and family room while Laura rinsed the dishes and put them in the dishwasher. She straightened from leaning over the dishwasher, reaching out for the plate being extended toward her automatically. Her head swung around when whoever held it refused to let go. She found herself staring up into a pair of penetrating blue eyes.

"Shane," she mumbled, stunned not only by his sudden presence but his nearness. Her gaze sank to the grim line of his firm lips. Against her will all the images and sensations of him leaning down and consuming her flooded her awareness.

A week had passed since they'd shared that torrid, tumultuous moment on her living room couch. Huey's funeral had occurred in the interim. The FBI's crime lab had issued a report that indicated that there was no evidence for considering Huey's death to be caused by anything other than the suicide his note alleged it to be. Her house had been broken into and she'd managed to either avoid or sidetrack Shane when he tried to get her to talk to him. She'd sold two of her sculptures and a painting during that time period and paid all the monthly bills, enormously relieved to have been able to pay off a good portion of Huey's remaining gambling debts.

Thousands of other things had occurred in the week since she'd burned beneath Shane on that couch. But it felt as if thirty seconds hadn't passed from that moment when she'd looked into his stormy eyes while his cock stretched and filled her.

From that moment when he'd forced her to *feel*.

She staggered back one step, her hip hitting the kitchen counter hard. She winced. His hand came up to her elbow to steady her, but his touch had the opposite effect on her. Her heartbeat began to drum unnaturally loud in her ears.

"Are you all right?"

"Of course I am," she replied coolly. She tried to look over Shane's shoulder to assure herself that no one was in the kitchen with him, but he was too tall . . . too broad in the shoulders for her to see.

And he stood too close, making it difficult for her to maintain an emotional distance. She yanked the empty plate from his grip and turned to resume her former activities.

"What do you want?" she finally asked when she noticed from the corner of her eye that he hadn't moved an inch.

"I want a lot of things."

She glanced over at the sound of his low, suggestive tone. For a few seconds she was once again caught in the snare of his eyes.

What did he see when he looked at her? Laura couldn't help but wonder. The woman who had betrayed him? An object of hatred? An object on which to expend his lust?

Bitter tears stung her eyes at the realization that it had all come to this.

She told herself to look away, but instead her gaze lowered over his hard, determined jaw.

She'd always found Shane's face compelling. There wasn't a trace of softness to be found anywhere in all those rugged angles and stark planes. With her artist's imagination she'd often envisioned his face beneath a Roman battle helm, one that might have once been worn by a Dominic ancestor. While his father had gifted him with his dark, Italian good looks, he'd received his blue eyes from his Irish-American mother. The effect of those eyes in his dark face was startling . . . breathtaking even. Laura guessed Shane had a similar effect on just about every woman he encountered.

He exuded a raw sexuality that drew her—intimidated her because it was almost impossible to resist. She'd been attracted to his quiet, forceful energy since they were children. Even as a boy Shane had possessed that inherent confidence, a genuine comfort in his own skin that drew people to him. His charisma had only grown as he matured. He'd been potent enough when he'd been her lover when he was twenty-four, but at the age of thirty-seven, Shane was clearly just entering his prime.

His magnetic pull on her had grown exponentially more powerful. If he knew the effect he had on her, he wouldn't hesitate to use it against her. Nevertheless she couldn't stop herself from gazing longingly at the cleft in his determined chin and recalling what the sexy indentation felt like beneath her lips and tongue.

She didn't realize she'd been staring until she saw one dark eyebrow arch up in mocking amusement.

"One of the things that I'd like more than anything is the truth, Laura," he murmured. "I wonder if you even know what that is anymore."

Her eyes widened in alarm when he stepped closer.

"Another thing I'd like is to be buried deep inside you again."

For a second she thought she'd hallucinated the words, imagined the manner in which his deep voice vibrated with barely restrained emotion. His nostrils flared slightly when she met his gaze. For a second or two she stood frozen, a deer caught in the harsh, stunning impact of high-beamed headlights.

She turned away, intent on escape, but he stopped her with a hand on her elbow.

"Let's go over to your place. We need to talk."

She yanked her arm out of his hold. Her gaze flickered over to the dining room. It was now empty.

"Looking for Randall Moody? He left five minutes ago. Let's go, Laura."

"Did you come here to question Joey?" she stalled, trying to find some secure footing on which to hold herself at a distance from Shane. He'd put his hand back on her upper arm and was molding her flesh softly, as though to soothe her skittishness. If anything his touch made her more nervous, however.

"No. I came here to find you," he stated bluntly. "I figured you couldn't avoid me at your own niece's party like you have all week. Now listen to what we're going to do. I'm going to leave in ten minutes or so. Carlotta wants to show me her new puppy out in the garage. Wait until you see Carlotta come back inside and leave a few minutes later. I'll wait for you in my car and follow you to your house."

"I'm not ready to leave yet," she said coldly, turning back to the counter.

"Maybe you want me to come up with some questions for Joey . . . like why he's so tight with Randall Moody? Is that it?"

She looked over her shoulder. "You're a bastard, Shane Dominic."

He leaned down until he was just inches away from her upturned face. "You haven't seen anything yet, Laura."

Shane blasted the heat but it had no discernable effect on the frigid temperature of the interior of his car for an uncomfortable minute. He kept his eyes trained on the front door of Joey's house.

Would she come? He had everything in place to carry out his plan, but he still hadn't completely decided if he was out of his mind for attempting it. The other part of him wondered if he wasn't just putting off the inevitable in the name of caution. He'd seen the way Randall Moody looked at Laura. She'd been too good at avoiding Moody's gaze not to have been hyperaware of it.

Laura wasn't safe. He could feel it in his bones.

When he'd told her that whoever had broken into her house had done so because they were looking for her, he'd seen the flicker in her eyes. She'd realized he was correct at that moment.

And then she'd proceeded to lie and tell him she had no idea what he was talking about.

Well, he was done with the lies that came out of her pretty little mouth. Laura's avoidance of him ended tonight.

After several more minutes of waiting for Laura, a flicker of light caught his attention out of the corner of his eye. For a suspended second he clearly saw the face of the man in the driver's seat parked a quarter of a block down the street, cigarette perched between his lips—thin, pale face, sandy-colored hair. A chord of recognition struck Shane's consciousness. It'd been twelve years since he'd last seen the man's face.

The man had been staring with hawklike intensity at Joey's front door in the second before his lighter went out. Shane'd just been looking expectantly at Joey's house as well . . . waiting for Laura.

Having already said his good-byes, Shane had left from a side door in the garage after Carlotta had proudly shown him the rambunctious golden retriever puppy she'd received for her birthday. He'd been cloaked in darkness as he made his way to his car. Although the smoking guy had likely noticed his headlights go on, he'd probably assumed Shane'd come out of one of the houses across the street from Joey's.

He slowly reached beneath his jacket and unsnapped the leather holster holding his gun.

The front door opened and Laura stood for a moment in the archway, light surrounding her. She leaned back and gave a kiss to someone standing just inside the door before she turned and walked down the front steps. The door shut behind her.

For a few uncomfortable seconds Shane couldn't see her as she made her way through the dark yard. He caught sight of her as she started down the sidewalk thanks to a dim streetlight. He opened his car door quietly, hearing her heels tapping on the frozen pavement.

He caught the sound of muffled voices as he crossed the street: the man's sounded clipped and a little anxious; Laura's surprised and breathless. Shane cocked his ear to catch their exchange.

"You need to come with me. I know what you're looking for. There's someone who wants to help you," the man said.

"What?" Laura gasped. Shane picked up his pace. Something in her sharp exhalation informed him that the man had just put his hands on her. "No. Let go of me. I don't know what you're talking about—"

"He knows and he's fixed on telling you for some reason. Won't have it any other way." The man suddenly grunted in pain. Laura must have hit or kicked him in an attempt to get away. "Why you little . . . Huey always did say you were a bitch. Had to go and call the police on me the other day when I dropped in to see you, didn't you? Okay, you want to do this the hard way? Fine. How's that feel? That change your mind any?"

Laura gave a muffled sound of dismay as Shane rushed the two of them in the darkness. There wasn't much room to maneuver with the man holding Laura so close to his body.

He grabbed his wrist and wrenched. It cracked audibly. He heard the metallic sound of a gun sliding across the sidewalk at the same time he covered Laura's attacker's face with his hand.

A scream of pain shattered the silence of the dark neighborhood.

Shane'd found the guy's eye sockets with his first two fingers and gouged. He held Laura too close for Shane to maneuver—and who knew what other weapons the asshole had stashed on him? The man reeled back blindly to protect himself, staggering in the snow, cursing disjointedly, both hands protecting his temporarily blinded eyes.

"Stand back, Laura."

One solid strike to the jaw followed by an uppercut to the liver region and the man fell, air punching out of his lungs when he hit the ground hard.

Shane roughly turned him over in the snow.

"Put your hands up above your head," Shane directed. Not being a field agent, he usually didn't carry cuffs on him. When the man started to struggle and curse, albeit weakly, Shane warned quietly, "Just try me. I've got plenty more for you, Ardos."

Telly Ardos started, obviously just as put off by hearing his name spoken out loud as he was by Shane's threat.

"What's going on out there?" someone shouted in the distance.

"Joey?" Shane called.

"Shane? What the hell's going on?" Joey repeated as he approached at a jog.

Shane could barely make out Laura's profile in the darkness.

"You'll have to ask your sister that, Joey."

An hour later Shane pulled into the driveway behind Laura. He started to get out when he noticed that she'd exited her car and was rapidly coming toward him down the driveway. He remained seated, not saying anything when she opened the door and sank into the passenger seat. She faced him as she slammed the door shut.

"If you have something to say to me you can say it here," she said, referring to the terse reminder he'd uttered not ten minutes ago after two patrolmen had arrested Telly Ardos in front of Joey's house.

"What are you afraid will happen if we go inside?"

She gave him a thin smile and turned forward. She wore her long hair up tonight in a twist on the back of her head. Her profile looked cold and beautiful in the dim moonlight. When she remained unmoving Shane realized that she wasn't even going to deign to answer his question.

Even though she refused to meet his eyes he knew how powerfully aware she was of him. He sensed her anxiety . . . and yes, he hadn't been too far off in his accusation. Laura was afraid of him.

She had good reason to be.

Fury still roiled in his gut at the memory of that two-bit criminal grabbing her, pulling a gun on her . . . trying to get her in his car against her will. What would have happened if Shane hadn't been there? His back teeth ground together at the thought. And after all that, Laura sat there cool and distant, her seemingly impenetrable façade locked back in place. *That* infuriated him as much as anything.

"Who's Telly Ardos to you, Laura?"

She gave him a glance of asperity. "You heard what I told the police. He was friends with Huey, but I barely know him. I saw him around the house once in a while."

"What did he mean when he said he was going to take you to someone?"

She shrugged. "How should I know? The man was raving."

Shane gave her a disgusted, give-me-a-break look. She returned his stare with cool disdain. She didn't bat an eye when he locked the doors.

"You didn't tell the police that Ardos admitted to being the one who broke into your house. You're protecting that slimeball for some reason. Why?"

Her eyes flashed in the dim light, but she remained mute.

"Okay, so I'll tell you what I know then," he said sarcastically. "Telly Ardos worked as an assistant to a well-respected jeweler about a dozen years ago. I don't think Telly's boss was so respectable though. In fact, I think he was a thieving asshole who repaid his customers' loyalty to him by keeping their rare stones for himself and returning them with a smile and thanks in a European accent, both of which were as fake as the jewels he put in his customers' settings. I know Telly and Huey were drug and sex buddies. Huey must have had him on the payroll for the theft ring as well. Or more correctly, Randall Moody did. Am I right, Laura?

"Have you slept with him before?" Shane pressed, his fury rising when she merely stared at him. She sat forward abruptly.

"No, not that it's any of your goddamned business."

The artificially heated air in the interior of his sedan crackled with electricity . . . like lightning was about to strike. Or maybe it was just his prickling nerves that made Shane feel that way. He took a deep breath.

"I'm going to give you one more opportunity to tell me the truth about what you know about all this," he said. "I think you've kept your silence for all these years because you're trying to protect someone. I'd guess it was Joey and his family."

She shook her head and smiled in the face of what she obviously considered pure audacity on his part.

"Just what is it that you think I know, Shane? Do you think I was privy to the daily activities of Huey's job? I knew just as much about his regular routine as he knew about the process of making a sculpture. You're engaged. How much do you know about what your fiancée does when she goes into work?"

"I know a fair amount," he countered. "You learn about things like that when you sit down and talk to your significant other. Are you saying that you and Huey never talked?"

"What I'm saying is that I don't know anything about what he was being accused of before he committed suicide. It's not going to matter if you ask me once or a thousand times, the answer is still going to be the same."

"Would you say that you and Huey were close?" Shane persisted, unperturbed.

She made a sound of disgust. "I don't have to answer these questions. Huey is dead. You can't put a dead man behind bars, Shane."

"The man I'm after is very much alive. I watched you tonight at Joey's. I think you know exactly who I'm talking about. Tell me what you know about Randall Moody. Tell me what you know about Huey's involvement with him in the theft ring. Did Moody ever come to this house? Did you ever see him and Huey meeting anywhere other than at work? Ever hear them talking on the phone?"

"I haven't got anything for you, Shane," she grated out.

He leaned across the console toward her.

"I'm desperate here. That's what you should understand. The cop that I'd hoped would give evidence on Moody is refusing to bargain. Moody must have a tighter hold on him than I'd thought. But even more important, you're in danger, Laura. Someone broke into this house looking for you. A man pulled a gun on you tonight. I won't sit by and watch while your stubbornness puts you in a grave."

Her contemptuous expression faltered slightly when he slowly began to dip his head toward hers.

"*Don't*, Shane," she whispered hoarsely.

"I don't have any choice. You've forced me to this," he said before he brushed his lips against hers. She made a soft, catchy sound. She stiffened when he put his hands on her back. Her body felt slender, curvy . . . enticing.

"I know you want me, Laura. There are some things you just can't hide from a man."

Her lips felt cool and dry, but he could feel her heat just beneath the surface. So he pressed closer. When he slid his tongue between her lips she moaned softly, her flesh becoming more supple, bending to his demand.

He brought her closer and swept the depths of her mouth. His cock swelled tight as he surrounded himself in her taste. Time and again he sampled her sweetness. He plundered, suckled, and coaxed until she fully participated in the kiss, her lips shaping his hungrily, her tongue sliding sensually against his.

The interior of his car suddenly felt as hot and sultry as the air on a tropical night.

She didn't protest when he slid one hand along her knee, lifting her skirt. He encountered a delicious length of silky thigh encased in smooth nylon. He paused a moment when he reached the top of her thigh-highs, sending two fingers beneath the elastic to rhythmically stroke the smooth, soft skin beneath it.

He groaned and leaned down farther over her, deepening their kiss. He probed beneath her panties, drawn to her heat. She gasped into his mouth when he worked his forefinger into her pussy. She was tight but a rush of warm liquid aided his cause considerably.

He drew his finger out only to plunge it back into her silky sheath. A considerable amount of her juices came with him when he withdrew the second time. He trailed his finger between her labia, lubricating her clit liberally. Her hips shifted restlessly against him and she moaned. Instead of giving her the pressure she wanted, however, he slid his wet finger along her lower belly, spreading her juices.

"*That's* honesty, Laura," he explained quietly. "Give me more of it."

"No," she whispered. She moved away from him, cloaking herself in the shadows.

He nodded his head slowly, having expected her answer. His hands slid down her arms. She gasped when he pushed her upper body forward and clasped her wrists, moving them behind her back. The sound of rattling metal broke the silence.

Her face registered mild confusion when he closed the handcuffs.

"What . . . what are you doing?" she asked, voice rising in incredulity when he leaned back into his seat. She twisted around, her eyes widening farther when she realized that she was truly bound. "Are you arresting me?"

Shane shook his head once. "I'm doing what I should have

done thirteen and a half years ago. I'm taking you away so you don't damage yourself any more than you already have."

"That's . . . that's ridiculous," she exclaimed shrilly. "That's *kidnapping*!"

He shrugged. "Call it what you like. I need the truth from you, Laura, and I'm going to get it. I've seen how you respond to me. If Huey Mays had the ability to get you to do whatever he wanted, I believe I can do the same. In fact, I think I can do better than he did at getting you to submit to my demands."

She went completely still. "You can't be serious."

"I'm serious all right. You're going away with me for a few days and I'm going to plumb the depths of your *honesty*!" He nodded grimly to her lap. "And you're going to discover the wisdom in telling me the truth about Huey."

"I can't believe this," she muttered slowly, clearly flattened by his actions. Just as he'd suspected, this had been the last thing she'd expected. Shane was still a little amazed himself at what he was doing, but that didn't deter him.

Something told him this was precisely the right thing to do. He knew he was breaking the law . . . was perfectly cognizant of the fact that he may go to jail for what he was doing.

But there was a higher law at work when it came to the issue of Laura. He needed to get her away, isolate her from whatever was influencing her. She'd been thrown back into his life again. He was convinced she was in danger because of something she knew. He would *not* let her go again without a fight.

Not this time.

Of course there was always the chance that he was deluding himself so that he could tie up the woman of his fantasies and have his way with her. Shane knew perfectly well that all criminals rationalized their actions, no matter how bizarre their logic had to become in order to justify what they'd done.

He also knew he couldn't continue living with the suspicion that Laura wasn't being honest with him because she was afraid. He'd seen how their desire for each other melted her defenses, if only temporarily. If he took her to a place where she couldn't escape him for several days, if he dominated her mind and body, her defenses against him would crumble. Maybe then she'd tell him what he needed to know.

He leaned over and secured her seat belt, ignoring her outraged protests.

"You plan to kidnap me, rape me—sacrifice everything you stand for just so that I'll tell you the truth about Huey's alleged criminal activities?" she asked in rising panic as he started to back out of her driveway.

"You know as well as I do that rape will never enter the picture. And I'm not doing this as an agent for the FBI. I'm doing this because of what you once were—what was between us."

"You're crazy. There was nothing between us but a summer sex fling between two kids!"

He threw her a scathing look. "I took your virginity, Laura. Do you really think I'm going to fall for the idea that you were a promiscuous slut who regularly engaged in sex flings?"

"That's what you think I am, isn't it? A promiscuous slut? You heard those tapes, didn't you? You heard me fucking all those men. Do you know why I did that? Because I *wanted* to . . . because I *loved* it," she shouted, fury lacing her tone.

After several seconds of silence Shane realized that he had a death grip on the steering wheel.

"Then what I have in mind should be right up your alley," he said eventually, forcing himself to loosen his hold.

CHAPTER **FIVE**

Laura swallowed and winced. She'd been alternating between shouting, scolding, and attempting to reason with Shane for the past hour and fifteen minutes and her throat had grown raw. He'd been equally impervious to every attempt she'd made. Panic roiled in her belly at the prospect of spending days alone with Shane . . . of being at his mercy.

The excitement that twined with her panic motivated her to try again.

"What about your fiancée? She's not going to want to have anything to do with you when she finds out about this." He rolled his strong jaw slightly as he stared straight ahead and drove.

"She's not my fiancée anymore," he growled.

Laura shook her head in incredulous disgust when he immediately sank back into silence after adding five more words to the dozen he'd spoken since backing out of her driveway.

"So she broke it off with you, did she? Found out the truth—that you're stark raving mad beneath that veneer of a smart, in-control FBI agent?" Laura taunted. She'd never known Shane to be distant. Angry, yes. Furious enough to strangle her, to be sure. Intellectually preoccupied, certainly.

But never impassive.

His coldness panicked her as much as anything. He'd always been there for her in her imagination, a looming, indestructible feature of her mental landscape, a touchstone of sanity during her darkest hours. Even knowing that he planned to marry hadn't entirely diminished the sense of his presence in her inner world.

"Well?" Laura used the last of her fading voice to try to pierce through his imperviousness with a shout. "Did your girlfriend find out that you get your jollies out of kidnapping unwilling women so that you can have your way with them?"

He merely nodded at a large lit-up billboard for a gas station on the side of the interstate. "That'll be the last public restroom for a while. Do you have to go?"

"Yes," she answered quickly.

"Don't even think about trying to yell out to someone. I travel this way frequently to our satellite offices in Rockford. The bathrooms are in the rear of the gas station and I'm going in with you."

"You are *not*." He looked at her for the first time in more than an hour. She inhaled shakily in relief when she saw the message of stark irritation in his eyes. It was a fragile connection, but connection nevertheless.

"Shane, listen to me . . . please. If I'm gone for three days, someone will notice."

"Joey's family is going skiing in Wisconsin this weekend. You can leave a message on the answering machine at your gallery that you won't be back until Tuesday. Who's going to notice or care that you're gone for the weekend, Laura?"

His piercing stare made her shift uneasily in her seat. "Surely you know how strangely you're acting. You're scaring me, Shane."

"Don't try to manipulate me," he said as he swung his sedan to an abrupt stop behind the empty gas station. "I've made up my mind on this."

Laura's shoulders sagged slightly when she heard that.

She knew Shane. Once he'd made a decision about something he was a stone. No, bigger than a stone . . . more unmoving than that indomitable, indestructible landscape that she compared him to in her mind.

"How the hell do you expect me to go to the bathroom when you have me handcuffed like this?"

He leaned over and uncuffed her wrists. Laura gasped in mixed pain and relief as she moved her hands in front of her for the first time in an hour and a half. She unobtrusively glanced into the backseat where Shane had put her purse. Her cell phone was inside it.

"If you try anything, I'll punish you."

"What are you going to do?" she challenged heatedly as she rubbed her chafed wrists. "Threaten me again with arresting Joey? At what point, exactly, did you become such a Nazi, Shane?"

"If Joey is arrested, it'll be because my people discover some solid evidence against him. I'm not gunning for Joey. This is about much more than that. I won't use anything that I learn from you in the next few days to nail your brother, but if he's guilty, there's nothing I can do to help Joey."

Laura felt like all the blood in her brain dropped on an express elevator ride down to her feet at his open admission that the FBI even considered Joey as a suspect.

"Joey's not crooked. How can you even think that, Shane? You played Little League baseball together. He spent every Christmas Eve at your house. You lived with us for two weeks when you came down with chicken pox because your mother's health was so frail and she'd never been exposed. After that, you always had a room in our home—both at my parents' and Uncle Derrick's. After everything you know about Joey, how can you believe he's a criminal?"

"Lots of things change over the years."

"Not something so basic. Not something so elemental! People can't change to that degree," she stated hotly before she noticed the way his dark head tilted to the right in a silent, wry query. She paused with her mouth open, her passionate defense of her brother frozen on her tongue.

She knew why he looked at her like that. He was trying to remind her of the way they once felt about each other. His raised eyebrows asked her silently why if it was true for Joey, it wasn't true for her.

"If Joey was colluding with Huey and the rest of them, . there's nothing I can do that will save him at this point. What's more, if he's innocent, no amount of convincing on your part is going to be what ultimately makes a difference. Only the truth matters now, Laura."

She swallowed with difficulty.

"Here," he said quietly as he reached in the backseat. He unscrewed the lid on a bottle of water and handed it to her. She hesitated only for a second before she took it and drank.

When she removed the bottle from her lips, he leaned close. She inhaled his scent—spicy, rich, and male.

"Do you really have to go to the bathroom, or were you just saying that so you could pull something?"

"I-I really do have to go."

"Okay."

He didn't unlock her door so she had to wait until he came around to get her. She gave him an irritated look when he put his hand around her upper arm and guided her to the bathroom door. She had to admit he'd chosen his location for a bathroom break well. The only thing she could see at the rear of the gas station was a vast frozen field. He released her arm and quickly, efficiently picked the flimsy lock on the bathroom door.

"You must be so proud of the things you've learned in your training," she snapped as he held open the door for her and switched on the light.

He merely closed the heavy metal door and leaned against it.

"You . . . you weren't serious about staying with me while I go," she exclaimed.

His blue eyes flicked down significantly to the dead bolt on the inside of the door. "I'm not going to stand outside in the cold while you lock me out and make a fuss until someone comes. Now, are you going to go, or not?"

"Not!" Laura replied, trying to ignore the ache of her full bladder.

He shrugged nonchalantly and straightened to his full height. He looked impossibly big in the tiny room beneath the harsh fluorescent lighting. He wore a rugged leather jacket that made his shoulders appear even broader than they already were.

"Suit yourself. Either way, I want you to take off your panties."

"Excuse me?" Laura muttered in disbelief. She took a step away from his tall, looming presence without being conscious of ever telling herself to move.

"You heard me."

"And why would I do that?"

He took two steps into the tiny bathroom and she took two steps back before she encountered the far wall.

"Because I said so," he explained almost casually before he reached out and delved his fingers deeply into her upswept hair.

He leaned down and seized her mouth in a kiss so ravenous that Laura couldn't help but wonder how long his hunger had been building. Had he been thinking about kissing her even while he stared straight ahead at the highway, his profile so cold and unmoving?

His lips molded and shaped her own, his tongue demanded entrance. His taste suffused her senses—both a new experience and a hauntingly familiar one at once. She groaned when he twisted his hand in her hair, turning her head so that he could penetrate her mouth deeper.

Why is he doing this? Laura wondered distantly even as she pressed closer to his hard body, drawn to his heat. But even as she asked herself, she knew the answer.

Tears leaked out of the corners of her eyelids as he continued to fuck her mouth boldly, branding her . . . staking his claim on her. Such a powerful wave of lust and longing surged through her at that moment that it seemed to obliterate all else in its wake. She kissed him back hungrily, obeying the law of her body and spirit for those brief moments instead of bowing down to harsh rules set by greedy men.

It took her a full five seconds to realize that he'd stopped kissing her. She opened her eyelids heavily.

Something flickered into his blue eyes as he uncurled his fingers from her hair and softly stroked her neck. Then he dropped his hand, his features settling once again into impassivity.

"If you choose not to use the toilet, that's your business. But you will take off your panties."

"Shane . . . *don't* do this," she entreated.

He stepped back. Despite the outrageousness of his actions, Laura found herself hating the absence of his weight against her. For a second she thought he'd relent, but then he merely cocked an eyebrow and glanced pointedly at the toilet.

Her hand shook slightly as she pulled toilet paper off the roll and placed it on the seat of the toilet. She forced herself to maintain eye contact with him while she lifted her skirt and bunched her panties around her knees.

"It's not going to work," she told him bitterly before she sat. Despite her bravado she found that she couldn't release her bladder while he watched her with his steady, blue-eyed stare.

She closed her eyes in temporary defeat.

"Take the panties off," he said succinctly once she'd finally finished.

"There's no way in hell," Laura hissed with a glare. Her heartbeat thundered in her ears while she waited to see what he'd do when she jerked up her panties and let her skirt drop. Would he rip them off her? She knew Shane would never really hurt her, but she kept thinking about his crazy allegation that he planned to dominate her sexually. He was wrong to assume she preferred her sex that way.

So she couldn't figure out why the thought of Shane restraining her, removing at least temporarily the necessity for keeping him at a distance . . . of him *forcing* her to feel caused a forbidden vein of excitement to throb to life inside of her.

He merely watched her with a stony stare, however, while

she washed and dried her hands before opening the door for her.

"Where are we going, anyway?" Laura asked thirty seconds later when Shane got into the driver's seat. He'd immediately relocked the doors once he'd seated her in the passenger seat, unlocking only the driver's-side door when he went around the car.

"To a cabin in the country, twenty miles or so from Galena, Illinois."

She snorted and settled in her seat, desperate to put up some emotional barriers after she'd once again succumbed to him so easily. "I see you haven't lost all your marbles. Still enough of an FBI agent not to take me across state lines."

She might as well not have spoken for all the effect her bitter words had on him.

"Lean forward. I'm going to cuff you again."

Despite everything that had come before, his words shocked her. "No! You have me locked in here. I'm not going anywhere."

"If I don't cuff you, you might try to hinder me while I'm driving. We could wreck."

"It's so nice to know you have my safety and well-being in mind," she said, her voice dripping with sarcasm.

It happened so quickly that she released her gasp of surprise with her forehead pressed against the leather surface of the driver's door armrest. She tried to move but Shane held her so firmly down in his lap with a forearm at her lower back that felt like it was a band of steel. While she still struggled in disoriented confusion, he efficiently recuffed her wrists behind her back.

"I *do* have your safety and well-being in mind."

"Goddamn you straight to hell, Shane Dominic," she cried out shakily. "You have no right—"

"If I have no right to cuff you then I certainly have no right to do this. But guess what, Laura?" he breathed out ominously from above her. "I'm going to do it anyway."

Laura stared blankly at the crevice between the leather

seat and the car door when she felt him yank up her skirt. The air inside the car felt cool against the bare skin just above her thigh-highs. Despite her struggling, Shane managed to successfully yank her underpants down to her knees. She yelped in surprise when he cracked the exposed flesh of her bottom with his palm once, then twice. It didn't hurt as much as it shocked her.

"Stop struggling or I'm gonna give you twice as many," she heard him say.

She clenched her teeth and determinedly twisted in his lap, but he held her down with an ease that infuriated her. When she shifted her pelvis off him, nearly tipping her body onto the floor of the car, he grabbed her hip, his fingers sinking deeply into her right buttock. Her muscles tensed when he cursed and released her, knowing what was to come. He landed a blistering spank on her right ass cheek, the crack of flesh against flesh sounding like gunfire in the confined space of the car.

"Stop it," she howled.

"I'll stop when you stop struggling and take your punishment. I'm tired of sitting here while you hurl insults at me. And the next time I tell you to take off an item of clothing I expect that you'll do it. Understood?"

Laura moaned uncontrollably. While he spoke he palmed her bare, stinging ass cheek and squeezed possessively.

"All right, fine," she said quickly. She would have said anything at that moment to stop him from touching her. "Just let me up."

"I told you I would. Once you take your punishment for being obstinate just for the sake of being obstinate."

"What? You . . . you already spanked me." She went still when his squeezing of her ass segued to a caress. He transferred his hand to the sensitive skin at the base of her spine just above the crevice of her bottom, caressing her with callused, gentle fingertips. Her mouth gaped open as she trailed that intimate caress with her mind.

"Lesson one, Laura. Any stroke you get on your ass while you're struggling doesn't count. I'm going to give you ten and if you don't keep completely still while I do it, you'll get one more for each time you resist. Do you understand?"

One long finger skimmed down the crevice of her ass in the silence that followed, lightly skimming the sensitive ring of her asshole. She shivered uncontrollably despite the heat that flooded her body.

"And then you'll let me up?" she clarified uneasily.

"If you promise to stop insulting me during the rest of the drive to Galena, yes."

She bit off a small moan when he rubbed her left ass cheek lightly with his fingertips and then palmed the tingling flesh greedily as if it were his to do with as he pleased. Laura pinched her eyelids closed in response to the rush of liquid warmth between her thighs. It felt shameful to be lying here, handcuffed and helpless in the lap of a man she had barely spoken to in thirteen years as he played with her bare ass—a bare ass that was still hot and tingling from his spankings.

Shameful and almost unbearably exciting, because Shane was that man.

"All right. Do it then," she ground out. Anything to get him to stop touching her.

But if she'd thought it was bad struggling against his touch, it was far worse to lie completely still and anticipate his cracking palm. He made her count as he spanked her, which humiliated her even further. By the time he smacked her burning, undoubtedly bright pink ass the last time, she was trembling in anger, shame, and arousal.

"I'll never forgive you for this," she informed him when he'd helped her back into a sitting position in the passenger seat and she'd winced at the stinging pain from putting weight on her bottom. She frowned when he slid her panties down over her boots and pocketed the black silk inside his jacket.

"Yes, you will," he countered calmly. She merely stared at him in impotent fury as he untied her wool coat before he refastened her seat belt.

"Oh . . . no, Shane," she cried out miserably when he lifted her skirt to her waist. She rested her head on the seat and turned her face away from him when he matter-of-factly pushed a finger between her labia. But she couldn't shut out the divine pleasure of his finger sliding against her clit . . . 'or the shameful, undisguised sound of him moving in the tight, wet crevice. Much to her chagrin, she ground her hips against him.

His chuckle sounded triumphant to her ears.

"Juicy," he murmured, his voice sounding a little awed. "You liked that, didn't you? It turns you on to have a man punish you."

"No."

Something in her tone must have made him pause. Laura bit her bottom lip in agony when he removed his finger from her burning, needy clit.

Neither of them spoke as he drove down the ramp and merged once again onto the interstate. Laura moved away from him, pressing the side of her forehead against the window. The cool surface felt good against her overheated body.

"There's nothing to be ashamed of, you know. You're a natural submissive. I knew it, even back when we were dating so many years ago," she heard him say after several minutes of silence. His familiar deep voice washed over her in the dim silence, awakening so many memories . . . so many feelings she'd thought long dead.

"Shut up."

She sensed him bristle next to her despite the fact that she couldn't see him from her hunkered down position. She sat bolt upright when he placed his hand on her knee and opened her legs.

"Keep them spread," he insisted when she instinctively began to close them again. The only light in the car came from the dim dashboard lights, but it was still sufficient enough for him to easily see between her thighs.

She made the mistake of looking into Shane's bold, handsome face as he stared into her lap. Her muscles locked into place, as though his desire commanded them and not her own will. For a moment he'd looked so intent, so hungry she'd been stunned.

His gaze flickered to the road and then back to her. He held her stare as he reached for her.

"There," he soothed softly as he stimulated her clit with a thick thumb. "Just give in to it, baby. Give me your trust."

Laura gasped raggedly at the intensity of the pleasure that flooded through her. It was like a volcano of emotion had brewed just beneath the surface for the past two weeks and Shane's touch supplied the outlet for an explosive eruption.

She tried to buck her hips against his hand, but he held her thigh firmly down on the seat as his thumb worked her. The dam broke loose. She sobbed uncontrollably as she came.

She sagged back into the seat a few seconds later, moaning when Shane shifted his hand and slicked his forefinger against her clit, eliciting several delicious post-orgasmic tremors from her. She'd never known that something could feel so incredibly good and intensely terrible all at once.

"How could *that* ever be something you'd be ashamed of?" he asked her after he'd finished strumming all the tremors from her flesh and removed his hand.

Laura slid her head back to the window and stared out into the impenetrable black night. His suggestion that she would have responded in such a fashion to any man was what had made her protest so vehemently before. But she couldn't tell him that he was dead wrong about his assumptions. Better he thought she responded so wholly with almost any man. If he ever discovered what he meant to her, he would use the knowledge to wrangle the truth from her.

And with her body being such a wicked betrayer, her secrets were the only weapons she possessed now.

CHAPTER **SIX**

Shane noticed fifteen minutes later when Laura closed her legs and shifted her hips toward the door . . . away from him.

"I told you to keep your legs spread."

"Fuck you" was her quiet, furious response.

"We'll get to that whenever I'm ready," he muttered grimly at the same time that he spread his hand across the stocking-covered thigh nearest to him and pulled it in his direction. His already erect cock throbbed painfully at the sensation of her shapely leg encased in cool silk. She jerked her leg away from him, denying him access.

"Do you want me to pull over and punish you again?" he asked. He'd rather not when he'd already turned her beautiful ass such a fetching shade of pink, but he accepted that it may be necessary in these early stages while she still resisted him.

She'd submit to him soon enough. He'd heard those tapes. It was in Laura's nature to submit. He'd never really doubted it. The juices running amply around his finger when he'd probed her pussy following her spanking certainly proved it.

It made his gut boil with anger to consider it, but Huey had trained Laura's body well.

Instead of fighting with her he removed his hand from her thigh.

"Obviously I didn't make my point earlier. I have a paddle in the trunk of the car. I'll pull off at the next exit and get it so I can make things a little clearer to you," he commented mildly. He watched out of the corner of his eye as she straightened in her seat and turned her outraged face toward him.

"No," she stated emphatically.

"Then keep your thighs spread," he replied just as firmly while he met her gaze.

He waited tensely for several seconds. When she spread her thighs slowly he merely said, "And lift your skirt higher."

"I can't believe you're doing this. I can't believe you're acting this way," she whispered as she lifted her skirt once again to her waist. Her incredibly smooth hips and thighs gleamed in the dim light.

"Believe it," he replied starkly, his eye glued to the trim thatch of dark hair between her thighs. Every time he glanced back at the road he wondered if the hairs surrounding her labia were as matted with moisture as they appeared to be. He finally gave up guessing and reached for her, slicking his forefinger against the swollen folds while he stared straight ahead at the relatively empty interstate.

She gasped raggedly.

It hadn't been his imagination. She was soaked. He ground his back teeth together in feral lust at the realization. He stroked her softly while he drove, keeping his eyes on the road, eating up the small, catchy whimpers that she unsuccessfully tried to stifle. His cock swelled furiously when, after a minute or two of stimulation, she pushed her pelvis against him, trying to get more pressure on her clit so she could come.

When he removed his hand completely she cried out in protest.

"What are you doing?" she asked when he grabbed the wheel with his left hand and leaned across her in order to lower the back of her seat. He sat up abruptly when the car swerved slightly to the right.

"That's better," he mumbled in grim satisfaction after he'd corkscrewed his forefinger in her tight, juicy channel, his action made easier by her adjusted position and her abundant cream. He continued to drive as he finger-fucked her slowly and she moaned.

"Keep your hips still," he ordered when she began to writhe against him, hungry for the release that he withheld from her with his slow, careful strokes. He refused to touch her swollen clit now, knowing that if he did she would detonate like a bomb.

He kept it up for a torturous fifteen minutes as they drove on the dark highway. Neither of them spoke as they engaged in a silent, tense battle of wills. He saw her bite down on her lower lip several times and knew that she restrained herself from begging him to allow her to come.

The idea of her denying herself from him infuriated him just like it had for thirteen and a half years.

Every time he sensed her nearing climax, he withdrew his finger until only the tip was buried fast in her heat and waited for her to cool. When he saw a brightly lit truck stop just off the interstate, he pulled away his hand completely from Laura's drenched pussy. He took the exit. She leaned back against the seat, her breathing coming shallow and fast.

"What do you want from me, Shane?" she asked in a choked voice when he parked the car in a solitary spot at the truck stop. There wasn't much car traffic, but several of the spots were filled in the truck parking a hundred or so feet away. Shane could see several truckers sitting in their cabs but he couldn't have cared less. He was so aroused from touching Laura's creaming pussy and hearing her stifled whimpers that he thought his cock would burst out of the stretched skin that covered it.

"I told you what I want," he said as he unfastened his seat belt and his jeans. He grimaced in genuine discomfort when he lowered his boxer briefs and pulled his cock free. He felt Laura's stare on him, the weight of it making him grit his teeth.

He unbuckled her seat belt and met her wide eyes before he glanced down at his straining erection.

"There's nothing much more honest than that, is there, Laura? Suck on it."

Her lush lower lip fell open in shock at his harsh words but the manner in which she eyed his cock hungrily made it lurch in his hand. He'd ravaged her hair earlier. It currently surrounded her delicate face in a wild, dark cloud. Her cheeks were stained bright pink with her arousal. He held up his heavy erection and palmed the back of her skull gently.

"Get down on it."

She glanced uneasily out the front window toward the line of trucks and the three figures in the seats.

"They can't see anything," he soothed at the same time that he applied more pressure on the back of her head.

He clenched his eyes shut and hissed a curse when she leaned over and inserted the tip of his cock between her pursed lips with no further encouragement. Her tongue, agile and supple, bathed the head in liquid heat. He lowered his hand to her shoulder, steadying her since she had no use of her hands, handcuffed as she was. Her lips slid down beneath the head and pistoned wetly for several hard strokes directly on his most sensitive spot.

He groaned gutturally in sublime pleasure. God *bless* it, it felt good.

He said nothing but lifted his head off the back of the seat in order to watch her moving in his lap. She worked more and more of his length into her mouth with each pass. He wished he could see her better as she sucked him, wished he could see her lips spread widely to accommodate his girth.

She had the talent, that much was certain. Because of the size of his cock a woman usually required the use of her hand in addition to her mouth to bring him off. But Laura would have him exploding in a matter of seconds if he let her continue. Her mouth was deliciously warm and wet.

How did she know to turn her head slightly on the upstroke, giving a tight, delicious twist directly on his sweet spot? Her lips held him in a secure clamp and her suck—

His head fell back on the seat. He growled in intense arousal at the sensation of her taking him deep, leaving only several inches neglected at the root. Her hunger stunned him. Was it really possible to train a woman to crave cock with so much intensity?

Fury mixed with his intense lust at the thought. When she slid the tip of his cock into her throat and he felt her constrict around him, pulling and taunting him, he promptly forgot about any other man touching her.

He put his hands on her shoulders and pulled her up. She stared at him from her bent-over position as he fumbled in his jean pocket for a condom, her exotically tilted green eyes glistening with a lust that even she couldn't deny.

It was nearly more temptation than he could master not to push her sweet mouth back onto his cock.

"Come here, baby," he ordered in a no-nonsense manner once he'd rolled the condom on his rock-hard erection and slid back his seat to give them a little extra room.

She sat up slowly at his command. She once again glanced warily out the window at the truckers in the distance.

"No, Shane," she whispered. "They'll be able to see."

"They might," he said in a steely soft voice. "But not any of the essentials. And I want my cock inside your pussy. Now come here."

He watched as she closed her eyes and licked her damp lower lip in an anxious manner. When she opened them her gaze fixed on his straining erection. He sensed her desire to please him, even as she pleasured herself, like a powerful stimulant being mainlined into his veins.

He reached for her.

She didn't fight him as he leaned back in his seat and drew her into his lap. Her breath came in warm, uneven puffs on his neck while he positioned her hips over him and guided the tip of his cock to her pussy. He inhaled her unique scent mixed with the intoxicating odor of her arousal.

"God you're so hot . . . so sweet," he muttered as he entered her. Her heat penetrated through the thin barrier of the condom immediately. He pulled her down on him, his desire clawing at his insides like sharp talons. She cried out at the impact of him embedding his cock in her so abruptly. Her head fell forward until her brow rested on his shoulder.

"Fuck me," he whispered next to her ear.

When she merely whimpered and the muscular walls of her pussy tightened around him he repeated more stringently, "Fuck me, Laura."

"I hate you," she muttered through clenched teeth at the same moment that she flexed her thighs, raising herself over him. She sank back onto half the length of his cock rapidly, causing a brisk whap of flesh against flesh.

He gripped her ass and added his own strength to her flexing thighs. "Keep it up, then, because it feels incredible."

"Shut up." She lifted her head and Shane saw that her cheeks were damp with perspiration and tears. He reached up and tenderly dried the wetness at the same time that he flexed his hips, powering his cock into the sleek tunnel of her pussy. He held her gaze. When he filled her she clenched her eyelids shut, her beautiful face tightening with pleasure.

The muscular walls of her vagina tormented him as he rocketed into her again and again. Every time he moved out of her she pulled and sucked at his cock, tempting him inward, taking him on a wild, chaotic ride of hedonistic pleasure. He was so lost in her that at first he didn't notice her pause in their frantic mating.

"Oh *God*, I can't believe you're making me do this," she whispered brokenly.

Shane blinked, allowing a sliver of reality to penetrate his thick arousal. He heard a truck honk its horn loudly only to be followed by another in quick succession. He tightened his grip on Laura's bare ass.

"Ignore them," he said, referring to the truck drivers. "They don't know you. The only thing you need to worry about is giving yourself to me, baby."

She sobbed spasmodically. He felt her trembling beneath

his hands, felt it around his buried, straining cock as well. He opened his mouth to soothe her when he felt her press down tightly into his lap and he realized she was coming.

Heat flooded around his cock.

"That's right, let go. You're mine."

He lifted her and pounded her down over his cock in rapid, short strokes, no longer aware of his surroundings, slicing himself again and again on the cruel, sharp blade of ecstasy that was Laura.

She didn't speak to him for the entire drive to the cabin except for once.

"Don't you think you're being self-destructive, Shane?" She'd curled into a fetal position, her face turned away from him, the moment he'd set her back in the passenger seat and fastened her seat belt twenty minutes ago. Shane had to strain to make out her words since her cheek was pressed into the back of the seat.

"Quite possibly," he responded grimly as he drove.

Her head came up slightly at that. "Why only *possibly*? From where I'm sitting there's no uncertainty in the matter. You're throwing away your career by doing this."

"You think I haven't thought about that?" he asked pointedly.

"Then why are you doing it?"

"Because there's more to my identity than just my career!"

She stared back, clearly surprised by his intensity.

He didn't say anything for several moments as he drove. He could tell by the way she put her head back on the seat resignedly that she thought he was too furious and stubborn to reason with.

Which was at least partially true.

"It all depends on you, Laura," he said quietly after a minute. "Either I'm one hell of a smart son of a bitch or a deluded idiot. If my bet was on the latter, we wouldn't be here right now."

He glanced over at her huddled figure, catching the glint of her open eyes watching him in the dim light.

Shane stared straight ahead grimly. She may not be talking yet, but one thing was for certain.

He'd gotten Laura's attention.

CHAPTER **SEVEN**

W hat is this place?" Laura asked as she peered through the front window into a nearly impenetrable black night. She'd been hyperalert ever since Shane pulled off the rural two-lane highway a half hour ago, her eyes seeking out signs and landmarks as to their location. She'd need any information available to her if she was to break free of Shane and make it to a phone.

At first she'd been heartened by all the houses and condominiums that they passed. She'd seen a sign as they entered the residential community welcoming them to Eagle River. Apparently the resort included a ski hill, a hotel, a spa, and several golf courses.

When Shane had turned off the main residential road onto a narrow rural route thirty minutes ago, however, and the lights of the cheery chalet-style houses had dimmed, Laura's hopes had dimmed along with them.

Shane turned off the engine of the car and then the headlights. Black night enveloped them.

"It belongs to my father. He bought it for fishing and hunting, but he hasn't been able to use it much in the past year."

Laura squinted to make out his profile in the darkness.

"Has . . . has your mother been ill?" she asked. Laura had loved Shane's mother once. Perhaps she still did. Who knew the full extent of the damage time wrought on the heart?

She heard Shane sigh but he remained unmoving. Through some cruel joke of fate Elizabeth Dominic's effervescent, vibrant personality had been housed in a frail body. "She had a stroke a year ago. She's still as sharp as ever mentally, but she has to use a cane now to get around and she tires easily."

Laura stifled the words of sympathy that flew to her tongue. Their exchange of words felt too intimate here in the darkness, as if the blackness could cloak the bizarreness of the fact that Shane had taken her captive . . . that he planned to make her submit to him.

He didn't seem to expect any condolences, however. More than likely he believed her to be bereft of human feeling—a belief that she'd harbored far too many times to count over the past decade, as well.

He got out of the car and slammed the door behind him. A light pierced the darkness and Laura realized that he held a small flashlight in his hand. He certainly needed it. Whatever luminescence that might have come from starlight seemed to be largely obscured by thick surrounding foliage. Apparently Alex Dominic had gone rustic in his choice of cabin and bought one in the midst of the woods.

"Uncuff me. My arms are killing me," Laura said after Shane had retrieved several bags, including what appeared to be groceries, from the trunk and came around to unlock and open her door.

"When we get inside."

She ground her teeth at his cool tone and the firm, impersonal grip he put on her elbow as he helped her out of the car. It was bad enough to consider how she'd been so drunk with lust that she'd fucked him in clear sight of a bunch of horny truck drivers just hours ago. But her humiliation seemed to amplify a hundredfold at his brisk, businesslike manner with her as he led her into the cabin. She really might have been a criminal under his jurisdiction, the way he was treating her.

"You said you would uncuff me," Laura reminded him acerbically several minutes later.

She sat on the couch shivering, watching Shane as he turned on lights and the furnace, checked the supplies in the luxurious kitchen, and put away the supplies he'd brought.

Alex Dominic had only taken his concept for a rustic cabin so far, Laura thought as she studied her surroundings. Alex and Elizabeth had never lacked for money, that much was certain. Shane had grown up in an enormous house on Chicago's affluent Gold Coast, the type of place that had been called a "townhome" in the nineteenth century but that people accurately labeled a mansion in this day and age.

The modern timber structure that Alex had purchased for outdoor sport had all the modern conveniences, including a kitchen with sleek stainless steel appliances and a gas furnace, although it would take a while for the heater to chase off the winter chill.

Shane didn't respond to her petulant comment immediately but just continued to survey the maple cabinets and what appeared to be a walk-in pantry. Laura could almost sense him making a list in that methodical brain of his of what was available. Eventually he came into the spacious living room, removed his coat, and flung it on the couch beside her.

"Come on," he said with a tilt of his chin. "There's a fireplace in the bedroom. A fire should keep us warm tonight."

Laura rose and walked down the only hallway in the otherwise open layout of the cabin, Shane following closely behind her. The hallway led to a large bedroom suite.

Laura's eyes skimmed over the comfortable, luxurious furnishings, lingering on the bed. When Shane signaled that she should sit on the bed while he went about building a fire, Laura sat in one of the upholstered chairs. His lips tilted slightly at her small show of defiance.

She watched dully as Shane laid and lit a fire. A wave of exhaustion had hit her, weighting her limbs. He sat back on his heels in front of the hearth. A single golden flame flickered upward, licking at first tentatively at the newspaper and kindling, then more hungrily. She stared, mesmerized by the sight of Shane's immobile, bold profile set against the growing blaze.

She blinked, forcing herself to look away and examine the room in which she found herself. The headboard of the bed was made of a matrix of wrought iron that resembled tree branches with leaves interspersed throughout. The color scheme of the bedding, pillows, upholstered chairs, and matching ottomans and draperies was a cozy burgundy, gold, and forest green. Laura thought she recognized Elizabeth Dominic's sure, knowledgeable hand in the cabin's homey decorating scheme. Despite the Dominics' wealth, Laura had never been in a more welcoming home than Shane's parents', largely due to Elizabeth's influence.

She stared in disbelief when she saw a landscape oil painting on the far wall.

"My mom has followed your work over the years. She never purchased any of it firsthand from your gallery. She thought it might make you feel uncomfortable if you knew she was the buyer. She's acquired several pieces though—another painting and several pieces of sculpture."

Laura turned, realizing Shane must have observed her looking at the painting. He nodded toward it as he stood.

"That one reminded her of the landscape in this area, what with the rolling hills and the way the trees turn so brilliantly in the fall."

"Why did your mother think I wouldn't want to see her?"

Shane shrugged and Laura suddenly understood. It was the same reason Joey didn't bring up Laura's name in Shane's presence, or why he so rarely spoke of Shane in front of Laura—because of their history together . . . and the strange, abrupt ending of that history.

She suppressed a sigh and swept the room once again with her gaze. It struck her that she felt familiar in these alien surroundings—familiar and *good*—almost like she'd come home.

The realization made her go on the offensive a few seconds later when Shane suggested that she use the bathroom first and then followed her to the entrance.

"You're going to create a far worse enemy than you already have if you try to come with me into this bathroom!"

"Actually, I was going to uncuff you," he murmured wryly.

He reached into his jean pocket and extracted a key. Laura stared up into his face warily as he leaned over her and reached behind her body. She winced in mixed pain and relief when he released her wrists and tucked the cuffs in the back pocket of his jeans.

She immediately tried to move away from Shane's overwhelming presence but he grasped her upper arms and began to massage them. A groan of discomfort escaped her throat as regular blood flow returned under his molding palms. Sharp prickles of pain tore through her flesh only to be followed by a tingling rush of warmth.

"Stop it," she muttered, twisting her chin and pressing it into the wool of her coat, trying to shut his rich scent out of her nose.

Much to her surprise he complied immediately.

"I'm agreeing to your request on this occasion only because the lock on the bathroom door is a joke. Don't bother locking it. If you do I'll break open the door," Shane said. He handed her one of the bags that he'd brought in from the trunk. "There are toiletries in there for you to use. If you're not out of here in five minutes flat, I'm coming in to get you."

"Please, you're overwhelming me with your benevolence," she said scathingly. She took a small measure of satisfaction in shutting the bathroom door in his face.

As soon as Shane was on the other side of the door, however, all of her composure melted. She turned and stared unseeingly at the marble countertop of the sink before she lunged forward and turned on the tap, panicked. The running water muffled her sobs. She sat on the closed lid of the toilet, trying desperately to control the intense emotion that surged up from her chest, gripping at her throat . . . holding her hostage just as surely as Shane Dominic did.

For a wild minute that stretched interminably she thought she wouldn't be able to bring herself under control. It infuriated her. *He* infuriated her for forcing her to feel so much.

She'd worked so hard . . . endured so much. Now that her

goal was within reach, Shane threatened to ruin everything she'd lived for these past years.

Now that she'd had the opportunity to think about the bizarre circumstances of Telly Ardos confronting her tonight, she was regretful she hadn't immediately gone with him and possibly avoided Shane altogether. She'd realized too late Ardos had been the anonymous caller. She'd been confused by Ardos's abrupt overture, frightened by the fact that he'd grabbed her and threatened her with a gun.

What if Ardos—or the mysterious person to whom he'd referred—truly had something of importance to tell her? Her impulsive resistance of Huey's old friend might have cost her the break she needed. Now Shane had kidnapped her and brought her to this cabin. What if the opportunity to get evidence against Moody had vanished by the time Shane allowed her to return home?

She cursed under her breath, her irritation at Shane helping her to get control of the powerful wave of emotion that had nearly overcome her. She rose and quickly removed her coat before she used the toilet, frowning when she thought of how Shane had watched her at the gas station earlier.

Arrogant bastard, she fumed.

Her frown faded when she noticed how wet things were between her thighs. She closed her eyes tightly, ordering her mind's focus away from the humiliating, arousing memories of Shane touching her.

She looked longingly at the large steam shower, wishing she could wash away the evidence of her body's betrayal, but decided there wasn't time. The last thing she needed for her composure was Shane bursting in on her while she was naked and vulnerable in the shower.

"Damn him," she muttered as she riffled through the toiletries he'd given her. She washed her face first, not wanting Shane to see the evidence of her tears . . . or her vulnerability. Let him believe that he could get to her sexually. See where it got him. She vowed then and there that her previous inability to resist his touch was the *only* manner in which Shane permeated her defenses.

Was this really happening? Laura wondered for the thousandth time as she brushed her teeth with one of the newly purchased toothbrushes she'd found in the bag. She'd been shocked before in her life, but never to the degree that she had been when Shane had handcuffed her earlier this evening and calmly told her that he was taking her as his captive until she talked.

His behavior was so irrational, so strange as to cast a surreal mental fog over the entire experience. And yet she sensed his steely resolve and methodical nature above all else. He was angry, but it wasn't his fury that primarily motivated him. The evidence of his grim resolve panicked her.

Shane wasn't the kind of man who did things halfway. He was a force to be reckoned with when he made up his mind on something and combined his will with a first-class intellect. The combination of an incisive understanding of human behavior, a steely determination, and unrelenting perseverance was undoubtedly a prime factor behind his success and rapid rise in the ranks of the FBI.

Did Shane really believe that even if she gave into him sexually that it implied she'd give him whatever information he needed in order to successfully complete his investigation?

He was wrong.

She had way too much at stake. She *wouldn't* relent to him. Not with her mind, anyway . . . even if her body and spirit did betray her cause.

Maybe she could use their intense sexual attraction for each other against him? Lull him into a sense of mastery over the situation so that she could try to escape. She needed to get back. If Randall Moody became suspicious of her whereabouts or her activities he might become desperate.

If he ever discovered she was with Shane Dominic, he'd resort to murder once again.

Moody got a perverse satisfaction from always mentioning how fond he was of her. Of course, Moody's definition of "fondness" meant that he hadn't yet had her killed, so Laura wasn't much comforted by his supposed benevolence.

She jumped nervously when Shane pounded heavily on the other side of the bathroom door.

"I'll be out in a minute," Laura seethed.

She spun around when the door swung open. He leaned in the doorway, a large, indomitable presence. What was it about being intruded upon in the bathroom that felt like the worst possible invasion of personal space?

"No. Now," he said calmly.

"I just need another minute."

"I told you five minutes."

"I'm not a criminal! How dare you treat me like one," she sputtered when he grabbed her elbow and drew her firmly into the bedroom. His dispassionate manner infuriated her all over again, making her forget her tentative plan to go along with him until he let down his guard. She stopped her instinctive struggling, gritted her teeth, and allowed him to lead her over to the bed.

"Do you want me to take off your clothes? Or would you rather do it yourself?"

Despite the fact that Laura had been expecting something like this, her mouth gaped open. "Do you really expect me to answer that?"

Shane shrugged. "I thought you might want to choose, that's all." His blue eyes looked glacial as they ran over her figure. "I'll do it, then. Lie down on the bed."

The protest on her tongue froze when she glanced down at the large bed. He'd been busy while she was in the bathroom. The comforter and top sheet had been folded back, the decorative pillows removed. But not only that, he'd fastened two black cuffs to the right side of the head of the bed. Her gaze flashed rapidly to the foot of the bed where she saw two more.

"What's wrong?" Shane asked softly when he saw her nervous glance. "Surely you didn't expect that I was going to give you free run of the place while I slept. You've been restrained plenty of times before, haven't you, Laura?"

CHAPTER **EIGHT**

She swallowed when she met his gaze, seeing the anger that simmered in his blue eyes. Despite his actions, the idea that Laura was accustomed to being tied up for sex clearly pissed him off royally.

Just as his belief that she was such an inveterate slut infuriated her in turn.

It more than angered her—it pained her like a physical wound that Shane believed so wholeheartedly such sordid things about her. But she *needed* him to believe if she wanted to continue this charade, and she really had no choice as to that. She never had. Just like Moody had said, *Huey's death doesn't change a thing in regard to you, Laura.*

Nothing mattered until she could finally wrap her hands around some tangible evidence. Then maybe she and Shane could be on the same side. But for now, Shane was as much her enemy as Randall Moody.

Laura didn't need Moody to tell her that nothing had changed after Huey's death. She'd known from the beginning that Huey was just one of many puppets. Moody himself was the one who jerked the string on his little army of soldiers. She'd been flabbergasted when Shane said Moody's name so matter-of-factly tonight at Joey's. Shocked and frightened.

The thought of Shane drawing too close to the fat, deadly spider in the center of his web terrified her.

Her anxious thoughts fueled her performance.

"What, are you worried I've got more experience in the bondage arena than you?" she asked, injecting as much scorn in her tone as she could muster.

He gave a small smile. "I think my experience will be sufficient. Now, are you going to lie down or what? The sooner you do, the sooner we can both get some rest."

Laura gave him a mutinous glance before she bent, unzipped her brown leather boots, and kicked them off carelessly.

"What did you mean by that? Do you *really* get into bondage?" she asked. Her tone was purposefully condescending, but she was curious about his response. She lay on her back on the bed, trying not to reveal her anxiety when he bent and leaned over her. Shane believed she had experience with being restrained on a regular basis, after all.

He didn't make eye contact with her as he began to unbutton her blouse in a brisk, matter-of-fact manner. Laura's skin pebbled and her nipples grew erect against the material of her bra when she was exposed to the cool air. He opened his mouth, as though he meant to answer her, but he went completely still instead.

She glanced down to where he stared so fixedly. The pendant on her necklace nestled in the valley of her breasts. A whimper rose in her throat when Shane touched the piece of cut glass with a long finger. The pendant was slightly larger than a quarter in diameter and approximately a half-inch thick toward the top. It had been shaped to roughly resemble a heart.

"Do you wear this often?"

"I . . . yes," Laura replied, confused by his intensity. "It . . . It's not real, but I always thought it was pretty anyway."

He looked up at her. "How do you know it's not a real emerald?"

Laura couldn't stop the blush from heating her cheeks. She knew because she'd taken all of the jewelry Huey had given her during the first year of their marriage—including her wedding ring—in order to sell it. Huey had gambled away his paychecks from the CPD even back then, and Laura could have used the assurance of a nest egg given the bizarre, tenuous circumstances in which she existed. She'd been vigilant about preparing for an emergency since the day she'd been horrified to discover that her bonds to Huey Mays were tied with steel knots.

She'd already suspected that the emerald was a fake: It was the type of gem one would expect in a prince's crown, not a cop's wife's jewelry box. But she'd at least expected some of the smaller items to be real.

At least her wedding ring.

But perhaps it made the most sense of all that her wedding ring was a fake. Not a particularly clever one either, Laura thought as she recalled the jewelry appraiser's glance of amused disbelief when she'd showed it to him.

"Don't you think I'd *know* if my own necklace was a piece of glass or a priceless emerald?" she asked Shane bitterly.

He didn't respond for a moment. His fingertip remained on the multifaceted surface of the pendant. She knew it was just her imagination but his touch seemed to enliven the trapped fires in the glass, making her skin tingle and burn.

"It's almost the precise color of your eyes."

Her heartbeat began to throb loudly in her ears at his low, intimate tone.

She breathed a shaky sigh of relief when he finally moved, reaching behind her to unhook her bra. She shivered when he whisked it off her shoulders and arms and tossed it aside. Laura couldn't say if she was disappointed or glad when he didn't even glance at her exposed flesh and reached for her wrists instead.

Her breasts felt strangely large . . . obvious and vulnerable prey even though Laura knew very well that they could be labeled medium-sized at best. She was acutely aware of her stretched naked torso as he secured her wrists inside the cuffs, then used an attached connector hook to attach her to the straps.

"You never answered me. Is bondage really your thing?" she asked as she tugged experimentally on the cuffs and straps once he'd finished. They seemed more than secure. Her fingers couldn't reach the silver buckle on the back of her wrists. Unlike the metal handcuffs that he'd used earlier, the straps restraining her snugly at present were made of soft, supple leather. She likely would grow stiff from having her arms over her head all night, but at least her elbows were bent and resting comfortably on the pillow.

Shane reached behind her to unzip her skirt. He eventually spoke but Laura wished he would have at least made eye contact with her when he went about this intimate business.

"Does that surprise you?" he asked gruffly. He wore a small smile as he swept her skirt down her thighs.

No, it didn't. Shane had always been a dominant, alpha male. People had responded to his calm confidence since they were children, looking to him instinctively for leadership and guidance. Even though he'd never used the paraphernalia of the trade on her, so to speak, when they'd been lovers in the past, he'd mastered her heart, mind, and senses effortlessly in his bed.

Still, his smug little smile irked her.

"My, *my*, this is news," she taunted. She gritted her teeth when he paused and stared down at her completely naked body with the exception of her thigh-high stockings. "Who'd have thought the all-American boy was into kink?"

"Who'd have thought the girl-next-door was?" he countered flatly as he attached the cuff to her right ankle.

Laura stared up at the ceiling as he pulled on her left ankle so that it reached the other restraint. She lay with her legs spread, her pussy completely bared. Why did the cool air tickle and caress it like a lover's touch even though Shane refused to look at her?

"You don't know anything about me, Shane. You don't know what you've gotten yourself into," she challenged when he'd finished.

He stood abruptly and met her eyes. "You're the one who doesn't understand, Laura. You're the one who has something to learn."

She just stared at him, speechless, as he drew the sheet up over her naked body, turned, and walked away. The bathroom door closed with a brisk bang behind him.

Laura's ears seemed to have been pitched to some hyperalert status as she listened to Shane move around in the bathroom. The fire made a crackling, cheerful sound that belied the heavy tension inherent to the situation. Laura already felt its heat warding off the chill in the room.

She tried to take advantage of Shane's absence to scope out where he'd placed things in the room—the location of the car keys, a cell phone . . . his gun.

Surely he'd brought his gun with him. Laura had grown up with cops. She'd lived with a policeman in the house since she was twelve. She'd gotten accustomed to the grim reality of a gun being in the house ever since her parents had died and she'd moved into her uncle Derrick's home.

The surfaces of the bedside tables were empty except for the lamps. If Shane had left keys or a cell phone anywhere, it was probably out in the living room or kitchen, far from where she could access it. What would she do with a cell phone anyway? Would she really have the nerve to turn Shane over to the police?

Laura admitted grimly that despite her fury at Shane, it wouldn't serve her ultimate purpose to have him arrested. Although the last thing she'd do was tell Shane that.

Escape was her only hope then.

Anxiety melded with anticipation, both of them rising to an alarming degree as she lay there waiting. Her pulse began to throb uncomfortably at her throat. Even though Shane had tossed the sheet over her, she felt very aware of her nakedness beneath it . . . of her stark vulnerability.

She forced herself to remain still even though her heart jumped a mile high in her chest when Shane opened the bathroom door abruptly. She told herself to close her eyes, to try her best to shut out his presence from her mind. But her eyes seemed to have a will of their own. For a full few seconds she didn't breathe, her entire body held captive by his male beauty.

He only wore his jeans, having removed his shirt in the bathroom. His skin stretched tightly over lean, rippling muscle, the color of it a rich olive tone. Laura recalled only too well how the summer sun treated Shane like a cherished lover, how easily he transformed into a bronzed Mediterranean god. She'd guess by the leanness of his torso and hips that he still ran to keep in shape. His arms, shoulders, and chest were thick with well-defined muscle, but he wasn't bulky or husky like some of the weight-lifting fanatics Laura had seen at her gym. Instead he was all long, lean power and graceful male movement.

He approached and paused on the opposite side of the bed, removed his wristwatch, and dropped it onto the bedside table. Laura clenched her eyes at the strangely erotic image of his strong, flexing forearms dusted with dark hair.

"Laura," he said. She felt the mattress give and knew that he'd sat down on the bed.

She opened her eyes cautiously.

"Are you comfortable?"

Laura thought of complaining just for the sake of complaining, but something in the tone of his deep voice had made her go mute. She nodded.

"If you become uncomfortable during the night, just call out to me and I'll change your position. I'm a light sleeper."

"I remember."

The intimate words had left her mouth before she'd had the opportunity to censor them. She saw the tiny flick of his eyelids as he watched her and knew that he'd been just as surprised by her admission as she had.

She felt like she couldn't draw air adequately when he suddenly stretched out beside her. He leaned on his elbow and looked down at her.

"What else do you remember?"

Laura stared up at the ceiling, refusing to be lulled by his seductive tone. "I remember lots of things about you. I have a good memory. I recall details about most of my lovers, even the ones who weren't particularly worth remembering."

"Is that right?"

Laura shrugged, still refraining from looking into his starkly handsome face. Something about his silky tone made her heartbeat escalate erratically, however.

"What about those friends of Huey's you entertained last month? Do you remember everything about them?"

"Why? Are you worried you won't match up?" she asked coolly. She gasped in surprise when he suddenly palmed her jaw and forced her to look at him. Despite the firmness of his hold, his forefinger gently stroked her cheek.

"You're a mean liar, Laura. But you're not a particularly good one."

Her eyes went wide in alarm. Could he see through her that easily? "What's that supposed to mean?"

"It means—" he began before he reached for the sheet that covered her, "that I know the way a woman sounds when she's out of her mind with desire and I know the sounds of a woman being dramatic to please her audience."

He whisked the sheet down until it crumpled around her knees.

Laura inhaled sharply when he lightly skimmed his fingertips across her hip bone and then her bare belly.

"Don't get me wrong," Shane said almost conversationally as she shivered beneath his slow caresses on her stomach and ribs. Her skin roughened and her nipples pulled into tight erection. "You sounded aroused enough on those tapes I heard. But there was a lot of showmanship mixed in. Huey's gorillas were either too stupid or too worried about coming to notice."

Laura stifled a moan when his callused fingertips skimmed lightly over the sensitive skin on the underside of her breast.

"A true dominant wants one thing above all else."

"W-what?" Laura couldn't stop herself from asking. She watched, wide-eyed, as his fingertip traced the shape of the aureole of her pebbled nipple, never really touching the pink crest, just lazily circling around and around . . . taunting her with his power over her.

"He wants to hear the sounds of his woman in an all-out frenzy of desire. He wants to take her to the core of honesty . . . to a place of raw, primitive need," he explained, his quiet, slightly rough voice making her skin prickle with heightened awareness. "He wants her to submit to that, to surrender to the truth. Do you understand, Laura? No dramatics. No lies can exist where I'm going to take you in the next few days. I want you to let yourself go, give up the responsibility you've been harboring into my hands. Do you understand what I'm saying?"

Laura shut her eyes tightly as emotion gripped at her throat. For a few seconds it felt as if she couldn't breathe. Oh God, why had he said that thing about giving over the responsibility to him? How had she known that it would pierce right through her defenses, tempt her with the promise of something that could never be?

"Just because you can make my body respond to you doesn't mean that you own me." A tiny cry of loss slipped past her lips when he removed his fingertips from her breast.

"No. But it's a damn good start."

When she felt his weight come off the bed she opened her eyes warily, on edge as to what he would do next. Her breath stuck in her throat when he stood, ripped open the button fly of his jeans, and hooked his thumbs in the elastic waistband of a pair of boxer briefs that looked starkly white against his dusky skin. He bent, preventing her from seeing more than a glimpse of the long, stiff penis that hung down his right thigh.

But then he stood before her naked. He didn't move, as though he knew perfectly well the effect he had on her.

Laura stared for a full moment, her eyes running over every inch of his hard body. When she shut her eyes they burned. His image remained on the back of her eyelids, however—the ridged muscles of his abdomen, the strip of black hair that made a swirling design around his taut belly button, the long, full cock just as dusky as his smooth skin but with an additional reddish hue. The head was erotically smooth and thick, its density weighing down the stalk.

She could perfectly imagine the delicious weight of it in her hand, the way that cock stretched and filled her, how it reached a place inside of her where no other man had begun to touch. She didn't really require his command to open her eyes because she'd already lifted her eyelids, hungry for more of the vision of him.

She watched, hypnotized by the image of him stroking his erection slowly. He pinned her with his stare, his eyes brilliantly alive in his otherwise impassive face when he came down on the bed next to her.

"I'd forgotten how beautiful your breasts are," he murmured, his lips just inches away from her left nipple. Laura moaned helplessly when he used the same hand that had been stroking his cock to massage a breast. She imagined that she felt the heat of his desire transferring to her own flesh. "Do you remember how crazy I used to be about them?"

Laura didn't know how to respond to the small, amused smile on his lips as he watched himself shaping her breast to his palm.

"Do you remember how I couldn't keep my hands off them . . . how shocked you were when I first told you I wanted to fuck them?" he asked, his voice gruff and intimate in the silent room. His lancing blue eyes suddenly leapt to her face. "It wasn't a rhetorical question."

"I-I—"

"Just be honest. Is it really that hard?"

"Yes," she replied on an exhale. "I remember."

He nodded slowly, holding her gaze. His hand lowered to skim across the sensitive sides of her torso and waist.

"You have the softest skin I've ever touched."

Laura made a strange, choking sound in her throat. He glanced up at her, his eyes pinning her in a fiery hold before he dipped his head suddenly. He lashed at a nipple with a warm, slightly rough tongue. Laura cried out, shocked by his abrupt movement and the stunning impact of his caress.

Before the cry had fully left her throat he began to suckle her. No buildup, no warning, no preamble—just a firm, hot, hungry suck.

Laura writhed beneath him, pulling on her restraints. It didn't hurt precisely—or it did a little. She couldn't be sure, because the primary sensation that struck her was need . . . the need for pressure, the need for friction on her pussy, her clit, the need to press his naked skin against her own.

Her hips shifted restlessly on the bed but she couldn't throw him off her breast. Not that she wanted to. God, it felt divine, but it was also nearly unbearable to have him hold her at his mercy this way.

She trembled beneath him when he made a low growling sound of male satisfaction deep in his throat and leaned up. Her nipple—reddened, glistening, and pointed—snapped out of his pursed lips with a popping noise.

"Shane . . ." she whispered, desperate to get his attention. But he ignored her and plumped the breast he held in his hand for his descending mouth. He gave her other nipple the same deft, slippery, slightly rough treatment that he had the first. Laura lifted her hips and pulled tight against her restraints, but no matter what she did she couldn't get the friction she needed on her increasingly hungry pussy.

She groaned in frustration. He lifted his dark head at the sound.

"Stop twisting around or I'll punish you. I'm doing this for my pleasure, not yours."

She stared at him, aghast.

"Why did you say all that crap about making me wild with desire then, if this is all for you?" she seethed.

He smiled as though her comment had genuinely pleased him before he leaned toward the bedside table. Laura's eyes went wide when she saw him extract a condom from the drawer. As she watched him slide the rubber over his enormous, swollen erection she promptly forgot what she'd just asked him.

Shane would give her the relief she needed. His beautiful cock rubbed her so deeply, agitated and enlivened secret flesh. He'd never failed to bring her the most electrifying orgasms imaginable . . .

"I'm going to fuck you now, but it's going to be for me. You're not allowed to come. Do you understand, Laura?"

Laura's reply stilled on her tongue when he gently swatted her right hip, his hand remaining on her flesh, his long fingers sinking deeply . . . greedily into her buttock, massaging her. "Hold very still," he commanded as he arrowed his cock into her spread pussy. She whimpered as the steely head slowly entered her, parting her flesh, demanding that her supple, slippery tissues give way to his burrowing cock.

He paused, the first several inches of his cock fully secured in her slit. Laura cried out sharply when he powered his full length into her with one stroke. Her eyes sprang wide. He braced himself over her on the metal headboard, still buried in her to the hilt, his testicles pressing to the sensitive skin at the entrance of her pussy.

"Tight," he whispered as he looked down at her. "You've got the sweetest little pussy." He grimaced in pleasure when he moved, drawing out of her several inches and sliding back in. He watched her reaction carefully as he stroked her deep.

"There," he said as he fucked her slowly.

Laura's eyes flickered back into her eye sockets. He knew what he was doing to her, the bastard. The thick ridge beneath the head of his cock stroked somewhere sublime. Did he have the same effect on all women or had he been formed perfectly to fill her flesh?

She moaned his name as he built the tension masterfully and she lay beneath him, bound and helpless with desire. She wondered if he'd read her mind when he spoke gruffly.

"Your pussy loves my cock, doesn't it?" he asked intently as he watched her and thrust with slow deliberation. "It shapes itself so tightly around it, squeezes me . . . taunts me."

Laura panted, her hips flexing desperately to get pressure on her clit. But he withheld himself from her, merely brushing against the sensitive opening of her pussy on his downstrokes, refusing to press on her clit. Still, the burn grew deliciously inside of her, making her want, making her crave—

"You're the one who's teasing me, Shane, and you know it."

"Maybe you're right," he murmured.

Laura gasped in mixed protest and arousal when he held himself off her even more, the muscles of his arms and chest bulging. He began fucking her in short, shallow thrusts using merely the first half of his cock.

"No." She couldn't stop herself from moaning in protest.

But he just continued to fuck her shallowly. An orgasm grew in her, ached in her, but he refused to give her the fuel she required to ignite.

He came up on the balls of his feet, his arms still braced on the metal branches of the headboard holding himself off her, six feet and several inches of grim determination and hard, flexing muscle. His facial features grew rigid with restraint. Despite the fact that she was furious at him for depriving her, she had to admit that what he was doing could hardly be called fucking solely for his pleasure.

What he was doing, more specifically, was trying to get her to beg. And she was so close to doing just that . . .

Laura bit her lip hard and groaned. The bed began to beat against the wall from Shane's short yet forceful thrusts. The only way he touched her body was by pumping the first half of his cock into her pussy again and again, faster and faster.

He closed his eyes and grunted with pleasure. A mist of sweat shone on his dusky skin. His small, dark brown nipples drew tight. But still he refused to offer her the extra pressure she required on her clit. Still he withheld the magical, rubbing knob of his cock from her deepest depths.

"Shane . . ." she moaned, the ache of need becoming a festering pain.

"What, baby?" he rasped.

She cried out in sheer frustration. The thick circumference of his pistoning cock created a low-level, yet insistent burn on her clit, which made her continually crave more pressure. She pulsed against him with the tiny centimeters of motion that her restraints allowed her. The burn amplified. She clenched her eyes shut and graphically imagined what it would be like to have Shane fuck her at full throttle while she was tied up spread-eagle on this bed, completely at his mercy.

Yes . . . yes . . . yes. He may be taunting her, but she would come anyway. She reached for orgasm, strained for it . . .

Her eyes flashed open at the sudden cruel deprivation of his cock. She saw him take his rigid erection in his palm and impatiently shuck off the condom. He knelt over her and pumped the glistening rod in his hand.

His cock swelled impossibly large, the veins popped from the surface, feeding his arousal. The head glistened wetly from the steady stream of pre-come leaking from the slit. She watched, transfixed, as his face clenched tight. He groaned gutturally at the same moment that his seed shot onto her belly, thick and abundant.

The scent of his semen reached her flared nostrils. Her womb constricted in an agony of desire.

She twisted her chin away from him as he grunted and moaned, his come continuing to spurt warmly on her belly. But she couldn't stop herself from seeing him in her mind's eye in all his primitive glory as he knelt over her—his fist eventually slowing on the shaft of his penis, the tension that had drawn his muscles tight as a cocked bowstring loosening . . . diminishing.

She refused to open her eyes a minute later when she felt him wipe the cooling come off her abdomen. Her breath stuck in her throat when she felt him gently place the pendant on the inner curve of her left breast, his fingers lingering on her skin for a brief, electric few seconds.

He covered her naked body with the sheet and blanket, securing it tightly around her to protect her from the cool air. She heard him shut off the bedside lamp, felt him lying down next to her. He didn't speak or try to touch her again.

"Why do you want me to hate you, Shane?"

The silence clung heavily.

He shifted in the bed, settling down to sleep. When he spoke, he sounded as though he faced in the opposite direction from her.

"You don't hate me. But even if you did, hatred is a powerful emotion. It's as good a place for us to begin again as any. At least it means I'm getting through to you, baby."

Laura lay awake staring at the dancing shadows cast by the fire long after Shane's breathing became deep and even.

CHAPTER **NINE**

S hane, wake up," Laura said early the next morning. He rustled in his sleep.

"Shane," she barked.

One blue eye popped open and met her gaze. He lay on his stomach, his left cheek pressed into the pillow. She saw the moment when recognition sparked into his awareness. He sat up. His short dark hair spilled forward onto his forehead and stuck out like a rooster tail on the crown. The trim on the pillowcase had made an indentation on his whiskered chin.

Laura steeled herself against the sight of his rumpled sexuality with determination.

"I thought you said you would wake up immediately if I was uncomfortable. My bladder is about to burst. I've been calling to you now for five minutes," she lied peevishly.

He threw her an annoyed look before he turned over and stood. The sheet slipped off his hips, revealing a pair of muscular buns covered by smooth, dusky skin. Laura stared up at the ceiling determinedly, her breath coming quicker.

"You have not been calling to me for five minutes," he

rumbled tiredly as he slid the jeans he'd worn yesterday over his thighs and tight ass, forgoing underwear.

She glared at him as he unfastened her ankles. "How would you know? *You* were unconscious."

He refused to be goaded into an altercation, however. He unfastened her arms, although Laura noticed that unlike the ankle cuffs, he left the leather cuffs around her wrists and merely unhooked them from the thick, woven cloth band. Laura threw him a look of deep loathing as she stood and passed, refusing to rush when she felt his stare on the back of her naked body.

She gnashed her teeth together in frustration when she turned on the shower several minutes later and Shane pounded on the door. She hastily wrapped a luxurious towel around her and opened it.

"What?" she asked acerbically.

"Don't shower yet. I'm going running, so you're going to have to go with me."

Her gaze lowered down over him. He had indeed changed into gray sweats, a long-sleeved dark blue undershirt, and a white Georgetown T-shirt that was ripped and frayed around the hem. Laura would have bet much-needed money at that moment that he'd bought the ancient shirt back when he was a graduate student studying criminology and psychology at the prestigious university.

"I'm not going anywhere," she countered calmly. With morning had come cold, harsh reality. She'd been kidnapped by a man who planned to use his history and his sexual hold on her to force her into giving him information that he needed for his investigation. The new day had thankfully granted her a little distance from the overwhelming, unquenched desire that had haunted her dreams.

At the moment, Laura experienced very little for Shane Dominic except a white-hot fury.

"You're going to come with me, all right," Shane replied pleasantly.

"Are you *nuts*?" Laura shouted. "I can't go jogging around in the snow in a skirt and high-heeled boots!"

His crooked, boyish smile took her off guard. She'd forgotten how effortlessly charming he could be. "I brought something for you to go running in."

Laura stared, slack-jawed as he held up a large shopping bag. "A couple pair of sweats, a jacket, socks, and tennis shoes. I guessed on your size, but if they're a little big for you it shouldn't matter. This cabin is isolated, not a soul for miles. I'm the only one who's going to see you."

"I am *not* going jogging," Laura repeated. He peered into the plastic bag and continued as though she'd never spoken.

"Since the fit of running shoes is so important, I bought you three different sizes—a seven, seven and a half, and an eight. I remembered that you wore a seven and a half, but I figured if you had a half-size wiggle room in either direction—"

"Shane, you're not listening," Laura grated out, trying her best to ignore her escalated heartbeat. He actually remembered her *shoe size*?

"You're going running with me. Do you know how I know that?"

"Because you're delusional?" Laura asked nastily.

"No. Because *I'm* going running. I run every day. And since you're going to be tied to me . . . you're going to have to run to keep up. I'm giving you two minutes or I'm going to come in and help you get dressed." He dropped the shopping bag on the bathroom floor and pulled the door closed in front of her shocked face.

Ten minutes later they stepped out onto the front porch and Shane pulled the door closed behind them. It had warmed up during the night to the low thirties, causing a light mist of evaporation to cling in the valleys of the surrounding hills. She'd never been to this portion of northern Illinois and was surprised by the gently rolling landscape.

Laura followed Shane before he had a chance to pull on the chain that he'd attached to the cuff around her wrist. He'd attached the other end of the light, but sturdy-looking chain to a loose woven band that he'd looped around his own wrist.

"Your body looks like you're in shape. Are you?" Shane asked matter-of-factly as they passed his car in the driveway and headed for the rural route—the only place they could run that had been completely cleared of snow.

Laura flushed. Even though he hadn't sounded remotely suggestive when he'd said it, she couldn't help but think of him inspecting her as she lay naked and tied to the bed.

"I swim and take yoga and aerobics classes several times a week," she muttered.

"Sounds pretty lightweight. Do you think you're up to jogging six or seven miles?"

"I can go whatever distance you do," she countered swiftly.

She saw the amused gleam in his blue eyes and knew that he'd goaded her right into a trap of compliance. Laura simmered over that fact for the first fifteen minutes of their jog. Soon she found herself relaxing into the brisk pace that Shane set, however. The cool, windless air soothed her heated body. The tension she'd been carrying in her muscles for weeks now, only to have it strung tighter last night by intense, unfulfilled desire, slowly eased out of her.

Shane glanced over at her. "You're not breathing very heavily. I think we can pick up the pace."

"No, I'm comfortable." She resisted—for the principle if nothing else.

He responded by subtly increasing his speed. Laura fumed as she watched the three-foot chain that had hung limply between them as they ran side by side start to lengthen and grow taut.

"I'm not a *dog*," she shouted. She sped up until she was in front of him and glared back at him. "If I lay down on this pavement you're not going to have a very satisfying run this morning, are you?"

"Maybe not, but it'll be damned satisfying to carry you back to the cabin and give your butt the paddling it deserves."

Laura blinked in the face of his gleaming eyes and calmly uttered threat. Her cheeks flushed with heat. She slowed her pace to match his, telling herself that it was best not to rock the boat at the moment.

Instead she inspected the gray, fog-cloaked hills. As far as the eye could see there were only trees and leaden gray sky. No farmhouse in sight that she might run to if she escaped.

The thought struck her that it was the sort of day that she typically found gloomy and oppressive. Why the cool air and leaden skies enlivened her as she jogged silently next to Shane—their breath making clouds of vapor around their mouths at a nearly identical rate, their footsteps synchronized thumps on the frozen pavement—was beyond Laura's understanding.

She cast a sidelong glance at him. "So what happened to your fiancée?"

"Nothing happened to her," he said as he continued to stare straight ahead.

Laura made a sound of disgust.

"Oh, I see. You're asking why she's not my fiancée anymore."

"Well?" Laura asked when he didn't continue for several seconds, hoping he didn't hear the anxious tremor in her query. He shrugged.

"Nothing earth-shattering. It just didn't work out."

"Did you break up with her?"

"I was the one who said that I didn't think we were meant to be married, yeah," he said, still not meeting her gaze.

"So it wasn't earth-shattering for you, in other words. It certainly must have been for her."

She rolled her eyes in frustration when he didn't respond and tried to control her breathing as they traveled up a long, slow upgrade. Her thoughts spun crazily, the vortex fueled by emotion she hadn't allowed herself to experience for a long, long time.

Had Shane broken off his engagement because of her—Laura?

"She deserved better than to have a guy who was constantly second-guessing himself when it came to marrying her," Shane said as they breached the summit of the small hill and began to jog down the other side. "I'd already postponed the wedding twice."

"Cold feet?" Laura wondered as she cautiously studied his profile.

"It just didn't feel right to me."

She couldn't stop herself from snorting in frustrated derision. "And you always have to go with your gut, isn't that right, Shane? That's what all this is supposed to be about," she said as she lifted her wrist and the chain that attached them swayed in the air.

"Yeah. I guess that pretty much sums it up." He glanced over at her, snagging her gaze with a warm, steady stare.

Laura swallowed and broke his gaze with difficulty. Neither of them spoke for the next five minutes as they ran.

"Oh," Laura exclaimed in pleasant surprise when they topped another rise. She paused, hardly noticing that Shane ceased jogging at the same moment. They stared down over a valley with a massive river flowing through it.

"It's the Mississippi," Shane said softly.

They stood for several moments, watching the mighty body of water cut its deep channel through the land. A lulling sense of peace stole over her just as gently as the fog encroached on the banks of the powerful river.

"Come on, we'd better turn back," Shane eventually said.

"It's supposed to snow later," Shane murmured in a mellow tone as he set a hot bowl of oatmeal topped with fruit and brown sugar and a steaming cup of tea in front of her forty-five minutes later.

Laura frowned as she stared down at the oatmeal. Shane had unfastened her wrist when they'd returned to the cabin and had ordered her to sit at the large oak kitchen table while he prepared them the simple breakfast. During the three-and-a-half-mile return jog back to the cabin, she'd had a chance to erect her barriers against him once again. The knowledge that she'd lowered her defenses without even being aware of it as they'd gazed together at the flowing river and the stark winter landscape had set Laura on edge.

"I'm not hungry. I'm all sweaty. May I go to take a shower now. *Please,* master?"

He didn't turn around as he spooned some oatmeal into a bowl for himself. "We'll take a shower after we eat."

"Screw that," Laura declared as she stood, shoving back her chair from the table. "I'm showering *now.*"

Her heart beat madly in her chest as she swept through the living room toward the hallway, mostly because she knew without having to look that Shane quickly closed the distance between them. She shouted in outrage when he encircled her with his arms from behind, lifted her, and swung her around to his right hip. His firm grip pressed her arms uselessly to their sides and the position made it so that her legs kicked at nothing but air behind him.

"Let go of me!"

"I don't think so. Not until you get what you were asking for," Shane muttered grimly before he sat down on the end of the bed and draped her over his lap with an effortless ease that infuriated her. He grabbed her outside wrist, joined it with the one that was trapped next to his body. He fastened the two leather cuffs with the small connector hooks quicker than Laura could finish her prolonged shout of pure, unmitigated fury.

She still shouted when he held her down with a restraining arm in his lap and jerked down her sweatpants, exposing her bare ass. She practically choked in outrage when he swatted a buttock.

"No," she squawked as he spanked her again and again and she jerked and writhed, trying unsuccessfully to avoid his palm.

"Remember what I told you in the car? Any stroke I give you while you struggle goes on top of your actual punishment."

"Will you stop this nonsense?" she shrieked as he smacked

her bottom again, resulting in a tingling burn in her flexing muscles.

"It would go easier on you if you just relaxed and took your punishment," he said as she wriggled in his hold and he held her down in his lap.

"Fuck you! *God*, I hate your *guts*, Shane Dominic," she snarled.

Laura had never experienced anything like this—such an intense, wild fury that felt as if it would explode out of her chest. She cried out when Shane spanked her briskly on the lower curve of her left buttock, her anguished shout not so much due to pain but a feeling of overwhelming helplessness. She spun in a cyclone of powerful, tumultuous emotions.

He paused for a moment, his hand remaining on her left ass cheek. Laura tried to ignore the way he slowly stroked her burning, sensitized flesh while she struggled and tears poured down her cheeks, some falling onto the deep pile carpeting.

His caress only tossed fuel on her inner turmoil. She increased her struggles, nearly succeeding in causing her wriggling body to spill off the end of his knees. He responded by smacking her bottom once, the brisk contact of flesh against flesh causing a sharp cracking sound, and then used his other arm to secure her in his lap, her left side pressing snuggly against his abdomen.

"Go ahead. Fight it if it'll make you feel better. It's not going to change anything. I'll still be here when you're done. I'm not going anywhere, Laura. You're going to have to give me what I want."

She gritted her teeth and gave one final feral growl of helpless outrage.

Her head fell limply forward as tears continued to pour from her eyes. Only once before had she felt so acutely out of control of her life. Laura had taken control then in the only way available to her.

And now Shane threatened what little advantage she'd bargained so desperately to gain.

Look at her—look at what he'd done to her in such a short period of time! She used to be able to remain calm around him. When he'd confronted her thirteen years ago about marrying Huey, she'd been matter-of-fact with him, impervious to his pleas. Now she was screeching like a fishwife, tears and snot running down her face while she struggled for what felt like her very existence and Shane spanked her bare bottom as though she were nothing but an ornery child.

The humiliation was almost too much to bear.

She inhaled raggedly, trying to catch her breath. She just needed to play along. That's all. If Shane wanted her to submit to him, to hand over control to him—fine. So be it. She would just have to do her best to pacify him.

The thought terrified her but what other option did she have, really? He couldn't keep her here as his captive forever. At some point he had to take her home. Then she'd do her best to repair whatever damage had been done to the wound he'd reopened on her heart and go on with her life.

She sagged in temporary defeat. In doing so, she became aware for the first time of every point of contact her body made with his—the hardness of his thighs beneath her gasping chest and belly, the column of his partially erect cock stretching along his thigh beneath her heaving ribs, the rate and pressure of his own escalated breathing from his abdomen pressing against her side.

And heat emanated off him. So did his scent—perspiration from his jog mixed with an intoxicating male musk and a residue of spicy aftershave and soap.

As if he knew somehow that she was suddenly aware of him sexually, his penis lurched against her rib cage, swelling noticeably in size. She stifled a groan.

"What do you want from me, Shane?" she asked miserably.

"You know what I want."

"You want me to sit still while you punish me?"

"That'll do for starters," he muttered with mild amusement from above her.

"Do it then. Get it over with," she grated out.

"You're not going to struggle?"

"No," she answered sarcastically. "I'll lay here like a good little girl and take it."

He chuckled and loosened his tight hold on her, his hand caressing her stinging bottom once before he completely released her.

"Actually, I think I'll have you stand and bend over."

CHAPTER **TEN**

He said it so lightly that at first Laura wasn't sure that she'd heard him correctly. Lying there in his forced hold while he spanked her was one thing—but willingly positioning herself to take her punishment was quite another.

Shane said nothing for the next several seconds. Laura got the impression he was waiting . . . curious as to how she would respond. It suddenly struck her that he no longer restrained her. She slid off his thighs and onto her knees. She grimaced in frustration when the desire to pull her pants up over her bare bottom hit her and she was stopped by the reality of her wrists being restrained behind her back.

"Stand up and bend over," Shane directed.

Laura glared at him in anger, but for some strange reason his request sent a surge of liquid warmth through her pussy. She felt simultaneously embarrassed, furious, and aroused when she'd done what he said, sticking her bare bottom in the air. He stood, came behind her, and lowered her sweatpants to her knees. She clenched her jaw, readying herself for the sharp sting that his palm would leave on her ass.

She glanced around in confusion a few seconds later,

however, when she heard the sound of a zipper from across the room.

"Bend back over," Shane said as he returned to her side.

Laura hadn't even realized that she'd straightened, fixated as she was on the black paddle Shane carried in his hand. It was unlike anything she'd ever seen before, being made of what looked like smooth, hard black rubber.

"Shane—" she began in a quivery voice.

"It'll be all right," he soothed as he approached. He came up next to her and placed his hand on her shoulder, pressing down gently, urging her to resume her former position. Laura bent over slowly, but he must have seen the doubt in her eyes. "I'll never give you any more than you can handle. You have to trust me, Laura."

She closed her eyes as his deep voice washed over her. He opened his hand across her shoulder. Laura jumped at the sudden sensation of the paddle touching her bare bottom— not with the brisk, stinging smack that she expected, but instead with a smooth, gliding caress.

"Bend your knees slightly," Shane demanded thickly.

Laura groaned in mixed humiliation and excitement. He waited while she followed his instruction, continuing to stroke her sensitive, tingling bottom with the surprisingly velvety soft surface of the paddle. She inhaled sharply when the paddle suddenly pressed tightly against her butt cheeks, garnering her attention.

"I call the shots while we're here. I decide when you're going to eat, sleep, fuck, and come. Do you understand?"

Laura's mouth gaped open, but before she had a chance to respond he drew back the paddle and swung. The resulting smack made air pop out of her throat. Before she had time to recover he paddled her again. She couldn't stop herself. She stepped away from him, instinctively trying to avoid the sharp sting of pain. She lost her balance due to the sweatpants gathered around her knees, but Shane steadied her with the hand on her shoulder.

"Dammit, that hurts, Shane!" she muttered fiercely. In truth, the sharp sting of the blow had already faded, leaving a hot, prickly sensation in the cheeks. She grimaced when she recognized that fiery sensation on her ass seemed to be spreading to her sex, tingling and enlivening the damp flesh. Was her arousal clear to Shane as she bent over like this with her thighs parted? Her ass cheeks must be glowing bright pink at this point, but could he see what his actions were doing to her traitorous pussy?

He responded to her accusation by rubbing the surface of the paddle up and down on her bottom with a frictionless glide. It soothed Laura's nerve endings, but his actions also caused a sharp, almost painful twinge of arousal on her clit.

Fire seemed to streak from her clit to her sacral area when he transferred the tip of the paddle to the base of her backbone, rubbing her gently. Why that relatively innocent caress had such a dramatic effect on her body, she had no idea. It'd had the same effect when Shane had caressed the skin just above her crack while he held her in his lap last night.

Perhaps the most disconcerting thing was that he somehow had knowledge of how sensitive she was there, even though Laura had never suspected it herself. Shane possessed far too much knowledge of her secrets.

She knew he was about to resume when he once again pressed the paddle tightly to her cheeks and circled it subtly against the flesh.

"Hold steady," he murmured.

Laura gritted her teeth together in preparation for the blow. She grunted when it landed with a loud crack. Once again, he soothed the sting with the smooth side of the paddle.

"Are you going to stop insulting me?" he asked.

"I'll try," Laura conceded.

He paddled her again, this blow angled slightly upward, landing on the sensitive lower curve of her bottom. She yelped. "All right. Yes."

"Yes what?" Shane queried softly as the paddle rubbed just inches away from her aching pussy.

"I'll stop insulting you," she moaned.

The paddle cracked her ass again. "And what else?"

"I-I'll eat when you tell me to . . . and shower whenever you tell me to," she added quickly when she felt the paddle leave her skin.

"And?"

Laura wiped her wet cheek on her shoulder. "I'll . . . I'll fuck when you say to . . . and come . . ." Her voice trailed off.

She grimaced when the paddle stung her again sharply.

". . . when you say to," she added tremulously. She tried her mightiest to restrain a sob, but didn't quite succeed when he again soothed her burning hot flesh, this time with his palm instead of the paddle.

He urged her gently to stand with his hand on her shoulder. Then he bent to pull her sweatpants back up over her hips and unfastened her cuffs. Laura was so stunned by the entire experience she just stood there mutely while he went to the bathroom. He returned a moment later with some tissues. She said nothing as he wiped off the tears and snot from her face with a tenderness that nearly undid her.

Her only defense was to refuse to meet his stare.

"Why do you fight it, Laura?"

She shook her head slowly, still staring steadfastly at the blue "H" of the *Hoyas* on his ancient T-shirt. "I don't know what you're talking about."

She couldn't believe it was possible, but fresh tears scuttled down her cheeks. She couldn't recall the last time she'd cried during the past decade or more and now it had become a regular occurrence since Shane had reentered her life. It was as if he'd flicked a switch in her . . . released a dam of emotion.

"Just tell me what you want me to say and I'll say it," she grated out, straining to regain control.

He never said "Look at me," so she had no idea why she did it. She felt compelled to look up and meet his stare. His eyes glowed brilliantly in his dark countenance.

"It's not forever, Laura. But for these three days, you will give me complete control. I don't know why for sure you believe you had to carry the burden of your secrets alone. All I know is it's going to stop between now and when we leave next Monday." He stepped closer. His long legs parted, cradling her hip. "I need to know what you know."

Laura ripped her gaze from his, staring straight ahead . . . willing herself not to be ensnared. He dipped his head. She felt his warm breath ghosting her ear.

"I'll never forget what it was like between us, baby. I can't let go of it. Tell me you remember."

"If I say it now you won't know if I'm doing it just to please you or not," she managed hoarsely. "Isn't that the shortcoming of this game?"

"This is no game, Laura. Just say it and I'll decide. Look at me."

Laura swallowed, steeling herself. She glanced up warily. His blue eyes glittered with emotion.

"I remember," she said.

For several seconds he didn't move. Then he stepped back several feet and turned around.

"Come out to the kitchen and finish your breakfast," he ordered before he exited the room.

Laura followed slowly, wondering what he'd seen in her face that resulted in his bold features stiffening in fury.

Neither of them spoke a word while they ate breakfast. Despite the tension, Laura found herself eating every last bit of the oatmeal topped with banana and brown sugar that Shane had set in front of her. She never added sugar to her cereal or oatmeal. At first she was irritated with him for having put it on there without asking her preference.

Typical, given the power trip Shane was pulling.

But then she'd taken a bite out of the still-warm cereal and discovered it tasted delicious. Much to her disbelief, she actually wanted more once she'd finished. She couldn't bring herself to ask, though, and just watched sullenly while Shane rinsed off their bowls and cups and put them in the dishwasher.

When he was done he looked at her and jerked his chin slightly, indicating he wanted her to get up. He followed her down the hallway to the bedroom and then passed her to turn on the lights in the bathroom.

"Come here," he said gruffly.

Laura eyed him warily as she entered the large bathroom.

"Do you have to go?" he asked bluntly.

"No," Laura replied, glad she was telling the truth. Otherwise Shane would have probably stood there and watched her while she went, in an attempt to further humiliate her.

"Go ahead and sit down while I shave, then."

Laura felt his stare on her even though she refused to meet his gaze. He was waiting for her to argue, she could tell. So she sat down on the closed lid of the toilet, refusing to give him the satisfaction.

Out of the corner of her eye she saw him whip first the T-shirt then the long-sleeved shirt over his head. Even though she tried to ignore him as he unzipped a leather toiletry bag and removed his shaving items, Laura found herself glancing over at him with increasing frequency. The sight of Shane stripped bare to the waist was a difficult one to ignore.

Besides, shaving was such a personal ritual . . . such a masculine one.

"Why don't you shave after you take a shower?" she asked as she watched him apply shaving cream, the foam starkly white against his dark complexion.

Shane shrugged and rinsed off his hands. "I don't know. I like to get it over with, I guess."

Laura had already noticed the elegant silver box that he'd removed from the leather bag. It looked like an antique. The initials "S.J.D." had been inscribed on the outside in a bold script. She watched as he opened the box and withdrew a chased silver razor. His morning growth was fairly heavy. The razor made a raspy sound as it passed over his skin.

"Those aren't your initials. Not your father's either," Laura commented idly as she watched him. Shane's father's name was Alexander and Shane's middle name was Marcus.

"It belonged to my grandfather," Shane muttered before

he stretched his mouth to one side and shaved a strip of skin beside his lips.

"What was his name?" Laura murmured, unaware that she'd leaned subtly closer to him.

"Salvador Joseph Dominic," Shane replied as he rinsed the razor that was also an heirloom and then swept it across his jaw. "My mother worked with her jeweler to modify it to fit modern razors."

Laura smiled. "That sounds like something Elizabeth would do. She could have been a jewelry designer herself she was so talented," she said, thinking how unfair it was that Elizabeth Dominic's frail body had never allowed her to explore to the fullest a myriad of artistic talents. Laura and Elizabeth had been kindred creative spirits. She hadn't said anything to Shane, but it had touched her deeply that Elizabeth had purchased some of her artwork without Laura's knowledge.

"So you remember my middle name?"

Laura stiffened at the abrupt question. She hadn't meant to reveal something so intimate.

"I told you. I remember a lot of things about you."

"Right," he said dryly before he resumed shaving. "Because you have a good memory."

Laura merely shrugged and turned away, refusing to watch him while he finished. Despite her actions, however, she was acutely aware of his movements beside her. Her heart seemed to swell unnaturally large in her chest a minute or two later, making it difficult for her lungs to find room to function adequately, when he removed his socks, then whisked his sweatpants and boxer briefs down his trim hips.

"Stand up."

Laura rose hesitantly. He stalked toward her, completely naked. She stood rigid as he bent his head and grabbed her wrist. She wanted to look down and watch him as he unbuckled the leather cuffs. Or more correctly, she wanted to look down to ogle his glorious nude body.

Being acutely aware of that desire was what made her

stare straight ahead at his chest while he removed the cuffs and set them on the counter.

"Take off your clothes." He moved past her, sliding open the glass shower doors and turning the knob on the tap, testing the water with his fingers. When he turned around a moment later, she still stood there, unmoving.

"I-I don't want to take a shower with you."

"I didn't ask your opinion on it," he said. "Take off your clothes and get in."

Laura hesitated but Shane's gaze suddenly flared with irritation. She quickly complied, not wanting a repeat of what had occurred earlier. Her bottom still smarted from her paddling.

Her hands felt clumsy and useless as she removed her clothing and her necklace, probably because Shane stood and watched her. She would have been better off following his order immediately and undressing while he turned on the shower.

Her step flagged when she saw that his cock had stiffened noticeably while she'd undressed.

"Get in," he said gruffly.

Her gaze swept down him anxiously as she approached. He didn't move. The space between him and the glass door was narrow. She squeezed past him, all too aware of his lengthening cock. She couldn't prevent the smooth, velvety-soft tip from brushing across her naked hip. It lurched upward at the brief, electric contact. She glanced up to meet his smoldering stare.

Laura stepped past him quickly beneath the warm jets of water. She wet her hair and let the water run over her face and body, shutting her eyes so that she didn't have to acknowledge the naked, aroused, gorgeous specimen of manhood who had just shut the shower door, forcing her to share the steamy, confined space with him.

Despite her tension it felt heavenly to wash herself. Had it really only been twenty-four hours since she'd last showered? It felt like an eternity.

The thought made her open her eyes and reach for the soap in the recessed holder on the wall, but Shane's large hand closed over the white bar before hers did. He reached over her head at the same time and grabbed a bottle of shampoo, handing it to her.

"You wash your hair. I'll do your body."

Laura's hand slowly rose to encircle the plastic bottle. He waited while she squirted some of the pink liquid in her hand and rubbed it into her scalp before replacing the bottle. She massaged the shampoo into her wet hair but her gaze stuck on the sight of Shane lathering the soap liberally between his big hands.

He reached out, sliding a white, foamy palm over her waist and upward. She stilled, realizing that her hair-washing had left her totally exposed with her hands on her head. Before she could drop her arms, however, he swept up with his soapy caress, cradling both of her breasts in his palm. He squeezed lightly as he washed her, slathering the foam over the damp globes, sliding his fingers over her erect nipples. Laura murmured in protest when he suddenly glided up to her underarms.

"Put your arms back up," he scolded, his lips twitching in amusement. Laura felt her cheeks heat as he cleaned her matter-of-factly, feeling embarrassed and yet strangely aroused by having him do something as intimate as washing her underarms. He moved on to lather up her shoulders and arms.

Her face wasn't the only thing that burned as he touched her body so intimately. Her pussy ached. Her clit simmered.

God, she needed to come.

She'd lain awake for hours last night listening to the sound of Shane's even breathing, her pussy aflame after Shane's purposeful depravation. Even her spanking and paddling had aroused her, although her lust had been mixed with fury and humiliation. Now she was forced to stand while Shane gently, almost lovingly caressed her vulnerable flesh with his large, capable hands.

It was really too much to bear.

She sighed shakily when he stepped closer to her and his

hands ran over the sensitive sides of her ribs. Her nipples pulled into painful erection as he slid both hands along the undersides of her breasts.

"I can't get over how soft your skin is . . . especially here. I've never felt anything like it," he complimented huskily as he shaped her breasts, pressing the turgid nipples against his palms. Laura felt painfully aware of the fact that if she tilted her neck back their mouths would be only inches apart. Instead she remained with her head downcast. She stared as the tip of his fully erect, water-glistening penis slid against her lower belly while he languorously fondled her breasts.

"Better rinse your hair," Shane rasped.

She closed her eyes and tilted her head back. The thick shampoo lather and warm water streamed down her back and neck, gliding over his wrists and hands as he continued to play with her breasts, running in rivulets down her belly and thighs.

His hands left her breasts for a moment, briefly breaking her spell of sensual arousal. She blinked the water out of her eyes and watched him as he rubbed more soap into his hands. And then he was caressing her again, massaging her hips and thighs. Her legs quivered as a delicious heat and torpor weighted her flesh.

"Open your eyes, Laura," he ordered gruffly as his palms smoothed over hips and his fingertips gently glided over the sensitive skin of her ass.

"No," Laura whispered. She sensed his irritation at her refusal, but Shane held her at his mercy. He couldn't expect to take everything from her.

"Then open your thighs," he demanded, his tone tinged with anger. That directive she followed eagerly.

"Oh, God," Laura cried out when she complied and he spread his lathered hand over her labia and rubbed, working his forefinger between the lips while his other fingers washed and sluiced warm water over the sensitive tissues of her outer sex. Laura clutched his shoulders, sinking her fingertips into the dense, warm muscle and held on for dear life.

It felt delicious . . . decadent. She whimpered in pleasure

when she felt the tip of his forefinger wash away the abundant cream at the entrance of her slit. The head of his cock, like a large, fleshy arrow tip, throbbed more insistently against her belly, the hard, smooth surface pressing against her wet skin, mounting her excitement exponentially.

"I'd be fighting a losing battle if I tried to wash away all those juices. Besides, I'm too selfish to do it. You wash me now."

Laura's eyes snapped open at the firm demand. She trembled in anguish when he removed his hands from her pussy.

She'd never known Shane to be cruel. Why was he taunting her this way? Although, Laura had to admit, to be given the opportunity to run her hands over Shane's glorious male body could hardly be called cruelty. But Laura wondered about that, as well, after she'd lathered up her hands and placed them on his rib cage.

For a moment she didn't move, the artist in her acutely attuned to the miraculous sculpture of masculine flesh that stood before her, his vibrant life force throbbing into her hands.

Remember this, treasure it, a voice in her head called out plaintively.

She slowly moved her foamy hands over his broad chest, relishing the feel of the wet, crinkly hair and the dense muscle beneath her fingertips. Neither of them spoke as she moved on to his neck, shoulders, and arms, her fingertips more than just washing, but exploring with sensual fascination the feeling of smooth, thick skin, the fascinating contours of muscle and bone. When she lathered up her hands again and transferred them to Shane's hips and then his firm, muscular ass, she wondered if Shane held his breath just like she did.

She dared to glance up at him then, one tight buttock curving into each of her palms. He watched her steadily, his eyes fiery blue flames. The sound of the water jetting from the showerhead and splattering onto the floor rivaled the drum of her pounding heart in her ears. Shane moved forward slightly, causing his heavy erection to slide along her belly, the thick head pressing against her belly button, the first few inches of the steely shaft rubbing against the softness of her abdomen.

"Touch me."

Even though she'd refused to look at him while he'd touched her, Laura found that she couldn't remove her eyes from his heady gaze now. She moved instantly, all too eager to comply when she was the one in charge of his pleasure. His handsome face convulsed slightly when she wrapped her soapy hand around the wet, thick shaft. She wondered if her own expression matched his at the moment as his facial muscles tightened with sublime excitement.

She gripped his cock tightly, but her fingers couldn't encircle the circumference completely. Her hand felt small and feminine on his steely length as she moved it up and down, her motions a frictionless glide due to the lather of the soap and warm water. A painful ache twanged her clit when she ventured downward to wash his testicles. Even though his large, heavy balls epitomized male power and potency, they felt strangely delicate in her gently massaging hand.

She watched his face closely, fascinated by the subtle tension she saw grow in his features as she moved her hand back up the thick root of his cock. When she tightened her fist and focused her up and down movements on the lower portion of the sensitive head and the few inches below, he groaned thickly. Laura increased the pressure and pace, twisting her wrist for extra pressure on her upward motion, loving the flame that leapt into his eyes every time she did it. She was suddenly wild with a need to see his rigid features tighten even further into a rictus of mindless pleasure, to witness him coming thickly in her hand.

Her fury of desire was interrupted suddenly, however, when he put his hands on her hips.

"Turn around."

She noticed that he tilted the showerhead so that the warm spray went to the side of both of them. He pushed her forward until her hands went out to brace herself on the wall. She moaned when she felt him caress her ass cheeks.

"Your bottom is still pink," he said thickly from behind her. "Are you sore?"

Laura bit her lip to prevent crying out in longing, to stop herself from begging him to put his beautiful cock in her seeping pussy. "N-not much," she muttered. In truth, her ass was still warm and tingling from her paddling earlier, but what was that compared to the dull ache in her womb and the sharp, nearly unbearable burn of her clit?

She glanced behind her, both anxious and eager to see what he was doing. Her eyes widened when she saw that he'd lathered up his hands again with a thick foam and now was reaching for the erection that jutted from his body. He slid his hand along the considerable length of his cock, spreading the lather. She groaned in anticipation when he came toward her.

But instead of arrowing that delicious cock into her hungry pussy, he slid the length of his thick column into the crack of her ass cheeks.

"Shane—" she cried out in confusion.

"Hush," he muttered as he put his hands on her buttocks and pulled them back while he pressed his cock deeper into the crevice. Then he switched the pressure, pressing her cheeks tightly together against his cock. Laura's knees nearly buckled at the erotic sensation of his thick, throbbing penis sandwiched between her ass cheeks.

"Your ass is gorgeous," he mumbled behind her, almost as though he was talking to himself. Laura moaned in combined pleasure and agony when he began to shift his hips, causing his lathered cock to piston up and down in the crack of her ass. She could perfectly feel the thick, defined head as it burrowed up and down the crevice, sliding along that sensitive patch of skin on her lower back. "It'll feel so good to come between these pink, paddled cheeks."

"No," Laura moaned. Her pussy needed to be filled with him so badly at that moment that it felt like an open wound. "Fuck me, Shane. *Please*."

"You'll see to my pleasure right now," he grated out behind her even as he flexed his hips at a faster tempo. His big hands molded her ass cheeks more tightly against his thrusting cock. "I was about to make you come, you know. Maybe the next time I tell you to open your eyes you'll do it."

Laura glanced over her shoulder at him. When she saw the way he watched his ruddy cock fixedly as it poked in and out of the crevice of her ass she cried out in frustration and dropped her hand to her clit. She rubbed wildly at the burning piece of flesh but just as she was about to get the pressure she required, Shane grabbed her hand and placed it back against the wall.

"What did I say?" he growled. He swatted her bottom once when she didn't reply. Laura yelped, not so much because the spanking hurt as she was taken by surprise by the wet popping sound of his palm against her ass.

"That . . . that I would see to your pleasure right now."

"That's right. And all you have to do is *hold still*."

Laura sobbed softly in mixed misery and stark arousal as he continued to slide his cock between her bottom cheeks. It felt as if he was masturbating, but using her flesh to do it instead of his hand. The realization humiliated and excited her at once, because part of her *wanted* Shane to use her for his pleasure.

She braced herself against the wall, tears spilling down her cheeks, while he pumped into the tight crevice with more force, his pistoning cock making lewd, sloshing noises as the thick cap plunged down into wet, lathered flesh, rubbing her intimately.

"You feel that against your little asshole? Do you like that, baby?"

God, yes, she liked it.

"Answer me," he grated out.

"Yes," she moaned.

She closed her eyes in anguish when he grunted a moment later and she felt his cock throb against her skin, then the erotic feeling of his warm come jetting onto her lower back and pooling in the crack of her ass. He growled like a well-satisfied animal as he continued to thrust while he came, his semen running down the crack thickly and anointing her sensitive asshole.

A sound of profound frustration and longing vibrated in her throat.

Shane straightened behind her, saying nothing as he moved the showerhead and rinsed his abundant emissions off her skin. She was glad he didn't make her turn around to face him when he drew her up so that she was no longer leaning against the wall. She stood there, staring sightlessly at the control knob for the shower while Shane flicked open the top of a bottle of conditioner and massaged some into her hair.

The taut, bitter silence continued while he quickly and efficiently washed his own hair, lathered up his underarms thoroughly and then rinsed them both. He shut off the shower and opened the glass doors. Steam billowed out into the rest of the bathroom. But Laura didn't even move she was so stiff defending against the pain of fury and thwarted desire.

"Get out," Shane said, the gentleness of his voice belying the terseness of the order.

Laura felt as though she experienced the world through a thick layer of insulation as he briskly dried her off. She glanced down in hazy disorientation when she felt Shane grasp her hand. The sight of him fastening the leather cuff around her wrist caused the bubble around her to pop.

A shout of white-hot rage exploded out of her chest.

CHAPTER **ELEVEN**

Even though he'd been half-expecting it, Laura still caught him by surprise. She howled in anger, her teeth clenched in a grimace of hatred as she lunged at him, raking his neck with her nails. She clobbered him once on the side of his head with a closed fist. The blow landed on his ear, the resulting blast of pain making his eyes water.

"Goddamn it," he muttered as he grabbed her forearms and pushed them behind her body. His eyes widened in disbelief when she kept coming at him, lowering her wet head and charging him like a bull. Before she could do any more damage he spun her around in his arms and lifted her. She kicked at the air when he briefly let go with one hand to open the bathroom door, almost successfully dislodging her flailing body from his arms.

"*Stop it,*" he bellowed, worried that she'd hurt herself in the midst of her wild turmoil. She responded with a hissed curse and renewed attempts to break free.

He'd wondered if she would fight him and suspected she might. In fact, he'd more than half-expected it. He knew what he'd just done in the shower had been hard on her. His gut instinct had warned him that the vulnerability she felt from her paddling hadn't abated.

His plan to take her captive for three days and make her submit to him sexually had been well thought out, and not just because he'd discovered that Laura possessed a proclivity to be dominated. He needed to break through her thick defenses somehow. Whatever she was keeping from him, whatever secrets she harbored needed to be brought to the surface . . . and it was going to take some drastic measures on his part to do it.

Something had happened to the exquisite young woman he'd fallen in love with fourteen years ago—something toxic to her spirit. Shane was determined to lance that poison from her once and for all.

He'd recalled that while her temperament was typically easygoing and calm, she could be stubborn—and, yes, even formidable—when she infrequently became angry. But he'd never seen her so furious as to become physical. He must really be pushing her buttons to get such a reaction from a trained submissive.

Shane hardly felt triumphant, however, when Laura planted a foot on the frame of the door and pushed with all of her might when he tried to carry her to the bedroom. He nearly lost his balance, growled in frustration, and swung her around, backing out of the door this time.

She screamed when he tossed her onto the bed. He kept his focus despite her struggling, managing to secure her left hand almost immediately to the restraint on the bed. She made him pay for the convenience, however, by scratching the back of his neck and grabbing his hair at the nape, wrenching tight with her fingers.

Shane grimaced in pain and cursed, his own temper inevitably pricked. He pried her fingers free from his hair and used his weight to keep her still while he restrained the other wrist.

"*Hate* you . . . How can you do this to me . . . ? Fucking bastard."

She continued to rage as he stood, using the protective

iron footboard of the bed to protect himself while he grabbed the ankles of her kicking, thrashing legs.

A moment later he came around the side of the bed, forcing himself to ignore her litany of curses and threats of what she planned to do to him when she got the chance. He checked to make sure that she was positioned securely and comfortably, righting the pillow that had come dislodged during her struggles so that her head rested in the middle of it.

"I'm gonna make sure the FBI fries your ass! I'm not going to rest until you're rotting in jail," she bawled. Shane met her blazing green eyes. Strands of her long, wet hair stuck in the tears on her cheeks. She panted raggedly, her bare breasts heaving.

He gently lifted her head and scooped her wet hair away from her face and neck before he set her back on the pillow.

"I had no idea you had such a bad temper," he said wryly.

"You don't know the first thing about me."

"Yes, I do," Shane said as he straightened. "That's what's got you so scared."

He swept the blanket over her naked body and grabbed one of his duffel bags, closing the door softly after him as he left the bedroom.

He listened at the doorway on and off for the next hour and a half, knowing he needed to leave her alone until her blaze of volatility cooled but still concerned about her well-being. The first time he'd pressed his ear to the door he'd reached for the knob hastily only to pull his hand back at the last second before he made contact. He'd turned around and headed out the front door.

He'd stood out on the small porch wearing nothing but his jeans as snow fell on his bare skin, the sound of Laura's wretched sobs replaying over and over again in his head, ripping at his heart.

"Ruthless asshole," he muttered bitterly.

When he realized that his hands were growing numb from cold he reentered the cabin and built a fire in the living room fireplace, trying to distract himself. He wanted nothing more than to go into that bedroom and pull Laura into his arms, soothe her with his touch and words and make slow, sweet love to her.

But she refused to give him an inch.

He knew she still cared for him. Saw it in her beautiful eyes, felt it in her sweet touch. When she'd looked at him earlier and told him she remembered, he'd read the truth in her gaze.

And he'd seen her desperation.

She was scared. Something . . . someone was scaring her. The thought infuriated him. Why couldn't she trust him enough to tell him the truth? He was a SAC at the FBI, for Christ's sake. If she was afraid of someone hurting her who better than him to help?

He called Mavis Bertram, telling her about the arrest of Telly Ardos and requesting a background report on Laura's attacker, filling her in on everything he already knew about him. He learned from Mavis that Vince Lazar was still refusing to talk in regard to knowledge of who pulled the strings for the theft ring at the CPD.

"He's a conceited son of a bitch," Mavis complained sourly. "Never tells you he doesn't know anything, like the other cops we busted. He makes it clear he knows who was in charge, all right. Says things like, 'Why would I tell you? What've you ever done for me, sweetheart?'"

Shane couldn't help but smile at Mavis's perfect impression of a six-foot-two-inch, brawny Italian-American with a South Side Chicago accent.

"He looks down his nose at you like you're the scum fungus lives off of. So I told him we might be able to get him free towel service for life at the Metropolitan Correctional Facility."

Shane gave a small smile. "I'm guessing he didn't like that."

"He's holding out for something, Dom, but I can't figure out what, and Lazar won't say. If I had to guess, he's got some goods—something beyond naming names. Or maybe he's just bluffing."

"What else does Lazar say?" Shane asked thoughtfully.

"Not much. Just the usual bilge. He told me once he knew my type. 'You do a favor for 'em and the next thing you know they're paying you back by drilling you in the ass.'"

"He's pissed off about something. He wants payback but he wants to make sure when he talks he gets the exact result he's aiming for," Shane said quietly.

"Probably PO'd that both Castaneda and Moody have left him to rot in lockup. I get the impression he'd love to get some revenge—"

"But still he won't talk for some reason." Shane knew from firsthand experience that a guy like Vince Lazar—a guy who looked like he came out of the womb cracking his knuckles threateningly—could have motivations that were highly incommensurate with his tough-guy image.

"Don't sweat it, Mavis. Maybe his nuts just don't quite fit in your cracker. Let Mac and Lorenzo have a go at him," Shane said before he hung up, his mind churning over what he'd learned from Mavis.

The next time he listened in at the bedroom door everything was silent. He peeked into the room and knew from Laura's utter stillness she was sleeping. He drew closer, wanting to assure himself she was comfortable and safe. Her right cheek was turned into the pillow but her left one was still damp with tears.

He picked up a corner of the sheet and gently dried the wetness, careful not to wake her. She rustled in her sleep, turning her head toward him, but her deep, even breathing resumed almost immediately. She seemed exhausted. Doubt swamped through him like a brackish torrential stream, an upsurge of emotion laced heavily with guilt.

He knew he was pushing her to the limit of what she could endure. If he pushed too far, she'd never forgive him. Shane wasn't going to lie and say that he didn't enjoy dominating her. Laura was the most stunning, sensual woman he'd ever encountered. Making her eyes shine with pure desire was an addictive experience.

All of that didn't change the fact that Shane's ultimate goal wasn't to step into Huey Mays's shoes as Laura's "master." He'd love to tie her up and spank her gorgeous ass anytime the mood struck him, but just as often he wanted to make slow, sweet love to her . . . to worship her with his fingertips and tongue, to see her lithesome arms in the air, beckoning him to her breast, her singular eyes glowing with pure, unleashed desire.

He took one last look at her face, now serene in sleep before he turned away with grim resolve. Maybe it was just a fool's dream, but if there was a chance of ever actually seeing it manifested in reality, he had to keep going. That vision had goaded and prodded at Shane for the last thirteen and a half years of his life.

He had to know Laura's secrets. He *needed* to keep her safe. Once he knew the truth—whether it be ugly or beautiful—then maybe he could finally find some peace within himself.

Laura was held captive while she slept, unable to escape a phantasm of pain and confusion. The dream was strange and nonsensical, but in the way of dreams, she never considered the irrationality of the sequence of events. Her reactions were purely emotional.

She dreamt that her mother, father, Shane, and Uncle Derrick met like a secret cadre to determine the appropriate guardian for her little brother, Peter. Laura came upon them sitting in a dark, oppressive room—a room that uncomfortably reminded her of the back room at Derrick's restaurant, Sunny Days. All four of them looked at her with condemnation when she flew through the door.

"No! I'll watch over Peter. He doesn't need anyone besides me," she exclaimed.

"It's rude to listen in at doors, Laura," Jean Vasquez said in an eerily cold voice that was nothing like her mother's usual tone. The expression of contempt on her beautiful mother's face left Laura feeling panicked. Her mother was always kind and loving. What had she done to deserve that look of distaste?

"You're nothing but a child, Laura. Peter needs a strong, protective adult," her father said sternly.

"Shane, we feel you'd be the best guardian but—"

"No!" Laura said, cutting off her mother. She examined Shane's impassive face doubtfully. "Shane has a very important job. He'll make that his priority, not Peter."

"Don't be ridiculous, Laura. Who else will protect him? *You?*" her uncle Derrick asked disdainfully.

She rushed farther into the room and knelt next to her father, eager to put an end to the unbearable anxiety that caused a choking sensation at the base of her throat at the thought of them taking Peter away from her. "Shane isn't family. I'll look after Peter. Let me do it! Dad?" she pleaded, desperate to have her father look at her. But Richard Vasquez merely stared straight ahead. He seemed so aloof . . . so far away from her. She couldn't reach him.

"Daddy?" she cried.

Her father turned toward his brother, ignoring her. "Shane is my choice, but it's true that he has a very demanding job. Maybe you could watch over Peter, Derrick?"

"No," Laura shouted.

Richard Vasquez's head swung around. His eyes looked inky black, like two holes that opened to vast, empty space. Laura whimpered in fear and tried to stand up to move away from him but her feet wouldn't work.

"We'll give Shane the responsibility, then."

"Noooo," Laura cried wretchedly, cowering in stark fear at the vacuum where her father's eyes should have been but still trying to beg . . . to plead. "I can do it. Let me take him. Let me. Let—"

"Laura. *Laura.*"

She glanced across the table at Shane in rising panic when he called out to her. He'd stood. His impassivity had melted away only to be replaced by a look of compassion and stark concern. He reached for her. Laura wavered, uncertain whether she should go into his arms.

"Laura, *wake up.*"

Her eyes flew open. She stared at the stark angles and planes of Shane Dominic's face. She blinked and glanced around her dazedly while the reality of the situation trickled into her awareness. Her heart drummed madly in her chest. What an awful, bizarre dream.

She tried to wipe away the sweat that had gathered at the back of her neck but her hand wouldn't lower. She squeaked in alarm when she saw the cuff on her wrist.

"You were dreaming," Shane soothed. He opened his hand on the side of her neck. He must have noticed how damp she'd become because he reached to a lower shelf on her bedside table for some tissues. Laura jerked her head away from him when he tried to dry her perspiration.

"I don't . . . I don't want you to do it," she mumbled uncertainly, the shadowy fingers of the nightmare still holding her in their grip.

Shane glanced at her with asperity. "You really don't have much of a choice, Laura."

She panted shallowly as her body's panic response slowed. Shane tossed aside the damp tissues and regarded her with concern.

"Are you all right?"

"Yes."

"You were talking in your sleep. You mentioned Peter."

Laura turned her cheek into the pillow.

"Do you still think about him a lot?" Shane asked quietly.

Laura merely nodded, not trusting her voice. She really didn't think she could take much more of this. It felt as if every defense she'd ever utilized in her life had been stolen from her. Emotion threatened to rip out of her chest, to erupt out of her throat at any given moment. It terrified her. She wanted to cover her face with her hands, but even that simple barrier had been taken from her.

A soft cry of surprise left her throat when she felt Shane's hands on her wrist, then on her ankles, freeing her of all the restraints but the one on her right hand. She curled into a fetal position. Knowing that he'd sensed her vulnerability only made her feel more transparent. Although her eyes were closed she was hyper-aware of Shane returning to the bed and sitting down next to her. A silence fell between them, full and gravid.

"He would have been thirty years old this September," Laura said eventually.

"I remember how much he loved the Chicago Bears."

Laura laughed softly. "He was out of his mind with excitement when your dad got tickets and took you, Joey, and him to that game that one year—"

"It was a good game," Shane said. Laura closed her eyes and sighed when he began to rub her back, his hands sure and soothing. "We watched the Bears beat San Francisco in the play-offs. Walter Peyton had a hundred and forty-eight yards rushing. I remember it snowed," Shane added, his tone a little wistful. "Joey and I were around fourteen. How old was Peter, do you think?"

"Eight," Laura whispered. She shifted and glanced over her shoulder at him. She swallowed when she saw the light scratches on his cheek and the more serious ones on his neck.

"Did you . . . did you put some disinfectant on them?"

"Yeah," Shane muttered as he watched her steadily.

Laura wondered if he waited for her to apologize for attacking him like she had. Would he punish her for it later? Somehow she didn't think so. Shane wanted something from her, but it wasn't the worshipful, rigid obedience that Huey's fragile self-esteem demanded from his women.

"Do you know—I'd bet that was one of Peter's best memories, that football game. Sort of sad, isn't it?" she murmured.

Shane's massaging hand paused. "What do you mean?"

"That his life was so short that going to a football game might have been one of his most prized memories."

He shrugged slightly before he resumed rubbing her back. "I don't know. It might be up there at the top for me, as well. Joey'd probably say the same. It was a fantastic game."

Laura just shook her head and laughed softly. Shane caught her eye and smiled. *Men*—so typical. She was so disarmed by his crooked grin that what he said next took her off guard.

"You weren't responsible for Peter's death, baby."

Laura stiffened.

"I never said I was."

"You don't have to. I remember how much you worried about him. I know how much family means to you. It doesn't take a psychologist to figure out that you shouldered a lot of the emotional burden for his accidental death."

"You're way off base, Shane," Laura said coldly as she turned away.

"Maybe, but I don't think so." Laura felt him rise from the bed. "I made lunch for us. Do you want to eat?"

"What did you fix?" she asked sullenly.

"Chicken noodle soup and turkey and Swiss cheese sandwiches."

"Will you take off these stupid cuffs?"

"No. You'll keep wearing the cuffs for now. I'm going to be restraining you again while I make love to you in a little while."

Laura spun around onto her back at his calm proclamation. "Oh you are, are you?"

"Yes. Would you rather I didn't tell you?"

Laura hesitated. She supposed it was better to know what he planned but she didn't relish the idea of waiting . . . anticipating the moment when he tied her down and touched and tortured her helpless flesh until she screamed for release.

"If you would just give into it and let go . . . if you'd just give me control, I'd give you pleasure."

Laura bit her lower lip, tempted beyond belief by his low, husky voice. Luckily Shane didn't appear to be expecting her to reply at the moment. He brought her another pair of the sweatpants that he'd bought for her and one of his T-shirts, laying them on the bed before he unfastened her last restraint.

"Get dressed and come eat something," he said before he left the room.

CHAPTER **TWELVE**

Laura went out into the kitchen several minutes later after dressing, using the bathroom, washing her tear-ravaged face, and rewetting and combing her hair. She wished she had some blush or lipstick to put on, but Shane had hidden her purse somewhere.

His simple lunch of canned soup and a sandwich tasted just as good as the oatmeal had this morning. Laura couldn't imagine why she was so ravenous. Maybe it was just the novelty of having someone prepare something for her. No one had made her a meal since she was twelve years old—when her mother had died. The fact that she was secretly enjoying Shane's nurturance made her feel guilty.

"I'll make our dinner tonight," she said as she took her bowl, plate, and glass into the kitchen. Shane already stood at the sink, rinsing out his bowl. Her eyes ran over him covetously, enjoying the opportunity to look at him uncensored while his back was turned. He wore a pair of well-worn jeans and a crimson-colored, casual long-sleeved shirt. She'd noticed earlier how the vibrant color enhanced his dusky skin color and brilliant blue eyes. His jeans certainly did their fair share in showing off his tight butt and long, strong thighs as well.

Laura jerked her eyes away from the tantalizing sight of Shane's denim-encased ass when he looked over his shoulder.

"We'll see," he said as he took her dishes.

His mellow tone irked her. "What . . . I can't even make us a meal if I want to? I thought you wanted to make me into a sex slave or something? You'd think you'd want me kowtowing to you, feeding you grapes, and making me kiss your feet."

He chuckled and took her glass out of her hands. "I never said I wanted you as a slave."

"Well, what is it that you *do* want, precisely?" Laura asked. She was irritated, but curious as well.

"I told you. I want you to submit to me. I want you to trust me enough to give me control," he stated calmly before he shooed her aside so that he could open the dishwasher. Laura went still when he looked up and speared her with his blue eyes. "You could have all along, you know."

"How can I trust you when you've kidnapped me and tied me to a bed?"

Shane considered her closely for a moment before he reached for the pan on the stove. "I brought you here and tied you to the bed because whatever you're keeping from me is putting you in danger, Laura."

"Maybe I'm not telling you because I don't appreciate you kidnapping me and tying me to a bed," she replied petulantly.

"So you admit you're not being honest."

"I never admitted any such thing!"

"Okay. So tell me what the deal was with Telly Ardos yesterday."

For a second she was confused. Had it *really* only been yesterday that she'd been to Carlotta's party and Shane had saved her from that unexpected attack by Telly Ardos? She shook her head to clear it. "I told you I don't know what he was talking about."

"You have *no* idea who it was Ardos said he wanted to take you to, or why he wanted to do it?" he asked, his tone thick with doubt.

"I don't *know*."

"Was he trying to bring you to Randall Moody, Laura?"

She inhaled sharply as though she'd just been struck. Despite the fact that she now knew Shane suspected the venerated chief of the CPD, panic fluttered in her gut every time she heard him mention his name.

"Shane, stay away from Randall Moody."

He turned slowly, his gaze on her intensifying, reminding Laura of radar closing in on a target. "What's that supposed to mean?"

Laura bit her lip uncertainly. Shit. She'd given him the scent. Shane would be ruthless about keeping it in his nose until he reached his quarry.

"Ardos and Huey have been friends for years. I didn't associate with him. He used to come into Sunny Days sometimes with Huey before we were married. He and—"

Laura froze, realizing too late she'd lured Shane off the trail only to circle around and lead him right back to the scent. She'd just recalled that Huey and Telly Ardos were usually accompanied by Vince Lazar—that big, hulking man whose intense, hot stares used to leave Laura in little doubt of what he thought of her.

And Vince Lazar was one of the cops that Shane'd had arrested along with Huey several weeks back—

"What, Laura? What were you going to say?"

She was so caught up in her anxious, chaotic thoughts that Shane's deep, quiet voice took her by surprise. She looked up in slight disorientation when she felt his hand cup her cheek gently. He stood close enough for her to catch his male scent, for her to see the almost wild look of concern in his blue eyes.

"I can see that you're scared, baby. Why don't you just tell me the truth? Why can't you just let it go? I'll keep you safe." His thumb caught the single tear that rolled down her face, tenderly wiping it away. "I promise I will. But you have to be honest with me. Give me the reins, Laura. You've held on for too long."

"Oh, *God*."

The two words felt like they were ripped out of her choking throat. Her body convulsed violently. She stepped away from Shane, nearly tripping on her own two feet in her haste, fearful that she'd throw herself into his arms . . . terrified that she'd do precisely what he asked of her.

Much to her surprise, Shane didn't stop her from turning and staggering away from him.

She was sitting at the corner of the couch when he entered the living room a few minutes later, her legs curled up in front of her. Her panic had faded somewhat as the heat from the fire warmed her skin and she stared at the heavy, gently falling snow outside the window. She'd been experiencing such a torrent of emotion for the past twenty hours that her energy seemed to be draining out of her like water trickling through a sieve.

She glanced over at Shane warily when he sat down on the couch beside her and picked up the remote control, clicking the television on.

"Are you all right?" he asked quietly after he'd found a station and returned the controller to the table. He spread his big hand on her thigh and rubbed her reassuringly.

Laura hesitated. The last thing she needed at this moment was for him to persist in questioning her. She couldn't give him the answers he wanted. She couldn't give him the answers that part of herself longed to give him . . . so what was the point of the whole exercise?

"Come here," Shane said. When he saw what must have been doubt on her face, he added, "I'm not going to pester you with more questions right now. I just want to touch you."

Laura swallowed heavily. Would it be so terrible for her to give into it . . . just a little? She still hadn't made a resolute decision one way or another but she found she didn't have the will to resist when he reached for her.

She leaned into his embrace, pressing her cheek to his chest. His arms closed around her. She shut her eyes and listened to the crackle of the fire and the dialogue from the movie Shane had switched to—*Raiders of the Lost Ark.*

Laura had always liked the Harrison Ford adventure but her eyelids felt too heavy to open in order to watch.

It could have been like this between her and Shane—should have been—curling up together on the couch to watch a movie during a weekend snowstorm, cherishing each other, their only concern a hectic day of work next week or the prospect of shoveling a foot of snow off the driveway.

It'd be a dream tomorrow. It was a reality today.

She breathed deeply of Shane's clean, spicy scent and felt herself melting against his flesh. It felt so good. Not to think. Not to act.

Just to give over to sensation . . . to let go.

Her lips opened but the protest never fell past her lips when Shane gently reached for her wrists and fastened the connector hooks. The ache between her thighs that had never fully dissipated since yesterday in the car flared to a dull throb.

"Is it so terrible a thing . . . to give me the control, Laura? You know I'll take care of you," he murmured in a low, sexy rumble that she found blatantly irresistible.

She couldn't stop it. Shane forced her to it. Slowly, almost imperceptibly her muscles relaxed and she ceased her resistance—at least for a little while.

He furrowed his fingers into her hair, stroking the length slowly. When he pressed down on her shoulder she dropped her head to his lap, her cheek resting against a hard thigh. How long she lay there with her hands restrained in front of her, her legs curled up while Shane played with her hair and gently stroked her neck and scalp with calloused fingertips she couldn't say. She didn't sleep—she was too caught up in the sensuality of the moment, feeling wildly anticipatory and paradoxically relaxed at once.

Her body became warm, heavy . . . pliable. Wetness accumulated between her thighs as her consciousness followed Shane's touch with a tight focus. He massaged the shoulder that wasn't pressed into the couch along with her upper back, kneading her muscles until she became so relaxed she wondered if she could move voluntarily.

Laura was only minimally aware of the rollicking score that always accompanied a chase scene in an Indiana Jones movie. It seemed that almost her entire self existed on the surface of her skin just below Shane's massaging fingertips and rubbing palm.

The fire crackled and snow silently blanketed the cabin while her sensual entrancement deepened. Shane's hand slid down the length of her arm, molding her shape to his palm. Heat emanated from his lap into her cheek. When he lightly ran his fingertips over the leather cuff, arousal stabbed sharply between her thighs, the strength of her reaction surprising her.

But then he continued to caress and stroke the fire-warmed skin of her arms, lulling her. She sighed deeply, much of her remaining resistance seeping out of her with her exhaling breath while another type of tension crept just as surely into her muscles.

It didn't surprise her when Shane matter-of-factly slipped his hand beneath the waistband of her sweatpants. This is what he'd been asking her to do, wasn't it—for her to melt at his touch? Why wouldn't he reward her for giving in to him? Was it so terrible to want to submit . . . to give herself wholly to him at least for a short while? Laura wondered desperately as he worked a finger between her cream-coated labia and she moaned softly.

Having Shane Dominic touch her was stuff straight from her most well-guarded, sweetest fantasies, after all.

He put a hand beneath her and turned her until she rested on her back, never stopping the delicious movements of his fingers on her clit. His other hand slid beneath her T-shirt and cradled a breast in his palm. His thumb and forefingers plucked at a nipple, making it peak—stiff and achy.

He circled, slid, and pressed on her clit until her body grew tense and rigid. She could feel how wet she was by the ease with which he glided over her burning flesh.

Her eyes remained sealed tight beneath her clenched eyelids. She was thankful that Shane didn't demand that she open them, that he gave her that small measure of protection as she lay in his embrace in the fire-warmed room and he strummed her most sensitive flesh until she panted shallowly in stark need.

His finger stirred in her cleft more forcefully, causing a wet rhythmic clicking sound to mix with Laura's breathy, uneven pants. The tempo of his pinching fingers on her nipple increased, causing fire to sear downward, amplifying the ache at her pussy.

She burned unbearably; she strained to ignite.

"Shane," she whispered in agony as her hips pressed desperately against the delicious friction he wrought.

"You can let go now, Laura. I've got you."

She exploded at his words, orgasm blasting through her. She left reality for a moment as pure sensation electrified every nerve in her body.

Laura sagged into the couch a moment later, stunned by the violence of her climax. Shane's deep voice sounded distant as he soothed her in her turned-inside-out state.

"You were meant to come for me. God, you're filling my hand with honey . . ."

Laura cried out when Shane worked a thick finger into her drenched slit. All the while he continued to rub her clit, coaxing wave after wave of delicious shivers from her flesh. She whimpered in pleasure, turning her face into his lap, drawn to his heat. Her nose and lips found his erection, mindlessly nuzzling and kissing the hard column of flesh that pressed against his jeans while Shane continued to nurse her through the most powerful orgasm she'd ever experienced.

He moaned, low and rough. His hand spread at the back of her head, pressing her closer. Laura welcomed the pressure, moving her lips anxiously over the steely length of his cock. When she scraped her teeth over the stiff ridge he growled and tightened his fist in the hair at her nape.

"Go to the bedroom," he ordered thickly.

Shane released her wrists and watched Laura while she stood. Her dark hair hung in a mussed cloud around her pink-stained cheeks. She glanced at him uncertainly before she began to walk to the bedroom, but Shane saw desire shining in her exotic green eyes as well.

He thought of her quaking in his arms as an obviously powerful climax shuddered through her flesh. He closed his eyes and took one deep, fortifying breath in an attempt at restraint.

When he entered the bedroom a few seconds later, she stood at the foot of the bed. She cast an anxious glance in his direction, but otherwise said nothing.

"Get out of your clothes," he directed quietly.

His cock swelled even thicker in his straining jeans when she complied, revealing every inch of her flawless, honey-colored skin to his hungry gaze.

"Go lie down," he said when his T-shirt joined her sweat-pants on the carpet.

His eyelids narrowed on the tantalizing image of the back of her naked body as she followed his instructions and went to the bed. For Shane, Laura defined female perfection. Her waist and rib cage were narrow but her hips and ass curved deliciously. Every time he saw her bare ass it sent an electric jolt of excitement through him, made him crave the sensation of her taut, rounded flesh in his palms.

The line of her backbone was delicate and graceful. He wanted to encircle her rib cage in his hands, to feel her heartbeat thudding with excitement into his palms while he cherished the exquisite knowledge of her existence.

"No. Leave it on," Shane said when he realized that she was unfastening her necklace. She glanced over her shoulder in mild surprise at his tense tone, but didn't argue.

He shrugged out of his shirt and dropped it in an uphol-stered chair as he passed, his eyes never leaving the sublime image of Laura lying on the bed naked, doing so of her own free will versus being forced there at his hands.

Her belly was a pale, smooth harbor. Her breasts rose and fell with her shallow, uneven breathing. The firm globes seemed to glow in the dim light of the bedroom. Shane saw no defined tan line to suggest that she'd sunbathed anytime in the past year or two, but years of covering them had left them paler than the rest of her honey-hued skin.

He saw the hesitation clearly on her face as he approached her. Nevertheless, when he nodded once she placed her wrists on the pillow next to her head. The submissive gesture made his cock lurch furiously. He wanted nothing more in that moment than to finish restraining her to the bed and fuck her until they both died together in a blaze of pure bliss.

And maybe he'd do just that but he had something else in mind first. He needed to take Laura deeper . . . to gently, firmly goad her until she ceded just a bit more of her control over to him.

CHAPTER **THIRTEEN**

Laura watched Shane with a mixture of anticipation and anxiety as he restrained her wrists to the bed. What did he plan to do this time when he had her at his mercy? Would he make her hunger unbearably once again, only to leave her ravenous and empty? Despite the explosive, intense orgasm he'd just given her, Laura was surprised to realize how excited she became as Shane bound her.

She couldn't keep her eyes off him. He made a compelling sight as he went about his erotic task, dusky skin on his taut abdomen, shoulders, and arms gleaming over flexing muscles as he moved with methodical, sure movements.

His cock strained beneath his jeans, the shape and contours of the thick shaft clearly visible next to his right thigh. Laura experienced the familiar sharp stab of arousal at her clit.

After he'd finished restraining her he came to the side of the bed and leaned down over her. Her breath stuck in her throat when he kissed her eyebrow and then her closed eyelid in a whisper-soft caress. The brief touch of his lips seemed to make her heart swell inside her rib cage. How could such a small kiss make her feel so indescribably cherished?

"You showed me trust out there on the couch, baby," Shane whispered gruffly next to her lips. "I want you to know that I realize how hard that was for you. Now I'm going to ask you to give me more trust. You can put yourself in my hands . . . and not with just your body. With the truth. Do you understand, Laura?"

This time she managed to stifle the sound of longing in her throat, but barely.

She watched him anxiously when he moved away from her across the room. Her eyes widened a few seconds later when he stood from reaching into one of the duffel bags he'd brought and she saw a black leather flogger in his hand.

Huey favored a flogger, she recalled as she tried to quash her rising panic.

Spankings and paddlings were one thing, but this was different . . . even if it *was* Shane at the helm.

She shook her head rapidly on the pillow. "No. I don't want to, Shane." She made eye contact with him as he came toward her, making sure that he understood she was serious. He paused midstride, obviously catching the stark anxiety in her tone.

"Why?" he asked as he came closer.

Laura shivered, her gaze fixed on the black leather straps that dangled next to his thigh. The flogger Shane held had straps that were shorter than the one Huey preferred, but still—

"I—I don't like to be whipped."

He didn't move for a few seconds. Her gaze leapt up to his face. He studied her with a fierce stare.

"I'd hardly call what I planned to do to you *whipping*. Surely you know about sensation play. I'd *never* cause you physical harm, Laura. The worst you'll ever experience at my hands is a sting and a burn, but it's meant to enhance sensation . . . to increase your pleasure. I'll never give you more than I think you can take, even with your punishments."

Her heart beat madly at her throat as she swallowed, trying to wet her suddenly dry throat. "I believe you. But I'm not . . . r-ready for that now."

He remained motionless.

"Did someone hurt you with a flogger?"

"No . . . I mean . . . yes . . ." Laura fumbled, knowing she somehow needed to explain her reaction or Shane would only become more suspicious than he was. He'd thought she'd sounded more than willing in those surveillance tapes, after all.

The vision of Huey rearing up over her, the flogger up over his head, a vicious leer of mixed lust and fury twisting his features flashed into her mind's eye. It'd only happened once. Moody had requested a demonstration of Huey's power over her soon after they were married . . . when Laura had stepped out of line.

The experience with the flogger had been unpleasant, but that wasn't what made her cringe. The flogger memory had blended with the far more powerfully frightening recollection of Huey leaning over her with a belt, lips stretched back over his teeth, the silver buckle gleaming. Laura clenched her eyelids together tightly as though she could squeeze out the frightening image until it held no power over her.

"Laura?" Shane asked tensely.

"Once," she said in a rush of honesty. "It happened once. And I made sure it never happened again." She looked up into his taut features. "You don't need to feel sorry for me. It's just . . . something else . . . I don't want the flogger."

Shane's brows knitted together furiously. For a split second Laura had the impression he was going to come down over her and shake her until the truth popped out of her unwilling throat.

But instead he abruptly turned and walked across the room toward the partially opened duffel bag on the floor.

He neared the bed this time carrying a crop with a thin, whippy handle and a two-and-a-half-inch round popper at the end of it. From his other hand streamed a nine-inch-long swatch of what appeared to be soft fibers—silk or maybe even horsehair? He set the skein of silky fibers on the bedside table and Laura saw they were attached to a black handle.

Shane must have read the dubious expression on her face because he gave a small smile.

"Are . . . are you going to punish me for attacking you earlier?" she asked in a quivery voice when her gaze once again lingered on the crop. For some reason she couldn't remove her gaze from the vision of his large, masculine hand holding the black leather handle. Despite her anxiety the image struck her as potently erotic.

"No," he said quietly. He reached down and stroked the skin on her belly and ribs, making Laura shiver with pleasure. Her nipples pulled into hard little darts as she watched his fingertips skim over her torso. "I can use the crop when you've been bad, but I can use it just as effectively to bring you pleasure." A low growl vibrated in his throat when he touched the underside of her breast. "Your skin is so amazingly soft."

"Thank you."

He glanced up and smiled when he heard her breathy whisper. "Have you ever been pleasured with a crop before?" he asked as he lazily stroked the side of her breast. Her nipple stood at full alert status, distended and red, begging for him to touch it, but instead his calloused fingertips moved to the sensitive skin at the side of her torso.

"Yes," Laura lied. Huey had tried to use his extensive cache of toys on her a few times just after they were married, but it was a joke to think she'd ever taken pleasure from it. Huey had quickly learned that Laura refused to play the worshipful, panting whore that he required to become aroused and find sexual fulfillment.

Besides, anything Huey did in regard to the sex act could hardly be called *pleasurable.*

In the end, her contemptuous gaze and scathing remarks about his lack of skill when it came to truly giving a woman what she needed made him avoid her altogether in the bedroom, preferring to pay to have prostitutes loudly shout their praises to his sexual prowess in front of his friends.

And Laura had been all too relieved to have him leave

her alone. They'd had to hide the fact that Laura wasn't the cowering wife that Randall Moody desired her to be. Thankfully Huey would have done anything to protect the legend of his supposed godlike, masterful lovemaking.

Her eyes widened when Shane raised the crop. She had her doubts about Shane giving her any pleasure using the type of toys that Huey used to collect. She *did* know that she wanted to give Shane pleasure.

And that she trusted him.

Wasn't that what he'd ultimately been asking her for?

She trailed the round little popper's path as he lowered it to the beaded nipple that had begged for his touch a moment ago. The surface of the slapper felt smooth and cool as he lightly rubbed the straining flesh. Laura moaned as her clit twanged with a stab of sympathy for what her nipple endured.

"Your breasts are so sensitive," Shane murmured as he moved the circular popper over them, lightly massaging her. It wasn't made of hard plastic, like Laura would have thought, but instead a more flexible material, like a pillow of turgid silicone. The fact that they both watched his actions with tight focus aroused Laura all the more. "Do they get sore easily?"

Laura blinked, breaking the hypnotic trance she'd been under as she watched the crop sliding across her other breast and rubbing against the aching nipple. "Yes," she muttered. "They get really sensitive during my period. Painfully so, sometimes. The nipples chafe against my bra. I have to be really careful about what I wear."

Shane made a growling noise and paused to unfasten the first few buttons of his jeans. Laura could understand why— things were getting pretty tight behind that button fly.

"Why would the idea of my breasts getting sore during my period turn you on?" she wondered, perplexed and amused.

"Because. It's an indicator of how nerve-packed your nipples are. It's exciting. Have you ever had an orgasm from nipple stimulation alone?" he asked gruffly as he ran the crop's circular tip over her ribs and belly. Laura squirmed in rising arousal.

"No."

Shane sucked in his breath slowly as he skimmed the slapper over her hip and then her thigh. Laura groaned when he ran it softly along her inner thigh, just an inch away from her spread pussy.

"Well, we'll just have to see if it's possible, won't we?" he asked, although he seemed too involved in his task of sliding the crop along her hip to expect an answer. "I'm going to give you some slaps now, baby—set your nerves on fire . . . make them hot and hungry. Are you ready?"

Laura merely nodded, too overwhelmed by his sexy proposal to form words. Shane raised the crop and snapped it down on the outside of her hip. *Pop. Pop. Pop.* She moaned and shifted restlessly in her restraints. It hadn't hurt really, but the slapper made her skin feel hot and prickly. He moved it after each slap, enlivening every inch of her hips and upper thighs.

She found the sound of it striking briskly against her skin almost unbearably exciting. Liquid heat bubbled out of her pussy, anointing the outer tissues. She wondered if Shane could see the wetness, spread as she was for his gaze. She writhed in arousal at the thought.

"Stay still," Shane directed. He kept the slapper positioned on her inner thigh until she calmed. When he resumed he brought the crop down on her belly, lightly slapping the sensitive skin until it blushed a light pink. He popped her hip with a bit more force and smiled.

"It makes a sweet sound on your firm flesh, doesn't it?" he murmured seductively. Laura opened her mouth but nothing left her lips because Shane had begun to lightly rub the crop on the sensitive skin on her pelvis directly next to her pubic hair.

She cried out in surprise when he suddenly pushed his forefinger into her slit, probing her pussy deeply before he withdrew. He plunged his finger into his mouth and sucked hungrily. When he saw her dazed expression of what must have been stunned lust, he smiled and withdrew his finger.

"Sorry. I couldn't resist that honey pot. You're soaking wet." He moved the crop tip to the sensitive skin on the side of her breast. "Should I make your breasts nice and pink, Laura? Would you like that?"

She moaned uncontrollably. "*Yes*."

His sexy smile widened as he brought down the crop, snapping underneath and the sides of her tender breasts. The pleasure that tore down to her pussy caused Laura to tighten in the restraints. Shane continued despite her struggle of agonized excitement, popping her other breast gently but briskly, carefully avoiding her distended nipples.

Laura's eyelids sprung open when Shane abruptly struck her hip—*whap*. The swat wasn't sufficient to cause significant pain, but it was certainly enough to deepen her arousal exponentially.

"Stop fighting it, honey."

Laura forced herself to relax her muscles, allowing her body to sink back into the bed. She stared at Shane, wide-eyed in anticipation. She bit off a moan when he slowly raised the crop back over her chest. Her panting caused her breasts to heave in rising excitement. The sensitive flesh burned and tingled. She watched the snapper with a sharp focus that matched Shane's.

They groaned in unison when he brought down the popper on her right breast.

"Look how it jiggles," he mumbled under his breath, his eyes glued to her breast.

His free hand went to his crotch, ripping at the remaining buttons on his jeans. He plunged his hand into his boxer briefs and pulled out inch after inch of dusky, thick cock. He pistoned his big hand just below the head for several strokes before he released it. His boxer briefs pressed against the thick column of blood-engorged flesh, but the head was too heavy for the elastic to keep pinned to his taut abdomen. It dropped forward and to the right, revealing several more inches of delicious cock.

"Oh, *God*, Shane," Laura cried out, her desire becoming desperate. Her clit burned unbearably, so needy for friction. Her hips rose up and she pulled once again on her restraints but she couldn't get the pressure she required.

Shane raised the crop a mere two inches over a tight, achy nipple.

"Tell me what you want, baby."

"The nipple . . . use it on the nipple," she whispered raggedly.

"Like this?" He popped the aching crest.

Laura's back arched in excitement, her body becoming a straining flame of sensation, eager to blaze hot and fast.

"More," she groaned in cresting desire when Shane snapped the other painfully erect nipple, making a sweet popping sound. "More. I need more!" she pleaded. She twisted in her restraints when he complied, snapping both stiff, eager nipples several more times. Laura was only vaguely aware of him leaning down over her, so caught up was she in her excitement.

But when he trapped the tip of one breast in his warm, wet mouth and lashed at the aching bud with his raspy tongue, Laura's eyes went wide. When he applied a taut, hungry suction, she shouted and exploded. Shane continued to suckle her nipple as she jerked helplessly in climax. After a few seconds, however, he stood and snapped the crop against her spread cunt.

Her shout escalated to a scream as her orgasm pitched up several notches in amplitude. She shuddered in pleasure for what felt like a glorious eternity as Shane prolonged her climax by gently, rhythmically swatting her swollen labia and clit.

Finally she sagged into the bed gasping, her brain and body overloaded by pleasure.

"Now that was a pretty thing."

She blinked dazedly, turning toward Shane's voice. Her eyes widened when she saw that he'd removed his jeans and underwear while she'd struggled to regain equilibrium.

"You please me beyond measure, Laura," he said huskily as he unfastened one ankle restraint and then the other.

Laura wanted to tell him that he was the one who pleased her beyond anything in her wildest dreams, but her body still clamored after her thunderous climax. She couldn't seem to catch her breath to tell him much of anything. Instead, she just watched him fixedly as he came around the foot of the bed, his taut muscles glistening with a light coat of perspiration, his cock stiff and swollen, a stream of clear pre-come running from the slit and moistening the head.

He must be pleased, Laura thought wryly as desire once again quickened in her womb. The sight of Shane's cock caused the miraculous. Her body pulsed with awakened arousal when she still hadn't yet caught her breath from an explosive climax.

She glanced up at Shane curiously when he began to release her wrists, as well. Was he finally going to let her run her hands all over his beautiful body and taste him at her leisure?

"I want you to turn over. I'm going to restrain your wrists again."

Her face fell in disappointment. "But I want to touch you, Shane."

His expression went rigid.

"I want that, too, baby. But not yet. Now turn over. That's it. Here, let me put some pillows under you."

When he was done arranging her the way he wanted, he lengthened the restraints so that he could reattach her wrist cuffs. She thought she'd felt vulnerable and exposed when he restrained her before, but this was even worse. He'd propped up her hips with the pillows so that her bottom stuck up in the air. Her cheek rested on the mattress. Her nipples just grazed the sheet, creating an arousing, low-grade chafing sensation on the hypersensitized crests. Because Shane had lengthened the restraint straps, her arms rested comfortably on the mattress above her head. She was up on her knees, her thighs opened widely.

Her nerves felt hyperaroused, her flesh tingly and flushed with hot, pumping blood running just below the surface of her skin. Even the cool air of the room seemed to stimulate and tease her wet, spread pussy.

She jumped when she felt the snapper of the crop slide along her bottom, caressing her. She cast a sideways glance up at Shane anxiously. He stood close to the edge of the bed.

His large, engorged penis filled her vision. She licked her lower lip.

"You look gorgeous, baby," he said as he ran the smooth surface of the popper all over her bare bottom and the sensitive patch of skin above the crack of her ass. "Your blush has faded from your paddling. Let's see if we can't turn this plump little ass just as pink as the front of you."

Laura turned her face into the mattress as he began to pop her bottom with the slapper repeatedly. It was nothing like being paddled; the burn was low-level and more precise. It also felt unbearably exciting to know that Shane stared at her while she held such a vulnerable pose, his hot blue eyes taking in every detail of her ass, spread thighs, and exposed, dripping pussy.

Having turned the temperature of her ass up to a slow simmer, the slapper progressed down her thighs, its frequent contact with her flesh filling the air with sharp, staccato whapping noises. Laura moaned when Shane changed his position slightly, working the crop so he could reach the sensitive skin of her inner thigh.

"Spread your legs farther," he ordered.

Laura complied, although embarrassment mixed with her arousal. She'd already been opened wide to him, her pussy fully exposed. But once she'd spread her knees an inch in each direction, she felt the cool air of the room not only touch more of her pussy's delicate tissues, but also the sensitive skin around her asshole.

"That's right," Shane rumbled, and Laura could tell by his low, sensual growl that he'd noticed what had been exposed.

By the time the snapper had reached within an inch of the lips of her labia Laura was calling out Shane's name. It felt unbearably exciting, feeling the crop pop in the dampness that seeped from her pussy. Her womb flexed inward almost painfully, aching to be filled. She arched her back, desperate to get the delicious friction of the sheets on her throbbing nipples.

"Why are you calling my name that way?" Shane asked in a soft, sensual rasp as he moved to the bedside table. He set down the crop. "Doesn't it feel good?"

Laura turned her head and opened one eye, taking in every detail of his appearance. A light sheen of sweat shone on his chest and belly. His tiny, dark brown nipples looked just as erect as her own. Pre-come streamed from the slit of his magnificent erection in a steady flow.

He looked down when he saw where she stared, chuckling when he saw the clear liquid. Laura watched wide-eyed as he caught the streaming fluid and closed his hand into a fist over the head, rubbing the pre-come into his cock, making it glisten . . .

"I asked you a question, baby."

"It feels wonderful," Laura whispered, her gaze never leaving the awesome sight of him stroking his big cock. "I just can't take any more. I need you to fuck me now."

His fist paused mid-shaft. Another drop of clear liquid swelled rapidly at the slit, making Laura moan in anguished longing. She licked her lower lip.

"Let me suck it."

She saw his already rigid muscles grow even tenser. She sensed his inner battle as he fought off a desire to grant her request.

"I don't think so, incredibly tempting though the offer is," he finally murmured, sounding bemused by the temporary break in his restraint. He let go of his cock and picked up the silky skein of hair. Before Laura had time to think, he ran the incredibly soft strands over the side of her torso and breast.

She groaned at the new brand of torture. The tickler felt delicious on her tingling flesh.

"Feel nice?" Shane asked as he ran the horsehairs over her other breast and studied her face. He seemed genuinely fascinated by her reaction.

"God, yes," Laura panted when he slid the silky fibers to the sensitive spot on her lower back just above the crack of her ass. He stayed there, tickling and firing the nerve endings for several seconds, making her asshole clench in excitement. He moved, gliding the wicked little instrument over her hot, burning bottom. When he trailed the silky skein down the crevice of her ass, teasing her asshole and making her vagina constrict unbearably tight with raw need, Laura begged.

"*Please*, Shane. No more. I can't take this another second."

"Tell me what you want then," he coaxed gently even as he continued to torture her by running the tickler up and down the crack of her spread ass cheeks.

"I want your cock," she shouted desperately. "And I want it *now*!"

"Far be it from me to deny such a sweet, docile request," he teased. But Laura heard the hard edge of desire in his tone . . . saw it in the tension of his muscles when he moved to the bedside table to retrieve a condom.

Laura grit her teeth in an anticipation unlike any she'd ever known before when she felt Shane's weight lower the mattress behind her. She waited in breathless excitement for the sensation of the broad head of his penis to press to her soaking wet slit. She cried out sharply in stunned pleasure when instead he spread his large hands over her buttocks and swiped his tongue between her labia, laving her hungry clit.

Every muscle in her body flexed to the breaking point when he suckled. She screamed as orgasm broke, shuddering through her flesh in electrifying waves. She barely was aware of him sliding a finger along her slick perineum, but she jerked in agonized ecstasy when he rubbed his thumb against her asshole and then penetrated her rectum with it.

He plunged his cock into her weeping pussy at the same moment.

"Oh, yeah. Such a sweet pussy . . . and what a hot little ass," she heard Shane grate out as if from a great distance. She was still lost in the throes of a delicious climax. His double penetration of her pussy and ass kicked it back up to the level of the first blasts.

Shane's cock slid into her to the hilt, stretching her hungry vagina and filling her near to bursting.

It took Laura a moment to realize she'd been shouting loud enough to make her hoarse. She'd been drowning in pleasure, overwhelmed . . . utterly overcome. She panted raggedly as her body clambered to recover from the explosive climax while at the same time trying to accustom herself to the welcome invasion of Shane's big cock. He twisted his thumb and pushed into her asshole to the bottom knuckle. Laura groaned as her rectum clenched around him uncontrollably. His cock lurched inside of her pussy in reaction.

"Okay?" he asked, his voice rough with restraint.

"I-I think so."

"You completely let go. I felt it. Do you know how much that means to me?"

Laura realized she was shaking when she felt her nipples scraping subtly against the sheet. Her pussy flexed at the sensation.

Shane growled.

"Answer me."

"Yes. I know. Shane?" she asked shakily.

"What, Laura?"

"I want *you* to completely let go. Right now."

He didn't respond for several full seconds. At first Laura thought he hadn't heard her.

Then he drew his thumb out of her ass and sunk it back in slowly. Laura sensed him watching his actions with his typical focused attention.

"You're admittedly difficult to resist for long." He flexed his hips and groaned, drawing several inches out of her and sliding back in until he was fully seated in her vagina once again. "So I think that's just what I'm going to do—take you for a nice, hard ride."

Yes, Laura thought triumphantly.

CHAPTER **FOURTEEN**

Shane watched his cock draw out of Laura slowly, relishing her whimpers of pleasure when he just as deliberately sank back into her. She fit him like no other woman ever had, taking him so completely and yet at the same time squeezing his cock in a tight, silken embrace.

Laura's pussy had spoiled him for other women long ago, he admitted to himself as he begun to fuck her more rapidly, still keeping his strokes long and thorough.

She cried out when he began to plunge his finger in and out of her ass at the same rate that he fucked her pussy. The heat that penetrated his finger made him escalate his thrusts.

"You like that, baby?"

"God, yes," she replied in a thready whisper. When the slaps of flesh striking flesh became more strident as he fucked her she began to bob her ass more enthusiastically. While Shane thoroughly enjoyed the sight of her plump, crop-pinkened bottom bouncing along as she pumped his dick, he knew from the tingling at the base of his spine she'd drain him before he was ready if she kept it up.

Shane held his hips steady with intense effort and popped her ass with his palm to get her attention. If this didn't mean so much to him he wouldn't have been able to find the restraint not to come in his wildest dreams.

But it *did* mean that much to him.

"Who's in control here, Laura?" He watched her in profile, her cheek pressed to the mattress, the other stained bright pink with arousal, her mouth gaping open as she sucked wildly for air.

So far from being impervious now, wasn't she? Her entire body trembled beneath him. He could feel the tiny, erotic tremors vibrate into his cock and into his thumb as she shivered into him.

God, she was about to explode like a cache of dynamite.

He plunged his thumb in and out of her ass, his lips curving into a grim smile when he felt her trembling increase.

"Laura?" he demanded in a hard voice.

"Y-you. *Shane*."

"That's right," he grated out as he removed his thumb from the hot tunnel of her asshole and grabbed the metal headboard with both hands. "So just let it happen, baby."

Shane only had the opportunity for a brief, bright moment of wonder as he began to fuck Laura long and hard, the brisk knock of the headboard and his own knuckles against the wall synchronizing perfectly with his heartbeat throbbing in his ears and Laura's sharp cries of pleasure.

She wailed in release. He saw her back muscles convulse even as he felt her pussy do the same around his cock, an eye-crossing sensation of liquid heat flooding around him at the same moment.

"Yeah, give it to me, give it," he demanded as he fucked her madly, drunk with a potent mixture of intense emotion and the type of sharp, mandatory pleasure that verged on pain.

He bucked into her sweet, climaxing pussy one last time, pressing deep. He roared as he came, orgasm ripping through his flesh and lungs, singeing him. What felt like forked lightning shot up his spine and through his cock at once, emptying out every drop of semen in his tightly drawn balls, leaving him raw and panting.

Scorched from the inside out.

His hands dropped to the mattress a moment later, his muscles quivering in the aftermath of his explosive orgasm. He blinked the sweat out of his eyes when he heard Laura's plaintive cry. His brows drew together in concern.

Christ, had he hurt her? He'd fucked her like a madman, after all.

"Laura?" he whispered gruffly as he nuzzled her neck. "Are you okay, baby?"

Her soft sob froze his breath in his lungs. The rapid withdrawal of his still-stiff, throbbing cock made them groan in unison.

Shane pushed Laura's hair out of her damp face, frustration hitting him when he realized he couldn't see her fully because of her position. He pressed a fevered kiss to her exposed cheek and forehead.

"Did I hurt you? I'm sorry, I was so excited—"

He felt her shaking her head beneath his lips and raised his head.

"You didn't hurt me, Shane. It felt so good. I just want . . ."

"What?" he asked in rising concern and confusion when her voice faded.

"To touch you."

Shane cursed under his breath as he hastily unhooked her from the restraints. "Come here," he whispered as he came down on his back beside her and lifted her into his arms. His eyes burned at the precious sensation of her weight against him, the top of her head pressed against his neck, her cheek against his pounding heart and her small hand gently stroking the sides of his torso and his ribs, soothing him while his lungs strained for air. He inhaled, her familiar scent made even more intoxicating by her perspiration-damp skin and the musky smell of their combined arousal.

Shane felt exquisitely attuned to her as their bodies strove to return to equilibrium, as if the connection hadn't been broken when his cock left the sweet harbor of her pussy . . . like their flesh had been fused somehow by their intense lovemaking.

She turned her face farther into his neck. Her small kiss penetrated deep to somewhere beyond mere flesh.

His hand came up to cradle her head.

"Okay?" he asked hoarsely. She nodded her head against his chest. Her movement spread wetness against his skin. He put his hand beneath her chin, silently asking her to look up at him. When she did so, something seemed to collapse in his chest.

"All I ever wanted to do was make you happy, Laura. How is it that the only thing I succeed in doing is making you cry?"

She shook her head and gave him one of her small, wistful smiles. "You never did get a woman's tears, Shane."

"What's that supposed to mean?" he asked incredulously.

"You used to panic when you saw me cry during a movie, like you were worried I was sick or something."

He idly raked his fingers through her hair, wondering at how soft it was. "You used to cry at *commercials*, Laura."

"I did not," she reprimanded. He groaned appreciatively when she ran her fingertips over one of his nipples. The light coat of sweat on his skin gave her caress a sweet glide. He was nuts to keep tying up a woman who possessed such a phenomenal touch.

Or he was smart. The feeling of her running her small hand and sensitive fingertips all over his naked skin was arousing him again with a rapidity that shocked him. How had he ever endured her doing it on a regular basis in bed without coming almost immediately every time?

"I hope you're not going to try to convince me that I misinterpreted your tears that time in Union Park," Shane said wryly, referring to the time when he'd chased off three jackasses who'd been harassing an eleven-year-old Laura. She smiled against his neck.

"No, you got it right that time. Kids can be so mean. There were three of them—all of them older than you—but you still stood up for me," she said, a hint of wonder spicing her tone.

"They might have been older and bigger, but they weren't

used to actually having to work for their supper. It was easier for them to just walk away," Shane murmured, thinking about how many times he'd run into the same phenomenon throughout his career. More often than not, bullies were just plain lazy.

"I was lucky you were there. You used to go to the park to read, I remember." She laughed softly, the delightful sound vibrating straight into his chest. "You were the only boy I ever knew who wasn't ashamed to read in front of his friends—read *anywhere*, for that matter. I admired you so much for that. Your teammates on the baseball and football teams—did they used to tease you about it?"

"Nah. They might've in the beginning, but they were good guys."

"Shane."

He blinked at the sound of her saying his name. There had been fondness in her tone, but something else as well, something deeper, richer. Or maybe it'd been wishful thinking on his part—

"You know, I cried when you surprised me by coming home from college early to attend my graduation ceremony," Laura murmured. She lifted her head and examined him. "You looked upset then, too. Just like a man not to recognize happy tears."

He stroked her cheek softly and held up his forefinger significantly. "And is that what these are? Happy tears?"

Her lower lip trembled. Instead of answering his question she rested her head back on his chest.

"Joey told me you really came back to Chicago that weekend because you were dating that girl from Northwestern—Robin Scherer—and she had some kind of sorority dance or something. But I was so happy to see you I didn't even care."

"Jesus. You really do have a good memory. I can't believe you remember that girl's name."

Her slight shrug shifted her breasts against his skin, making him hyperaware of her stiff nipples pressing into his ribs. Laura had the prettiest breasts he'd ever seen—so firm that a bra was a convention not a necessity, softer than silk against his sensitive lips, the most responsive nipples imaginable—

"I remember all your girlfriends' names," she said softly, pulling his focus back to the topic at hand with effort.

He cradled the back of her head, urging her to look up at him, but she remained with her cheek on his chest.

"Joey got it wrong, you know."

"What do you mean?" she asked.

"I might have had something else going on that weekend, but I specifically came back on that Friday night to go to your graduation."

She lifted her head and stared. "You did?"

Her expression of wide-eyed amazement touched him . . . pleased him. He leaned up to kiss her parted lips softly. She tasted so sweet that he lingered before he spoke, molding and shaping her mouth with his own, relishing her tiny whimper of pleasure.

"I may have been too much of an idiot to notice that you'd become a beautiful woman, but I always cared about you, Laura. Surely you knew that."

Her smile struck him as a little sad. "I knew you cared. That didn't stop me from wishing like hell that you'd lust after me like you did Robin Scherer or Nicole Todd or one of the many other members of your harem."

He pushed her onto her back and came down over her, laughter bubbling up from deep in his chest. His mood must have affected Laura because she gifted him with one of her luminous smiles. God, what he'd give to make that sublime smile of hers a regular occurrence instead of a rarity.

"Maybe you didn't approve of my timing, but surely I get some credit for sheer volume. Because once I got around to lusting after you, I did it at superhuman levels." His gaze lowered over her beautiful face and elegant neck, lingering on the green heart-shaped stone that lay between her flushed breasts. His cock throbbed against her thigh insistently as he met her stare. "I still do, you know."

She sighed his name against his lips before their mouths

met in a questing, gentle kiss that quickly became hot and demanding.

A loud knocking at the front door shattered the spell of their mounting desire. Laura started in his hold, her gaze snapping to meet his when he broke their kiss.

He lurched off the bed and stalked rapidly into the bathroom, disposing of the condom before he grabbed his jeans. He retrieved his gun from the small safe his father had had installed in the closet, quickly checking that the safety was in place before he shoved it into the waistband at the back of his jeans.

"Don't . . . you . . . move," he told Laura when he turned around, enunciating each word succinctly. He waited for a response. She sat up in the bed, clutching the sheet to her breasts.

"Yes. All right," she agreed when whoever was at the front door started pounding again. He gave Laura one more fierce, warning glance before he shoved his head into the collar of his shirt and left the bedroom, closing the door behind him.

He moved cautiously through the living room, standing with his back to the wall as he lifted the edge of the curtain in order to glance outside. The snow continued to fall thickly. A pickup truck with a snowplow attached to the front sat on the road in front of the cabin. A quick surveillance from the opposite end of the window decided him on opening the front door, albeit warily.

The thin, angular man who stood on the front porch nodded once politely through the outer glass door before Shane opened it a few inches.

"My apologies for bothering you. I saw the car in the driveway and thought I should stop and make sure you had a shovel before I plowed the road in front of your car. Snow's already thick. You can see what a pileup the plow is making."

Shane nodded although he never removed his gaze from the man. "There's a shovel in the back."

The man's gaunt face brightened beneath his Milwaukee Brewers baseball cap. "You must be Alex Dominic's son?

He's mentioned you and I can see the resemblance. I usually sell your dad firewood when he's here. Do the basic maintenance on the hot tub, too."

"Oh . . . right. I've heard Dad speak of you as well. Tim, isn't it?"

"Tim Brandt. I've got a farm east of Eagle River."

Tim ripped off his worn leather glove and extended his hand. Shane shook it and introduced himself. He'd already noticed the cords of snow-covered firewood in the back of the man's truck and vaguely recalled his dad mentioning the man's name when Shane had visited the cabin in the past. Tim Brandt appeared to be just who he said he was. Still, Shane's stance remained wary.

"Thanks for the concern, but it'll be all right. I might have to shovel us out but it's more important that the road is clear."

"You sure?" Tim asked uncertainly. "I'll try to make another pass tomorrow morning, but we're supposed to get another foot or so before it stops. Hope you weren't planning on leaving anytime today."

"We're not going anywhere for a while."

"Did you come up with your dad?" Tim asked as he put his glove back on his hand.

Shane felt his irritation rise but he tried to contain it. Tim was just being neighborly, not nosy. "Nah, Dad's still in Chicago. I'm here with a friend."

Tim nodded. "Don't suppose you need any more firewood?"

Shane forced his lips into a grin, thoughts of a warm, soft Laura lying in bed making it difficult for him to concentrate on chitchat. " 'Fraid not. You've kept Dad pretty well supplied it looks like. We're keeping nice and toasty."

Tim started to reply but stopped abruptly when he glanced to the left of Shane.

"Oh. This must be your friend."

Shane froze as Tim removed his Brewers hat, revealing a thatch of straw-colored hair. "Hello, ma'am."

Shane sucked air into his lungs and turned slowly toward Laura.

It was no wonder Tim looked so flustered, Shane thought grudgingly. She looked gorgeous wearing sweatpants and one of his old sweatshirts, a sexy, tousled mane of dark hair spilling around her back and shoulders. Her cheeks still glowed lividly pink from their lovemaking.

She looked exactly like what she was—a woman who had just crawled out of bed after being well loved.

Her green eyes flickered up to meet his glower ever so briefly before she looked at Tim. She opened her lush lips and Shane was sure she was about to scream at the top of her lungs that Shane had kidnapped her . . . to beg Tim Brandt to get her the hell away from him.

"Hello," she said instead, her voice low and husky. "It's really coming down, isn't it?"

Tim's sallow cheeks turned every bit as pink as Laura's. He stepped back and shoved his hat back on his head. "Supposed to get a foot and a half to two feet by the time it's through. Well, I'll let you folks get back to whatever you were do—" Tim stopped abruptly, reddening even deeper. "Have a good evening, then," he finished awkwardly before he turned.

Laura said "Good evening," at the same time that Shane offered his thanks. He shut the door and double-locked it as his fury slowly mounted.

"What the hell did you think you were doing?" he asked once he'd slowly turned to face her.

Her lips fell open in surprise. "I wasn't doing anything. I just said hello."

He took one step closer to her, forcing her to tilt her head back to look up at him. "I told you not to move. You agreed."

"Shane, I could have begged that man to take me with him, but I didn't. Did you think about *that*?"

"Yeah. I thought about it. And so did you. I could tell when you looked at me before you talked to him," he said grimly before he walked away. He took out some of his irritation on the logs in the fire as he stirred them with a poker with unnecessary force, causing sparks to fly everywhere like a swarm of tiny glowing bugs.

"So what if I did think about it? Would it be surprising? You did bring me here against my will, Shane."

"That's not what I'm talking about," he said over his shoulder with a pointed glare. "What if whoever had been at the door hadn't been Neighbor Tim? I told you to stay where you were for your safety, not because I was trying to bully you."

"You *are* bullying me, Shane! How else would you describe what you've done by bringing me here? Handcuffing me, tying me to a bed—"

"Making you scream," he finished through clenched teeth as he turned and faced her. She paled beneath her pink cheeks. "Don't be pissed off at me for giving you what you want."

"What *I* want? You think that's what I *want*?" she asked shrilly. "You're crazy, Shane Dominic!"

Shane closed his eyes briefly, trying to reign in his temper. The poker clattered loudly when he tossed it back in the metal holder. "Are you really going to stand there and try to tell me you didn't like that?" He gave a meaningful nod toward the bedroom.

"I-I didn't say that."

"*You think that's what I want*?" Shane repeated her words as he came toward her. He wondered just how pissed off he looked when she took one step back before she steeled herself and held her ground. He grasped her shoulders. "When I ask you to do something for your safety and you agree, I expect you to keep your promise."

"You don't really expect that someone would come out to this cabin and try to . . . *attack* us or something, do you?"

"I don't know what to expect. That's the problem. Maybe you never noticed, baby, but Huey wasn't a nice guy. Neither were his buddies. One of them broke into your house and just yesterday pulled a gun on you. Do you remember that?" She didn't answer, but Shane hadn't really expected her to, either, given his sarcastic tone. "And since you refuse to tell me the truth about any of that, it's not too surprising that I don't know what to expect, is it? Now. Tell me that if I ask you to do something like, 'stay in the bedroom and don't move' ever again, you'll do it and not just say you will. I'll turn you over my knee the next time you pull something like that!"

"Shane—"

"*Promise* me."

"Oh, all right," she replied exasperatedly. "I promise. There. Are you happy?"

"No. Not really."

"Why not?"

"What did you mean when you implied that being dominated wasn't what you want? Did Huey force you to have sex that way?"

Her face stiffened. "No, Shane. It wasn't like that."

He nodded his head slowly, his eyes taking in every nuance of her features. He felt her shoulder muscles tense beneath his fingertips.

"Then tell me how it was," he said, his tone gentle but firm. He easily sensed her anxiety but he wasn't going to let her get away until she answered him. She lowered her gaze to his collar, denying him access to her expressive eyes.

"Laura?"

"Why do you want to hurt me this way? Why do you want to hurt yourself?" she asked in a rush of frustration.

"The answer to how it was between you and Huey will hurt me. Is that what you're saying?" he prodded.

"I don't want to talk about this."

Shane's heart began to thud in his ears when she pulled out of his hold and turned toward the bedroom. His grip loosened and slid down her arms, but he caught her hand at the last minute, stilling her.

"I care too much about you to just let this go."

His gentle pull on her arm had caused her dark, lustrous hair to fall forward, obscuring her face. He saw her shoulders rise as she took a slow, deep breath.

"It's not going to work, Shane."

Bitter fury rose like bile in his throat when he heard the glacial quality of her tone. The distant, untouchable woman was back, making him doubt his sanity in recalling the Laura he'd just been holding in his arms minutes ago, the warm, generous, sexy creature with the sweet touch and sublime smile.

"What's not going to work?"

"What you're trying to do by bringing me here. You're not going to succeed in seducing me to your cause . . . convince me to tell you something that will assist in the FBI's investigation of the CPD."

"Is that what you really think this is all about? The Bureau's investigation?"

Despite the fact that she wore a baggy sweatshirt and her hair was a wild tangle she looked as regal and impervious as a queen when she turned and met his stare with chin held high.

"That's what you *told* me it was about in front of my house yesterday. You brought me to this cabin, tied me to that bed . . . and used our past together to try to break down my defenses and get me to tell you some detail that will bolster your floundering investigation. But like I said—it's not going to work."

"Is that right?" Shane growled as he narrowed the distance between them.

"Yes."

"So nothing I do or say for the next few days is going to penetrate that heart of ice, is that right, Laura?"

He saw her throat convulse as she swallowed. "If that's how you want to word it, fine. No. Nothing is going to work."

"That sounds like a challenge."

"Call it whatever you want. You've got a losing hand, Shane."

"That's a pretty cocky statement coming from someone who hasn't even figured out the game yet."

He took a small measure of satisfaction in seeing her eyes widen. He smiled grimly as he tightened his hold on her hand and pulled her back to the bedroom with him. "I'll tell you what I do have—two more nights. The game isn't over yet."

CHAPTER **FIFTEEN**

Laura took refuge in silence as Shane restrained her to the bed once again by her wrists. She didn't struggle but she didn't help his cause, either, letting her arms go limp and heavy and giving him her best bored, contemptuous stare. Within the first week of her association with Huey Mays, she'd practiced and honed that look until it was sheer perfection.

Unfortunately, while that glare literally wilted Huey it just bounced right off the surface of Shane's confident, bold personality.

She fumed at the evidence, even though a small voice in her head told her *she* was the one who deserved the disdain. Apparently she needed to gird herself for battle against a part of herself—not Shane.

How dare he accuse *her* of having a heart of ice? Her heart was clearly hot and gullible, not to mention perfidious. Shane was the one with a frozen stone lying behind that beautiful chest of his—the same chest that she'd snuggled against so warmly not ten minutes ago while his low laughter vibrated into her cheek. Now he was back to tying her up to this bed again, his expression fixed and furious.

How could she have been so stupid? How could she have just allowed that man, Tim, to walk away without asking him to take her with him? What if Moody had noticed that she'd left town so soon after Huey's death? How many people had she endangered with a childhood infatuation that stubbornly refused to die?

Shane had lulled her with his soft caresses, erotic love play and sultry kisses. She'd been bewitched by his whispered temptations to let go . . . to give him control. He'd forced her to forget herself until she'd been luxuriating in his strong arms, remembering the old times together . . . falling deeper and deeper into his sensual trap.

She didn't even bother to watch him once he'd restrained her wrists and walked to the other side of the room. She just stared up at the ceiling, willing herself not to think . . . not to feel. A whimper of protest left her throat, however, when Shane matter-of-factly jerked down her sweatpants a moment later, pulled them off, and tossed them next to her on the bed.

He held something in his right hand but she couldn't make out what it was as he grabbed one of her ankles.

"What are you doing?" she asked when he laced both of her feet through what looked like thin black straps. The next thing she knew he pulled them up her legs, almost as if he were putting a pair of underwear on her. He didn't respond but merely went about his task in a brisk, businesslike manner. It wasn't until he'd pulled up the straps near her waist that she felt one of them slide snugly into her butt crack like a thong.

Laura's breath stuck in her throat when he pressed something against her labia with his fingers and fastened the black straps against her hips. Her eyes went wide when she saw what was pressed just above her clit—a one-by-two-inch little golden bee.

"Wha—"

"It's a vibrator."

Her gaze flew up to meet Shane's stare. He must have noticed her perplexed expression. He didn't say anything else though, just reached once again for her sweatpants and laced her ankles through them. When he'd secured them around her waist once again he unhooked her wrist cuffs from the restraints.

"Let's go."

"Where?" she asked, injecting as much contempt into her tone as possible to cover her confusion.

"I'll show you. Just stand up."

Laura realized when she stood that a thin cord was attached both to the golden bee on her pussy and a black box that Shane carried in his hand. She knew that Shane would be triumphant to know it—and that pissed her off as much as anything—but the sight of that thin black cord linking her and Shane together and the slight weight of the little bee on her clit created a slow, hot simmer of anticipation in her pussy.

And he hasn't even turned the damn vibrator on yet, Laura thought resentfully as she followed him into the living room.

Shane pulled out one of the backless bar stools tucked beneath the high shelf of the kitchen counter. He nodded once, indicating he wanted her to sit down on it.

The living, dining, and kitchen area of the cabin all coexisted in the open space of the great room. The place where she sat overlooked the kitchen but also was close enough to the living room fire for Laura to appreciate the warmth.

"What are you going to do?" Laura asked uneasily.

"Make dinner." She blinked in surprise at his unexpected answer. He placed the black box on the lower shelf of the kitchen counter and added a log to the fire before going to the kitchen. "Would you like a glass of wine?"

"No. I don't drink."

He made a face as he reached for the bottle of wine on the counter and flung open a drawer. "You used to have a glass of wine once in a while."

"Times change," she replied coldly, refusing to watch him as he uncorked the bottle. Even though she and Huey essentially led separate existences, being around his alcoholic excesses over the years had tended to put a damper on her enjoyment of even a good glass of wine. She refused to comment when Shane set down a wineglass filled with the crimson liquid in front of her. He said nothing about her disgusted look but merely began to go about the business of preparing their meal.

Despite her attempts to remain aloof she couldn't help but be curious when she saw all the ingredients that Shane had put on the counter: a pork tenderloin wrapped in white butcher's paper, a box of Buttery brand premium crackers, salt, pepper, eggs, cooking oil, an enormous skillet, a cutting board, and a meat tenderizer.

"You're not . . ."

"What?" Shane asked casually when her voice faded off.

"You're not going to make your mother's breaded pork tenderloins, are you?"

"You remember that, too?"

Her gaze skated up to his face. His blue eyes seemed to glow with amusement as he regarded her.

"Obviously I remember."

His mouth twitched slightly and Laura suddenly knew for a fact that he was still irritated with her. "I almost forgot."

"The recipe?" Laura wondered.

"No. This."

She jumped slightly when he flipped the switch on the black box and the bee began to vibrate against her sensitive labia and clit. She made a choking sound at the powerful sensation. Having never used a vibrator she hadn't expected the precision of the little instrument. Heat flooded her cheeks.

"Giving you a nice little buzz, baby?"

She dragged her gaze up to see Shane studying her reaction with a heavy-lidded stare.

"Too much, I think. You've got a sensitive little clit, haven't you?" he murmured as he turned a small dial on the box. Laura breathed in raggedly when the golden bee began to buzz less strenuously. Against her will she pressed her pelvis forward in the stool, hungry for more of the delicious sensation. When she saw Shane's eyelids narrow she forced her face into a neutral expression. She picked up the glass of wine in front of her and took a healthy swallow without ever telling herself to do so.

Shane smiled without a trace of irritation this time and resumed his meal preparation.

Laura sat there in mounting misery for the next several minutes, trying to think of anything but the bee buzzing industriously on her clit and silently scolding her hips for moving against her will, making tiny little hungry undulations against the vibrator.

"You okay, baby?" Shane asked. He'd just ground the entire box of Buttery crackers into fine crumbs in a bowl using the head of the meat tenderizer and an astonishing display of flexing muscle and male exuberance. He picked up the knife and began cutting the loin. "Do you want another glass of wine?"

Laura stared down at her empty glass and blinked in surprise. "Shane, have you ever actually made your mother's tenderloins before?"

"No. But I told her I was making them this weekend and she gave me the recipe. Why? Am I doing something wrong?"

Laura pressed her mouth together in annoyance. She felt dampness on her upper lip and knew that it came from that damn little bee, not the warmth of the fire on her back.

"You're cutting the meat too thin."

"More like that?" he asked, adjusting the knife on the tenderloin. He glanced up at her for confirmation and Laura nodded. "I forgot my mom taught you how to make them."

"You did not," Laura muttered. She'd tried to sound disgusted but the combined effects of the buzzing bee, the glass of wine, and the novelty of watching Shane cook a meal for them made her voice sound bemused instead of annoyed. "Joey went on about them so much after having them at your house that Elizabeth asked me if I'd like to learn how to make them so Joey could have them at home."

"I don't get why she didn't offer to show *Joey* how to do it," Shane mumbled.

"You know I cooked for everyone after my mom died."

"Yeah. I do."

Laura glanced up at his tone only to find him watching her steadily. He resumed cutting the meat almost immediately. "Derrick shouldn't have allowed that."

"For me to cook?" Laura asked in amazement.

"Not just cook. Cook for everyone. Take care of everyone. You were just a little girl yourself. Who was taking care of you?"

Laura shrugged. "My mother taught me to do all of those things. My father and Derrick grew up in Cuba. It's a different culture. Women do things like that for men."

Shane's raised eyebrows told her he wasn't buying her argument.

"I *wanted* to cook for them. I wanted to look out for Joey . . . and especially for Peter. Mom's and Dad's death hit him hardest of all."

"That doesn't mean that you didn't need someone looking out for you as well."

Laura was too preoccupied to contradict him. He'd pushed the sleeves of his shirt up while he worked. Laura licked the sweat off her upper lip, mesmerized by the sight of his strong hands and flexing, hair-sprinkled forearms as he cut the tenderloin. Against her will she graphically recalled what he'd looked like holding that crop earlier.

Her pussy squeezed tight at the same time that her clit pinched in stark arousal.

He was so tall that the counter hit him at the tops of his thigh. Her gaze latched on to the fullness below his fly, pictured his big, firm testicles nestling there. She knew he wasn't wearing any underwear. She could see the shaft of his penis pressing against the denim. He wasn't rock hard, but he appeared to be in a state of semi-arousal.

And all the while she ate up Shane with her gaze the bee continued to buzz mercilessly on her needy, aching, craving clit. She had to hand it to him. Shane knew precisely what to do to melt her stiff, icy resolve to a puddle of warm jelly. Laura nearly groaned out loud at the literal interpretation of her thoughts when she felt the warm, abundant juices wetting her thighs. She pressed her hips forward but the friction just wasn't enough . . .

"Shane," she gasped.

"Yeah?" He stopped cutting, obviously put off by her strange tone.

"I have . . . I have to go to the bathroom."

"Okay."

He turned to the sink and washed his hands with soap and water.

"You don't need to escort me to the bathroom," Laura told him with a scowl a few seconds later. He carried the black box of torture in one hand and held her elbow with the other hand, guiding her like he thought she was a sick invalid or something. In truth, Laura did feel feverish and lightheaded . . . and so aroused she thought she would scream from frustration.

When they reached the bathroom Shane unplugged the black cord from the box. Laura's body shuddered in mixed relief and agony when the golden bee stopped buzzing. Her clit continued to ache and torment, however.

God she needed to come—

"We'll leave the door open, I think."

"Wha . . . No, Shane!" she exclaimed wildly.

He shook his head like he couldn't believe she thought he was so stupid. "Do you think I don't know you're about to detonate, baby? I'm the one who's going to make you come, not a damn vibrator and not your own hand. Now . . . are you going to go or not?"

She stared at him mutinously.

"Just keep your hands in clear sight while you go and I won't stare. Come on, hurry up. I'm starting to get hungry."

It took Laura twice as long to go as usual, even though Shane was true to his word and kept his eyes averted. Laura suspected more of the problem in releasing her bladder on this occasion was her acute arousal.

Besides, it was nice to get a break from the tortuous little bee.

After she'd washed and stepped out of the bathroom Shane stopped her with a hand on her shoulder. He matter-of-factly shoved her sweatpants down her hips.

Shit, Laura thought as she stared up at the ceiling and he readjusted the vibrator to its original position. She had hoped he wouldn't notice that she'd shifted the golden bee into a location where it wouldn't be quite so damned precise. He switched on the vicious little vibrator again.

"You're gonna get some more buzz for that, baby. I think I'm going to have to restrain your hands, as well. You can't be trusted, can you?" Shane taunted softly, his blue eyes gleaming in the dim bedroom.

Laura pursed her lips together, refusing to give him the satisfaction of speaking to him or even looking at him. Yeah. He was right. She couldn't be trusted.

Or at least her pussy couldn't be.

She maintained her silence, utilizing a supreme effort of will when they returned to the kitchen. She bit her tongue on several occasions as she sat on the stool and watched Shane cook. He made a lot of mistakes, but he usually self-corrected his own errors with relative rapidity. It irritated her to know that he could make the meal successfully without her help.

Shane paused after hammering out the tenderloins with the meat tenderizer and took a drink of his wine while he studied her. The higher setting on the vibrator was taking its toll on her although the setting was still insufficient to make her come. She panted shallowly. Sweat glazed her hot cheeks and neck.

"Is there something you want to ask me, Laura?" he asked in a mellow tone. He took another leisurely sip of his wine. "Anything you need?"

Laura shook her head rapidly.

"A little more wine, maybe?"

Laura hesitated and then nodded—anything to distract her from her concentrated hatred of the golden bee. She couldn't think of anything but its wicked buzz, couldn't stop obsessing about how fantastic it would feel to gush in climax onto Shane's cock and escape its evil tortures.

Shane filled her wineglass and came around the counter with it. He'd restrained her hands in front of her and then set them on the counter where he could see them upon their return to the kitchen. Laura could have drank on her own if he'd put the wineglass in her hand, but she kept her vow not to speak to him when he placed his hand on the back of her head and lifted the wine to her mouth.

A strange sort of taut anticipation overcame her as he slowly tilted the glass and she waited for the red liquid to slide onto her tongue. She suddenly felt parched, like she hadn't drunk anything all day. She craned forward and swallowed thirstily.

"Whoa." Shane chuckled, obviously surprised by her greediness. "It's wine, not water, baby."

Laura licked her lips and tried to catch her breath while he set the glass on the counter. Her senses had pitched to a hyperalert level. Shane's scent filled her nose. The delicious smell of him seemed to make her already hot blood boil in her veins. Shane's hand at the back of her head transferred to her neck.

"You're so hot," he murmured. He moved decisively, unhooking her wrist cuffs and whipping his sweatshirt over her head. He tossed it on the back of the couch. Laura made a loud, gasping sound when he ran a big hand along the sides of her breasts and ribs. "Jesus. You're burning up."

He hooked her wrists together again before he went to the fire, using the poker to shove one of the logs back in order to bank the flames. He returned to her side when he was done, once again torturing her further by sliding his hands along her sweat-slick neck and shoulders. She shivered despite her fever of arousal. She tried to steel herself when he leaned down and nuzzled her hair aside so that he could kiss her ear. Her defenses were useless against Shane, however. She cried out sharply in agonized pleasure even at his simple, chaste kiss.

"If you want to come, all you have to do is ask me." His low, gruff whisper near her ear caused a fine tremor to rise in her flesh. She reached deep into her reserves and turned her chin away from him.

"Okay, I guess you don't want to come yet. Fine by me. Let's just lower these sweatpants a little before you really do sweat to death in them," he murmured silkily but it was the steel lacing through his tone that made Laura tense warily. Her mouth gaped open in surprise when he pushed her stool toward the counter several inches, grabbed her hips and slid her bottom slightly off the back of the seat. Laura leaned forward, her restrained forearms on the bar holding the majority of her upper body weight.

Shane shoved her sweatpants down. Not all the way, Laura realized with growing humiliation. Just below the lower curve of her buttocks, leaving her ass bare and hanging slightly off the edge of the stool. The bee buzzed away energetically at her clit, as though the little bugger actually sensed that the new angle of her body provided it with new levels of torture.

"Hmmm," Shane murmured as if considering something while he lightly caressed a buttock and then skimmed his fingertips on the sensitive pad of flesh above her butt crack. She felt the fly of his jeans lightly brush her ass, the sensation making her whimper.

She opened her mouth at that moment, a plea on her tongue. But he walked away suddenly, leaving her staring after him in angry confusion. When he returned from the bedroom he carried several things in his hands, but Laura couldn't see what they were when he set them down in an upholstered chair behind her, his body blocking her vision.

But then he turned and she saw that he held the ankle cuffs from the bed in his hand.

Her heart thundered loudly in her ears when he knelt and buckled the cuffs to her ankles. He pulled her feet to the side and then the back of the stool, forcing her knees to open, using a short restraining strap to affix the cuffs to the rear metal leg.

A small, thoroughly male grin of satisfaction curved his handsome mouth when he stood. Laura's head fell forward onto her forearms, an agonized moan vibrating her throat. She was almost completely naked. Shane'd positioned her so that her knees were spread and her body weight pressed down and forward on the stool, giving her much-desired extra pressure on her pussy. Her bare bottom hung lewdly off the back of the stool.

She *hated* him, Laura thought wildly as she panted. But God she was about to explode with what must be the best fucking orgasm in the history of mankind.

CHAPTER **SIXTEEN**

Shane reached hastily and flipped the switch on the vibrator controller. Laura's body shuddered slightly and for a moment he thought he was too late.

Then she let out a growl of pure frustration and lifted her head off her forearms. Her cheeks and lips glowed bright red. Her baleful glare couldn't undo the fact that her green eyes were glazed with distilled lust. Her lush lips parted slightly as she panted, the sight causing shockingly graphic fantasies to leap into his brain concerning what he'd like to do to that beautiful mouth. The green heart glimmering between her heaving breasts made his gaze lower.

Her nipples were stiff, the center nubbins distended as though she'd just been suckled nice and hard.

Jesus fucking Christ, Shane thought in mild disorientation. His cock lurched furiously in his jeans like a snake at the strike. She was a fantasy come true, although Shane had to admit he didn't think his imagination could have ever conjured up anything as beautiful and blatantly sexual as Laura at that moment.

Of course the ultimate fantasy would be for her to beg

him to make her come right now. He'd be only too happy to comply. He waited in taut anticipation when her lush, reddened lips opened even farther.

But the only thing that left them was her soughing breath.

He averted his eyes from the jaw-dropping vision and turned the vibrator to a lower setting before he flipped it back on. It was hard to focus on breading the tenderloins and dropping them in the hot oil when he was so aware of the sound of Laura's uneven pants and occasional stifled whimper or when he kept envisioning how outrageously tempting she'd looked with her firm, plump bottom hanging over the edge of the stool, her suspended breasts trembling as her ribs expanded and contracted wildly for air.

"You're the most stubborn woman I know, Laura," he said softly a moment later as he removed several golden brown tenderloins, placing them in a pan to keep warm in the oven. Despite his irritation, his heart went out to her when he risked looking up. Her face had the slightly pinched look of someone in pain. The spatula clattered loudly when he tossed it onto the stove. He leaned forward on the counter, pinning her with his stare.

"If you tell me how it is you want me to make you come right now, I'll do it. Just say the words. Anything you want. If you don't, I'm going to make you come anyway. But I'm hornier than I've ever been in my life, baby. You might not like the way I go about it."

Her hands fisted on the counter, causing her knuckles to go white. Her shining, incredibly sexy eyes lowered over his body hungrily . . . But damn her. She still refused to speak. If Shane knew the mystery of how to slay the poisonous silence that always came between them he'd be one hell of an ecstatic man.

Fuck it.

He turned down the burner on the skillet and briskly tossed the control box for the vibrator on the upper shelf. He saw the trepidation in her expression when he came around the counter but her eyes gleamed with something else—anticipation.

"You know what you're going to get, don't you?" he asked in a gravely voice.

She twisted on the stool to watch him when he moved behind her. He didn't miss the anxious widening of her eyes when he picked up the bottle of lubricant from the chair. Okay, so she *hadn't* known.

She was still gonna get it anyway.

A few seconds later his lubricated forefinger penetrated the tiny pink rosette of her rectum. She gasped, her head falling forward, her long hair brushing her forearms. Her body naturally resisted his invasion, but he pushed forward determinedly.

"God your ass is on fire," he mumbled almost incoherently as he finger-fucked her with increasing ease and rapidity. She groaned loudly and Shane considered shutting off the vibrator completely.

He didn't want her exploding until his cock was buried deep in her asshole.

He'd fantasized about doing it for years, hadn't yet built up the nerve to suggest it to her when they were young. She'd been so innocent and sweet, always a little shocked when he suggested different methods of lovemaking but always more than interested and willing to try out his suggestions.

But things were different now. Neither one of them was innocent anymore. And he was determined to take her in this intimate way even if she did stubbornly refuse to acknowledge her desire for him. The truth was in her beautiful eyes. It would be in the shudders of her orgasm as they vibrated from her flesh into his thrusting cock, as well.

That's what Shane felt desperate to be buried in at that moment—the truth.

He squeezed a taut ass cheek, prying it back so that he could watch as a second finger penetrated her tiny hole. He stroked her slowly and then more forcefully when she cried out in pleasure and began bobbing her ass in a counter rhythm to his thrusts. He was deeply gratified when a shout erupted out of her throat, ending her silence.

"Oh, God. Oh, God," she wailed.

"What, baby?"

"Please," she sobbed, her forehead falling down to her forearms. "*Please* make me come."

"You can come when you take my cock in your ass."

Her bobbing bottom stilled momentarily before she slowly started pushing back against his fucking finger again.

"Do you want to come, baby?"

"Yes, yes!" she screamed.

Shane hesitated. He'd brought along a dildo that he'd planned to use to prepare her to take his cock in the ass. But he couldn't keep Laura on the edge like this for much longer. It was cruel, as desperate as she clearly was. Besides, he thought he might come in his jeans if he kept staring at himself finger-fucking her delicious ass while she was restrained to this stool.

She bit off a moan when he removed his fingers from her smooth, tight channel and reached for the lubricant, unfastening his fly hastily at the same time. He hissed when he liberally applied the silky lubricant to his cock, rubbing it over every straining inch.

He felt Laura's body go rigid when he spread her ass cheeks with one hand and pressed the tip of his cock to her asshole.

"Shhh, baby. It'll be okay. Just try to relax," he soothed. She cried out in pain, however, when he pushed and the wide girth of the head of his cock slipped into her ass.

Shane cursed. Heat penetrated the tip of his cock. The tight ring of her rectum squeezed him like an elastic band. He used all his willpower to keep his hips steady—to not flex forward into her heat, but also to stay fixed in place as her muscular ass tried to reject him from her body.

The bones of Laura's ribs showed as she panted wildly, her breasts quivering like ripe, lush fruit waiting to be plucked. She didn't appear to be in pain anymore, but Shane reached and turned up the dial on the vibrator just in case.

"Put more of your weight on the counter, babe," Shane rasped, finding it difficult to find his voice he was so aroused.

He waited while Laura adjusted herself slightly, lowering her forehead to rest on her arms and arching her back slightly, presenting her ass even more conspicuously than it already had been.

Shane closed his eyes and took a deep inhalation, praying for restraint.

He spread his thighs slightly and found the perfect angle for penetration. He opened his hands on her hips, his thumbs lifting up and separating Laura's ass cheeks.

His hips flexed forward slowly, only to stop almost immediately when she clenched around him and her muscles went rigid in his hands.

"You know what to do, baby. Press your ass against my cock. Don't fight me, that'll make it harder on you."

This time when he thrust she resisted the pressure and he pushed the stalk of his cock into her hot, tight tunnel several inches. He grimaced in unbearable excitement while Laura moaned shakily. Sweat dampened the front of his shirt. He absentmindedly swiped the moisture on his abdomen with the fabric before he whipped the shirt over his head and tossed it aside, his hands back on Laura's smooth hips in a second.

"That's good, baby. Now a little more," he urged as he pressed deeper. He felt her flesh trembling into his hands and vibrating his cock when he penetrated her to mid-staff. It felt so damn good for a second Shane didn't know if it was Laura shaking or him.

"Are you about to come?" he asked.

"Yes," Laura squeaked.

Shane's brow furrowed in sympathy for her. She sounded wild . . . crazed. He hadn't planned to let her come until she'd taken him completely but he found he couldn't deny her any longer when she was in so much pain.

He couldn't deny himself.

He began to fuck her utilizing the first half of his cock, careful not to plunge farther into her heat but riding her fast and forcefully nonetheless. A shout erupted out of Laura's throat. She screamed for what seemed like an eternity while he fucked her shallowly, his semen boiling in his balls. By the time she finally sucked air to her lungs, Shane couldn't take any more.

He growled gutturally as he came, his burning seed erupting into her ass. He kept thrusting for the length of his climax, his shouts of pleasure as orgasm slammed through him again and again twining with Laura's sharp cries.

"Are you okay?" Shane panted a while later. Miraculously, he'd hardly paused in his stroking of Laura's ass. His cock was still hard as a pike and her ass felt just as eye-crossingly fantastic squeezing his cock in its divine grip as it had before his thunderous climax.

"Yes," he heard her reply from beneath the curtain of her dark hair.

"Good," he mumbled. She moaned when he turned up the dial on her vibrator another notch, felt her rock her hips against it as she enjoyed the amplified buzz. "Cuz I'm not done yet."

He grasped her hips tightly and thrust with a steady determination. He thought sure he'd die in that moment if he couldn't bury himself in Laura to the hilt. This time he didn't need to remind her to resist the pressure. She stiffened her arms on the countertop, pushing back on him so forcefully that he slid into her several more inches. They groaned in mutual gratification.

"That's right," Shane rasped as he began to fuck her more deeply, his stare fixed on the erotic site of his ruddy, glistening cock plunging back and forth into Laura's sweet ass. He figured the erotic vision would be tattooed on his memory banks for an eternity. "Do you like that, baby?"

The answer he got was a low, guttural moan accompanied by the sensation of Laura pushing her ass back on him firmly, begging for more of his cock without words. Shane gave it to her, growling like an animal when his balls finally pressed to her plump ass cheeks.

"Fuck *yeah*," he grated out mindlessly as his drove into her to the hilt and was finally completely surrounded by her penetrating heat. Her whimpers of pleasure drove him wild when he began to drive in and out of her with short thrusts, his pelvis and thighs slapping into her ass cheeks with brisk smacks of flesh against flesh. Her whimpers escalated to sharp cries as his strokes became longer and more forceful.

Her soft, firm flesh began to tremble in his hands again.

"You like that, don't you? You like being ridden hard?"

When she didn't answer but the fine tremors in her flesh became more pronounced he slid into her to the hilt with a loud smacking noise. He leaned toward her.

"Answer me."

"Yes, I love it . . . I *love* . . ." She cried out suddenly, wiggling her hips as much as she could with him pinning her with his cock. Every muscle in his body went rigid in ecstasy when she convulsed in another orgasm and her ass gripped his cock even tighter.

His vision went red for the next few seconds as he fucked her while she came, granting her no mercy because she clearly didn't want it. She bucked her bottom along his shaft wildly as she shrieked in orgasm, taking him on a swift, relentless ride. His body was pulled so tight on the rack of pleasure, he wondered distantly if his muscles would break from the tension.

He grabbed her lush bottom, stilling her when a scalding orgasm ripped through his flesh. He lifted her several inches off the bar stool and held her to him desperately as he emptied himself into her yet again.

His ears still rang with his harsh roar of release a half minute later. He gently set Laura's bottom back down on the stool, encircling her waist with his hands as he leaned over her and tried to catch his breath.

"Maybe I should ask my dad if I can buy these stools off him," he mumbled as he leaned forward and pressed a kiss along Laura's elegant spine.

She made a harsh sound that he initially thought was disgust. It was difficult to tell for sure when she leaned forward with her forehead on her arms, her hair completely covering her face. But then he heard—he *felt* the exquisite sensation of her laughter vibrating into his cock, hands, and lips. He smiled.

He knew Laura'd never believe him in a million years if he admitted it, but that sound was every bit as precious to his ears as her screams of pleasure had been.

CHAPTER **SEVENTEEN**

Open."

Laura shook her head in Shane's lap but she couldn't help but laugh as she parted her lips and Shane popped another bite of pork tenderloin between them. She chewed, savoring the decadently rich flavor.

"You know there's more cholesterol and fat in two of those things than there are in about twelve hot fudge sundaes. I'm surprised the American Heart Association hasn't put out an official ban on Buttery crackers," she murmured lazily as she watched Shane stab two bites with his fork and eat with relish. He looked like a gorgeous sybarite feasting as he leaned back on the couch, gloriously bared to the waist as the firelight cast gold light and shadows over his taut muscles covered in dusky skin—one of the members of his worshipful harem lying in his lap.

Her grin widened at the thought.

They'd showered after they'd made love and then come back out to the kitchen to finish preparing the breaded tenderloins, this time working together. Laura admonished herself for having such a good time doing it, but Shane's appeal was irresistible. They'd both been too tired and hungry to make the salad he'd planned to serve, so they'd retired in front of the fireplace with a plate heaped high with the delicious golden brown tenderloins.

"I'm gonna love every second of my equivalent of one hundred and forty-four hot fudge sundaes. I'm going hog wild tonight on my favorites," Shane informed her before he dropped a kiss on her mouth. He lingered, tasting her lower lip before penetrating her depths with his tongue in a leisurely yet thorough possession.

His sensual hunger never ceased to amaze her. The fact that her own desire for him easily matched it left her stunned and deeply gratified. She'd been deprived of the rich pleasures of her sexuality for nearly her entire adult life, after all. To have Shane reintroduce her to the pleasures of the flesh—to have him intensify them exponentially—was a powerful experience.

The emotions that accompanied his sensual onslaught overwhelmed her. Had he known this was how she'd react? Is that why he'd done something so outlandish? Laura wondered.

She took the bite that he offered her and watched him as he ate another forkful.

"Hmm, pork tenderloins and Laura Vasquez. That's a combination worth dying for," he murmured softly as he nipped at her lips.

Laura's vision blurred as she stared up at his handsome face. She blinked dazedly a second later when Shane held up another forked offering to her sealed mouth.

"Are you already full? I thought you would have worked up more of an appetite than that," he told her with a dead-sexy, crooked smile. His eyebrows pinched together in puzzlement when she continued to refuse to open her mouth for the food, however. "What's wrong? I thought you said they were just as good as my mom's."

She sat up abruptly.

"Laura?"

That's a combination worth dying for.

The fire in the dimly lit room seemed to highlight the

creases of concern on Shane's face. She forced a smile. "It's okay. I'm just a little tired. I'm not really used to drinking wine."

Shane slowly lowered the fork, setting it on the plate on the coffee table. "Come here." He beckoned with his hands.

Laura stiffened at the enticement but then went to him. She clenched her eyelids together tightly when his arms encircled her and her cheek was pressed to his warm, bare chest.

"I can hear your heart beating," she whispered.

His big hand opened on the back of her head and laced his fingers in her hair. "It's a strong little bugger. It'll take a lot more than breaded tenderloins to put it out of commission."

"Shane? What are you planning on doing?"

"You mean right now? I was thinking about putting you to bed. It's no wonder you're so exhausted, two glasses of wine aside."

"No. I mean once we go home. What are you planning?"

His fingers stilled in her hair for a second before he resumed caressing it. "That depends on you, Laura."

Laura opened her eyes and watched the flames leaping, their frantic movements seeming to echo the beating of her heart.

"I know what you're thinking."

She glanced up at his tone. "What?"

"You're thinking I'm asking too much of you. But I have to do it. I have no other choice."

"No. It's me who has no choice, Shane."

His features stiffened. "I'm gonna *kill* the son of a bitch who made you feel that way."

He stopped her with a hand on her shoulder when she tried to sit up again. "I'm sorry, I shouldn't have said that. I didn't mean to upset you."

"Shane, *please* take me home," Laura pleaded.

"Goddamn it, Laura, we're not here because I want to be your adversary! I want to help you. Why won't you let me?"

"You're not helping me, you're hurting me."

His face collapsed for a brief second before he rallied,

leaning toward her intently. "I know I'm being hard. But I can't think how else to get through to you . . . to the woman I used to know."

Laura's shoulders sagged. "You're making a mistake. You're looking for something that's not there. The Laura you used to know is gone, Shane."

"I know you're not the same as you were when you were twenty years old. I'm not that stupid." He cupped her jaw and turned her head so that she'd meet his gaze. "But the essentials don't change. You said so yourself. Don't give up. *Don't.*"

Her eyes widened in amazement at his stark intensity. His forceful will, his sheer charisma hooked and held her at his mercy.

"We still have tonight. We have tomorrow and tomorrow night. I'm not taking you back to Chicago until Monday either way, Laura. It's only us here. No one else. Nothing else. Two more nights. Don't you think what we once had warrants that, at least?"

Laura closed her eyes, wanting to guard Shane from the longing she was sure he would see in her gaze . . . wishing she could shield herself—

"Do you want me to tell you a truth I'm not particularly proud of, Laura?"

Her eyelids slowly came unglued at that.

"The Chicago media has been implying that I've been obsessed with the FBI's investigation of corruption in the CPD. They've even hinted I might have a personal agenda for it. I've had to do a mini-PR campaign along with Jake Moriarity, the superintendent of the CPD, to assure the public that the investigation was to increase the public trust in the CPD, not decrease it."

"I'm sorry the press has been giving you a hard time. I think you're right. If you don't expose the corruption and punish the wrongdoers, how is someone like Moriarity ever going to be able to make the changes necessary to ensure police corruption, especially at that level, never occurs again?"

Shane's expression looked a little stunned and Laura thought she knew why. It was the first time she'd ever admitted to him she knew there was corruption at the CPD, let alone condemned it. For a second she thought he was going to interrogate her about her views, but he seemed to stop himself at the last second.

"Thanks for the vote of confidence, but what I was trying to actually tell you was that there's more than a grain of truth to the press's suspicions about me and the personal agenda. Not that the investigation wasn't called for or that it doesn't fall completely within the domain of the FBI's jurisdiction. Investigating corruption in public officials is one of our prime directives. It's just that . . ." His voice dropped in volume and Laura realized whatever he wanted to say was difficult for him.

"Remember how I told you about how I knew who Telly Ardos was because of his boss running a scam back in the nineties, replacing valuable gems with fakes while he was supposed to be creating new settings for the stones, cleaning jewelry, stuff like that?"

Laura nodded.

"The thief's name was Orvantes. The way I found out about that wasn't professional. The incident became personal on more levels than one."

"What do you mean?" Laura asked slowly. A thought occurred to her. Shane's mother possessed some magnificent jewels, both heirlooms from her family and gifts from her husband. She also enjoyed sketching ideas for jewelry designs, both for her own gems and for some of her close friends who recognized her talent. "Did Elizabeth give some of her jewelry to Orvantes?"

Shane nodded, his blue eyes gleaming from the light of the fire. "Yeah. She gave him some of her older jewelry in order to have it reset in her own designs. Apparently Orvantes didn't count on the fact that Mom knew what she was doing when it came to stone appraisal. She and Dad called the police on Orvantes and had him arrested, although nothing could ever be pinned on Orvantes's assistant, Telly Ardos.

"Even though I wasn't officially involved in the investigation, I poked around a little bit. Enough to find a connection between Orvantes's little operation and Huey Mays. Enough to give me some information that led to some pretty unsavory suspicions about your husband. I didn't have enough solid evidence to bring anything to the police, and at that time, the case didn't fall under the Bureau's jurisdiction. But I'd started to wonder about Huey and whether he was abusing his position as a police officer in order to commit crimes even back then, Laura."

"I don't understand why you're telling me this, Shane."

He raked his fingers through his dark hair and stared up at the ceiling for a few seconds, as though choosing his words carefully.

"I'm telling you because I was already itching to expose Huey Mays for what he was more than twelve years ago. I've lived in two other cities in the interim because of promotions at the Bureau. I've been on hundreds of different cases, done truckloads of administrative paperwork. A lot of years went by—a lot of water under the bridge. But I never forgot, Laura. I never forgot how much I wanted to nail Huey Mays."

"And when you came back to Chicago, this time as the Special Agent in Charge of the Chicago offices . . . that's what you did," Laura added quietly.

He shook his head slowly. "What I'm really trying to confess is that I was gunning for Huey Mays from day one upon my return to Chicago. It just so happens that his abuse of power and crimes were much graver and further reaching than I'd ever imagined. The point is, I went after Huey because I wanted to expose him. Not to his honest, hardworking peers and not to the Chicago community. I wanted *you* to see him for what he was, Laura."

A log fell in the fireplace, sending up sizzling sparks in the silence that followed. The flash of orange flame highlighted Shane's intense, bold features.

"I never forgot. I never could let it go completely. I never could let you go."

Laura watched him through a veil of tears.

"Almost fourteen years. And all I'm asking of you is two more nights. Say you'll at least give me that."

Emotion gripped her throat, making speech impossible. Anything . . . *Anything* to make this torture end.

She nodded her head once.

And the next thing she knew she was in his arms.

They went to the bedroom soon afterward and Laura lay on the bed naked. Shane held her gaze as he restrained her wrists. She sensed he would have left her unrestrained if she requested it. But in all honesty, she'd grown to love having him restrain her so that he could worship, torment, and pleasure her, forever pushing at the boundaries of what she thought she could endure.

It felt so wonderful just to let go.

Shane kicked off his pajama bottoms and proceeded to make slow, sweet, thorough love to her, touching her everywhere, tasting her everywhere, insisting she survive in the center of the white-hot fire even as he amplified the temperature in her burning flesh.

Laura stared up at him later in wonder as he fucked her slow and deep. He'd bent her knees back into her chest, demanding she take everything he had to offer. She wanted to memorize how he looked at that moment, the torment of ecstasy tensing his bold features, every muscle in his beautiful body flexed tightly. His eyes pierced straight through her when he met her gaze and leaned his upper body on the headboard of the bed.

"You're mine, Laura."

She gasped when he began to ride her hard, straining for the release he'd denied himself as he pleasured her again and again. The thick ridge beneath the head of his cock stimulated her hard, deep, and fast, forcing her to go beyond submitting to her desire; demanding she drown in it. The headboard and his gripping knuckles knocked against the wall at a tempo that matched the blood pounding in her ears and the staccato beat of their bodies crashing together in a violent storm of ecstasy.

"Say it. Say it's true. You're mine," Shane snarled.

"Yes. It's *true*."

He slammed into her one last time, the sensation of his jerking, spasming cock lodged deep inside her flesh igniting her yet again.

"Shane?" she murmured softly minutes later against his neck. His breathing had become slow and regular but she wasn't sure if he slept. He'd released her wrist restraints and turned off the bedside lamp. They both lay on their sides belly to belly, their limbs wrapped fast around the other so that they formed a secure, fleshy knot.

"Hmm?"

"Do you remember when Peter found that bird with the broken wing?"

His head twisted, causing his chin to caress the top of her head. "Yes. He fed it with an eyedropper and kept it in one of Joey's old hamster cages. Joey was the big-brother voice of doom, always predicting its death."

"I thought it would die, too," Laura murmured. "But it didn't. And then it got better, and it started to flap at the cage. Peter was beside himself with worry that it'd redamage the wing he'd healed."

"Using a Popsicle stick as a splint," Shane added with amusement. "Kid probably would have become a doctor."

Laura smiled sadly. They'd never know what Peter would have become. "Derrick told him he had to let it go. The noise of its wings batting against the cage was terrible."

Neither of them spoke for a minute. Shane's hand spread across the back of her skull. He kissed her once on the forehead.

"You, Joey, and I went with Peter across the street to Union Park to let the bird go. Derrick was adamant that Peter couldn't keep it," Laura reminisced.

"Poor Peter. He was so solemn. It was like he was attending an execution or something."

"Do you . . . do you remember what you told Peter before he let the bird out of the cage?"

For a stretched moment she thought Shane wasn't going to reply.

"I remember. My dad had said the same thing to me when I took home a stray puppy when I was seven years old and the original owner eventually showed up to claim it."

"If you love it, let it go. If it comes back to you, it's yours. If it doesn't, then it never was," she whispered against his neck.

She felt Shane nod and swallowed a painful knot in her throat.

"Go to sleep, babe," Shane murmured, kissing the top of her head again. "Gotta get you rested up for tomorrow."

"Why? So you can use more of those implements of torture you keep pulling out of that bag over there?"

He chuckled and swept his big hand down the sensitive skin at the side of her torso. She shivered with pleasure before he pulled up the sheet around her. "No, so you can help me shovel us out of this mountain of snow. Maybe after you've done some good hard labor, I'll consider torturing you some more."

"A girl can only hope," she mumbled.

"I believe it pays to treat my captives well," he growled near her ear. "Laura?"

Her eyes blinked open at the change of his tone. "Yes?"

"Tomorrow you're going to tell me. Everything. We'll weather the truth together. No matter what it is. Okay?"

It seemed for a stretched moment that her heart completely stopped in her chest. When it resumed, it did so sluggishly, as though a weight pressed on it.

"Yes," she whispered. She took his head in her hands, the degree to which she cherished him nearly overwhelming her. Even though she knew Shane couldn't see her in the darkness, she smiled up at him as she spoke, her soul in her eyes. "Tomorrow."

She lay awake until Shane's breathing became deep and even, refusing to sleep, needing to treasure the feeling of being in his arms.

What Shane had told Peter about his bird had been kind . . . quaint. But Laura knew the hard truth of the matter. There were so many reasons a creature may not return to the hearth where it belonged, where it was most loved, reasons that had *nothing* to do with the heart's true desire.

Laura awoke to the delicious sensation of Shane mouthing her neck. When she murmured in profound contentment and proceeded to fall back into the warm cocoon of Shane's arms and sleep, he nipped at her sensitive skin teasingly.

"Ouch," she muttered even though it hadn't really hurt much. She blinked her eyes open and saw that the room was still cloaked in darkness.

"Don't go back to sleep," Shane preempted when her eyelids sagged heavily.

"Shane, it's not even dawn yet," she complained.

"It'll be light soon enough. I've only got so much time with you here. I don't want to spend too much of it sleeping."

That forced her into alertness. She only had so much time, too.

"What did you have in mind?"

"Come on. Put on your sweats and a pair of socks. No shirt needed. You'll have on your coat."

"Wait . . . we're not going outside, are we? Shane, we're in the middle of a snowstorm!"

"The snow stopped over an hour ago. Come on, don't be a wuss," he said as he sat up and prodded her ribs with his fingers before segueing into a tickle.

Laura snorted with laughter before she bolted out of bed quicker than a startled cat. Damn him. He'd remembered that the sure way to torture her was to tickle her. Joey and Shane had frequently brought her into a frantic state of combined laughter and tears by tickling her.

"You really have turned ruthless in your old age." She ducked her head to hide her smile. Shane turned on a bedside lamp. She yelped when he swatted her bare butt as she bent over to retrieve her sweatpants from the floor. Her cry of surprise segued to a soft moan when he boldly trailed his long forefinger along the crack of her ass.

"You gotta be cruel to be kind," he murmured under his breath on the way to the bathroom.

A few minutes later they stood at the back door of the cabin fully dressed, Shane holding two towels in one hand.

"Just stay here for a minute and I'll come back to get you," Shane instructed as he opened the door, grabbing the shovel that leaned against the wall. He switched on an outdoor light. Laura's eyes widened when she saw the nearly three-foot-tall drift that had accumulated against the door. Shane just lifted his long legs and plowed right into it, holding the shovel over his head.

"Shane?" Laura protested, but he ignored her. Understanding of his actions slowly dawned when she saw him shovel the snow over a raised hillock in the backyard and finally lift a cover. Steam billowed up around him. He pushed down on what appeared to be a button near his feet and Laura heard the distant sound of agitated water. She laughed when he came back to retrieve her and lifted her into his arms.

"I didn't know there was a hot tub out here," Laura murmured with delight next to his ear. He carried her through the thick accumulation of snow and set her down next to the hot tub he'd just uncovered.

"I'd forgotten about it, too, until Tim Brandt mentioned it. He maintains it when my dad is away for extended periods."

"Oh . . . wait," Laura exclaimed when Shane reached up under her coat and jerked down her sweatpants. Cool air struck her bare skin, raising goose bumps all over her body.

"Come on, buck up. The sooner you strip the sooner you can get in the water."

She shivered as he pulled on one foot, then the other, whipping off her socks. She stood on the concrete enclosure for the hot tub wearing nothing but her coat over her naked body, her feet quickly turning to blocks of ice.

Shane whipped off his own spare clothing. Laura's gaze

stuck to his muscular back and flexing bare ass before he submerged himself in the water. He groaned in sensual satisfaction.

"Feels great. It's not that bad outside, you know. There's no wind and it must be in the low thirties." He sat on the deepest step of the tub and stared up at her, amusement gleaming in his blue eyes. "Go on, baby. Strip and get in."

Her chilled fingers fumbled clumsily with the belt of her coat. She held both sides securely together at her waist, dreading the moment of full exposure. She finally held her breath and whipped the coat over her shoulders. Her nipples pulled tight at the blast of frigid air. She carefully arranged her coat on the other clothing and the towels to keep it off the snow, sensing Shane's stare on her all the while like a tingling caress.

She stepped into the water and met Shane's gaze before she plunged into his arms. He laughed, the warm, masculine sound striking her as being every bit as delicious as the steamy water.

"Oh, this is nice," Laura said once she'd spread her knees and settled in Shane's lap, their faces just inches apart. She hooked her forearms behind his neck. Her skin prickled and tingled from the abrupt contrast of going from cold air to hot water. She purred in sensual delight when Shane began to stroke her body along her sides from hip to below her armpit.

He'd been right. It was relatively warm for a winter day, the temperature hovering just around the freezing mark. Not a breeze tickled her cheek as she luxuriated both in the hot water and Shane's equally steamy stare. An outdoor lamppost cast enough light for her to see that the surrounding trees looked like they'd been dipped in thick white icing. Dawn must be coming soon, Laura thought, because the night sky seemed impenetrable and black.

Shane must have noticed her gazing upward.

"Always darkest before the dawn," he murmured.

She glanced down at him and they shared a smile.

"It's just like being at a ski resort, isn't it?"

"Hmmm?" Laura murmured distractedly as he stroked the sensitive sides of her breasts with his long fingers. "Oh . . . I wouldn't know. I've never been."

He considered her thoughtfully. "Why not? You must have wanted to, considering all those travel brochures you've been collecting."

Laura studiously examined one of his wet, muscular shoulders. "Those were just some dreams I had."

He placed a hand on her chin and tilted her face toward him.

"Why were they just dreams?" he asked gently.

"I don't know. I guess I was always too busy with the studio," she lied. Like most prisoners, Laura continually dreamed of escape. She could tell by Shane's furrowed brow he was about ready to pursue the subject so she headed him off at the pass.

"Do you like to ski?"

"Sure," he said slowly after a few seconds. "It's a rite of passage to strip down and get in the hot tub during a snowstorm." His hands spanned her hips, nudging her forward. "Come here."

Laura bit her lip in rising sensual awareness when she pressed against Shane's growing erection. He lifted and settled her so that her right ass cheek and thigh rested on his cock. He burned beneath her, feeling even hotter than the water.

"Put your mouth on me," he ordered gruffly.

"Where?" Laura asked, surprised by his request.

"Anywhere you fancy will do."

Laura's smile lingered as she leaned forward and lightly brushed her lips against his. The vapor made them feel warm and damp beneath her. He remained motionless, letting her nip and pluck at his mouth at her leisure.

"Is that what you want?" she whispered as she slid her lips against his seductively. His cock throbbed beneath her.

"It'll do for starters."

She smiled wider and traced his lips with the tip of her tongue.

"You have the sexiest mouth in existence," Shane told her quietly while she continued to nibble and tease.

She took advantage of his parted lips and plunged her tongue between them. He groaned and tightened his hold around her waist, bringing their bellies flush together. Laura kissed him deep and thorough before she backed up. He came after her, a man-beast suddenly deprived of its meal. She chuckled.

"Wait. I thought you said *I* was supposed to put my mouth on *you*."

"So *put* it on me," he growled, craning toward her.

"Sit still. I'll come to you at my own pace," she directed despite the allure of his seeking lips and steamy, determined stare. She could tell by the hard line of his mouth he didn't like it, but he leaned his head back on the edge of the tub and waited for her to come to him.

It felt decadent to sit in Shane's lap with that hot water bubbling around them, sipping at his firm lips at her own pace, tasting him with her tongue . . . indulging in a sensual feast. He held out for longer than she would have expected, knowing what she knew of his demanding, dominant nature. But when she bit lightly at his lower lip and sucked it between her teeth, he tilted his head, pulled her tightly against him, and consumed her.

They kissed voraciously, then sensually, then with wild abandon again for delicious, suspended moments. She grew so lightheaded from the heat, Shane's caresses on her ass, hips, and waist, and a kiss that could have been the main event for sex versus merely foreplay. Eventually, however, Shane lifted her hips and set her down next to him on the seat.

"What are you doing?" she whispered hoarsely as he stood before her. She stared in stunned lust when he put one foot on the seat next to her and lifted his cock fully from the water, the smooth, ruddy, mushroom-shaped head gleaming just inches from her face. She squeezed her thighs together tightly over the pinch of excitement at her clit. He loomed over her as he slowly stroked his cock, his pose blatantly, unapologetically dominant.

"Now it's your turn to keep still while I sample that pretty, teasing mouth." He furrowed his fingers into her hair and spread them across her skull, keeping her steady.

He leaned forward.

Laura was so hungry for him that she strained against his hold, lips spread wide. But he tightened his grip and kept her in place.

"Put your hands behind your head and lean against the tub. That's right. Now don't move."

Laura did as he directed, her gaze fixed on the thick head of his penis. She felt the saliva pool on her tongue as he slowly . . . deliberately speared his cock between her lips.

She ran her tongue over the thick head in mounting excitement and then applied a steady suck.

"That's a girl," Shane murmured as he flexed his hips forward.

Shane watched her through eyelids weighted with intense arousal. Her lips clamped tightly around the tip of his cock, her tongue dancing around the head to taste his pre-come. He pressed forward, using his foot on the seat to steady himself. He grimaced in pleasure at the sensation of sliding his cock along her tongue into her delicious, humid heat. His hips moved, pumping her mouth rhythmically while she applied a firm, eye-crossing suction. The cold air around his wet torso cooled a raging internal inferno.

"That's right," Shane murmured as he fucked the most beautiful face he'd ever seen in his life. Every time she strained forward to try to control the movements, he tightened his grip in her hair. His cock stretched her lips wide. He knew her hunger from her strong, thirsty suck. She seemed to want more so he gave it to her.

"Try to relax," he whispered as he watched her struggle to take him down her throat. "Ahhh, yeah," he moaned in ecstasy a moment later when he breached her body's defenses and the tip of his cock penetrated her tight opening. He slid back along her tongue and plunged deep once more. He felt the familiar tingling at the base of his spine.

"I'm going to come now," he grated out.

He thrust deep, feeling her muscles constrict around the tip of his cock, squeezing him tightly. A roar erupted out of his lungs and ripped at his throat as he climaxed. It felt so damned good that he nearly didn't have the presence of mind to unblock her throat. He still shot what felt like gallons of come on her tongue when he withdrew, fucking her mouth shallowly. Laura stared up at him, her eyes huge and glistening with sexual excitement as she slurped on the end of his cock, swallowing every last drop of what he gave her.

How could she trust him not to hurt her while he face-fucked her forcefully, and yet be unwilling to entrust him with anything else? An urge to totally possess her, to show her exactly to whom she belonged, overwhelmed him.

He savored his final stroke in her hot mouth before he slid the length of his cock out of her clamping lips.

"Thank you, baby. That felt so good. Now it's your turn," he muttered. He turned and reached for one of the towels, folding it at the edge of the hot tub. "Sit up here."

He helped her stand because she looked a little unsteady on her feet. The intense heat must be getting to her. His gaze toured her slender, curvy naked body hungrily when she placed her bottom on the towel. Her breasts looked round and full, the nipples fat and succulent from the heat. Mist rose rapidly all over her flushed skin. He parted her thighs and knelt in front of her on the tub step.

"Have I ever told you you're the most beautiful woman I've ever seen?"

She merely shook her head, her slanted green eyes glistening as she looked down at him.

"Well you are." He reached around her, his fingertips burrowing into the deliciously cold snow. "Look at all the steam coming off you. You're so hot. Let's see if we can't cool you off a little."

She jumped when he covered a relaxed pink nipple with snow. "Shane!"

"Shhh," he soothed as he rubbed the frozen water over her, the contact with both of their heated bodies melting it almost instantly. He smiled when he felt her nipple pebble against his fingertips. She cried out brokenly and grasped his head when he placed his mouth over the turgid peak, both agitating and soothing the chilled flesh with his tongue.

"Ummm," he murmured, giving a tender bite to the firm flesh surrounding the nipple and finding it succulent. Laura's nipples were made for a man's mouth—made for *his* mouth. He suckled the sweet tip until it turned dark pink and distended and all vestiges of snow had turned to steam.

Then he turned his attentions to the other breast until Laura clutched at his head, clamped her thighs together tightly and wiggled her hips against the towel. He put his hands on her knees and spread her thighs, exposing the tempting, slick folds of her pink pussy.

He held her gaze as he grabbed more snow.

"No," she protested softly when he reached between her thighs.

"Yes," he whispered. They both watched as he pressed up on her firmly with a snow-covered hand. Laura gasped and trembled. Shane grunted in tense arousal. "Look at the steam coming off you. Nothing's going to chill that hot little pussy."

"Shane, *please*."

He looked up into her beautiful, steam-glazed face.

"Lean back a little," he instructed.

She cried out sharply when he placed his mouth over her snowy pussy, his tongue avidly seeking out the warm cream lying beneath the ice. Melting snow flooded his mouth, but he suckled and swallowed greedily, eager to have Laura's musky sweetness running down his throat instead. Soon every last drop of cold water was gone and only hot, delicious woman-flesh remained for his tongue and lips to plunder.

He ran his tongue languidly over her labia, savoring her flavor. She thrashed her hips against him desperately, but he restrained her with his hands. When he sensed her rising desperation, he stabbed at her erect clit with a stiffened, relentless tongue.

She screamed as she quaked against him in orgasm, her fingers forming claws in his hair. He continued to eat her throughout her climax, refusing to let her escape his rubbing tongue. When she slowed and quieted he turned his head and sucked her clit firmly, enormously gratified when she cried out with renewed tremors of climax.

He pulled her into the tub with him a moment later, kissing her neck ardently.

"Let's go inside," he whispered hoarsely. "I want inside that hot little pussy."

"Yes, yes," Laura murmured in mindless agreement before their lips met and fastened in a heated kiss. "I need you, too."

Shane awoke hours later to the sound of a snowplow in the distance. He blinked dazedly. Morning light peeked around the curtains. He usually didn't sleep so heavily, but a combination of the wine last night, the steamy early morning hot tub foray with Laura, and a sense of profound contentment must have kept him in the clutches of deep sleep.

He immediately knew something was wrong . . . something was missing. He leaned up on his elbows, instantly alert. His quick survey of the bedroom told him he was alone.

"Laura?"

The only sound to answer his strained query was the scraping of the metal snowplow on the frozen road. His gaze shot over to the side of the mantel where he'd set aside Laura's leather boots. The corner was empty.

"No."

He flew up out of the bed and scuttled into a pair of jeans. When he stormed into the great room a second later he instinctively knew it was empty. By the time he fumbled barefoot down the front porch steps, nearly falling on his face in the deep drifts of snow, Tim Brandt's dark blue pickup truck was already fifty yards down the rural route. He saw the figure in the passenger seat of the truck turn and look back at him.

Frustration coursed through him when his frantic gaze landed on his snow-covered car. Thanks to Brandt's snow-plow, a five-foot-high wall of snow barricaded the exit of the driveway. Until he shoveled himself out, he was as trapped as a tiger pacing in its cage.

"Fuck," he muttered viciously.

After the way she'd given herself to him last night . . . after she'd told him she was his, Laura had tricked him.

Left him.

Shane thought he'd explode clear through his skin in a blast of helpless rage.

CHAPTER **EIGHTEEN**

Shane had cleared the driveway, showered, packed, and dressed within an hour and a half of Laura's departure. Under the guise of wanting to purchase firewood, he found out where Tim Brandt lived from the clerk at a gas station in Eagle River.

"Doubt he's at home, though," the clerk had added as he'd rung up Shane's bottle of water and mints. "Just saw him headed for the highway a little over an hour ago and haven't seen him come back this way since."

Shane had grunted his thanks and headed for his car. He'd hidden Laura's purse at the cabin, so she didn't have any credit cards or money. He had little doubt, however, given the way Tim Brandt was staring at her yesterday, as if he'd just been gifted with the vision of a goddess, that he would have volunteered to take her anywhere she wanted to go.

On his drive back to the city he checked Laura's cell phone for received messages over the weekend. Her incoming included two calls from a blocked caller identification and one from an unlisted number with a 312 area code. He tried to access her voice messages but she had them password protected. He tried Laura's and Joey's birth dates, but came up short. The blocked caller didn't pick up when Shane dialed the number, nor was there any type of voice mail message.

The unlisted call looked like an institutional number, the kind that a caller needed an extension to access. He already had a suspicion of what that institution was before he called it.

Sure enough, it was the main trunk line for a myriad of Cook County institutions—including the Cook County Jail. He made a quick call to Mavis Bertram. When she told him that Telly Ardos was out of the Cook County Jail on bail, Shane pressed harder on the accelerator.

"Do me a favor, will you? Wait outside Laura Mays's house until she gets home, then make sure she's okay until I arrive? I have a feeling Telly Ardos might try to go after her again."

A long silence ensued.

"Yeah, okay. But Dom . . . is there anything you need to tell me about Laura Mays? Does this really have to do with our case? Or is it personal?"

"It has everything to do with the case. Not only did Ardos break into her house and pull a gun on Laura the other night, he implied he wanted to take her to someone who wanted to talk to Laura specifically. That won't have changed just because Ardos got thrown in jail. I told you yesterday I think Ardos was Huey's connection to the jewelry industry."

"So you think Laura Mays is somehow involved, as well."

Shane's knuckles went white on the wheel. "She knows something but she's not talking."

"Yeah, there's a lot of that going on around here." Mavis grunted. "We did have a bit of luck though, Dom. I was about to call you about it."

Shane listened for the next minute as a weight seemed to grow heavier and heavier on his chest.

"So what do you think? Should we bring him in for questioning?" Mavis asked finally.

"*Questioning?* The evidence you have is pretty damning, Mavis. It justifies arrest. "

"I realize that," Mavis said uneasily. "But I know Vasquez was a friend of yours from way back. I thought—"

"The evidence speaks for itself," Shane said dully. "Bring in Joey Vasquez. If you can't locate him, just have a couple agents wait at his house. He and his family are on a ski trip in Wisconsin but they should be returning anytime now. Wait until I get there to question him, though. I'm not going to be involved. I just want to hear what he has to say . . . see his face when he says it."

The sky had grown dark by the time Shane finally walked out of one of the interrogation rooms at the First Precinct. He'd chosen John McNamara and Andre Lorenzo to question Joey.

The weight of dread pressing down on Shane's chest since Mavis had mentioned Joey's name this morning seemed to magnify tenfold when he saw Shelly and Carlotta Vasquez sitting in the waiting area by the precinct front desk. Shelly rose from her chair when she saw Shane.

"Dom, what's going on? They said I needed to call our lawyer. Where's Joey?"

Shane inhaled slowly, his gaze falling to Carlotta. The teenager looked as drawn with anxiety as her mother.

"I need to talk to you a moment in private, Shelly."

"No, Dom! I want to hear what's happening to my dad," Carlotta exclaimed. "Mom?"

Shelly swallowed convulsively and nodded once, mutely granting her permission to hear. Shane grimaced.

Christ, this whole situation sucked.

"Joey's being booked on a federal charge of racketeering conspiracy. I'm sorry, Shelly. I wish I could spare you this." He grasped Shelly's elbow when she swayed on her feet and gently urged her back on the plastic chair. Something behind him thudded dully on the dingy tile floor. Coffee seeped around his shoes. He turned around.

"I can't believe it. I can't *believe* you arrested Joey."

Laura stood there, her green eyes looking huge in her shocked face. Mavis had reported to him hours ago that Laura had been dropped off safely by Tim Brandt at her home and then left again soon afterward. Shelly had likely called her about Joey being picked up and Laura had come down to the police station to offer support.

Her hair had been pulled back into a ponytail. She wore jeans and a form-fitting dark green sweater. He saw the gold chain on her neck and knew the pendant nestled between her breasts. Despite the fact that the incandescent lights and anxiety washed out every trace of color in her face, her beauty struck Shane anew, feeling like a kick to the gut. She still held one full cup of coffee in her hand. He bent and picked up the now empty paper cup from the floor.

"Let me get you another cup."

"We don't want anything from you," Laura muttered between clenched teeth.

Shane paused in the action of throwing the cup into the garbage when he heard the sheer fury in her tone. He met Laura's eyes.

"May I have a word with you for a moment, please?"

"What's going to happen to Joey? Where will they take him?" Laura demanded, ignoring his request. A movement at the entrance caught Shane's eye. Blaine Howard, that vulture reporter from Channel Eight News, entered the police station with one of his cameramen. Jesus, this just kept getting better and better, didn't it? How'd that asshole get tipped off so quickly?

"Excuse me for a moment," Shane murmured. He talked to the sergeant at the front desk. The sergeant stood and approached Blaine Howard. He noticed the reporter looking over the sergeant's shoulder at Shane, and then glancing at Laura hungrily. The sergeant shooed them out, but Shane knew Blaine Howard would be outside the precinct doors waiting to pounce. He'd tell the sergeant to show Shelly and Carlotta out a rear entrance.

He'd prefer if Laura came with him right now. Shane sighed tiredly when he approached her again and realized the unlikelihood of that occurring, however. Her scowl hadn't diminished. He'd been expecting this reaction from

Laura—dreaded it. Still, no amount of preparation could have readied him for the hurt and anger in her eyes.

"Like I said, I need to talk to you privately," he said.

"I've got nothing to say to you in private. Just tell us what's going to happen to Joey," she replied stiffly.

"He'll go before a judge at the Dirksen Federal Building for a preliminary hearing in the morning. You'll need to think about posting bail," Shane said, glancing at Shelly. Tears spilled down Carlotta's cheeks.

"Mom?"

"Shhh, it's going to be all right, honey," Shelly murmured shakily. She hugged the girl and rocked her in her arms as Carlotta sobbed.

"You bastard," Laura hissed softly, so only Shane heard.

"Do you think this is easy for me?"

"I don't care what it is for you." Laura held his gaze as she sat down in the chair next to Carlotta and rubbed her niece's back as she cried. "You got what you wanted, Shane. Now leave us alone."

Shane bit back a sarcastic reply when he glanced over and saw Carlotta's wet cheeks and crumpled face. He left the station, accepting defeat for the moment only because he knew he had no other choice.

Just as Blaine Howard noticed him coming down the precinct's front steps, Shane's cell phone rang. He glanced down at the number and hit the receive button.

"Hi, Dad," he mumbled quietly as he sidestepped Howard.

"You okay, Shane?" Alex Dominic asked.

"Yeah. I'm fine. *No comment,*" Shane said when Howard asked him if the rumors were true about another police officer being arrested in the CPD corruption case. Shane's pointed, furious glare caused Howard to hesitate. Shane strode past him.

"Sounds like you're in the middle of something," his father commented. Having been a corporate lawyer, Alex Dominic was always sensitive to what might be happening with Shane's work, sometimes more so than Shane wanted him to be.

Shane's brow furrowed. "It's not a problem. What's wrong? You sound tired."

"Now I don't want you to worry too much—the doctor says your mom is going to be fine—but we're down here at Rush St. Luke's Hospital. Your mother had another stroke, son."

CHAPTER **NINETEEN**

Shane peered at the entrance of Laura's Fulton River District gallery as a middle-aged couple exited the front door and walked down the sidewalk holding hands. He'd been sitting there in his car for more than two hours and he'd grown stiff. Neither muscles nor his patience were in practice anymore for doing surveillance work, although he'd been doing his fair share of watching over Laura in the past few days.

The Lake Street L train rattled loudly as it passed. Laura's gallery was located on the West Side of Chicago in an area that had been the city's meat-packing district and which had recently been revitalized by fashionable restaurants and the art community. Still, Laura's gallery was on the fringes of the neighborhood. In Shane's opinion, the area was distressingly desolate, even at one o'clock in the afternoon. It made him nervous knowing she was in there all alone with the front door of her gallery open to all comers.

He hadn't spoken to her for three days—ever since her dismissal of him in the police station waiting room. If he wasn't the Special Agent in Charge at the Chicago offices of the FBI, he'd probably have been written up by now for missing so much work. Good thing he had a reputation for spending too much time at the office versus not enough or people would have started questioning his sporadic work schedule. If anything, however, his staff just assumed he was frequently absent and preoccupied because of his mother's most recent stroke, and they wouldn't have been entirely wrong in that estimation.

He did visit his mother in the hospital in the evenings, but she grew tired easily after her therapies and was usually asleep by eight p.m. Her stroke had been a minor one, thank God, especially in comparison to the one she'd suffered last year. She was on the rehabilitation ward currently, doing physical, occupational, and speech therapy to address the new impairments caused by her stroke. She was doing well, however, and was supposed to return home tomorrow.

It'd been like acid icing on a poison cake, as far as Shane was concerned, to have so many shitty things happen at once—first Laura's hurt and fury following Joey's arrest, and then his mother's stroke. They said bad things happened in threes.

He was as wired and jittery as he'd ever been in his life waiting for that third thing.

He'd contacted Shelly the day after Joey's arrest to tell her about the time for Joey's preliminary hearing and what to expect. While Joey's wife had been chilly with him on the phone, her reaction had nowhere near equaled Laura's fury. And her tone had even softened infinitesimally when he'd asked her confidentially if she needed any money to post Joey's bail.

Shane was left to face the fact that taking Laura to his cabin had been a mistake. His whole intention had been to encourage her to let him in, to trust him. But as things stood, Laura was keeping him at a distance more than she ever had before. She'd refused to return his calls and had even hung up on him twice when he'd reached her at her house. He knew she was upset about Joey's arrest. Still . . . Shane couldn't help but feel the opportunity also provided her with the foothold she required to push Shane away again after having allowed herself to become vulnerable to him over the weekend.

He'd misjudged her. He'd known she was stubborn, but hadn't realized the extent of her sheer bullheadedness.

Meanwhile he grew increasingly nervous about her safety with every passing minute. He couldn't watch over her constantly and couldn't ask Mavis or one of the other special agents in the Organized Crime Squad to do it for fear of raising suspicions that Laura was somehow implicated in the theft ring.

Shane still wasn't sure just how Laura was involved, but there was little doubt in his mind that she kept something from him. He could only pray that his suspicions were correct and she wasn't guilty of colluding with Huey, Moody, or even Joey in anything illegal. He didn't know how he'd react if he found out he was wrong in that assumption . . .

Didn't even want to think about it.

Movement across the street caught his eye. He cursed under his breath when the man turned his face slightly in Shane's direction before he entered Laura's gallery.

When Shane burst through the front door a few seconds later he saw nothing but Laura's paintings and sculptures in the main showroom. He raced toward the rear of the building, his gun drawn. A doorway behind the desk at the back of the showroom led to a narrow hallway, which opened up on what appeared to be a studio, given the kiln Laura used to fire her sculptures and the blank canvases stacked against the wall.

"Raise your hands and move away from her."

Telly Ardos looked over his shoulder.

"Do it," Shane barked.

Ardos lifted his hands, but not before Laura took a piece of paper from him. Shane saw her shove the paper into her skirt pocket.

"Shane—what in the world?" Laura exclaimed. "Put that gun down."

"Move away from her," Shane demanded.

"Shane, you have no right—"

He crossed the room in three long strides, putting himself between Laura and Ardos. He grabbed Ardos's collar and shoved. "I said to get away from her." Ardos stumbled on the leg of an easel but righted himself. He glared at Shane as he pulled his shirt back into place. Shane saw that he wore a cast on his forearm and recalled that he'd snapped his wrist when he'd been coercing Laura on the street. The memory gave him a grim feeling of satisfaction.

"What do you think you're doing?" Laura asked from beside him.

Shane looked at her incredulously. "Don't tell me you want this scum here."

"That's none of your business. You're the one who's trespassing, Shane."

"Forget it. I was just leaving anyway," Ardos said contemptuously. Shane followed the man out to the main showroom to ensure he truly vacated the premises.

"If I see you near her again I'm going to shoot first and ask questions later," Shane promised.

Ardos glowered at him before he forcefully pushed open the heavy wood and glass door, making it bang on the outside wall. Once he'd stalked down the street Shane closed the door and reached for the lock. Laura caught his hand.

"The only way that door is going to be locked is if you're on the other side of it," she challenged.

His nostrils flared as he looked down at her. He unintentionally caught a hint of her fresh floral perfume and the singular scent of Laura just beneath it. A potent mixture of adrenaline, anger, and lust pumped through his veins.

Goddamn it, he was sick of it. Sick and tired of Laura Vasquez denying him. Denying *them*.

"Come here," Shane bit out as he grabbed her hand.

"Shane? Let go of me. What are you doing? If you think I won't call the police on you this time because I didn't before, you're mistaken."

She stumbled behind him as he dragged her back to her studio. He pulled on her hand, bringing her around in front of him and pushed her back into the only seating in the room—a wooden armchair.

"Why *didn't* you call the police?" Shane breathed out quietly as he bent down over her, his hands on the arms of the chair essentially trapping her in place. He brought his face to within inches of hers. He saw her pupils constrict, her dark pink lips drop open.

"I'm a very private person," she said hoarsely.

"It's because you didn't want to have to tell the cops about how you loved every second of your captivity. Isn't that the truth, Laura?"

She shot him a fulminating look. "If that's true, why'd I leave, Shane?"

He lowered over her an inch, her breath striking his face in choppy, fragrant bursts. "You left because you were afraid."

"I'm not afraid of you."

"Yes, you are. More important, you're afraid of the truth. That's why you've been avoiding me."

She glared at him mutinously.

"There," he spat, pointing with his finger.

"What?" Laura asked in rising confusion. She followed his finger. When she saw what he pointed at—the sculpture of a teenaged boy with his hair partially covering his eyes as he intently read a book that was prominently displayed on a column—her face settled into a mask.

"It must be an important piece to you," Shane challenged. "It's the only thing you have on display in your studio."

"I don't know what you mean. I often put up pieces that I've just completed on that column before I sell them. This one is no different."

"Liar."

Her green eyes shot up to his face when she heard his cold disdain.

"You made that sculpture over a dozen years ago."

"How . . . why would you think that?" she asked slowly.

He leaned down farther until he could see the tiny points of green fractured light in her irises.

"I *know* it. I also know it's a sculpture of me—reading in Union Park when I was a kid. Why've you kept something like that, Laura? Why do you have it displayed so significantly in a place where you spend so much of your time?"

Her eyes went wide. She shook her head. "I don't know where you got that idea, Shane, but I assure you that you're mistak—"

"I'm sick of your lies," he snarled. "What did that asshole Ardos want? What did he give you?" Shane queried as he looked down pointedly to her skirt pocket where she'd secreted the piece of paper.

"I don't know where or why you've gotten the impression that you're the king of my universe, Shane, but you couldn't be more wrong," she grated out between clenched teeth. "Haven't you done enough damage to my family?"

"If you would have just let me explain about Joey instead of acting like a spoiled little brat, I would have. Those phone records my agents uncovered were solid evidence that Joey was involved in the theft ring, Laura. An informant gave my agents a tip that the members of the theft ring used a common calling card to talk about plans for their jobs. The records show that Joey repeatedly contacted Huey and Vince Lazar, among others, in several cases just before and after successful heists. They show him making calls to known jewelry, fur, and rare coin fences, in addition to a lock company that's been known to make keys for thieves. What did you want me to do? I told you from the very beginning neither one of us could save Joey if he was truly involved."

He took in the stunned look on Laura's face and wondered if Shelly hadn't fully explained all the charges against Joey.

"There has to be some kind of mistake," she said.

"There's no mistake. The judge agreed my agents provided more than ample evidence against Joey for an indictment."

"He's been set up!" Laura exclaimed heatedly.

"Set up by whom?"

"I-I don't know."

"Ah, come on, Laura. You're going to have to do better than that," he goaded.

"Fuck you."

"If you're not going to give me anything else worthwhile, that'll work just fine for now," Shane muttered viciously before he palmed the back of her head and sunk his tongue between her lips. When she tried to rise up off the chair he pushed her shoulders down and kept her in place for his punishing kiss.

He'd been going mad with worry and anxiety . . . with longing for her. At night when he lay alone, thoughts of making love to her would plague him ruthlessly until he'd finally give up and get out of bed, eventually falling asleep on the couch in his den in the wee hours of the morning. He kept seeing her rare, luminous smile when she looked up at him while she lay in his arms, kept recalling in far too much graphic detail the feeling of her trembling in orgasm as she lay in his lap before the fire, giving herself to him despite her nearly tangible fear in doing so.

He'd started to wonder if he'd been born with a hard-on.

She kept a goddamned sculpture she'd made of him ages ago displayed in prominence in her studio, for Christ's sake. How stupid did she think he was, trying to convince him that he meant nothing to her?

"You told me you were mine," he accused savagely against her lips when he finally felt her stop fighting the kiss.

"I lied," she whispered as she looked up at him with shiny eyes. "I would have said anything to get away from you."

He shook his head slowly. "You would have said anything to escape the *truth*. I don't care what you say with that lying mouth, Laura. You are mine."

She cried out softly when he kissed her again, the muted sound reminding him poignantly of a wounded creature. Despite that sad sound, her hands were all over him, as though she'd been as starved for the sensation of touching him as he was her. He growled at the realization and reached down to lift her skirt to her hips.

A bubbling brew of emotions surged up in him, even more powerful than that night he'd taken Laura on the couch in her living room. As impossible as it seemed, Laura seemed just as wild and desperate as him, making him wonder how big the explosion would be when their erupting emotions combined.

Laura gasped when he worked his fingers beneath the silk panties she wore, seeking out her delicious heat. She bit like a wild, trapped animal at his lips, chin, and jaw when he tried to gain entry to her body, her small, scraping teeth hurting him a little and arousing him a lot. She shifted her hips in the chair, altering the angle of them so he could plunge into her slit.

Their desperate groans merged in the humid air next to their parted, touching lips. She'd been moist on the exterior but inside her pussy was filled with warm cream. He held her gaze as he stroked her and they panted into each other's mouths. A fine tremor arose in her flesh when he whisked his finger out of her pussy and spread her abundant juices onto her erect clit.

"Shane? Please?"

He shook his head incredulously when he heard her beseeching tone. "You *ask* me? You *beg*? I'm yours, Laura. None other's. I always have been."

Her beautiful face stiffened into the determined lines of a warrior. She reached for him, unbuckling his belt and unfastening his pants, her movements hasty and frantic. She pushed the pants down over his hips and shoved her hand into his boxer briefs.

Shane clamped his eyes shut at the feeling of her hand closing around the root of his swollen cock. He regretfully removed his fingers from Laura's weeping sex and straightened slightly. She watched herself as she withdrew his erection from his boxer briefs, but Shane couldn't keep his eyes off her face as she stared at his cock. She licked her lower lip as she stroked him, her green eyes glowing with sensual hunger. She spread a hand on one of his tensed ass cheeks and squeezed, pulling him closer to her.

He moaned when she flicked her wrist, pistoning his cock rapidly with her fist, smearing her fingers in a stream of pre-come and spreading it on the head until it glistened. Shane pushed his boxer briefs down his thighs and gripped the root of his cock, pumping himself with short strokes while Laura focused on the end. They carried on like that for a moment, the silence broken by Shane's grunts of pleasure as Laura became more insistent.

"I want to come inside your pussy so bad I can taste it. But I don't have a condom," he muttered miserably as she continued to jack his cock with cruel precision.

"I just finished my period. The chances of pregnancy are negligible. Just don't come inside of me."

"Ahh, baby, don't tempt me," he implored, already imagining the sheer nirvana of what it would be like to be naked in her hot, shrink-wrapped pussy.

Her pumping fist on his cock slowed and then stopped altogether. Something slid across Laura's features . . . something he didn't understand.

"You're worried I'm going to give you something, aren't you?" she asked.

"What?" Shane mumbled.

She let go of his cock. "You think I might have a disease or something . . . because of those tapes you heard . . . because you think I'm so promiscuous."

Shane blinked, recognizing her expression as hurt. He shook his head incredulously.

"Why deny it? What man in his right mind would have unprotected intercourse with a woman who had sex with so many men? Isn't that what you were thinking?"

"Laura—"

"You are *such* an asshole, Shane," she bit out viciously.

He gaped at her as he tried to wrap his mind about what was occurring. She'd been more than eager—even suggesting he fuck her without a condom—and now . . .

"I'm an asshole because I thought of protected sex?"

"No," Laura whispered at the same time that she shoved hard on his stomach with a sharp elbow. He grunted in pain and stepped back from the chair. She stood and darted around him.

"You're an asshole because you never miss a chance to lecture me about *trusting* you and *giving in* to what's between us . . . and all along, you have no compunction about giving me nothing . . . not even the benefit of the doubt. You have no difficulty painting me as a slut in your mind. You want me to trust you completely and then call me a whore with your next breath, isn't that right, Shane? Every man wants a whore in his bed."

"I never called you that."

"No, but you *think* it," she shouted. She moved several feet away from him, her stance wary. "*'That's right, Laura, suck him nice and deep like a good little wife. Show him how nice we treat our guests.'* Sound familiar, Shane?"

He panted shallowly as he stared at her. *Jeez, how had this gone from heaven to hell in five seconds flat?* Shane wondered in bemusement. He slowly drew his underwear over his throbbing erection.

"I was wrong to taunt you with my knowledge of those tapes. I was furious . . . hurt," he conceded.

She crossed her arms beneath her breasts defensively.

"Do you actually believe that even if that *was* me recorded on those tapes you could really get past the idea that I'd done those things with other men? You're supposed to be the expert on human behavior. How likely is *that*, Shane?"

He just gaped at her. She shook her head in disgust. "Like I said, you are *such* an asshole," she added, her contempt so thick he could have sliced it with a knife.

But Shane's mind was fixated on something else entirely.

"What do you mean, *'even if that was me recorded on those tapes'*?" he asked slowly.

CHAPTER **TWENTY**

Laura dropped her arms and held them rigidly at her sides, her nails biting into the palms of her hands. She welcomed the pain. It helped clear her vision from the blinding haze of fury she experienced.

God, she hated Shane in that moment . . . even more so than she had when she heard him tell Shelly that Joey was being charged with a federal crime. Yes, *hated* him, despite the fact that she was crazy in love with the jerk.

It felt as if her rage could set her hair aflame.

"It . . . means . . . that . . . it . . . wasn't . . . me . . . you . . . ass," she explained, enunciating each word succinctly. "It means that Huey must have known the FBI was listening and thought it'd be a good joke on you. *That's* what it means."

"But—"

"There's no buts about it. It wasn't me. So it's not too much of a stretch for me to believe it wasn't Joey making those phone calls either! If they could set me up, try to hurt me . . . why not Joey? Huey purposefully staged that little scene in the basement—probably with one of his many whores colluding with him—knowing that Shane Dominic would eventually hear the tapes. He and his friends probably thought it was great fun, even if they did feel you breathing down their backs for their crimes. You yourself told me that you never learned anything of consequence from the surveillance in the basement. You didn't discover anything because he knew you were listening."

"Do you mean to tell—"

"Get out."

He paused in the process of moving toward her. Laura took advantage of his moment of hesitation and dodged past him. She rushed to the front door of the gallery and flung it open, knowing Shane dogged her heels.

"Get *out* and stay the hell away from me," she shrieked, knowing she hung on the slick fibers of the last strands of her final rope. "If you want to get yourself killed, so be it, but I won't have you hurting anyone else that I love because you want to get your rocks off."

Laura experienced a moment of regret and trepidation for her hurtful words when he flashed a dark glance from beneath his lowered brow as he zipped up his pants. Knowing she'd accused him of selfish lechery when she was just as guilty hardly helped her frothing emotions. His cock still looked thick and full. She could even make out the rim beneath the mushroom-shaped head pressing tightly against the fabric of his dark gray dress pants. It'd felt so good stroking him in her hand, having him at her mercy while he stared down at her with hot, wanting eyes.

Then he'd had to go and ruin it all by reminding her that he thought her promiscuous enough to act in the way she did with him with *any* man. With one doubtful look he'd ripped away the special quality, the uniqueness of how she responded to *him* out of a love she could never hope to deny . . . despite the undeniable necessity of doing precisely that.

Laura couldn't take waging this constant battle anymore. So many emotions warred inside her breast she felt as though she'd literally explode from the friction.

"Why didn't you just tell me it wasn't you on the tapes?" Shane asked when he'd finished buckling his belt.

"Because you're so sanctimonious and cocky you wouldn't have believed me. Just like you don't believe Joey."

"Joey's not claiming his innocence, Laura. The agent in charge of the investigation thinks she can get him to plead guilty and give evidence against other people who were involved in hopes for a lighter sentence."

Laura's heart seized. "You lie."

"Why would I lie about that?" he asked bitterly.

Laura didn't have the wherewithal to respond. Joey had given no indication of anything like this when she'd visited at the house for the past few days. Of course, she'd hardly given him the opportunity, being cheerful and optimistic about his eventual acquittal. He'd been pale and withdrawn, but that hardly surprised her given the circumstances. The concept of Joey being guilty, of him colluding with Huey and Moody, made her feel like vomiting.

It *had* to be a setup.

Shane placed his hand on her jaw and stepped closer.

"I would have believed you, Laura. I would have loved to believe you. You didn't tell me the truth about that orgy in your basement for a reason, and it wasn't because you thought I was too smug to believe you. You let me believe it because it aided your cause for me to believe it."

"Leave!" She was mortified when she sobbed, the noise sounding ragged, harsh, and miserable to her own ears. She shut her eyes tightly, wishing like hell he would just walk away . . . tormented because she also knew that was the last thing she wanted.

"I don't think so," Shane murmured, his tone no longer cold and angry. *Oh no,* she couldn't mount a resistance against his compassion, against his tenderness. Not at that moment, she couldn't. She was too raw . . . too confused.

"Open your eyes, Laura."

Slowly she pried open her eyelids. A shudder went through her when she read the message in Shane's fiery blue eyes. She felt her emotions bubbling at the back of her throat, burning and scoring the tissues. She feared they would literally explode out of her mouth in a rushing torrent of love, fear, fury, and honesty.

"Shane, I'm afraid—"

His head went around like a hound's that had caught the scent.

"Shit."

A series of sounds, sensations, and images impinged on her consciousness all at once. Shane grabbed her and pushed her into the gallery, falling heavily on her body. A sound like two firecrackers popped in quick succession before a car's tires screeched as they bit into the pavement, the elevated metal tracks of the L making the noise echo eerily on the empty street.

Laura stared at Shane in rising confusion as he withdrew his weapon from his shoulder holster, wincing as he did so. He grabbed her and slid her body across the slick wood floor, leaving her to rest at the wall between two windows.

"Stay down and don't move."

"Wha . . . what . . ." Laura never got out a coherent question before Shane had army-crawled over to the door, then shut and locked it.

When he reached for his cell phone Laura saw the blood on his white shirt.

"Shane!" she shrieked. She slid up on her knees and started to crawl toward him.

He moved quickly. The next thing she knew he was back on top of her, both of their bodies against the wall. Laura stared at the spreading crimson flower on his shirt. She could smell his blood—sweet and metallic. Horror rushed through her veins like ice water.

"Oh my God, oh my God, you were shot."

"Laura."

She couldn't remove her eyes from the growing stain of blood. She'd done it once again. The first time she'd killed Peter and now Shane—

"Laura."

Laura jumped at Shane's barking voice, her gaze flying to

his face. He didn't look like he was dying. He looked worried as his blue eyes scanned her face.

"Baby, it's not bad," he spoke softly, now that he had her attention. "I'm gonna be fine. A bullet grazed my shoulder. The blood's leaking down to my chest. I need to call the police, now. Are you going to be okay?"

Laura nodded, staving off her panic. The last thing Shane needed was for her to flip out on him. "Of course I am. I'll make the call."

He examined her closely for a second before he passed her the phone. "You call it and give it to me when they come on. I need to give my badge number."

Laura recognized that he encouraged her because he wanted to distract her, get her to focus on something besides the blood soaking his shirt. If that was the case, it helped. Laura felt a little more grounded by the time Shane hit the disconnect button on his cell phone.

"I think you should lie on your back, Shane. And . . . and we need to use something to apply pressure to the wound."

Shane stopped her when she reached between their bodies and began unbuttoning her blouse.

"If you want to take off your blouse, I'm all for that. But there's no need to ruin it for this little scratch." She slapped away his restraining hand and continued to unfasten her blouse. "Laura, look at me."

When she did he leaned down and kissed her.

"Shane." Laura tried to twist away, scandalized by the fact that he wanted to make out when he'd just been shot. He chuckled next to her lips.

"I told you . . . there's nothing for you to get so upset about. It's just a scratch. They bleed the most. Whoever shot at us wouldn't be stupid enough to hang around." He plucked coaxingly at her immobile lips. "Come on, baby, kiss me. I can't think of anything I'd like to do more while we wait for the ambulance."

"I know what you're doing. You're trying to distract me," Laura mumbled while he nibbled at her lower lip.

"Is it working?"

She met his blue-eyed stare. A shudder went through her as she gently put her hands on his back, embracing him with all of her being. Her heart seemed to expand in her chest as she sent up a silent plea to heaven to keep him safe.

"Yes," Laura lied, before she craned up to meet him, her kiss every bit as fervent as her prayers.

CHAPTER **TWENTY-ONE**

L aura Mays?"
Laura looked up from where she was sitting in the emergency room of Rush University Medical Center. An attractive African-American woman in her late thirties with a smooth, rich brown complexion stared down at her. Laura recognized her as the woman who had accompanied Shane when he came to her house after the break-in.

"Yes. I'm Laura Vasquez."

The woman put out her hand. "I'm Special Agent Mavis Bertram. I work with Dominic at the Bureau." She flashed a white grin as Laura shook her hand. "More correctly, I work *for* him. I understand you've known him since you were both kids."

"Yes," Laura agreed as Mavis sat down in the gray plastic chair next to her.

"So I guess you can tell me if he's always been this stubborn or if he acquired it at some later stage. He's back there bossing that poor resident around, insisting he's not going to stay in the hospital overnight, and if they don't want to give him the instructions for dressing his wound right now, he'll just leave and wing it."

"Oh, no," Laura muttered.

They'd allowed her to wait with Shane until the resident came to examine him in the emergency room. A Chicago cop had taken down both of their accounts of the shooting incident before the doctor arrived.

Laura'd sagged with relief when the physician—who, in Laura's anxiety, looked as if he was only a few years older than her niece, Carlotta—explained that Shane's wound was superficial, although the bullet was still lodged at the surface of Shane's deltoid muscle. Her relief had only amplified when the charge physician examined Shane and concurred with the resident's opinion.

They'd given Shane a local anesthetic in preparation of removal of the bullet and asked Laura to go to the waiting room. She'd reluctantly left Shane. She stood now upon hearing Mavis Bertram's news, intent on talking some sense into Shane.

He couldn't just walk out of the hospital when he'd just been shot, for Christ's sake!

Special Agent Bertram put a hand on her shoulder, stilling her.

"Do yourself a favor and don't bother. While I'm beginning to suspect Dom would listen to your advice above all others, this is one instance when your pleas will fall on deaf ears."

"Why is that?" Laura asked as she slowly resumed her seat.

"Because he won't allow himself to be holed up in the hospital while you're in danger."

Laura's mouth fell open in disbelief. "While *I'm* in danger? He was the one who was shot."

Special Agent Bertram studied her with a penetrating brown-eyed gaze. Laura easily sensed the woman's intelligence . . . her toughness. "Dom thinks the shots were meant for you. He told me about Telly Ardos being at your gallery just before the incident."

Laura shook her head hastily, desperate to correct the misunderstanding. "No . . . *no*, it wasn't Telly Ardos. I don't believe that. And whoever *was* shooting that gun was aiming for Shane, not me."

Bertram straightened in her chair, her expression growing dead serious. "How do you know that, Ms. Vasquez?"

"I-I just do. Who would want to kill me?"

"Dom seems to think whoever is in charge of the racketeering operation at the CPD is responsible. He thinks you know something that could make you dangerous," Mavis Bertram replied in a flinty voice.

Laura met the other woman's stare.

"You didn't answer my question, Ms. Vasquez."

"What question?"

"The one about how you knew it was Dom the shooter was aiming for."

"It just makes sense. Shane has spearheaded this whole CPD investigation."

"As the leader of the Organized Crime Squad, I'm actually in charge of it. I haven't noticed anyone taking potshots at me. No . . . I think Dom got shot because of his relationship with you, Ms. Vasquez."

Laura held the agent's stare for a long moment. Bertram clearly was suspicious of her, furious at her, even, for putting Shane in harm's way. Obviously she thought the world of Shane, which didn't surprise Laura in the least. Shane inspired respect and loyalty wherever he went.

"I would do anything in my power, *anything* to ensure Shane Dominic's safety," Laura stated hoarsely. "If you think I'm a threat to him in any way, tell him to stay away from me."

Bertram's brows furrowed as she studied Laura. Finally she exhaled slowly, her smooth face hardening into a mask. "Trust me. I already have. Much good it'll do. Dom also told me you think your brother Joey is being set up."

Laura nodded.

"What makes you think that?"

"I just know Joey wouldn't do the things you've accused him of, that's all."

"That doesn't give me much to go on, Ms. Vasquez."

Laura stared at her hands in her lap before she met Bertram's gaze. "I realize that. Shane said the same thing. I'm going to try to get you the proof that you need."

Special Agent Bertram's eyebrows rose on her forehead. "Better just to tell me what's on your mind . . . what you suspect. I don't advise you trying to get any proof yourself. These men are dangerous. If they suspect you're gathering evidence against them they're going to . . ." Mavis's eyes widened. "Is *that* why you were shot at?" she demanded.

"I told you. Those shots were meant for Shane," Laura said, her gaze entreating the other woman to believe her.

"Is this all you're going to say about the matter?"

"Yes. For now." Laura glanced up in time to see Shane walk through the swinging doors that led to the ER, his left arm in a sling to keep it immobile. His blue eyes immediately found her in the crowded waiting room. He looked a little peaked beneath his dark complexion, but his step was brisk, his expression sharp. She distantly marveled at his strength and vibrancy. Laura would never guess in a million years he'd just been shot. She'd thought the same thing a thousand times in the past few hours, mostly while Shane had kissed her thoroughly while they waited for the ambulance. By the time the wailing sirens had stopped outside her gallery he'd had a steamy look in his blue eyes and his cock had throbbed next to her sex and belly.

The man was a force of nature.

Special Agent Bertram glanced over to where she was staring and then back to Laura's face. She spoke quietly.

"I guess I have no choice but to give Dom the benefit of the doubt when it comes to you, Ms. Vasquez. But I don't trust you. And if anything happens to him, and I find out you were in any way responsible . . . better watch your back."

Laura didn't respond as they both stood to greet Shane. She understood perfectly. And she sensed Mavis Bertram knew that about her as well.

Mavis said her good nights in the hospital lobby several minutes later. Laura and Shane both watched her push through the lobby doors, then turned to look at each other at the same moment.

"Are you in pain?" she asked.

He shook his head. "Laura, about what you said back there at the gallery—"

"I don't want to talk about that now, Shane," she exclaimed. "You've just been *shot*."

"By a bullet that was meant for you. Someone's been blackmailing you, haven't they, Laura? That's why you let me believe it was you on those tapes. You were using Huey's trick to keep me at a distance. Don't you think it's time you told me the truth, or do we have to wait until one of us is in the morgue before you see the wisdom in trusting me?"

He cursed under his breath for his harshness when she paled notably. "Shit. I'm sorry. I shouldn't have said that. I'm never going to let anything happen to you."

"You let something happen to Joey."

"I told you from the beginning there were no strings I could pull for Joey if the evidence against him was incriminating. Now I'm willing to listen to what you have to say on the matter, but as things stand, there was more than enough evidence against Joey to arrest him."

Her shoulders sagged. Her pallor alarmed him, but it also served to highlight the dark pink color of her full lips. He'd kissed her thoroughly at the gallery, deepening their natural color even further. He found himself staring at her mouth, thirsty for her sweetness once again, longing for the heady sensation of her lips molding to his own . . . of her giving herself to him.

"I'm hungry," he mumbled, his eyes still on the pink bow of Laura's mouth. He cleared his throat when he realized he was staring. "Let's go get something to eat. But first, there's someone here you might like to see."

He saw her hesitate and figured she was thinking up an excuse to leave. He wasn't going to let her get away easily, though. He grabbed her elbow and steered her toward a bank of elevators.

After the shooting tonight, Shane'd had good reason to

request an agent be put in charge of tailing Laura for protective purposes. Mavis and he had both agreed the surveillance was needed and that the agent should stay in the background. Their motivations for Laura's secret surveillance were different, though. Shane knew she was in danger, but also guessed that Laura would never agree to have someone shadow her.

Mavis, on the other hand, wanted Laura followed because she didn't trust her.

Shane knew that Laura was innocent of any wrongdoing, so Mavis's suspicions didn't bother him overly much. Mavis was just concerned about him, that's all.

The important thing was for Laura to have twenty-four-hour protection. But FBI surveillance aside, Shane planned on having Laura as near to him as he could possibly manage given their work schedules.

Now that Laura was talking to him again, she was *not* going to be spending her nights alone, even if it meant tying her up to his bed like he had at the cabin. Besides, she'd been so close to breaking down and telling him her secrets tonight. Shane could almost taste the truth like a vapor flavoring the air between them.

At that very moment, however, Laura looked predictably hesitant about being by his side.

"Shane, I wanted to make sure you're all right but I can't stay."

He glanced down significantly at his arm in the sling as the elevator door opened with a ding. He felt like an idiot wearing the damn thing, but for the moment the obvious testament to his injury aided his cause with Laura.

"I told the doctor I had someone to help me change the dressing."

He nudged her toward the elevator while she eyed his shoulder and chewed at her lower lip indecisively.

"Surely the dressing doesn't need to be changed tonight," she reasoned.

He shrugged and winced in an exaggerated fashion, gratified to see Laura's face crease with concern.

"It will need to be changed in the morning before work.

And I'll need someone to help me out with things until I get used to it."

Laura scowled but he hit the button for the sixth floor, causing the doors to close before she could flee.

"Who would we be visiting in the hospital?" Laura asked. Her green eyes widened in alarm. "*Elizabeth* isn't here, is she?"

Shane nodded.

"Oh, Shane. I'm so sorry . . . and with everything else going on as well," she whispered, her eyes dropping to his shoulder.

"She had another stroke but it was a minor one. She's supposed to be released tomorrow. You'll see for yourself, baby. My mom's tougher than she looks," Shane added when he fully took in her stricken expression.

"But won't it upset her to know you were shot?"

"It'd upset her more if I didn't bring you to see her."

He was surprised to see Laura nervously smoothing her skirt and hair once they got off the elevator. He squeezed her upper arm in a reassuring gesture.

"What are you worried about? You look beautiful."

"It's just I haven't seen your parents for so long . . ."

Shane thought he understood when she trailed off uncertainly. The last time Elizabeth and Alex Dominic had seen Laura, she'd been involved in a passionate love affair with their son—only to abruptly marry another man, leaving their son decimated in the process.

"Are you sure your mother will want to see me?"

"Yes."

Despite the conviction in his tone, Laura still looked nervous when Shane led her to his mother's private room and knocked on the open door.

"Look who I brought to see you," he called out as he pulled Laura, whose body had gone stiff as a board, into the hospital room with him.

Elizabeth Dominic sat up in bed while her husband sat in a chair beside her. Laura was saddened to see how thin the older woman's wrist looked where it lay in Alex Dominic's hold. Her brilliant blue eyes sharpened on Laura, however, and Laura sensed the power of Shane's mother's vibrant spirit.

A small, knowing grin curved her pale lips. The slight droop in Elizabeth's left cheek, a remnant of her most recent stroke, couldn't prevent the radiance of her widening smile.

"Laura Vasquez. I hoped I'd have the pleasure of seeing you walk in my door again one day."

For a few seconds Laura's throat was clogged with emotion as she held Elizabeth's gaze.

"Elizabeth. Alex. It's . . . it's so good to see you again," Laura murmured with feeling. She freed her hand from Shane's grip and approached the bed. Alex stood to his full height, which was within a hairsbreadth of Shane's six feet and three inches. Laura gently kissed Elizabeth's cheek before she turned to Alex, giving him a big hug.

"How are you feeling, Elizabeth?" Laura asked once Alex had released her from his hearty embrace.

"The only thing I'm suffering from at the moment is a healthy case of homesickness. And seeing your face has gone a long way toward alleviating that."

"Told you she'd be glad to see you," Shane said from behind her.

"We were sorry to hear about your husband's death," Alex consoled.

"Thank you," Laura murmured, looking away uncomfortably.

"What happened to you?" Alex boomed. Shane's parents both stared at their son's sling. Shane shook his head dismissively.

"This? It's nothing. A scratch. They patched me up in the ER and told me to get out of the way and make room for people who were really sick."

Laura glared at Shane for his blatant lie. Still, she said nothing. He obviously just didn't want to overburden his parents with more worries.

Alex insisted on getting more chairs for them. Laura's

anxieties in regard to how Shane's parents would react to her being there with their son had vanished by the second minute of conversation. Alex and Elizabeth Dominic were two of the warmest, kindest people she'd ever met.

It especially did her a world of good to see Elizabeth. They'd always been kindred spirits. Laura was touched to learn that neither time nor circumstances had damaged her love for Shane's mother.

Nor, it would seem, Elizabeth's love for her.

The realization made something squeeze tight in her chest. How many years had Laura lost . . . years she might have shared a special relationship with this woman who she'd once considered as dear as a mother? She was embarrassed to see that Elizabeth noticed when she surreptitiously wiped a tear from her cheek.

"Why don't you and Shane walk down to those vending machines down the way and get us all something to drink?" Elizabeth suggested to Alex.

Shane stood with his father—two big, handsome men whose relationship to each other was poignantly obvious. Shane cast a sidelong glance at Laura before he followed his dad.

"A room seems to go hollow in their absence, doesn't it?" Elizabeth said.

Laura smiled tremulously. Hollow . . . yes. That's what her life had been for the past thirteen years. Hollow was what you were when you weren't only empty, but you knew precisely what *should* have been in that gaping hole in your spirit.

"Come closer," Elizabeth beckoned. She patted the side of her bed when Laura rose and came to her bedside. When she sat, Elizabeth took her hand. Laura smiled when the familiar scent enveloped her.

"I'd forgotten you always wore Shalimar."

"It's hard for us old dames to change our habits." Elizabeth paused for a moment to study Laura's face. "Things have just been hard on you in general, haven't they Laura?"

Laura felt herself blushing beneath a stare that was both

penetrating and kind at once. She opened her lips and it just came out without her ever intending it to—the truth.

"Yes," she whispered.

A piercing awareness of her loss sliced into Laura at that moment. Elizabeth's hold on her hand tightened in sympathy for her grief. Elizabeth finally broke the full silence.

"Do you know when Alex first asked me to marry him I was eighteen years old? He was a first-generation Italian, so handsome the devil would have been jealous. When we met he was working at a men's clothing store on Michigan Avenue, putting himself through college. I'd accompanied my father to the store while he was fitted for several new suits."

Laura smiled as she tried to picture it—the tall, good-looking, dark young man and the delicate, fair, Irish princess. Laura knew Elizabeth's father had been a baron of finance and industry and that as an only child Elizabeth had been an heiress of a vast fortune. Elizabeth and Alex would have been leagues apart socially and economically, but none of that had mattered when they'd first looked into each other's eyes.

Laura wagered none of that would have even existed.

"You two must have been blown away by each other."

Elizabeth gave a toothy grin that made her look years younger. "We fell madly in love. My parents forbid me to see Alex. I defied them, of course, and dated him behind their backs. He asked me to marry him seven different times. I was scared to accept, you see. Fearful of the unknown. I loved him, but what would it be like to live with no money, no health insurance . . . no *guarantees.*"

"So what happened?" Laura asked.

"Well I married him anyway, of course. Who could have resisted him for long?" They both laughed. "My parents disowned me at first. They didn't come around until later. I'd finished college by then and Alex was in law school. He worked part-time at the university library and I worked as a guide at the Art Institute." Her eyes gleamed when they met Laura's. "They were some of the best years of my life."

Laura squeezed her hand in shared understanding.

"I always regretted the years I didn't spend as Alex's wife because I was afraid. I should have had more faith in him."

Tears blurred Laura's vision as she stared down at their joined hands. Elizabeth had been talking about much more than her and Alex's romance. She started to speak once but found her throat was closed. Her second attempt was more successful.

"Elizabeth, I want you to know . . . Shane and I . . . everything that happened back then . . . it's got nothing to do with faith."

"No. It's got *everything* to do with faith."

Laura raised her head at Elizabeth's steadfast tone. It felt as if her warm smile was a benediction. She glanced down in surprise when Elizabeth reached up and slipped a cool, elegant finger beneath the chain around her throat, lifting the necklace out of her blouse. If Laura had to describe the expression on Elizabeth Dominic's face when she studied the green pendant it would be "smug satisfaction."

"I'm so pleased you wear the emerald."

The hairs on the back of Laura's neck stood on end. Was Elizabeth all right? They must be tiring her with their visit. She was losing touch with reality.

"Elizabeth, you should rest."

"It's been in my family for three generations, you know," Elizabeth continued as though she hadn't spoken. "Well . . . Shane is the fourth, actually."

"Elizabeth . . . it's just a piece of paste. Huey gave it to me years back."

"No. Shane gave it to you. He asked for my permission to do it when he realized that awful man had copied my design for the setting and stolen the emerald. It all happened years ago. I got back most of my jewelry, including the emerald. The jeweler was caught, of course. I think Shane looked into that criminal's records and saw your husband had purchased a copy—a fake. Shane was angry at you for marrying Huey Mays. Bitter. Still . . . he couldn't bear the idea of you being fooled."

As Laura stared into Elizabeth's eyes she got the strangest

feeling that somehow Elizabeth knew the truth. She was talking about more than Huey giving her a piece of fake jewelry. Despite the fact that she still whirled with confusion, she muttered, "I was never fooled. I always knew the truth."

Elizabeth shook her head slowly and held up the pendant. Its captive fires flashed in the dim light.

"No. Here is the truth. I don't understand why you married that man, Mays, but I'm guessing whatever the reason, there was tragedy and heartache involved. I don't know precisely what's happening between you and my son now, although all I have to do is look into Shane's eyes to know he's even more in love with you than ever. What I know for certain is that I found a precious family gem that I'd long ago planned to give to Shane for his wife. I found it worn next to your heart. What finer truth is there than that, Laura?"

Laura gaped in dawning amazement. Elizabeth's moist eyes flickered over her shoulder. Laura turned to see Shane watching them, his puzzled gaze dropping to where Elizabeth held the emerald in her hand. She saw his strong throat muscles convulse as he swallowed. Something he'd said at the cabin came back to Laura at that moment.

The thief's name was Orvantes. The way I found out about that wasn't professional. The incident became personal—on more levels than one.

Shane's eyes rose slowly to meet hers. Laura stared in disbelieving awe at the truth she saw in his gaze.

Alex cleared his throat loudly and Laura realized she'd been caught in Shane's soulful stare for an untold amount of time. She stood shakily.

"I . . ." She began before she glanced back at Shane. "We probably should be going so that you can get some rest, Elizabeth."

"Come and visit me at home, won't you, dear? I have two gorgeous new oils from a Spanish artist I want to show you."

"I will," Laura promised as she kissed the older woman's cheek, thinking that when it came to hers and Elizabeth's relationship, at least, it was as if thirteen years had passed in the blink of an eye.

CHAPTER **TWENTY-TWO**

Shane sat on the couch and watched Laura as she walked around his study, examining his framed lithographs on the wall and the contents of his bookcase. He wondered if she was nervous being here in his home with him alone.

She'd relayed to him on the way from the hospital what Elizabeth had told her about the emerald. When she'd asked him if it were true, he'd admitted it was. He'd been a little concerned that she hadn't asked him anything about it since, just commenting on mundane topics like the convenience of the location of his Gold Coast high-rise and the comfort of his condominium.

He couldn't be quite sure what Laura was thinking as she prowled around his study with her elegant hand curled around a brandy snifter. She took a sip occasionally, but mostly she just rolled the liquor in the bowl of the glass thoughtfully.

"I can't believe all your awards," she murmured as she examined a letter of commendation for his work on counter-terrorism efforts from the United States Attorney General. She set the frame back in the bookcase and gave him a warm glance. "Or rather, I can. It just seems . . . so strange to see firsthand proof of what you've been doing all these years."

He shrugged, feeling a little self-conscious about displaying the awards and letters of commendation. In truth, there were several more that he'd never bought frames for. The few he had put up in his office were the ones he was particularly proud of.

"The federal government is pretty proficient when it comes to stamping out some words on a piece of paper. Hell of a lot cheaper way to handle things than springing for a bonus or a gold watch."

Laura turned to face him and perched her bottom on the edge of his desk. The smile she gave him made him ache with longing.

"You're not going to convince me those awards are meaningless pieces of paper, Shane. They commemorate something special—you: your courage and dedication." She took a sip of the brandy and lowered the snifter, her gaze remaining steady on him the whole time. "When did you do it?"

"When did I do what?" he asked distractedly, most of his attention on the movement of her elegant throat when she swallowed. An intimate, sensual spell seemed to have been cast between them. Their voices had become hushed, an unintentional sign of respect for the sacredness of the unfolding moment. He was almost preternaturally aware of Laura's actions, of the thrilling rise and fall of her breasts beneath her silk blouse, of the delicate pulse at her throat.

"When did you exchange the piece of paste that Huey had bought for me for this?"

His breath stuck in his throat and his cock ached dully when she placed her fingers between her breasts, parting the fabric of her blouse so that she could touch the emerald.

"Twelve years ago," he replied huskily.

She shook her head slowly, her loose hair making a sensual swishing sound against the silk of her blouse.

"Why? Why did you do it?"

He met her gaze. "I told you before. I couldn't let go of you. I *can't*."

For a stretched moment neither of them spoke.

"Even though you believed I'd betrayed you by marrying another man?"

"Are you telling me I'm a fool, Laura?"

"No. I'm not."

She set down the brandy snifter on his desk, never breaking their stare, and came toward him. When she reached him she carefully removed his glass from his hand and set it on a nearby table. Shane just watched her, made mute by longing, as she kicked off her pumps and straddled his hips on the couch, settling her weight in his lap. His good hand spread along her hip and lower back.

"You're not a fool because you were right. I never betrayed you, Shane. Not with my body. Not with my heart."

He thought of how he'd gripped on so tightly to his belief of her having sex with Huey and his friends in that basement, even though the knowledge had cut him . . . wounded him.

"I had no right to throw what I'd learned—what I *thought* I'd learned," he corrected, "on those surveillance tapes in your face, Laura. I've hardly been a monk these past thirteen years. I've had my share of women. I almost married one of them."

She shook her head in wonderment. "You believe what I said is true about Huey setting it up so that you would hear that orgy and assume it was me? You *believe*—just like that?"

He sighed. "I should have guessed the truth. Problem was, I knew what a sleaze Huey was. I also knew you'd married him. I assumed you must have shared his preferences, that you liked being dominated by him . . . being used for Huey's and his friends' pleasure. It was hell for me to think it but when I heard those tapes I felt like I couldn't kid myself anymore. I couldn't deny the truth."

"So you took me up to that cabin and tied me up to that bed, thinking if Huey could make me submit to his every demand, surely you could, as well."

He pushed on her back until she came closer. Their foreheads touched. Her long, thick hair surrounded them like a curtain. His nostrils flared to catch her singular scent. "I don't regret it, Laura. I needed to do something to break through to you."

"I don't either. And you're right. It was what I needed, to have you force me to the truth. It felt so good to give in to you," she replied in a hushed tone. "But only because it was *you*. Shane."

He gave a small grin. "Does that mean you're still going to let me tie you up?"

She wiggled in his lap, getting friction on her pussy and stimulating his cock in the process. His smile widened.

"I'll take that as a yes," he murmured. He lifted her blouse and ran his hand along the satiny expanse of her back, needing to touch her skin to skin.

He felt the fine tremor in her flesh.

"Laura, if it's true that Joey is being set up, you have to tell me what you know. You'd never forgive yourself if you didn't."

"I know." She inhaled raggedly. "I'm ready to tell you."

His hand slid beneath the waistband of her skirt, his fingers stretching to stroke the sensitive spot just above the crevice of her buttocks. She moaned softly at the intimate caress, shifting up in his lap and stroking his cock with her pussy. His erection strained against his boxer briefs, eager to be released from its confines. Laura must have felt his cock surging beneath her because she dropped a fervent kiss on his neck.

"Funny," he whispered as he turned his face, his lips brushing against her soft cheek.

"What?" Laura queried between kisses that were becoming increasingly feverish on his neck and ear. She emanated a heat that he longed to bury himself in.

"I would have guessed that when the moment came when you finally told me your secrets, when you explained to me why you married Huey Mays all those years ago, that there would have been nothing more important for me to do than to listen."

"And is there something more important, Shane?" Laura whispered as she ground her pussy against his aching cock.

"Yes." He raised his hand to her shoulder, pushing her back slightly. "You're more important than the truth. We are. I should have believed that from the beginning . . . despite how you pushed me away."

"Shane—"

"No. Let me finish. You were coerced into marrying Huey Mays. Weren't you?"

He felt her soft yes in every cell of his being. Their stare held, full and gravid.

"Because of something you knew? Something you overheard?"

Her long hair whisked across his hand when she gave a small nod.

"And I just threw you to the wolves by doing nothing. Didn't I?"

"No." She shook her head rapidly. Tears moistened her large eyes. "You did everything you could. You tried to get me to explain, but they threatened me. In the beginning, soon after my sham of a marriage to Huey, I considered telling you the truth, despite their warnings. I scheduled a meeting with you. Do you remember?"

Shane nodded. "Yes. But then Derrick wrecked the car and he and Peter were killed. I tried to talk to you at Peter's funeral to schedule another meeting, but you were too grief-stricken to consider it. Every time I tried to speak to you after that, you were so cold . . ." He paused, his mouth falling open as the truth struck him. "They were responsible for Peter and Derrick's car accident, weren't they? And you were afraid to speak to me after that for fear of more retaliation?"

This time the swish of her hair as she nodded felt like fine little blades cutting into flesh.

"Oh, *God*, Laura."

"No, *please*. Don't blame yourself," she whispered fervently when she saw his face collapse in anguish and accurately intuited the origins of his pain. "It was Uncle Derrick. He was one of the leaders of the illegal CPD operation from the beginning. And . . . and when I accidentally overheard them plotting their next theft one night in the back room at Sunny Days Derrick caught me at it and dragged me in front of all those men. He forbade me to tell the truth. They . . . they threatened me in so many ways. When I defied them, they made a point of assuring me their threats were genuine."

Shane stared at her in rising horror. "I don't understand . . . Derrick died as well in that car wreck with Peter. Are you sure it wasn't an accident?"

"Oh, yes. I'm certain of it."

"Why?"

He saw her throat constrict as if the muscles themselves had been coerced into not speaking the truth and rebelled against it even now.

"Randall Moody and Derrick both vied for the leadership position of the theft ring," Laura said in a voice barely above a whisper. "Derrick'd disagreed with Moody's decision to marry me off to Huey Mays when I discovered what they were doing—to make Huey my jailer. But Moody had overridden him. Later, when Derrick had understood that I'd been threatened with Peter's life as well, he balked. Him threatening me was one thing, but other people threatening his family outside of his jurisdiction was too much, even for a bastard like Derrick.

"Derrick's and Moody's positioning for power put Derrick at as much risk as Peter," she continued, her volume increasing some when she expressed the degree of her hatred for Derrick Vasquez. "When Huey discovered that I'd contacted you back then, soon after I'd been forced to marry him, they retaliated. One of them—I still don't know which—ran Derrick and Peter off the road into an embankment. It looked like Derrick had lost control and went off the road, but it was murder. Pure and simple."

Laura must have felt him shudder. She leaned forward and brushed her lips against his. "Please . . . please don't regret anything. What else *could* you have done given the circumstances? I gave you no reason to suspect . . . I made *sure* you had no reason to hope. I did everything in my power to turn you away. Some of the things I said were so hurtful."

Her choking sob ripped at him. "I'm the one who's sorry, Shane."

He couldn't be sure if it was his or her tears that dampened both their faces as she kissed him feverishly, but he suspected it was both. He tasted their combined misery and ecstasy on his tongue when she penetrated his lips, kissing him with a pressured intensity.

She leaned back a moment later and began frantically unbuttoning her blouse. Both of them panted shallowly when she finally parted the fabric, revealing her dewy, honey-hued skin and her full breasts encased in thin white satin and lace. The vision of her beauty made his eyes burn and his heartbeat throb dully in his cock. She touched the emerald that hung between her breasts, her heart in her eyes as she met his gaze.

"I'm the one who gave up hope, Shane. I'm the one who let evil men rule my destiny. You never did. Here's the proof of it."

"It means nothing," he said roughly. "It wasn't enough."

"It means you never gave up . . . even when I had. It means *everything*," she corrected urgently as she stood, lifting her skirt and whisking her panties down her thighs. She turned her attention to his belt and the fastenings of his pants. He watched her numbly, finally lifting his hips when she tried to drag his clothing down his thighs.

Her franticness finally pierced his fog of shock and regret. By the time she lifted his stiff cock, stroking it as she repositioned herself in his lap, her urgent need to join, to rejoice in their continued mutual existence, had spread to him as well.

It was like the night of Huey's suicide when he'd pushed her onto the couch, but with Laura being the one who demanded they acknowledge their connection despite the harsh reality that surrounded them.

She perched on her knees as she brought the head of his cock to her slick, warm slit. At that moment, Shane couldn't comprehend how he'd lived for the past thirteen and a half years without that divine sensation . . . without this sharp anticipation of joining himself to her, of blending with Laura. Pain throbbed in his injured shoulder when he instinctively tried to grab her waist to help position her.

"Stay still. Let me do this. Let me come to you, Shane."

"Laura . . ." he groaned.

"Shhh, I need you, too," she soothed shakily as she lowered down over him several inches, fixing him in her flesh. Her hands went to the back of the couch to steady herself. She looked into his face, both of them wincing at the cruelty of the pleasure as she slid slowly down his length. He felt himself stretching her warm, muscular walls, sensed her body trying to accommodate his cock even as it clasped him like a velvet fist.

By the time she sat in his lap, his cock fully enfolded in her body, both of them shook. He sensed when her muscles tensed in preparation to ride him to their fiery deaths.

"I'm not going to be able to last. It feels too good," he rasped.

"You don't need to last," she replied simply. "There will always be another time. Always."

She gave the sweetest sigh as she began to pump him with her sleek, tight pussy. He lowered his head to her breasts as she fucked him, burying his face in the fragrant valley. The emerald scraped his cheek when he turned and pressed his lips to a bobbing breast, but he welcomed the small pain, embraced it because it would help him endure this agony of bliss for just a little longer.

He pushed down the fabric of her bra, freeing the curving flesh from its confines. The material pushed up her already firm breasts into further pronouncement, the image the equivalent of distilled desire being plunged into Shane's veins. He placed his lips on the incredible softness of the inner swell as she bucked up and down on his cock with increasing force.

His face convulsed tightly as pleasure and emotion overcame him.

"There's never been another, Laura."

"Never for me, either. Let go now, love," she insisted as she dropped her weight on him, her ass smacking into his tensed thighs. His lips parted and fastened on her nipple as an orgasm slammed into him, the power of it knocking him clean out of this world for an ecstatic, interminable period of time.

When he came back to himself it was to the sensation of Laura riding his still spasming cock, fast and furious. His good hand rose to cradle her jaw. Her face looked surreal in its beauty at that moment, clenched as it was with pleasure and a love that seemed too vast to measure.

God, she was beautiful. And she was his. She always had been.

The only thing left was to hear the details of her story so he could make every last person who'd hurt her pay.

The sound of a phone ringing penetrated Laura's satiation. She slumped in Shane's lap, his cock still inside her body, her face pressed against his uninjured shoulder. Both of them still panted in the aftermath of their frenzied, pressured mating. Neither of them moved and the phone eventually stopped ringing. When it started ringing again thirty seconds later, Shane leaned his head back on the couch and groaned in frustration.

"I should probably get it. I'm technically on company time," he muttered regretfully.

Laura lifted herself off of him and reached for his jacket at the end of the couch. She found the ringing phone in an inside pocket and handed it to him. Shane glanced at the incoming number, frowned slightly, and answered it.

"Yeah?"

His dark eyebrows knitted together intently as he listened to whoever had called. Laura loved having the opportunity to study his face while his attention was so focused elsewhere. She knew she'd never tire of looking at his bold, ruggedly handsome features. She smiled when she glanced down at his lap and saw his cock lying along his thigh. He was still semi-erect and glistened with a combination of her juices and his own seed. The sight was singularly compelling. She couldn't regret that they hadn't used a condom.

Their lovemaking had been too intensely emotional . . . too special to warrant regrets.

"Has he talked to his lawyer?" Laura heard Shane ask as

she settled on the couch next to him. She gave him a small grin when he glanced down at her, but although some powerful emotion Laura couldn't identify flashed in his blue eyes, he didn't return her smile.

"Yeah . . . Okay. I'll talk to him about it—explain I can't become directly involved. We need to be careful we don't make any mistakes that would make his testimony inadmissible . . . Yeah . . . It's not like we weren't expecting this. I'll see you at headquarters in a bit."

"You have to go into work?" Laura asked when he'd hung up. The way Shane stared at the phone for several seconds without speaking made her wary for some reason.

"Yeah." His eyes rose to meet hers. "You're going to have to go with me at some point, Laura. In order to make a statement."

Her eyes dropped. "I know. I'm ready."

"I want to hear everything you have to say first," he said gently. "You can tell me when I come home later. I have to leave for a while. Joey just informed Mavis Bertram that he wants to plead guilty. He's going to give evidence against those who haven't been caught yet in hopes of a lighter sentence."

Silence reigned in the study for a taut moment.

"I don't understand." Laura sat up slowly. "How can Joey name names when he's not involved? I know he's innocent. He's been set up."

Shane's face became masklike. "I don't know, baby. All I know is he's specifically asked for me. I guess we're going to find out what Joey has to say," he said grimly as he grabbed his pants and underwear and stood, jerking them up over his thighs.

Laura put her hand on his arm. "You've got to tell him not to do it, Shane. He doesn't have to say something that's not true just to get out of this mess. Tell him we'll get the evidence to prove his innocence. Will you tell him that, Shane?"

She didn't care for the shadow of sadness that crossed his features when he looked down at her. Her hand slowly dropped from his arm. Was he *pitying* her? Her mind went back to what he'd just said on the phone before she'd understood he was talking about Joey.

We need to be careful we don't make any mistakes that would make his testimony inadmissible . . . Yeah . . . It's not like we weren't expecting this.

"You never believed me about Joey being set up?" Laura whispered incredulously. Hurt spread from her neck down to her gut like hot, liquid lead.

"That's not true. I wanted to believe you. But the evidence against Joey is overwhelming, Laura, and now—"

"You just wanted me to tell you the truth and you used Joey as an excuse to get me to do it."

Anger and incredulity pinched his features. "How can you say that to me? I wanted you to be honest—I want you to be honest with me—because it's the right thing to do. Your damn secrets have kept us apart all these years. You can't believe for a second it's right to let these criminals blackmail you."

She stared up at him, her pain and confusion making her temporarily mute.

Shane sighed, shutting his eyes in frustration for a few seconds. "Look. I need to go right now. I'll come back as soon as I can. You and I still have a lot to discuss," he reminded her as he zipped his pants. "I want you to stay right here. Double lock the door after I go and don't let anyone inside.

"Laura? Do you understand?" he probed when she just stared at him unseeingly, her thoughts whirring with the news about her brother. She delved her hand into her skirt pocket, her fingers clutching the piece of paper Telly Ardos had given her earlier today.

How could Joey possibly justify giving evidence for crimes he wasn't involved in? Was he so desperate to avoid the possibility of going to prison? Shane had said the evidence against him was strong. The thought of Joey being implicated in all this sordid ugliness on top of Uncle Derrick left her feeling weak and nauseated.

What if what Shane said was true? What if Joey had known all along how she suffered? What if he'd sold her to a miserable fate in order to beef up his bank account, or so that he could buy that vacation home in Wisconsin?

She barely contained her rising panic.

"Tell him not to do it, Shane," she begged, her voice shaking. "Tell Joey his innocence will be proven once and for all. Shane? You'll tell him, won't you?"

"Laura, I won't be the one who actually takes his testimony. I've taken myself off any formal proceedings because of Joey's and my friendship and history together. Although he's specifically asked for me, I'll have to go and explain that I can't be involved in taking his statement. But of *course* I'll encourage him to tell the truth."

"I'm going with you," she said, standing.

"No. They won't allow you to be involved in the interrogation. Now, I'm going to go wash up and leave, but I want your promise before I do that you're going to stay put until I get back."

Laura nodded rapidly, but she hardly knew what she agreed to. Her mind was completely wrapped up in one thought and one thought alone.

She had to get solid evidence against Moody . . . something he couldn't just deny like he could her or Joey's allegations. She had to stop him before he destroyed everything that was dear to her. And if the evidence truly existed, like it'd been hinted to her that it did, she might be the only one who could access it.

"Laura?" She met Shane's stare dazedly. "I know you're upset, both with me and this situation. But I want your word you'll stay here where it's safe. I want you to say it."

"Of course I will," she assured him.

He'd forgive her for lying straight to his face when she gave him all the evidence the federal government needed to prosecute the true criminals in the CPD theft ring. Shane could no longer deny the truth about Joey when he saw the proof she would lay in his hands.

And perhaps more important, Shane would be safe from Randall Moody's encroaching reach.

CHAPTER **TWENTY-THREE**

Shane stared blankly at the beige walls of one of the interrogation rooms at Bureau headquarters. It was more comfortable for him to stare at the wall than at his old friend. Even though Joey slumped in his chair like a defeated man, Shane still had to resist a primitive urge to grab his hair and slam his face into the wood table at which they both sat.

Anger tightened his throat so he cleared it before he spoke.

"This is going to kill Laura."

Joey clenched his dark eyes shut and cursed under his breath. "You think I don't know that? It's going to kill Shelly and Carlotta as well. I don't need you to remind me of that, Dom."

Shane turned his furious gaze onto Joey. "I'm talking about more than just your admission that you took part in the theft ring. Don't you get that?"

Joey looked confused. "What do you mean?"

Shane slammed the table so hard Joey jumped back in his chair. "I mean that Laura has been emotionally blackmailed by these sons of bitches for years because she discovered what they were up to. That must have been before you joined their little club. They've been threatening Laura with hurting you and your family, and she had good cause to believe them. According to her, Randall Moody had Derrick and Peter killed when she stepped out of line. She was coerced into marrying Huey Mays so he could act as her jailer all these years, ensuring she kept quiet. And she did—do you know why, Joey? Because she thought she was protecting her family. And all along, you were colluding with the assholes that threatened her . . . *hurt* her . . . murdered your own brother. That's what I mean, you selfish bastard."

Joey's lips turned white around the edges.

"I don't understand. I don't know what you're talking about. Laura never gave any indication she didn't want to be with Huey. True, I always thought it was bizarre the way they eloped all of a sudden . . . and she certainly seemed chilly toward him, but—"

"You never bothered to ask her about it though, did you?" Shane interrupted savagely. "You saw whatever you wanted to see. Laura says she's happy, so of *course* she must be."

"Jesus Christ, Dom, I'm not some kind of psychologist or a mind reader or something. Laura never indicated there was anything wrong with her marriage. What was I supposed to think?"

Shane leaned forward aggressively, both his forearms on the table. "Don't tell me you spent all that time with Huey Mays while you two were using your badges to rough up and steal from innocent people and you never noticed a thing about Mays's obsession with hookers. Or that he was a raging alcoholic and drug abuser. You're the detective, Joey. What more indication do you *need* that your sister was more than likely miserable being married to that creep? Or were you right there with Huey, enjoying all his drugs and whores?"

"Fuck you, Dom. You know how much I love Shelly."

"I don't know the first thing about you, apparently."

"If you knew all those fucking things about Laura, why didn't you do anything?" Joey accused bitterly.

Shane had slid his chair next to Joey and had his good

hand around his throat almost before the last syllable died on Joey's tongue. Joey made a choking sound beneath Shane's squeezing hand but he didn't fight him. He just stared at him with those dark eyes—eyes Shane had been familiar with for more than thirty years.

Joey gasped loudly when Shane released him. Shane stood and bolted for the door.

"I had my . . . own life to consider . . . my own problems," Joey sputtered angrily between coughs.

"I don't want to hear about your *problems*," Shane growled. "If you want to spill your guts, more power to you. I'll send Special Agent Bertram in to hear your sob story. Don't expect any special treatment on my part, though. You bought your ticket knowingly. Don't plan on coming to me now and complaining about it being a shitty ride."

Shane paused outside the interrogation room door, back against the wall, head bent, eyes closed, trying to regain his equilibrium. Rage and adrenaline pumped through his veins. He felt his boiling blood pounding in his injured shoulder, the resulting pain like a throbbing toothache.

He'd held out hope that Laura was right, that there was a small chance Joey really had been set up. Stranger things had happened in conspiracy cases like this one. He knew when he'd gotten that phone call from Mavis earlier that the chances of that were nil, however.

Seeing Laura's confusion and disillusionment when he'd told her that her brother was about to plead guilty and give evidence on his coconspirators had just about killed him. But hearing Joey confess his involvement and, at the same time, deny his knowledge of Laura's suffering had him ready to break something—most preferably Joey's face.

The thing of it was, he suspected Joey was telling the truth. He'd known Joey since he was a kid, recognized he had a tendency to cut corners to get what he wanted versus engaging in hard, honest labor. But Joey wasn't cruel by nature. He didn't—*couldn't*—believe that Joey Vasquez had knowingly conspired with his brother's murderers and his sister's jailers.

"Really shitty day all around, huh?" Mavis Bertram asked.

Shane blinked his eyes open. "Yeah. Joey's ready for you to question him, but don't get your hopes up. Mays kept him pretty insulated from Moody. Most of what he has of relevance for testimony is in regard to a few fellow officers."

"Shit," said Mavis.

"Yeah. I was actually hoping Joey knew something." It would have helped their case if Laura wasn't the sole witness against Moody.

Shane's gaze sharpened when he saw Mavis's uncomfortable expression and shifting feet. "What is it?"

"Agent Patterson just made contact."

Shane paused in the action of wiping his brow. Patterson was the agent Mavis had put in charge of tailing Laura. Was Mavis going to chew him out for taking a potential witness on her case to his condominium? He doubted it, since he hadn't yet told Mavis that Laura was going to confess—that she *had* confessed, at least partially.

"What's wrong?" Shane demanded.

"It seems that Laura Mays left your condominium soon after you did," Mavis replied, casting her gaze at the floor, probably to prevent from giving her boss an accusing stare, Shane thought. He inhaled slowly.

"Where'd she go?"

Mavis met his eyes. "The Metropolitan Correctional Facility."

"*What?*" Shane exploded.

"She completed a request to speak with a prisoner, Dom. Laura Mays is having a visit with Vince Lazar even as we speak."

Shane's mind went blank for a second. The first thought that popped into his head made his heart feel like it dropped into his gut. "Visitor conversations in federal lockup are all recorded."

Mavis nodded. "That's right. So unless your girl made an appointment to discuss the weather with her husband's old crime buddy, we're likely going to have something significant on tape."

"Let's go," Shane muttered.

What the hell could Laura be thinking? Shane thought furiously as he charged down the hallway, Mavis jogging to keep up with him. Hadn't he specifically asked her to stay in his condominium where it was safe? And instead she'd traipsed off to the MCF and requested a meeting with an accused federal felon?

Worse, if she said anything that implicated her on that tape, there wasn't a damn thing Shane could do to help her.

Yeah, this day just kept getting better and better.

Shane squinted while he watched the black-and-white video recording, not so much because the quality of the tape was poor, but because it pained him to see Laura's beautiful face—a face he considered precious and special and *his*—transmitted on a video screen for not only himself, but Mavis Bertram, John McNamara, Andre Lorenzo, and the man who handled the surveillance tapes at the MCF.

The camera angle was above and to the right of her. Although he observed her only in profile at a distance of about five feet, he sensed her anxiety as she spoke through the telephone to Vince Lazar and watched him through a pane of bulletproof glass.

"Can you replay the whole thing from the beginning?" Mac asked the technician in charge of the surveillance. "I didn't catch any of that. Were they talking in code or something?"

"They both knew they were being taped," Mavis murmured, "It's federal policy to tell visitors about surveillance. I got the impression she didn't understand what Lazar was trying to tell her, though. And what was all that stuff about 'checking with the other Cubans?' Does Laura Mays have other family members that might be involved in the theft ring? Dom?" she prompted when Shane didn't immediately answer the question she'd clearly intended for him.

Shane was busy grinding the enamel off his back teeth. God *damn* Laura for backing him into this position. He'd seen something on the tape all right—something only he, who knew Laura so well, might notice. If he said anything, though, he might get Laura into some kind of trouble. Although that would imply Laura was guilty of something . . . which he didn't believe.

Did he?

He wouldn't have initially guessed Joey Vasquez, his childhood friend and companion, could have knowingly agreed to take part in these crimes, either, even though his belief in his guilt had grown commensurately with the evidence that piled up against him.

He was furious at Laura for exposing herself this way. He stewed in a kettle of helplessness and rage. What the hell did she think she was doing by meeting with scum like Vince Lazar? And why had she gone behind his back, just when they seemed to have finally shattered the long-standing barriers that stood between them?

He stared at the snow on the video screen for a moment before he realized all the people in the room were looking at him expectantly.

"Are you okay, Dom?" Mavis asked, concern wrinkling her smooth brow. "Your shoulder bothering you?"

He didn't have any choice. He believed Laura wasn't involved, but he resented her for backing him into a corner where he might reveal something that put her in the FBI's crosshairs.

"Actually, we just need to look at the last minute of their conversation," Shane told the technician, ignoring Mavis's question. He thought of that subtle shift that had occurred on Laura's face there at the end of the recording. Understanding had hit her in that moment. She'd "gotten" whatever it was Lazar was trying to covertly tell her.

Shane's mouth twisted in anger as he watched the last part of the tape again. Vince Lazar ate up the vision of Laura like a perv at a peep show as he leaned as close to the window as possible.

"I never liked the way they treated you, Laura," Lazar muttered unctuously into the phone. "If it'd been me, I would have been sweet with you. Now I'm locked up in here with no one on the outside who gives a rat's ass. You and me are alike that way . . . our families betrayed us. So I'm gonna tell you a little secret, one that I acquired from a family member who *did* care about me, but who's no longer alive. You know I've always liked you, so I kept it there . . . close to you. Just in case the shit flew, which I knew it would. Check with the other Cubans. With that and what else you received, you'll have all the evidence you need."

The first two times Lazar had mentioned the Cubans Laura had stared at him like he was mad. Shane knew Laura's facial expressions too well not to recognize the precise moment when comprehension had struck her. She'd stiffly thanked him. Lazar had leered at her ass as she walked away, the phone dangling uselessly in his hand.

Their conversation had actually taken place less than a half hour ago.

"The details about what Vince Lazar was trying to tell her don't matter," Shane said softly when Laura and Lazar's interview came to an end once again on the video. "The important thing is that Laura understood what Lazar said. First, she'll go to her house and retrieve something. I don't know where she'll go next, but all we have to do is follow her to know what Lazar wanted her to find."

Mavis pulled out her cell phone and called the agent tailing Laura. Shane felt Mavis's gaze on him once she'd uttered a few terse sentences into the phone and hung up.

"You were right, Dom. Laura went to her house, was inside it for less than a minute or two, came out, and got in her car again. She's headed north on Ashland as we speak. I've given Patterson instructions to call us as soon as she reaches her destination."

"We'll be in the car," Mac told Mavis as he and Lorenzo left the room. "Give us a call when you find out her location."

"Dom? Are you coming?"

He stood and walked out of the room behind Mavis, Lorenzo, and Mac. Mavis gave him a wary look and let the others get ahead of them a bit. She spoke in a soft voice.

"Are you worried that if Laura finds anything the courts will say it's inadmissible evidence because of your relationship to her?"

"The thought crossed my mind. Among other things."

"We have the tape of her and Lazar talking. He's the one who tipped her off. You had nothing to do with it. If there's evidence, it'll be admissible. So don't beat yourself up about that."

Shane didn't say anything as they got on the elevator, but he'd already come to the same conclusion about the admissibility of any evidence that might be uncovered. That wasn't what had him so preoccupied.

Laura had put him in the untenable position of choosing her safety and well-being over his integrity and mission as a law enforcement officer. He couldn't lie to his staff about what he'd seen on that tape. Who knew what kind of trouble she was getting herself into? They'd just found their way back to each other after nearly fourteen years. Now she'd gone and done this.

He'd stand by her, no matter what. But he was going to turn her over his knee the first chance he got for willfully making herself a target not only for the investigators in this case, but the guilty men who had nothing to lose at this point by harming her.

Or worse.

The frightening thought galvanized him, punching through exhaustion wrought by stress and his injury.

"Call Patterson back and tell him to make sure he never loses sight of her," Shane told Mavis as they got on the elevators that led to the parking garage. "Tell him there's a possibility someone else could be following her to see where she goes after her visit with Vince Lazar."

CHAPTER **TWENTY-FOUR**

Y ou were right about Lazar holding out to tell someone what he knew. He wanted to tell Laura Mays for some weird reason. What did you see on the tape, Dom?" Mavis asked as Shane pulled out of the parking garage and headed toward Ashland Avenue. "How did you know Laura would go to her house before she went wherever Lazar suggested?"

"Laura doesn't have any family left except for Joey in the United States who qualify as 'Cubans'—even though Laura and Joey are only half Cuban. So unless Lazar wanted her to check with every Cuban émigré in Chicago, he wasn't talking about people."

"Yeah . . . so?"

"Lazar said he put whatever she needed close to her in case the shit flew. Lazar was down in that basement with Mays on any number of occasions. It was their party central. I'm hazarding a guess he referred to a humidor Huey Mays kept at his bar in the basement," Shane murmured, thinking of how he'd seen the electronically regulated storage box for cigars years back when he'd broken into Laura's home. He'd seen the same humidor recently at Huey's bar when he'd checked Laura's house following Huey's suicide.

"Cubans. He was talking about *cigars*?" Mavis asked. "What do you think Lazar put in the humidor?"

Shane shrugged as he turned north on Ashland and slammed his foot on the accelerator. Laura had quite a head start on them. "I'm guessing he hid a key of some sort. Whatever it is will give her access to something along with the information on the piece of paper Telly Ardos gave her earlier at her gallery."

"You didn't tell me about any piece of paper." Mavis shot him an accusing glare.

"I didn't get its significance until now," Shane said truthfully. "Lazar must have passed on half the information to Ardos and kept the other half to give to Laura himself. It ensured he wouldn't give away too much in the surveillance tapes."

"I don't get why he wanted to tell Laura and not us, aside from the fact that the guy was slobbering all over that pane of glass between him and Laura. Lazar obviously leches after her, but that's not a good enough reason for him to do what he did," Mavis mused.

"It's just like he said. He felt a commonality with her because they'd both been betrayed by their families. Laura told me earlier this afternoon that her uncle, Derrick Vasquez, was a leader in the cop theft ring."

"He was? So you think Lazar was talking about his cousin, Eddie Mercado? But he's dead."

"Alvie Castaneda isn't. Randall Moody isn't. Neither crime boss has stepped forward to help Vince. Both of them must think Lazar will either stay quiet or are betting his criminal background will make him an untrustworthy witness against them. Neither think he's got anything worthwhile on them. The Chicago mob and the men in the theft ring are the family Lazar referred to, and if I don't miss my guess, Eddie Mercado—Alvie Castaneda's one-time first lieutenant and Lazar's cousin—is who Lazar meant when he said he had a family member who *did* care, but was dead."

Shane stared out the front window grimly. "I'm thinking it was Eddie Mercado who gave his cousin Lazar something worthwhile on this case—something either Castaneda or Moody or both didn't know about."

"And that *something* is what Laura Mays is going after at this moment," Mavis said with dawning understanding. "But what does she plan to do with whatever it is? She thinks it'll vindicate her brother. She hinted that much at the emergency room. But Joey Vasquez is guilty by his own admission—"

"We just need to get there and fast," Shane interrupted. "I'm more worried about Moody or one of his boys tailing her like we are after her visit with Lazar. Moody knows everything that happens in this city."

Mavis flipped open her cell phone when it rang a second later. She pulled out a pad of paper and pen from the breast pocket of her overcoat. "Okay, go ahead. Got it. We should be there in ten minutes, tops."

"Tell Patterson to stay fixed unless he sees someone go in after Laura or she leaves before we get there," Shane said.

Mavis relayed his instructions to Agent Patterson and hung up before she called Mac to tell him their destination.

"Mac and Lorenzo are a few blocks behind us. It looks like you were right again, Dom. Laura pulled up at one of those warehouses where you can rent spaces for storage. It's located on Racine and Loomis. Patterson said she had a card key to get into the building."

Shane cursed when the light turned red and the cars in front of him slowed. "Shit. We're still seven or eight minutes away."

The ceiling was twenty feet high inside the warehouse although the newly built storage rooms only went up eight feet. All that open space above her head combined with the narrow hallway made Laura feel jittery, like something was looming above her, waiting for the right moment to swoop down and strike.

It was so eerily quiet she had the strangest urge to tiptoe

down the vast hallway lined with doors. She resisted the stupid temptation, however, and located locker number fifty-eight accompanied by the sound of her pumps clicking briskly on the tile floor.

She used the keypad to the left of the door to enter the seven digit code Telly Ardos had given her earlier today along with Vince Lazar's name. The light on the keypad turned green. Her breath burned in her lungs as she once again utilized the card key she'd found inserted beneath the felt lining at the bottom of Huey's humidor.

The lock on the door clicked, the noise sounding unnaturally loud in the empty, silent facility. Laura reached for the knob, her heart hammering in her chest. She flipped the switch on the wall and the room was bathed in harsh fluorescent light.

She didn't know what she'd been expecting, but the ten-by-ten-foot room stacked with boxes seemed a little anticlimactic. A quick inspection of one of the top boxes told her it was filled with what appeared to be reels of audiotape, each one labeled with a date and names. The one she picked up read: sunny days—SEPTEMBER 28, 1992, PENSACOLA, FLORIDA.

Her heartbeat pounded even louder in her ears. Sunny Days had been Derrick's restaurant, the place where Laura first overheard the cops planning for a jewelry heist. For as long as she could remember Sunny Days had been a cop hangout. For a select few, however, those meetings took place late at night in the back room.

She opened several other boxes in quick succession and saw that most of the tapes were labeled with the restaurant name.

After a few more minutes of investigation Laura realized that the tapes were arranged by year. She couldn't get back to the tapes in the far right-hand corner without clearing out the entire room to make way for herself, but a cursory count told her there must be at least fifty boxes there and they weren't all filled with audiotape. One contained electronic equipment and another bulletproof vests.

In another she found notebooks filled with writing, most

of it in a single hand. Laura couldn't be sure, but it appeared the names and drawings represented some sort of plans or worksheets for multiple-member crimes like the jewelry heists. A memory flashed into her mind's eye, a recollection that anxiety and fear had made fragmented and blurry, of Derrick dragging her before a group of eight men sitting around a table. She saw flashing images: Huey's hungry, furious gaze; Vince Lazar's lascivious expression, so unchanged from the one she'd seen today through the bulletproof glass; Randall Moody inspecting her coldly with those chilling light blue eyes as he held a pen in his hand, a notebook on the table before him.

Well, well, what's this? A sneak? Didn't your uncle ever teach you it is rude to listen in at doors, Laura? Randall Moody had asked, a small, cold smile curving his thin lips.

A shiver leapt down her spine at the memory. She forced her attention back to the notebooks. She thought she recognized some of the locations written both on the tapes and on the notebooks: Pensacola, Florida; Andersonville, Indiana; Green Bay, Wisconsin. They were the locations for some of the jewelry and rare coin exhibitions that Huey and the other cops had been accused of hitting.

Were the tapes of them planning for their heists? And if so, why in the world would the members of the theft ring purposefully make and save such incriminating evidence against themselves?

Unless somebody else besides Moody and his gang was secretly recording the meetings. But who? It couldn't have been the federal or state government or it would have been mentioned in Joey's preliminary hearing. Besides, the evidence was all locked away in private storage, not in a government facility.

Excitement fluttered in her belly. This could be it—her ticket to freedom after all these years; a guarantee of safety for Joey, his family, and Shane.

Shane needed to know about these tapes. All she could do was pray that whatever was on them was a stake to Randall Moody's heart.

She randomly grabbed two of the reels and shoved them into her bag before she shut out the light and made sure the door was locked behind her. The hallway seemed dim in comparison with the superbright lights in the storage room. It was chilly, too. Apparently the owners of the facility didn't waste money on heat. She rushed down the gloomy corridor, eager to be out of the vast, silent warehouse so she could call Shane. He'd be irritated with her for leaving his condo when she'd promised she wouldn't, but what was inside that storage facility would go a long way toward getting him over his anger.

The temperature had dropped a good ten degrees with nightfall, Laura realized when she stepped into the parking lot. The chirping sound her car made when she hit the unlock button on her key chain echoed off the surrounding warehouses and abandoned-looking brick buildings. Just as she reached for the handle of her driver's-side door, someone wrapped his forearm around her throat and jerked her head back painfully. Her scream froze in her throat when she felt the sharp edge of a knife biting into her skin.

"You've been a bad girl, Laura. Maybe Huey was right when he said we should have gotten rid of you from the first. You always were a nosy little sneak," Randall Moody murmured into her ear.

Shane parked his car a quarter of a block down the street from the storage warehouse.

"Patterson says she's still inside," Mavis said after she'd flipped closed her cell phone.

"He hasn't seen anyone else near the storage facility?"

Mavis shook her head. "Laura's car is the only one in the parking lot. All he's seen is an occasional car passing."

"You, Patterson, Mac, and Lorenzo stay put for now. I'm going to meet with her when she comes out, see if I can just talk her into showing us point-blank what Lazar wanted her to see," Shane said as he unbuckled his belt.

"Do you want me to move to a closer position to the entrance?"

Shane shook his head. "Patterson should have her in his sights once she leaves. I'll call you as soon as I know what's going on."

Laura's cry of mounting fear was cut off by the pain from Moody's knife cutting farther into her skin.

"Stop struggling or I'll finish you off here and now."

Laura went completely still, sensing the truth of his words not only in the viciousness of his tone but the sensation of warm blood seeping down her neck.

"That's better. I'm going to ease up with this knife, but don't get any ideas. I have a gun, as well."

Laura gasped for much-needed air when he released her slowly.

"Now we're going right back inside the storage facility," Moody stated from behind her.

Laura's eyes sprung wide and she cried out sharply in pain when he suddenly tightened his hold on her again, the knife pressing to the cut he'd already made on her throat.

"Drop the knife."

Laura flinched when she tried to lower her gaze to see who had spoken and encountered the barrier of Randall Moody's knife. She forced her eyes down without moving her head. When she saw a stranger wearing a gray overcoat pointing a gun at them she struggled against Moody's hold. Moody might be nearly sixty years old, but he was still strong. His forearm pressed back against her larynx, choking her, even as the knife dug farther into the side of her neck, the pain making tears rush down her cheeks.

"Drop the gun or I'll cut her throat." Moody shifted her in his arms so that Laura almost completely covered his torso and head, blocking him from a potential bullet from the man with the gun.

"I *said* drop the gun or she dies," Moody shouted more forcefully.

Laura winced in a silent agony of pain when the sharp edge of the knife dug deeper into her neck. She wanted to howl in frustration and fear when she heard the metallic sound of the man's gun hitting the gravel.

"Let her go. I'm a federal agent. I'm not the only one here. You're not going to get away," Laura heard the other man say.

Moody's choke hold tightened on her at the same moment she felt his hand moving behind her. He was trying to get at his gun! Something told her she had to move.

Now.

She elbowed Moody in the gut as hard as she could with her left arm. He grunted in pain and cursed, his body instinctively dropping to guard against the blow. His brutal hold on her gave slightly, allowing Laura to move in the opposite direction from the knife that sunk its teeth into her throat.

A shot sounded, the noise sharp and precise in the cold night air. Laura panicked at the sudden increased pressure of Moody's arm against her throat, choking her. Moody dragged her backward with him. She fell on the gravel pavement, gasping in pain at the impact. It was the fullest breath of air she'd taken since Moody grabbed her.

Moody's arm slithered down her chest. The knife slid across her coat and landed with a dull metallic sound on the gravel. She heard footsteps running toward her and tried to sit up. A wave of vertigo hit her and she fell back, her elbow hitting the gravel hard.

"Call for backup and an ambulance."

"Shane?" Laura called out, immediately recognizing that voice. She tried to sit up a second time, this time with more success.

"Keep still for a minute, baby," Shane murmured. He knelt next to her. A vision of his handsome face creased with concern swam before her eyes. He gently moved aside the collar of her blouse, wincing when he saw the blood at her neck.

"It's not deep. I'm okay," Laura assured him, her voice gruff from Moody's strangling hold. It felt like heaven when Shane gently took her into his arms, settling her against his thighs. He dug in the breast pocket of his coat and withdrew a neatly folded, crisp white handkerchief.

"Shhh, I'm sorry," he muttered when he pressed the cloth to her bleeding neck and Laura cried out in pain. "I'm trying to stop the bleeding."

"It's a scratch. They bleed the most," she quoted him. God, had it really just been this afternoon Shane'd uttered those words to her after being shot in the shoulder? She cast her gaze behind her, seeing Moody's legs sprawled on the gravel.

"Is he—"

"He's not going to be threatening you again," Shane said. "Ever."

Laura peered up into Shane's face. He looked ashen but the surrounding ambience from the city and the lights in the parking lot allowed her to see the fierce gleam in his blue eyes. She saw his pulse throbbing at his throat just above his black overcoat.

"Your shoulder . . . are you all right?" she asked.

"My shoulder's just dandy," he muttered before he leaned down and pressed his lips to her temple. "You moved away from him at just the right moment, baby. I was getting closer in the shadows of the warehouse but I couldn't get off a shot with you so close to him. Just stay still. Everything's going to be fine."

"Inside. There's a room full of audiotapes and other evidence," Laura said, her voice scraping at her raw throat. "I was going to call you about it, so you could come see it, but then Moody—" She paused, inhaling raggedly. God her throat hurt. "Take the card key and the password in my pocket. Maybe whatever is in there will vindicate Joey."

He kissed her again, this time more urgently.

"The only thing I'm going to do right now is hold you until the ambulance gets here. Then I'm going to hold you some more. Whatever's in that storage locker can wait. This can't," he murmured gruffly before his arms tightened around her waist. "We've waited long enough, Laura."

CHAPTER **TWENTY-FIVE**

The sound of Laura's sobs echoed in Shane's ears even when Mavis got up and abruptly shut off the tape recording. He blinked when Mavis shoved a cup filled with water along the surface of the table. He was hardly aware that Lorenzo, Mac, and two other agents from the Organized Crime Squad got up and filed out of the room.

"Drink, Dom."

He picked up the cup and swallowed automatically, not even one hundred percent sure of what he was doing. The sounds of a twenty-year-old Laura's screams of agony as she was beaten by Huey Mays while a group of men observed— one of them her uncle and guardian—echoed repeatedly inside his head. Through a haze of shock and rising nausea, Shane wondered if he'd ever be able to shut out those cries of pain and betrayal.

"Stay away from her neck and face, Huey, and don't scar her. There's no need to mar so much beauty unless she makes it a necessity. There's no better way to bring a woman around to your way of thinking than to threaten her with a disfigured face, you know," Moody had said to someone during Laura's beating, his tone pleasant and conversational.

You'd have thought he was chatting with friends while they watched a DVD.

But scarring Laura's beautiful face hadn't been what forced her into the prison of a marriage with Huey Mays. It hadn't been what so effectively held her tongue all these years.

"Shane?" Mavis asked cautiously.

He started out of the poisonous memories and tried his best to focus on Mavis.

"It's not your fault. You couldn't have known."

Shane just stared at her blankly for several seconds.

Mavis sighed unevenly. "I know. That hardly makes it any easier."

Neither of them said anything for several moments, both of them staring at the tape recorder. The reels, notebooks, and photos Laura had found in the storage facility contained more than enough evidence to incriminate Randall Moody and the other members of the theft ring that hadn't yet been caught.

There were ten men in total, eight of them either current or former CPD officers and one a former convicted felon named Rudy Baker, who Shane was guessing Moody used for some of the dirtier jobs, two of which were likely forcing Derrick and Peter Vasquez off the road into an embankment and another taking a shot at either Shane or Laura at her gallery several days ago. They'd found and arrested Baker in a posh Wicker Park condominium, a residence worth well over half a million dollars. Baker owned the condo despite the fact that according to the public record he'd never worked more than a year solid in his entire forty-seven years of existence.

The tenth member of the gang had been Telly Ardos. They'd issued a warrant for Ardos's arrest, but he'd obviously been forewarned of impending events by Vince Lazar and was currently nowhere to be found.

"The devils keep checks on each other, don't they?" Mavis murmured, shaking her head. "All those years Moody was masterminding the criminal activities of this little group of corrupt cops, the mob was keeping tabs on *him*, taping all his secret meetings, photographing them. Eddie Mercado must have had Lazar steal Moody's notebooks, as well. Lazar was a double agent, carrying out the orders of the mob and also working for the cop theft ring. Why do you think Eddie Mercado kept such close tabs on Moody and his activities?"

"It's just like I told you," Shane muttered gruffly. "The mob probably was involved because of the amount of money Moody was bringing in, not only from the theft ring, but from extorting bookies, drug dealers, and other petty criminals. They were probably taking a cut from Moody and wanted to ensure that they knew about everything he was involved in so they wouldn't get shortchanged. Thus, the surveillance."

Another tense silence ensued.

Mavis cleared her throat uncomfortably. "I'm . . . a . . . I'm guessing from your reaction to the tape just now you didn't know the ultimate threat they used to bring Laura Mays to heel was to threaten your life?"

Shane's eyes clamped shut when Mavis's words brought back the blistering memory of Derrick Vasquez's harsh voice.

What about your boyfriend, Shane Dominic, Laura? Did you think I didn't realize you've been letting him fuck you? Would you like to have his blood on your hands? No? Then quit your squealing and listen to how it's going to be from now on.

Laura had sobbed then on the tape, the sound cutting at Shane even deeper than her former desperate pleas for Derrick to intervene, her curses at Huey, and her subsequent grunts and cries of pain and stark betrayal as she was beaten.

After they'd threatened her with Shane's death, she'd gone quiet except for those muffled, wretched sobs.

That had been when Mavis had gotten up and shut off the tape.

Laura's reaction to what Derrick had said had been marked enough that Shane doubted men as vicious as Moody, Mays, and even Derrick himself would have had any qualms about reminding her of that particular threat whenever she stepped out of line. After Moody had ordered Derrick's and

Peter's deaths, Laura must have been literally terrified into silence.

"I never felt like I knew Derrick Vasquez as well as I did Laura's father. I may have had a suspicion about him a time or two in regard to the theft ring, but I would have *never* expected he'd turn on a family member in such a . . ." Shane trailed off and shook his head. ". . . *vicious* manner. Derrick was her guardian. Laura was his own flesh and blood. He always seemed so protective of her."

"Yeah. I'm sure from the testimony she gave here yesterday she'd long ago stopped considering him as 'family,' even though he did stand up for her there at the end when he discovered Moody and Mays were using her little brother to threaten Laura in addition to blackmailing her with your life. No wonder she was so adamant that Joey Vasquez couldn't be involved. Who'd want to believe that one brother was colluding with the other brother's murderers? Her refusal to accept the evidence came honestly." Mavis shook her head, disgust writ large on her face. "I'm glad you killed that rat bastard Moody."

Shane grunted in agreement. He'd checked Randall Moody's pulse two nights ago while they'd waited for the arrival of the ambulance but he'd never found one. He wasn't surprised. He'd been aiming for the base of the man's skull—an area that was the farthest distance from Laura and also one of the most lethal places if pierced.

Shane was typically an excellent shot. Once Laura had moved her head away from Moody's he'd seen a clear target and never hesitated. He couldn't risk merely injuring Laura's assailant for fear of his muscles seizing up or him jerking back in pain, cutting Laura's throat in the process.

The only shot that would do was a lethal one to an area of the brain that shut down all muscular control.

Instantly.

"I, uh . . . I guess Laura is still pretty upset about her brother being on a few of those tapes, huh?"

Shane nodded grimly. "She refused to talk to me yesterday when I told her."

Mavis stood from where she'd been perched on the edge of the table. "She'll come around, Shane. People do and say things under stress they don't really mean. Surely she'll come to see that her brother's involvement wasn't *your* fault."

"After her parents died, all she had left was Derrick, Peter, and Joey. Derrick betrayed her. Moody had Peter killed . . . and Derrick, too. It's no wonder she's bitter over the fact that her last family member was in league with the devil, as well."

"She's got her sister-in-law and her niece. She's got you, Dom." Mavis sighed when he didn't respond. Shane wasn't feeling so confident at this point whether or not Laura considered him as being someone she wanted in her corner.

After they'd bandaged her neck at the emergency room two nights ago and they'd both given their statements about the evidence in the storage room and Moody's death, Laura had agreed to stay with him at his condominium. They'd lain in his bed and held each other like two survivors of a catastrophic storm. She'd slept for a while, but Shane had remained awake and vigilant, thanking God for the thousandth time for the precious gift of her life.

He kept replaying those moments in his head as he'd stealthily made his way along the dark shadows of the storage warehouse, restraining himself from rushing, from moving in haste and panic and possibly attracting Moody's attention. The lights in the parking lot revealed the look of terrified shock on Laura's face, the gleam of Moody's knife . . . the blood running along the blade and down Laura's neck. He honestly couldn't have said what he would have done if Randall Moody had slit her throat right there in front of him.

The only thing he knew for certain is it wouldn't have been pretty.

When Laura had awoken later that night she'd finally spoken to him about what had happened to her so many years ago. She'd told him about how Derrick had discovered her listening in on their meeting at Sunny Days and how they'd cowed her by threatening the lives of people she loved. She explained that the men had all turned to that patriarch of that cadre of thieves and extortionists, Randall Moody, silently asking what they should do with her. And Moody, in his infinite sadistic wisdom, seeing how Laura cringed at the sight of Huey Mays, had proclaimed that she would be tied to them through Huey.

Laura had told him bitterly about Derrick Vasquez protesting at the suggestion that she marry Huey Mays. There wasn't a one of them present who didn't know the depths of Mays's depravity and seediness, especially when it came to women. But Derrick's protests had only seemed to fuel Moody's decision to "give" Laura to Mays.

Moody and her uncle Derrick had been vying for the ultimate leadership position of the gang. Laura's discovery of their illegal activities by overhearing them at the door one night after she finished cleaning up at Sunny Days had been Moody's excuse to trump any aspirations Derrick Vasquez may have had for heading up the group. Besides, Moody wanted her under his number one soldier's control—Huey Mays—versus leaving her in his adversary's domain.

"They arranged a marriage the following day, if that's what you want to call that farce of a ceremony," Laura had muttered as she lay in Shane's arms and dawn had peaked around the blinds of his room. "They said the man who presided was a priest, but I swear he was either demented, drunk, or both. I have no idea to this day if it was legal."

"What better candidate for the job at hand? And it *wasn't* legal," Shane had assured her as he had smoothed his palm over her soft hair. "If it was done under duress—which it clearly was—it wasn't a legal proceeding."

Afterward she'd slept again for a while. All the questions Shane had about how Huey Mays had treated Laura for thirteen years, living in the same house, had burned on his tongue, but he'd never asked her because she hadn't offered the information.

And maybe he was afraid of what her answer would have been.

But when she'd awakened she'd examined him in the pale morning light. "You're wondering what it was like between Huey and me, aren't you?"

He'd merely met her gaze and he knew she'd seen the answer in his eyes.

"It wasn't as bad as you're thinking, Shane," she whispered shakily. "The beginning was the worst. Huey played the part Moody wanted him to play. He'd bully me. He'd beat me on Moody's command. He'd . . . force me to have sex with him several times . . . in the beginning."

Shane had winced when she'd said those words.

"But it . . . it wasn't like what you're thinking, Shane. He couldn't. He couldn't do it."

"What do you mean?"

"Huey couldn't . . . perform unless a woman played up to his image . . . unless she screamed how wonderful he was. Once I got over my initial fear of him after he'd beat me in front of those other cops, he . . . he didn't seem to know what to do with me, to be honest with you, didn't know how to react to a thinking, breathing woman who used deodorant and had to rush to get to school or work in the morning. Women for him were just a stimulant, like liquor or drugs. He'd never lived in the same house with one. Fortunately, his reaction to the bizarre situation Moody forced him into was to essentially ignore me. In regard to Moody, Huey and I became unintentional partners. Both of us needed Moody to believe that Huey dominated and controlled me, that he kept me at heel. I wanted Moody to be convinced so I'd drop off his radar screen. The more he believed I'd come to accept my fate and had even grown attached to Huey, the less he'd consider harming the people I loved. I did my best to convince him I no longer cared about you, although I could never be sure if Moody truly believed that. Huey played along for different reasons . . . to keep up his image with Moody and the men who looked up to him.

"I confused Huey," Laura'd continued. "I was supposed to be his wife. I was a woman. But I clearly didn't want him. He couldn't compute that. He tried flattery. He tried to buy me off by giving me what he implied was expensive jewelry, but in reality were fakes. He forced me into sex several times, but I suppose because of his history of paying women for it, he couldn't become aroused without having a woman who—"

"Praised his bedroom skills to the high heavens and every friend he possessed, besides?"

"Yes," Laura agreed tremulously.

When he'd seen the look in Laura's eyes he'd tightened his hold around her.

Everything had been fine between Laura and him until later that morning when Mavis had called and requested that Laura come down to FBI headquarters to clear up some unanswered questions. She and Shane had given their statements already in regard to Moody's attack on Laura, but Laura hadn't yet given testimony about the coercion she'd endured for the past thirteen and a half years.

After she'd made her statement to Mavis yesterday, Laura had sat down with Shane, who'd told her about Jocy being on the tapes. To say she'd been decimated would have been the understatement of the century, especially since she'd been the one to hand over the evidence against her brother. Shane's insistence that Joey had already confessed, and that the tapes hardly mattered in his case, had bounced right off the hard surface of Laura's dismay.

"Where's Laura right now?" Mavis asked Shane, bringing him back to the present.

He rubbed his eyelids, feeling the familiar burn. "She said she wanted to go back to her house yesterday. I couldn't talk her into going to my place but I was able to finally get her to agree to stay at my parents' house."

Mavis checked her watch. "It's going on six. Why don't you go on over to your folks' house and see her? I'm sure she's had time to think things through by now. It wouldn't be rational for her to blame you for any of this. You saved her life, for God's sake—"

"No. I'm staying to hear the rest of the tape."

"Dom, *no,*" Mavis protested. "That's not healthy for you. I'll give you a report on whatever's important—"

"Laura went through it. It was hardly *healthy* for her," Shane grated out. "I'm not going to shove my head in the sand, Mavis."

"I never said you were. More like engaging in self-flagellation, I'd say. I think it'd do both you and Laura a hell of a lot more good if you were together instead of torturing yourselves apart. Haven't these assholes kept you two separated long enough?"

"Laura's the one keeping us apart at present. Now, are you going to get the others so we can continue? Or should I?"

Mavis rolled her eyes and shook her head in disgust.

"*Men*," she muttered under her breath as she headed for the conference room door.

CHAPTER **TWENTY-SIX**

Laura stilled in the process of raising her teacup to her mouth when Elizabeth joyfully called out her son's name. For a moment she remained frozen as Shane's stare pierced straight through her from across Elizabeth's large, cozy kitchen.

Even though she'd last seen him twenty-four hours ago, it struck her how awesome he looked to her . . . so new and exotic, as though she hadn't seen him in years. A five-o'clock shadow darkened his jaw. His tie hung loose and limp around his neck. He'd removed the sling on the night of Moody's shooting and stubbornly refused to put it back on again. His dark hair looked mussed. For some reason Laura was reminded of the way he'd looked when he awoke in the morning at the cabin, rumpled and naked and deliciously sexy. She'd been restrained to the bed at the time, both furious and lusting for him at the same time.

Her cheeks burned at the turn of her thoughts. A dull ache of need spread between her thighs, making her shift uneasily on the couch. She saw Shane's gaze narrow on her and wondered if he'd noticed.

"Would you like some dinner heated up, Shane?" Elizabeth asked. Shane's mother had incorporated a warm, comfortable sitting area at the far end of her kitchen, which is where she and Laura had been drinking tea and chatting.

"Spinach lasagna," Alex Dominic said, patting his belly as he followed his son into the kitchen. "Laura made it. Delicious, even with the low-fat cheese."

"No, I'm not hungry," Shane responded, his gaze never leaving Laura's blushing cheeks. "I've come to take Laura home."

Laura noticed Alex's salt-and-pepper eyebrows go up at Shane's firm proclamation. Elizabeth, on the other hand, took note of Laura's bemused expression and responded with more aplomb.

"It's been so wonderful having you here, Laura. Promise me you'll come to visit again soon, won't you?"

Laura cleared her throat and stood. For a split second she'd considered acting offended at Shane's caveman tactics. But the fact of the matter was, she'd treated him unfairly yesterday and she knew it. It still hurt, like rubbing sandpaper on an open wound, every time she considered Joey conspiring with Huey and Randall Moody.

But her brother's treachery hadn't been Shane's fault. A full night of sleep and the cold, clear light of day had reminded her of that. Nor had Laura been at fault for locating those tapes. Joey had dug his own grave, and it would be stubborn and petulant on her part to lie in it with him for the sake of principle.

She leaned down and kissed Elizabeth's cheek. Fate worked in such strange ways. Just as she'd been forced to face the fact that her entire family had been taken from her by death or treachery, another family had been given to her: Alex, Elizabeth . . . and Shane.

Shane above all else. She felt as if she stood on the very edge of a fantasy, her foot poised to step into it. Her eyes unexpectedly filled with tears and she ducked her head to hide them. For a few seconds she thought she wouldn't be able to contain the tight feeling in her chest that threatened to burst free.

"I'll help you," Shane said gruffly as she walked past him.

"No." She saw his eyes widen when she gave him a fleeting smile. "It'll just take me a moment."

Neither one of them spoke on the short car ride over to Shane's condominium. To Shane, the interior of the car felt just as gravid and electric as on the night he'd taken Laura captive.

"Shane—"

"Laura," Shane said at the same moment once they'd entered his condominium and hung up their coats. He watched, spellbound, as her throat convulsed in a swallow. A part of him felt like weeping when he saw the white bandage next to her gold-tinted skin. Another part—a much more insistent part—just wanted to take her up to his bed and prove to her once and for all that she belonged there . . . with him.

He'd almost lost her. This time for good.

"I want you to know that I'm sorry," she murmured huskily.

Shane dragged his eyes from the regal column of her throat to meet her gaze.

"It was wrong of me to accuse you the other evening of using Joey as an excuse to get the truth out of me. For blaming you in any way for his mistakes."

"I know how you are about family. You're as fierce as a lioness protecting her cubs."

She gave a sharp bark of laughter that struck him as anything but funny. "If that were true, I'd be a pretty pitiful lioness." Her smile faded slowly. "My den is empty, Shane."

He shook his head and went to her, his hand cradling her jaw. "No. It's not empty. You have Shelly and Carlotta and Joey, too. He's not going to be in prison forever, Laura. I know your feelings about what he's done are even more complicated than mine are, but I'm not going to abandon him. I doubt you will either."

"You're right. I won't," she whispered. She moved closer to him, her jeans brushing against his pants, the edges of his opened suit jacket bumping against her breasts. She tilted her head back and watched him with those exotically tilted green eyes—the same green eyes he'd once prayed would stop haunting his dreams.

He knew now those prayers had been useless because a much more crucial aspect of himself never wanted to forget Laura. Never wanted to let go. His hand fell and he palmed the muscle of her shoulder.

Never *would* let her go.

"You have my mother and father. They love you. Surely you know that."

A bewitching smile flickered across her lips. "And?"

He leaned down and brushed his smile across her temple, inhaling her singular scent. "Ahh, you need to hear it, is that it?"

"Yes. I've been waiting to hear it since I was six years old," she murmured in that low, husky voice that always had the effect of nails softly scraping down his spine.

"Okay. Here it is, then. You have me, Laura. From this moment on, I'm your family. And you're mine." He nuzzled her nose with his own before he brushed his lips against her parted ones. "And I'm not ever going to let you forget it . . . deny it . . . or tell me differently. So don't even think about it."

"I'd just as soon say the sky was yellow."

"Good," he muttered before he turned his head and seized her lips, molding and shaping them with his own. He kissed her ravenously, staking his claim and glorying in the richness of it all at once. When he lifted his head a moment later Laura's skin looked flushed and her eyes had grown limpid.

"I want you to recognize the absolute craziness of the mere idea of me letting you go. The sky can turn chartreuse, for all I care, and you're still not going anywhere except to admire a green sunset while you're in my arms. Understood?"

A small, intoxicating smile twitched her lips. "I remember that tone. I'd be a fool to say anything but 'yes.'"

"You'd be a fool to do anything but mean it." His finger brushed against the exquisite line of her angular jaw. His cock throbbed sharply, his need for her incredibly powerful. "Now I'd go full out caveman for you here, because I know how much you'd love it, but I can't sling you over my shoulder and take you to bed like I want to right now because of my damn arm. But if you could get your lovely butt upstairs and get out of these annoying clothes, I'll make it up to you."

Laura looked over her shoulder seductively as she led him toward the stairs. "Just how do you plan on making up for it?"

He released her hand and swatted her luscious jean-clad fanny, hiding his grin when she hopped slightly in surprise. "Did you forget what I said I was going to do to you if you ever defied me again when I asked you to do something for your safety and you agreed to it?"

His cock strained furiously against his boxer briefs when he saw her wide-eyed trepidation and the way her already pink cheeks deepened in color to a dusky rose shade.

"Go on up to the bedroom, Laura," he said softly. "Surely you've learned by now it's best just to take your punishment."

When they got up to his bedroom he closed the door and leaned against it, watching Laura as she stood at the foot of the bed.

"You know what to do," he muttered, completely enraptured by her beauty and the anxious, yet clearly seductive glance she gave him over her shoulder. He remained rigid—a fixed, hungry flame—as he watched her remove her clothing. Once she'd removed her panties she stood before him wearing nothing but the emerald.

"I never told you about how I gave that to you," he said gruffly, his gaze glued to the vision of her firm, lush breasts and the gem lying between them. He continued, sensing her curiosity even though he couldn't remove his eyes from the erotic vision of her. "I broke into your house one night over a dozen years ago. By that point, Peter and Derrick had been killed. You refused to speak to me. I was angry at you. Furious. But when I learned accidentally that Huey was giving you fake jewelry, more than likely trying to pass if off as genuine, and that one of the pieces he'd given you had been based off my mother's design for the emerald, I knew I had to do something. Even if it was stupid and useless."

Her breasts heaved as she inhaled deeply. His eyes rose to her face as she said, "It wasn't stupid or useless, Shane.

Who knows why I always chose to wear what I thought was a pretty piece of glass? Maybe it was God's subtle way of connecting us even when all hope seemed lost."

"I was stunned when I saw you wearing it that night at the cabin."

Laura nodded, clearly as amazed by the poignant strangeness of it as he was.

"The night I broke into your house to leave you the real emerald, I saw the sculpture of me as a boy—the one you keep in your studio," Shane said after a pregnant pause.

"You were right about that. I kept it near to me always—a reminder of that beautiful, perfect boy I'd always loved," she whispered.

He levered his body away from the door and took two steps toward her, unbuttoning his shirt as he did but never breaking their weighty stare. When he reached her he opened his palm along her waist and lightly dug his fingertips into the soft, firm feminine flesh of her hip.

"I watched you while you took a shower that night. I wanted you so bad it was like the pain from a bone-deep wound . . ." His voice faded as he thought of that cruel memory of seeing her naked as water ran in rivulets down her honey-hued skin, so much more separating them than a distance of ten feet and a pane of glass. When Laura whispered his name feelingly and placed her hand on his cheek he realized how lost he must have looked for a few seconds.

He rallied with a grin.

"It's okay, baby. Circumstances may have kept us apart for fourteen years, but we're going to make up for it. That's a promise."

He unbuttoned his cuffs and removed his shirt, hiding a wince at the dull ache the motion caused in his shoulder. He sat on the edge of the bed.

"Come here."

She glided toward him, her eyes a little wary.

"Lie across my lap," he directed.

For a second he thought she was going to refuse, but then he saw her studying his naked torso hungrily. It was on the tip of his tongue to tell her to forget it, to lay her down on the bed and bury his cock in her sweet pussy with no further ado, but he persevered. There was a point he wanted to make.

There was a point he would make.

"Randall Moody nearly killed you the other night, Laura. He would have if we hadn't been there to stop him. I nearly lost you, and all because you were too stubborn just to tell me the truth. Even after what had happened between us earlier that night . . . even after you'd promised you'd stay here behind a locked door."

"I only wanted to—"

"I know what you wanted," he interrupted softly. "But I didn't ask it of you lightly and you knew that. I didn't request it lightly at the cabin, either, when I asked you to stay in the bedroom. If I ask and you agree, that's got to be a sacred trust between us. You broke your promise to me the other night because you wanted to protect Joey. You wanted to protect me. I love you for that, Laura. I do. But I'm not going to let anything keep us apart in the future. Not even your stubbornness. Now lie down," he repeated, glancing down at his lap.

She inhaled deeply and knelt on the bed next to him. He arranged her how he wanted her with slight nudges on her shoulders and hips. When she finally settled, the lower curve of her breasts pressed to his outer thigh, her belly pressed against his thick erection and her round, lush bottom curved around his other thigh. He'd turned on only a single lamp when they entered the room. Her smooth, flawless skin glowed in the ambient light.

He ran his hand over her back, hips, ass, and thighs. He cupped a round buttock from below and squeezed at the same rhythmic rate that his pulse pounded in his cock.

Laura turned her face into the mattress and moaned.

Shane reached back and gave her a satisfying spank on the lush lower curve of a cheek. His cock surged painfully at the arousing sound of flesh smacking against flesh. He gritted his teeth when she wiggled her body along the length of his aching erection.

"Keep still," he ordered quietly. When she froze and

moaned as she anticipated the next spanking, he gave it to her, lingering to soothe and massage the warming buttock with a caress. "You've had too much experience with looking out for everyone in your life, baby. From now on, *I'm* going to look out for you. I'm going to be the one doing the protecting." He lifted his hand and smacked a tight cheek, staring in fascination as his blow quivered in her firm flesh. He liked what he saw and touched so well he repeated the spanking on the opposite cheek.

"Do you understand, Laura?" When she didn't immediately respond he smacked her ass again.

"Yes," she moaned.

"Good," he murmured. He grimaced slightly as he lifted his left hand and pain throbbed in his shoulder. The sensation nowhere near approximated the ache of his cock as he lay with Laura naked in his lap, his spankings starting to turn her plump ass pink.

So he endured.

"Spread your legs some," he ordered. When she opened her thighs several inches he used both hands to part her cheeks. Her chest and belly began to expand more rapidly next to his straining cock when he silently inspected the treasures he'd uncovered: her glossy pink pussy and the tiny, puckered rosette of her asshole.

"That's a pretty sight," he murmured.

"Shane, please," Laura pleaded, and he knew she wasn't begging for him to stop. She moaned gutturally when he smacked her ass twice in a row, this time both luscious cheeks at once. She writhed in his lap, pressing her clit to his thigh as she became more aroused.

"Keep still," he muttered before he landed several more crisp spanks, the smacking noise going off like gunfire in the still room.

He paused and filled his palm with tight, hot flesh.

"Do you think you've gotten my point, Laura?"

She leaned up and looked over her shoulder. An explosion of need detonated in him when he saw how vividly pink her cheeks were from arousal.

"Yes," she whispered softly. "You're going to take care of me."

"That's right." He rubbed his fingertips softly over the sensitive patch of skin above the crack of her ass. She inhaled sharply.

"I think I'd like to see you wearing your cuffs again, baby. Would you like that?"

She bit her lower lip to restrain a groan. She nodded her head, her eyes huge in her face.

"Stand up, then, and I'll get them for you."

He went to his chest of drawers and withdrew the black leather cuffs she'd worn much of the time they'd been at the cabin. Once he'd fastened them to her wrists he stood back and inspected her with a hot stare.

"You know, I don't know how you could possibly ever top this outfit. I'd be a happy man if all you ever wore were these leather cuffs." He smiled when he saw her open her mouth, a protest undoubtedly forming on her tongue. "And my heart between your breasts," he added softly.

She just stared at him for a moment, her lips gaping open and her green eyes glistening.

"Shane Dominic," she whispered. "You can say the damnedest things."

After spanking her until her bottom blushed hotly and slaying her with his unexpected, sweet words, Laura was all too willing to do whatever Shane asked her. She was like putty in his hands.

And my heart between your breasts.

Who was she kidding, anyway? She'd be putty in Shane's hands if he quoted the Sunday comics to her.

"Come here," he said quietly, leading her over to the head of his king-sized bed. He was such a big man, the giant wrought-iron sleigh bed suited him perfectly. And was apparently perfectly suited for restraining a willing woman, as well, Laura thought with amusement as she followed Shane's instructions and slid her hands behind one of the iron posts.

Once he'd joined the cuffs behind both a vertical and horizontal post she was restrained.

"Lie on your right side on the bed," he whispered, his voice growing hoarse from the same arousal that fired her own flesh and turned her pussy wet and hot.

She groaned in protest once she'd positioned herself on the bed and Shane lay down behind her without removing his pants.

"Shane, I need you," she moaned.

"I need you, too. That's what this is all about, isn't it?" he asked as he ran a hand over the curve of her hip and along the sensitive skin at the side of her torso. She shivered with mounting excitement. Her nipples drew painfully tight. He leaned down over her and kissed her ear, the suction he applied and then his warm tongue making her squirm on the bed.

"Tell me what it is you need," he whispered hotly next to her ear.

"I need you." She gasped when he plunged a thick forefinger into her pussy.

"Care to be a little more specific?" he coaxed.

She groaned as he moved his finger inside of her. Her clit throbbed, aching to be touched. Even the soles of her feet burned she was so aroused. She pulled down on her restraints, thrusting out her breasts and grinding her hips down onto his hand.

"Your cock," she whispered shakily.

His finger paused inside of her. "You're trembling, baby. And your pussy is so wet." Laura moaned in an agony of need when he withdrew from her. "Turn your face to me. Keep your lips parted." She twisted her head around. He held her hostage with his fiery eyes as he traced her lips with a finger lubricated by her juices.

"Suck it. It's sweet," he ordered hoarsely.

Laura closed her lips and suckled her own musky essence while Shane pushed his finger in and out of her mouth. She loved it; loved tasting herself mingling with the subtle taste of his skin. She drew on him so hungrily he growled deep in stark arousal and began to attack the zipper on his pants.

His underwear and pants never made it far past the middle of his long, strong thighs before he was fisting his cock and pressing the fat head to her slit.

Laura wanted him inside of her so badly. His absence felt like a pain. Shane pushed her upper leg forward on the bed, opening her body to him. He growled, primitive and deep, and pushed his cock into her pussy several inches.

She gasped. He groaned.

"Don't hurt your shoulder," she panted.

"Fuck my shoulder."

"No . . . fuck *me*. Oh . . . *Shane*."

Laura grabbed the wrought-iron bedpost she was restrained to and pushed back forcefully with her hips, seating his cock fully in her body. He began to pump her shallow and hard, the thick rim of the head of his penis massaging deep, delicious flesh.

"That's how you like it, isn't it, baby?" he asked as he held himself off her with his good arm and watched her face.

It was how she liked it, all right. She wanted to tell him so but she was too full of him to speak. Her mouth hung open slackly as he smacked their flesh together again and again. It had never felt so intense for her. Every muscle in her body grew rigid. She pulled desperately at her restraints, not because she wanted to be free . . . but because she wanted Shane closer, nearer, deeper.

"Oh, God!" she cried out in agony. He kept her coasting right on the crest of a powerful wave of climax. Sweat slicked her body as he pounded into her and she strained for release.

Shane held her hip and began thrusting into her pussy with longer strokes. Her eyelids cracked open and she glanced over her shoulder. His handsome face was rigid with excitement. He looked primal, his dusky skin covered with a thin coat of sweat, muscles flexed, his hips powering his cock into her mercilessly.

"Nothing. Nothing will keep me from you again," he told her fiercely.

She whimpered at the sensation of his cock swelling in

her pussy. He slammed into her. He roared, his face convulsing with pleasure. Laura whimpered at the sensation of his cock jerking inside her as he came. The sensation tipped her over the edge, igniting her. It was as if her explosion amplified his, and Shane's her own, until they existed at the core of a blinding, white-hot conflagration of bliss.

"Let me loose," Laura said sometime later. Shane spooned her, their naked skin pressed tight. Once his wild panting had slowed, his head dropped to hers and he began to mouth and nibble at her neck lazily. It felt delicious.

But she wanted to touch him.

He released her wrists and she turned onto her back. She smiled up at him as he leaned over her. She used her forefinger to explore the sexy cleft in his chin, feeling like the queen of the universe when her actions brought a small, crooked grin to his lips.

"I'm glad you won't let anything come between us again," she murmured. "But I hope your plan for keeping me safe doesn't consist solely of tying me up to your bed and having your way with me whenever the mood strikes you."

He turned his chin and bit playfully at her finger. She laughed softly. "It wouldn't be fair to you to keep you tied up twenty-four hours a day. I have a feeling that's how often the mood is going to strike. I have fourteen years of making love to you to compensate for, you know."

She caressed his chest near his bandaged shoulder, treasuring the preciousness of that simple touch in a way that a person who took a loved one for granted could never understand. She promised herself then and there to do her best to always remember how fragile life could be . . . how indescribably amazing it was to be here with Shane. He must have noticed her expression because he cupped her face with his hand.

"Why so serious, baby?"

She smiled and shook her head, feeling foolish at the tears that sprang to her eyes.

"For all those years, something like this"—she paused and glanced down at them pressed together, skin to skin—

"would have been a dream. I can't quite believe I'm here with you. That I can stay . . ."

Her voice trailed off as emotion gripped at her throat. Shane's face convulsed slightly.

"It's not all going to be fun, games, and being tied up to my bed, you know. I'm an old bachelor. I'll probably drive you nuts with my bad habits."

Her smile widened. "Bad habits? Like feeling the need to tease me into a good mood the second you see a tear? You're probably right. You will drive me nuts. I guess you'll have to be extra sweet to me when you're not being old and crotchety to make up for it."

His white teeth flashing in his dark face made her heart squeeze in her chest. God, she was every bit as head over heels for him as she had been as a girl of seventeen . . . more so, now that a woman's heart beat in her breast.

"I think I have an idea to sweeten the weight of your heavy burden right from the starting gates," Shane murmured as he ducked his head and nuzzled the emerald heart between her breasts. "Why don't you find that folder filled with all the places you used to dream about going to and pick one of them? We'll go. Next week if you want. Anywhere your heart desires."

Laura laughed softly.

"What? You're laughing at my gift to you?" he asked, pretending to be offended. "I thought you said you used to dream of going to those places. Now you can."

She shook her head. She wondered if her vast love for him was broadcast in her eyes when she saw his rugged features soften.

"I used to dream about those places because I wanted to escape. I don't want to go anywhere now unless it's with you," she whispered as she touched his cheek. "I've finally come home, Shane. Being with you . . . anywhere. *That's* always been my true dream."

About the Author

Beth Kery grew up in a huge house, built in the nineteenth century, where she cultivated her love of mystery and romance. When she wasn't hunting for secret passageways and ghosts with her friends, she was gobbling up fantasy and adventure novels along with any other books she could get her hands on. Currently, she juggles the demands of two careers, her love of the city and the arts, and a busy family life. Her writing reflects her passion for all of the above. Find out more about Beth and her books at bethkery.com.

Turn the page for a sneak peek
at Beth Kery's novel

EXPLOSIVE

Coming in February 2014
from Berkley Sensation!

She was so caught up in the lazy mood of the first evening on her summer holiday that at first she couldn't compute the fact that Thomas Nicasio was standing on her dock. He stared fixedly at the rippling lake, the golden sunlight bringing out the burnished highlights in his uncharacteristically mussed brown hair. If it weren't for that singular profile she would never have recognized him in these surroundings.

Thomas was an inhabitant of her work world, after all, a denizen of the city and the high-rise where they both worked. For Sophie, he only lived within the confines of 209 South LaSalle, wearing his perfectly tailored Armani suits, always moving with a brisk sense of purpose through the corridors or paging through his BlackBerry distractedly while he waited for his brother in the waiting room of the medical practice where Sophie worked.

They'd shared nothing more until that moment but heated glances, a few flirtatious conversations. On several occasions, she'd noticed Thomas sitting in the waiting room, studying her covertly while she interacted with her patients as she escorted them to the reception desk. It was clear to

Sophie that Thomas was attracted to her, but he'd always seemed to make a point of keeping his distance.

The single exception to their sterile acquaintance had been the charged, brief exchange they'd shared in the waiting room of her office just last evening. Thomas certainly hadn't seemed contained or aloof on that occasion.

Still, until that moment he'd always hovered on the periphery of her life, never fully entering it, but never totally absent from it, either. She thought of Thomas Nicasio a lot, usually in a sympathetic manner following her consultations with her psychologist friend, Andy Lancaster.

More recently, she had good reason to consider Thomas with compassion while watching the ten o'clock news.

He might occasionally creep up into her thoughts whenever she saw another tall man out of the corner of her eye while she was grocery shopping or jogging by Lake Michigan. Certainly the faces of her fantasy lovers often morphed into Thomas the closer she got to climax, but surely that was no surprise. Sophie suspected the same was true of a majority of the women who caught sight of him.

Still . . . she wondered at times if his sober, watchful gaze had the same effect on most females that it did on her.

Usually Thomas existed for Sophie only within the confines of her office lobby or the eight-by-eight confines of a crowded elevator, his head easy to see over the other early-morning elevator riders, his eyes unfailingly meeting hers, his gruff, quiet, "Good morning, Doctor," tickling her ear before the elevator doors opened and Sophie stepped off on the twenty-third floor.

The overlap of their lives was so minimal that it made her wonder if she was hallucinating—conjuring her dreams into reality—when she saw him standing on her dock wearing a pair of jeans and a black T-shirt.

Her brain just couldn't seem to get a handle on the image.

And there was something about his stance that caused a muted alarm to start ringing in her head. She considered calling Andy Lancaster, who had been treating Thomas's brother, Rick. Thomas had been asking to see Andy just last night.

But what could Andy do, even if she got a hold of him? He was in Chicago, after all, over one hundred fifty miles upstate.

And *Thomas* had never been his patient.

Sophie knew that multiple tragedies had befallen Thomas Nicasio's family recently. His brother and nephew were dead. Thomas's adoptive father, Joseph Carlisle, was being investigated for several federal crimes. The FBI was in the midst of building an indictment against the wealthy businessman.

Did those things relate to the fact that Thomas was standing on her dock, looking dazed and shell-shocked? And if so, what was he doing here? There was no way he could understand that she, of all people, knew details about the dark labyrinth of his family life.

She placed the paintbrush she'd been gripping into a coffee can filled with water and headed toward the side door. She glanced down at herself, hesitating. A few swipes of dried lavender tempura paint decorated her bare ribs and abdomen. She wore a bikini with a pair of jean shorts pulled over the bottoms and white canvas tennis shoes that were so ancient the cloth was separating from the soles in spots.

She should go and change—throw on a shirt at the very least.

But then she recalled the way his head hung at a queer angle as he stared at the sunset-infused lake and she descended the steps.

The closer she got to his rigid figure, the more anxious she became. Before her feet hit the dock, she saw the way that his rib cage moved in and out. It struck her as strange—eerie, even—how he stood so still and yet appeared to be panting, as though from some invisible exertion.

She gasped when he spun around as her foot hit the wooden dock, looking like a ready, lethal warrior anticipating attack. A sensation like flowing, hot liquid sank through her lower belly.

For a few seconds, they just stood frozen in each other's sights, his stare unnerving her. His jaw was covered with whiskers that were two shades darker than the hair on his head. He typically combed his long bangs back in a conservative style that suited his polished work image. Currently, they hung loose, bracketing his dark brows and eyes that had always reminded Sophie of a deep forest wood with shards of sunlight breaking through the topmost branches.

Sophie heard a speedboat motor hum in the distance through the increasingly loud throb of the heartbeat in her ears.

After a moment she summoned her voice, trying to grasp on to a fleeing sense of reality.

"Thomas? What a surprise. It's me—Dr. Gable? Sophie? From Dr. Lancaster's office?" She waved lamely at the glistening waters and laughed. "I hadn't realized we shared space at Haven Lake as well."

Despite her growing uncertainty, she'd forced her voice into the level, reassuring tone she took with someone who was agitated or panicked. She'd had her share of crisis training to become a physician, but even before she'd gone to medical school she'd worked for a year as a clinical social worker with abused children. She'd long ago learned to soothe instinctively . . . without thought.

She was so caught up in the bizarre, electric moment that it never occurred to her to question why she would treat a six foot four male in his prime, a man who typically moved through the minutes of his life with the easy grace of a prince, like an agitated child. Especially since Thomas Nicasio hardly seemed childlike to her at that moment. If anything, he reminded her of a wild, cornered animal.

A wild, *dangerous* animal?

The worn black T-shirt he wore carried the inexplicable caption *Mighty are those that flirt with fate, EOD*. The material skimmed across his long, lean torso, making it easy for her to see his rapid breathing. She'd never seen him in anything but a suit before, but she had to admit his broad shoulders, narrow hips, strong thighs, and long legs were perfectly suited to jeans. Her gaze skittered across his crotch. She glanced guiltily back up to his rigid face in time to see a spark ignite in his eyes.

Her heartbeat amplified in her ears.

A strong sexual current had often leapt between them in the past, but at the moment, Sophie felt burned by the heat of his stare. She tensed when he took a step toward her.

"Tom. Call me Tom."

Her mouth fell open at the sound of his deep, hoarse voice. Why did he sound like he hadn't spoken in days? Her expert eye took in the pinched look of his bold, masculine features, the whiteness at the corners of his mouth, the look of exhaustion that seemed to reside behind the maniclike intensity of his gaze.

She turned her shoulder to him in a nonthreatening stance and beckoned with her hand.

"Why don't you come inside, Tom. You must be thirsty."

For a few seconds she had no idea what he would do, this man who was both familiar to her and yet a stranger, a man who had never said much more than a few dozen words to her at a time if he spoke at all. He might have laughed. He might have flown at her in a rage. Anything and everything seemed possible in that gravid moment. Considering her readiness for catastrophe, what he did next should have seemed mild.

Instead, it jolted her to the core of her being.

He walked toward her with a long-legged stride that ate up the space between them in a second. She tensed and a tingling sensation ran beneath her skin when his gaze traveled over her naked torso.

He halted less than a foot away from her.

Close.

Closer than casual human contact.

"I came looking for you."

She felt his warm breath tickle her upturned face. He reached for her. His hand felt hot and dry encircling her own, as if he had a furnace working overtime inside him. She just stared up at him, speechless.

"I came looking for you, Sophie," he repeated.

"Why?"

He just nodded soberly toward her house. She was still stunned when he gently urged her to accompany him, his stare never leaving her face.

The wraparound porch was a landscape of golden light and shadow when they approached the side entrance to the house. The door squeaked open, and she led him onto the screened-in portion of the porch. Their hands were still locked, so she felt it when he paused. She turned back to see him staring at her work in progress. He glanced from the painting to the lake, and back at the canvas again, his expression unreadable.

"It's not very good. I just do it for fun," she said, wondering why she whispered. Maybe it was because the atmosphere suddenly seemed electrically charged, expectant . . . like the air before a storm. Her breath stilled when he suddenly transferred his gaze to her naked abdomen.

"I was wondering why you had purple paint on you."

She gave a small laugh when she saw how his well-shaped lips quirked—very slightly—in amusement.

"I used to tell Rick you were like the little girl in the neighborhood who was always so clean; the kind that Mama wouldn't let play rough with the other kids . . . the kind that was never allowed to get dirty." His palpable gaze flickered over her breasts and neck before he met her stare.

Her mirth faded.

"Rick said that was just my lame excuse not to ask you out," he finished.

Sophie swallowed thickly. This situation just kept getting more and more bizarre. She knew from her friend Andy how close Thomas had been to his brother, Rick Carlisle. Not that she wouldn't have already guessed it the few times she'd witnessed the two men's easy camaraderie when she'd glimpsed them together in her office or in the building.

"You must be upset, Tom," she whispered. "Is that why you're here? Are you hurting . . . after your brother's and nephew's death?"

His eyes glittered with emotion in an otherwise masklike countenance.

"Come inside." She tightened her hold on his hand and

guided him down the dim hallway to the kitchen. The windows there faced east, depriving them of the sunset light. She flipped a switch, chasing away the dark shadows.

If she'd thought that electric lights and her cheery, homey kitchen would bring a sense of normalcy to this surreal situation, she'd thought wrong. One glance at Thomas's tall, whipcord lean body and rigid features and she existed in the *Twilight Zone* all over again. Perhaps it was the thick, nearly tangible cloud of tension that surrounded him that contributed to her sense of floundering for familiar territory.

She released his hand and headed toward the refrigerator, trying to shake off her sense of unease.

"I made fresh lemonade earlier today. Would you care for some?"

"Do you have anything harder?" he rasped.

She glanced back over her shoulder. "I have some wine in the pantry."

"Never mind. Lemonade is fine."

She studied him anxiously. Under the bright fluorescent lights, she could more easily see that a fine sheen of sweat covered his face.

Fever, she thought.

"Why don't you sit down at the bar," she suggested before she headed toward the refrigerator. She filled two glasses with ice and lemonade and handed him one. He hadn't taken her advice to sit down and still stood in the precise spot where she'd left him. He took the glass and drained the contents in two seconds. When he'd finished, she took the empty glass and gave him the other one. While he drank, she encircled the wrist of his free hand with her own.

He swallowed the second glass of lemonade almost as quickly as the first. When he'd finished, she sensed him watching her from above, his head lowered while she concentrated and counted the beats of his rapid, strong pulse while watching the seconds pass on her kitchen clock.

The silence seemed to press on them like a thick cloak.

"Would you like some more?" she asked after she'd finished and dropped his wrist.

"No. I've had enough."

"Tom, you're ill," she said, looking up at him.

He blinked. He glanced around her kitchen with a slight scowl on his features. His confusion seemed to fade when he looked at her face again.

"You might be right. I'm not sure how I got here."

She took the glass he held from his stiff grip and set it along with the other one on the kitchen island.

"Do you mean you don't remember?"

For a few seconds he seemed uncertain. "I remember driving here. I had to get away."

"Had to get away from what?" she asked slowly.

He just stared at her with those brooding green eyes flecked with gold. Sophie supposed that given everything that had happened to Thomas Nicasio lately, he had plenty of reasons for needing an escape.

He remained immobile when she reached up to touch his forehead and cheek. His skin felt clammy. She mentally cursed when she recalled she didn't have a thermometer in the lake house. Still, she'd guess that if he ran a fever, it wasn't an alarming one.

Her fingers delved through thick, surprisingly soft hair, searching for wounds on his scalp. A shiver coursed through him when her hand reached the base of his skull. She caught his scent. Despite his obvious illness and uncharacteristically disheveled state, Thomas Nicasio smelled *good*.

Cautiously, she met his stare.

For a few seconds, neither of them moved. Sophie suspected neither of them breathed.

"Did you hit your head, Tom?" she asked eventually, her fingers resuming their careful search.

"I don't think so."

"Have you been drinking?" she asked, even though she'd inhaled his breath and already suspected that he wasn't drunk. He shook his head.

"Drugs?"

Again, he shook his head. She pushed back his hair. Her

gaze shot to his when she saw the discoloration near his hairline on his left temple.

"You *have* been hit." She reached for the wrist of his right arm, holding his stare all the while. Her mind churned when she glanced down and saw the abrasions and flecks of dried blood on his knuckle.

"You've been in a fight," she stated tersely. Did a shadow of defiance cross his features, or was that her imagination? Well, perhaps she had sounded accusatory. It wasn't her place to judge him, after all. "Are you in any pain?"

"No."

"Sick to your stomach?"

He shrugged negligently.

"How is it that you're *here*, Tom?" she asked, despite the memory of what he'd said earlier.

I came looking for you, Sophie.

He wasn't entirely lucid, after all.

"Do you know someone who lives near here?" she prompted when he didn't speak.

"No. I only know you."

"Well . . . why did you come looking for me?" she couldn't resist asking in an anxious rush. "Did you find yourself getting ill on the road and need a doctor? Did you remember me telling you I was vacationing here, at Haven Lake?"

A spasm went through him and he cupped his right brow with his palm, squeezing his eyes shut.

"I'm taking you to the emergency room in Effingham," she declared, alarmed by the sight of what must have been a jolt of intense pain going through him.

"I'm not going anywhere."

"But you've got to, you're not well and—"

"I'm not going to the hospital," he grated out between clenched teeth.

She went completely still at his harsh tone. She considered calling the police, but then he opened his eyes.

"All right."

The two words leaving her own lips surprised her a little,

but she felt as if she didn't have a choice once she'd looked into those twin pools of turmoil and anguish. "You might have a concussion, but you're feverish, as well. I'll get you some Tylenol and then you need to rest. Will you at least promise me to do that for now?"

"I'm not sleepy," he said hoarsely. His gaze lowered. Heat flooded her cheeks. He stared at her breasts covered in the thin bikini top. Her body responded to his blatantly sexual gaze against her will. Her nipples stiffened beneath the flimsy fabric.

He stepped toward her.

Sophie stepped back.

"You're ill. You need to rest. Is there someone you want me to call? Will someone be missing you in Chicago? Never mind. Come on," she said when he just stared at her. She waved her hand and led him down the dim hallway to the guest bedroom. She turned on the light and inspected the state of the room. She hadn't been in it since early June, just after Andy and his wife, Sheila, had visited for a weekend.

Her mind sifted through his symptoms, trying to make sense of his bizarre presentation as she bustled around in the guest bath, laying out clean towels and getting Tylenol out of the medicine cabinet. His feverish state implied that something physical was going on, but the pain she'd seen in his eyes just moments ago argued for something psychological. The bruise on his temple wasn't massive, but she knew the brain could sustain considerable injury from a blow without any obvious external trauma.

Of course there was no reason why his condition couldn't be *both* physical and psychological, considering the amount of stress Thomas must have been under recently.

Who had he been fighting with, and why? Oddly, it didn't surprise her to consider Thomas engaging in a brawl, despite the fact that she was used to seeing only his polished work image. She'd always sensed a rebel existed beneath the smooth exterior of his perfectly tailored suits. Maybe it was the tilt of his jaw that made her think it, or the gold flecks that flashed and burned in the deep green of his eyes; or a smile that was sweet, but just a tad cocky . . . slow in coming and breathtaking upon arrival.

Or maybe it was just because Sophie knew he'd spent the first years of his life in a working-class Southside neighborhood far from the perfectly manicured, sweeping green lawns and multimillion-dollar homes of Lake Forest, where Thomas had gone to live with the family that adopted him, the Carlisles. A kid growing up in Morgan Park would have known how to use his fists. Besides, he'd only worked in the private sector for the past few years. Before he'd taken up the reins of his own business, he'd been in the military, but Sophie couldn't recall at the moment if Andy had ever mentioned in what branch he'd served or what his duties had involved.

She grimaced as she filled a glass with water from the tap. She felt guilty for not taking him to the hospital, even though the chances were that the emergency room physician would recommend nothing more than close observation of Thomas's symptoms for the next forty-eight hours.

And either way, Thomas had flatly refused to go, so what choice did she have?

Her level of anxiety upon entering the bedroom was unprecedented since her first year of medical school.

She carried the Tylenol in one hand and the glass of water in the other. He still stood just inside the threshold of the door. She was relieved when he took the Tylenol without argument. He stood behind her while she turned down the bed, making her highly self-conscious of her bent-over position.

She added his blatant sexual stare into her formulary of symptoms, even though Thomas Nicasio's hot eyes hardly left her feeling analytical. Was he in a manic state, perhaps? That would explain his hypersexuality, the sudden need to impulsively escape . . .

. . . but not the bruise, fever, or dazed confusion.

Was she *safe* with him there in the house with her? She glanced back at him and their gazes held. She exhaled slowly.

"Why don't you get into bed?" she asked, glad to hear

that her voice didn't audibly tremble. He stepped toward her and Sophie glanced down, avoiding that laserlike stare. She knew she should have backed away, but she didn't.

Not even when he spread one hand along her naked hip.

She held her breath and clamped her eyes shut when she felt his thumb gently rub across a dried smear of paint. Her lungs burned by the time he bent his long legs at the knees, and he wrapped her in his arms.

He encompassed her. In that full, fertile moment, she felt Thomas Nicasio in every cell of her being.

He nudged her hair back with his nose and pressed his entire face to the side of her neck. His hardness pressed against her softness, stark and potent.

"Sophie."

Her heart throbbed erratically in her chest at the sensation of his hot mouth moving next to her sensitive skin.

"Sleep with me, Sophie. I need your cleanness so much right now."

All it takes is one moment for your life to change—
One night of desire to make you feel alive...

FROM *NEW YORK TIMES* BESTSELLING AUTHOR
BETH KERY
writing as
BETHANY KANE

Addicted to You

A One Night of Passion Novel

Irish film director Rill Pierce fled to the tiny backwoods town of Vulture's Canyon seeking sanctuary and solitude after a devastating tragedy. Once, his raw sex appeal and sultry Irish accent made women across the globe swoon. Now, he's barely recognizable...

But Katie Hughes, his best friend's sister, is not the type of woman to give up on a man like Rill. She blazes into Vulture's Canyon, determined to save him from himself. Instead, she finds herself unleashing years of pent-up passion. In a storm of hunger and need, Katie and Rill forget themselves and the world. But will Rill's insatiable attraction to Katie heal his pain—or will it just feed the darkness within him?

"Really packs an emotional punch."
—*Smexy Books*

"Explosive and intense."
—Lisa Marie Rice

bethkery.com
facebook.com/beth.kery
facebook.com/LoveAlwaysBooks
penguin.com

M1345T0713

FOR THE FIRST TIME IN PRINT!

FROM *NEW YORK TIMES* BESTSELLING AUTHOR

BETH KERY

Because You Are Mine

The moment Francesca and Ian met, the attraction was mutual: an exquisitely physical charge that ignited between them. For Ian, Francesca was the kind of woman he couldn't resist. She was a true innocent. For Francesca, Ian was the kind of man she feared *and* desired—dark, extreme, commanding, and forbidden. What happened between them couldn't be ignored—only indulged, evolving into an inescapable bond.

From a private jet to an interlude in Paris, from a daring tryst in a public museum to the intimacy of a luxury hotel, Francesca and Ian come together whenever their need is aroused. But as their relationship grows more intense, Francesca discovers something about Ian—and herself—that forever changes the game and the players. It's something they never expected, something that sends both their lives spinning deliriously out of control . . .

"Addictive and delicious."
—*USA Today* Happily Ever After Blog

"One of the best erotic romances I've ever read."
—*All About Romance*

"Nearly singed my eyebrows."
—*Dear Author*

bethkery.com
facebook.com/beth.kery
facebook.com/LoveAlwaysBooks
penguin.com

M1209T1112